LETTICE DEVEREUX WAS BEAUTIFUL, SOPHISTICATED, AND IMPETUOUS . . .

And she was used to getting her way. Her unbridled passions were exceeded only by her scheming mind.

Lettice married the Earl of Leicester, stealing him away from another woman. And Lettice was the mother of the Earl of Essex, who would one day break that same woman's heart. It was Lettice who was the constant figure in a love triangle.

And who was the woman she constantly thwarted? None other than Elizabeth I, the great Queen of England. . . .

MY ENEMY THE QUEEN—A story unsurpassed for its color and pageantry—a novel only Victoria Holt could write. . . . "Dramatically moving."
—*Pittsburgh Press*

"AN IRRESISTIBLE TREAT . . ."
—*Cosmopolitan*

Victoria Holt

My Enemy
the Queen

FAWCETT CREST • NEW YORK

MY ENEMY THE QUEEN

THIS BOOK CONTAINS THE COMPLETE TEXT OF
THE ORIGINAL HARDCOVER EDITION.

Published by Fawcett Crest Books, a unit of CBS Publications,
the Consumer Publishing Division of CBS Inc., by arrange-
ment with Doubleday and Company, Inc.

Copyright © 1978 by Victoria Holt

ALL RIGHTS RESERVED

ISBN: 0-449-23979-9

Selection of the Literary Guild
Selection of the Reader's Digest Condensed Book Club

Printed in the United States of America

10   9   8   7   6   5   4   3   2   1

The Old Lady of Drayton Basset

Blame not my Lute! for he must sound
Of this or that as liketh me;
For lack of wit the Lute is bound
To give such tunes as pleaseth me;
Though my songs be somewhat strange,
And speak such words as touch thy change,
Blame not my Lute.

SIR THOMAS WYATT
1503–1542

I never go to Court now. I stay in my house at Drayton Basset. I am getting old, and it is permissible for old women to sit and dream. They say: "My lady goes on. How old is she? Few have reached her age. It seems my lady will live forever."

I sometimes think that too. How many people now alive can remember that November day in the year 1558 when Queen Mary—whom people had begun to call Bloody Mary—died, causing no great sorrow to her people except to those supporters who had feared what her passing would mean to them? How many can remember when my kinswoman, Elizabeth, was proclaimed Queen throughout the land? Yet I remember it well. We were in Germany then. My father had thought fit to flee the country when Mary came to the throne, for life could be dangerous to those who by nature of their birth and religion looked to the young Elizabeth.

We were all summoned together and made to kneel and thank God, for my father was a very religious man. Moreover my mother was Elizabeth's cousin—so the new reign should bring good to our family.

I was just past seventeen at the time. I had heard a great deal about Elizabeth and her mother, Queen Anne Boleyn. After all, my mother's mother was Mary Boleyn, Anne's sister, and stories of our brilliant fascinating kinswoman Anne were part of our family legends. When I saw Elizabeth I knew what that brilliance meant because she possessed it too—in a different way from her mother, but it was there all the same. Elizabeth had other qualities also. *She* would never have suffered from the executioner's sword. She was too clever for that; she had shown even during her early life a genius for self-preservation. But, for all her coquetry and dazzling adjuncts to beauty, she lacked the essential appeal which her mother must have had, and which my grandmother, Mary Boleyn—who had had the good sense to be the King's mistress and not bargain for a crown—had possessed in great measure; and if I am to write truthfully, I must not impede myself with false modesty and must say that I had inherited this appeal from my grandmother. Elizabeth was to discover this—there was little she did not discover—and she hated me for it.

When she came to the throne, she was full of good intentions, which I have to admit she tried to keep. Elizabeth had one important love affair in her life, and that was with the crown. She allowed herself a little dalliance, though; she liked to play with fire, but in the first year of her reign she was so badly scorched that I believed she was forever after determined it should never happen again. Never would she be unfaithful to the greatest love of her life—the glorious, glittering symbol of her power— the crown.

I could never resist taunting Robert with this even during our most passionate encounters—and there were many of those. He would become violently angry with me then; but I had the satisfaction of knowing that I was more important to him than she was. Apart from her crown.

There were the three of us—a challenge to fate. Those two who strutted across the stage were the two most brilliant, awe-inspiring figures of their time. I, the third member of the trio, was often kept in the background of their lives, yet I never failed to make my presence felt. Try as she might, Elizabeth never succeeded in shutting me out completely. In due course there was no one at Court whom the Queen hated as she hated me; no other woman so aroused that overwhelming jealousy. She had wanted Robert, and he became mine . . . of his own free will; and the three of us knew that although she might have given him the crown—and he was as passionately in love with it as Elizabeth herself—yet *I* was the woman he wanted.

I often dream I am back in those days. I feel the exhilaration, the excitement creeping over me, and I forget that I am an old woman, and I long to make love with Robert again and do battle with Elizabeth.

But they are in their graves long since and only I live on.

So my consolation is to ponder on the past, and I live it all again, and sometimes I wonder how much of it I dreamed and how much was real.

I am reformed now—the Lady of the Manor. Some go to convents when they have lived lives such as I have; they repent their sins and pray twenty times a day for forgiveness in the hope that their last-minute piety will assure them a place in heaven. I have devoted myself to good works. I am the bountiful lady. My children die, but I live on; and now it has struck me that I will write it down as it happened, and that will be the best way to live it all again.

I shall try to be honest. It is the only way I can relive the past. I shall try to see us as we really were—a brilliant triangle, for any must be brilliant with those two scintillating at two points, so brightly often as to obscure the vision. And myself there too, as important to them—for all their power—as they were to me. What emotions shook that triangle: Robert's love for me, which made me the Queen's rival; her hatred of me born of jealousy and the knowledge that I could please him as she never could; those rages of hers which somehow never allowed her to lose sight of her own advantage. How she loathed me, calling me "That She-Wolf," which others imitated rather to please her than out of contempt for me. Yet I—only I— of all the women in her life was to cost her so much in jealousy and anguish—and only she would cost me so much. We were in conflict, and she had the advantage. It was her power against my beauty—and Robert, being the man he was, was drawn this way and that between the two of us.

Perhaps she was the winner. Who shall say? Sometimes

I am not sure. I took him from her, but then she took him from me—and death cheated us both.

She had her revenge on me and it was a bitter one—but I still have the fire and the passion left me, old as I am, to tell our story. I want to convince myself of the way it happened. I want to tell the truth about myself . . . about the Queen and the two men we loved.

The Exile

While the city is covered with gibbets and the public buildings so crowded with the heads of the bravest men in the kingdom, the Princess Elizabeth, for whom no better fate is foreseen, is lying ill about seven or eight miles from hence, so swollen and disfigured, that her death is expected.

ANTOINE DE NOAILLES, *the French Ambassador, commenting on one of Elizabeth's "favourable" illnesses at the time of the Wyatt Rebellion.*

I was born in the year 1541, five years after Elizabeth's mother had been executed. Elizabeth herself was eight years old. It was the year after the King had married another kinswoman of mine, Catherine Howard. Poor child, the following year a fate similar to that of Anne Boleyn overtook her, and Catherine too was beheaded at the King's command.

I had been christened Letitia after my paternal grandmother, but I was always known as Lettice. We were a large family, for I had seven brothers and three sisters. My parents were affectionate and often stern, though only for our own good, as we were often reminded.

My early years were spent in the country at Rotherfield Greys, which the King's recognition of my father's good services had secured him some three years before I was born. The estate had come to my father through his, but the King had a habit of taking for his own any country mansion he fancied—Hampton Court was the outstanding example of this royal avarice—so that it was comforting to know that he accepted my father's claim to his own property.

My father was away from home a good deal on the King's business, but my mother rarely went to Court. It might well have been that her close connection to the King's second wife could have aroused memories in Henry's mind which he would have preferred to be without. It could hardly be expected that a member of the Boleyn family would be welcome. So we lived quietly, and in the days of my childhood I was content enough; it was only as I grew older that I became restive and impatient to escape.

There were what seemed to me interminable lessons in the schoolroom with its leaded windows and deep window seats, its long table at which we bent over our laborious tasks. My mother often came to the schoolroom to see us with our tutors and she would go through our books and listen to reports on our progress. If they were bad or even indifferent, we would be summoned to the solarium, where we would take up our needlework and listen to a lecture on the importance of education to people of our rank. Our brothers did not join us in the schoolroom. After the custom of the day they were to go to the houses of illustrious families and were brought up there until the time came for them to go to Oxford or Cambridge. Henry had already left home; the others, William, Edward, Robert, Richard and Francis, were as yet too young. As for Thomas, he was but a baby.

It was during those lectures that I and my sisters, Cecilia, Catherine and Anne, were made aware of Elizabeth. "My first cousin," my mother explained proudly. Elizabeth, we were told, was a model for us all to follow. At the age of five, it seemed, she was almost a Latin scholar, and as familiar with Greek as she was with the English tongue, besides being fluent in French and Italian. How different from her Knollys cousins, whose minds strayed from these important matters and who gazed out of the windows when their eyes should have been on their books so that their good tutors had no alternative but to complain to their mother of their inaptitude and inattention.

I was noted for saying the first thing which came into my mind, so I declared: "Elizabeth sounds dull. I dareswear that if she knows Latin and all those other languages she knows little else."

"I forbid you to speak of the Lady Elizabeth in that way again," cried my mother. "Do you know who she is?"

"She is the daughter of the King and Queen Anne Boleyn. You have told us often enough."

"Don't you understand what that means? She is of royal blood, and it is not impossible that she could be Queen one day."

We listened because our mother could easily be led to forget the purpose of our presence in the solarium and to

13

talk of the days of her childhood; and of course that was more entertaining to us girls than a lecture on the need to apply ourselves to our lessons; and when she was thus enthralled she would not notice that our hands lay idle in our laps.

How young we were! How innocent of the world! I must have been six years old when I first began to take notice, and by then we were in the last stages of the old King's reign.

My mother talked not of the present time, which could have been dangerous, but of the past glories at Hever when as a child she had been taken to the castle to visit her grandparents. Those were the days of glory when the Boleyns' fortunes were rising fast, which was natural because they had a queen in the family.

"I saw her once or twice," said my mother. "I shall never forget her. There was a certain wildness in her then. It was after the birth of Elizabeth and Anne had been desperately hoping for a son. Only a male heir could have saved her then. My uncle George was there at Hever—one of the handsomest men I ever saw. . . ." There was sadness in her voice; we did not press her to tell us of Uncle George. We knew from experience that such a request might put an end to the narrative and remind her that she was talking to young children of matters beyond their understanding. In due course we discovered that handsome Uncle George was executed at the same time as his sister—accused of committing incest with her. Falsely accused, of course, because the King wished to be rid of Anne in order to marry Jane Seymour.

I often remarked to Cecilia that it was exciting belonging to a family like ours. Death was something we accepted in the nursery. Children—and particularly children of our station—thought lightly of it. When one looked at the family portraits it was said: "This one lost his head. He disagreed with the King." That heads were very precariously held on the place intended for them was a fact of life.

But in the solarium our mother made us see Hever again with its moat and portcullis and the courtyard and the hall where the King had often dined and the long gallery where he had courted our famous relative, the enchanting Anne. Our mother used to sing the songs which had been sung by the minstrels there—some composed by the King himself—and when she strummed on her lute, her eyes would grow glazed with the memories of the brief and dazzling glory of the Boleyns.

Now great-grandfather Thomas Boleyn lay buried in the church at Hever, but our grandmother Mary came to see us now and then. We were all fond of our grandmother. It was sometimes hard to imagine that she had once been the old King's mistress. She was not exactly beautiful, but she had that certain quality which I have mentioned before and which she had passed on to me. I very quickly learned that I possessed it and it delighted me, for I knew it would bring me much of what I wanted. It was indefinable—a certain appeal to the opposite sex which they found irresistible. In my grandmother Mary it had been a softness, a promise of easy yielding; not so with me. I would be calculating, watchful for advantage. Yet it was there in both of us.

In time we learned of that sad May day at the Greenwich joust when Anne had been taken to the Tower with her brother and her friends, and from which she had only emerged to be led to the scaffold. We knew of the King's immediate marriage thereafter to Jane Seymour and the birth of the King's only legitimate son, Edward, who became our King in the year 1547.

Poor Jane Seymour, dying in childbirth, had no chance to enjoy her triumph, but the little Prince lived and was the hope of the nation. Then had followed the King's brief marriage with Anne of Cleves, and after its abrupt dissolution the ill-fated union with Catherine Howard. Only his last wife, Katharine Parr, survived him and it was said she would have gone the same way as Anne Boleyn and Catherine Howard if she had not been such a good nurse and the King's ulcerous leg so painful and he too far gone in years to care much for women.

So we entered a new reign—that of Edward VI. Our young King was only ten years old at the time of his accession—not much older than I; and the paragon, Elizabeth, was four years his senior. I remember my father's coming down to Rotherfield Greys, rather pleased with the turn of events. Edward Seymour, the young King's uncle, had been made Protector of the Realm, the title of Duke of Somerset having been bestowed on him; and this now all-important gentleman was a Protestant who would instill the new faith into his young nephew.

My father was leaning more and more towards Protestantism, and as he remarked to my mother the greatest calamity which could befall the country—and incidentally the Knollys family—would be the accession to the throne of Catholic Mary, the King's elder daughter by Catherine of Aragon.

"Then," prophesied my father, "the scaffolds would be stained with the blood of good Englishmen and women, and the dreaded Inquisition which flourishes in Spain would be introduced into this country. So let us thank God for the young King and ask that through His clemency and loving care, Edward VI may long reign over us."

So we knelt and prayed—a custom which I already felt was followed too zealously in our family—while our father thanked God for His goodness to England and asked Him to go on looking after that country, keeping a particular eye on the Knollys family.

Life went on as usual for a few years while we lived as country gentry do, continuing with our studies. It was a tradition in our family that even daughters of the household must be well educated; special attention was paid to music and dancing; we were taught to play lute and harpsichord, and whenever a new dance was introduced at Court we must try it. Our parents were determined to make us ready in case we should suddenly be called to Court. We used to sing madrigals in the gallery or play our instruments there.

We dined at eleven of the clock in the main hall, and when we had visitors we would sit over our meal until three in the afternoon, listening to the talk which enthralled me, for during young Edward's reign, I was growing up fast and taking a great interest in what was happening outside Rotherfield Greys. Then we would sup at six. There was always a good table and a certain amount of excitement because we could never be sure who would arrive to join us. Like most families of our standing we kept open house, for my father would not have had it thought that we could not afford hospitality. There would be great joints of beef and mutton and meat pies of all kind flavored with herbs from our gardens, venison and fish accompanied by sauces as well as conserves of fruit, marchpane, gingerbread and sugar bread. If anything was left the servants would finish it, and there were always beggars at the gates—that community, my mother was constantly remarking, had increased a thousandfold since King Henry had dissolved the monasteries.

There were celebrations at Christmas when we children amused ourselves by dressing up and performing plays. There was great excitement among us as to which one should find the silver penny in the big cake which was made for Twelfth Night and be King—or Queen—for the day; and innocently we believed it would go on like that forever.

Of course, had we been wise we should have seen the portents. Our parents did, and that was why my father often looked very grave. The King was delicate and if any-

17

thing should happen to him, the heir to the throne was that Mary whom we feared—and we were not the only ones. The most powerful man in the country shared my father's apprehension. This was John Dudley, Duke of Northumberland, who had made himself virtual ruler of England. If Mary came to the throne it would be the end of Dudley, and as he did not relish spending the rest of his days in prison, nor yet surrendering his head to the ax, he was making plans.

I heard my parents discussing this and it was clear to me that they were very uneasy. My father was essentially a law-abiding man and, try as he might, he could not but accept the fact that the majority of the people would say that Mary was the true heir to the throne. It was an extraordinary situation because if Mary was legitimate, Elizabeth could not be. Mary's mother had been displaced when the King, eager to marry Anne Boleyn, decreed that his marriage of more than twenty years to Catherine of Aragon, was not legal. It was simple logic that if his marriage to Catherine *was* legal, then his marriage to Anne Boleyn was not, and Anne's child, Elizabeth, a bastard. My family —out of Boleyn loyalty and self-advancement—must of course believe that the King's first marriage was illegal; but because my father was a logical man in most matters, I guessed he had a certain difficulty in preserving his belief in Elizabeth's legitimacy.

He told my mother that he believed Northumberland was going to try to put the Lady Jane Grey on the throne. She had a certain claim, it was true, through her grandmother, Henry VIII's sister, but it was one which few people would accept. The strong Catholic factions throughout the land would stand firmly behind Mary. So it was small wonder that young King Edward's sickness gave my father great misgiving.

He did not, however, put himself on the side of Northumberland. How could he, married to a Boleyn, support anyone but the Princess Elizabeth? And Elizabeth, as the King's daughter, surely came before Lady Jane Grey. Unfortunately there was Mary—daughter of the Spanish Princess—a fierce Catholic and the King's elder daughter.

Those were days when it was necessary to be watchful. The Duke of Northumberland had staked everything on Jane Grey by marrying her to his son, Lord Guildford Dudley.

That was the state of affairs during the last year of the young King's reign. I was then twelve years old. My sisters and I were more interested in the gossip we heard through the servants, particularly that which concerned our illustrious cousin Elizabeth. Through this we acquired a different image of her from that which our mother had instilled of the scholar of Greek and Latin, a shining example to her less virtuous and less intellectual Knollys cousins.

After the death of King Henry VIII, she had been sent to live with her stepmother, Katharine Parr, at the Dower House in Chelsea, and Katharine Parr had married Thomas Seymour, who was one of the handsomest and most attractive men in England.

"They say," one of the servants told us, "that he has a fancy for the Princess Elizabeth."

I was always interested in what the anonymous "They" said. Quite a lot of it was, of course, conjecture and should perhaps be dismissed as idle gossip, but I think there was often a germ of truth in it. However, "They" said that there were exciting "goings on" at the Dower House and that there was some relationship between Elizabeth and her stepmother's husband which was inappropriate to her station as well as her character. He crept into her bedroom and tickled her when she was in bed; she ran screaming with laughter from him, but it was the kind of screaming which was not without an invitation. Once in the garden when Elizabeth was wearing a new silk gown, he, urged on by his wife, took scissors and playfully cut it to shreds.

"Poor Katharine Parr," said "They." Did she know the true nature of these frolics. Of course she must, and to give them that air of respectability which could cover the impropriety of it all, she joined in them.

I liked to think of the scholarly Elizabeth being chased around her bedroom or having her gown slashed to pieces, being tickled by the jovial Seymour with the glint in his eyes while his pregnant wife tried to pretend that the jollity was a family affair.

Then finally Katharine Parr had caught her amorous husband kissing the young Princess in a far from avuncular manner so that even she could no longer pretend, and the result was that Elizabeth left the Dower House. Naturally scandal followed her. "They" were at it again, and a rumor was spread that the Princess had been delivered of a fair young lady who was Thomas Seymour's daughter.

There were stout denials of this and indeed it seemed highly unlikely, but how interesting it was to us girls who had lived in the shadow of her virtues all those years.

It was not long afterwards when Thomas Seymour, involved in ambitious political schemes for his own advancement, was brought to trial and beheaded. Meanwhile the sad little King's health was declining. Dudley induced the dying boy to make a will passing over both Mary and Elizabeth and naming Lady Jane Grey sole heir to the throne. She had by this time married Lord Guildford. I often pondered on that in the days to come. It might so easily have been Guildford's brother Robert who was the chosen bridegroom. Robert, though, had already committed the folly—if so it could be called in view of what happened later—of marrying at the age of seventeen the daughter of Sir John Robsart. He soon tired of her, of course—but that is another story. It often appalled me later to contemplate that, but for Robert's marriage, my life—and Elizabeth Tudor's—would have been drastically different. Robert would certainly have been considered more suitable than Guildford, who was weak and far less handsome, for Robert must have been outstanding even in his youth. Heaven knows he later quickly became the brightest star at Court at the Queen's accession and remained so till his death. However, fate was looking after Robert—as she so often did—and it was poor Guildford, his younger brother, who became the husband of the ill-fated Lady Jane Grey.

As everyone knows, when the King died Northumberland put Jane on the throne, and, poor girl, she reigned for only nine days before Mary's Catholic supporters were triumphant.

My father did not join in the conflict. How could he? Mary's accession, whether legitimate or not, would be disastrous for him, but neither could he support Protestant Jane. She had no just claim in his eyes. There was one and one only whom he wanted to see on the throne. So he did what wise men do at such times. He removed himself from Court and did not take sides.

When it became clear that Jane's brief reign was over and she, with Guildford Dudley, his father and his brother Robert, were lodged in the Tower, we were summoned to the great hall and there our father told us that it was no longer safe for us to remain in England. These were not going to be good days for Protestants; the position of the Princess Elizabeth was very precarious indeed, and as it was known that we were her kinsfolk, he had come to the conclusion that the wisest steps to be taken were those which would lead us out of England.

Within a few days we were on our way to Germany.

We remained in Germany for five years, and as I grew from a child to a woman, I was aware of great restlessness and dissatisfaction with life. It is hard to be exiled from one's own country; we all felt it deeply, my parents most of all, but they seemed to take refuge in religion. If my father had previously leaned heavily toward Protestantism, he was, at the end of his sojourn in Germany, one of its strongest adherents. The news from England was one of the main reasons for his conviction. Queen Mary's marriage with King Philip of Spain had sent him into depths of despair.

"Now," he said, "we shall have the Inquisition in England."

Fortunately it did not get as far as that.

"There is one thing," he used to say to us, for naturally we saw more of him than we ever did in England when he was engaged on Court matters, "the people's dissatisfaction with the Queen will turn them to Elizabeth. But meanwhile the great fear is that Mary will have a child."

We prayed for her infertility, and I found it ironic to contemplate that she was praying equally fervently for the opposite.

"I wonder," I said flippantly to my sister Cecilia, "whose petition will be the more favorably received. They say Mary is very devout, but then so is our father. I wonder whose side God is on—Catholic or Protestant."

My sisters were shocked by my talk. So were my parents.

My father used to say: "Lettice, you will have to guard your tongue."

That was the last thing I wanted to do because my outspoken comments amused me and certainly had their effect on other people. They were a characteristic—like my smooth, delicately tinted complexion—which set me apart from other girls and made me more attractive.

My father never ceased to congratulate himself on his wisdom in escaping from the country while it was possible, though when she first came to the throne Mary showed

22

signs of leniency. She freed Lady Jane's father, the Duke of Suffolk, and was reluctant even to sign the death warrant for Northumberland, who had been the puppet master pulling the strings he had attached to poor Jane and Guildford which had made them Queen and Queen's Consort for their brief nine days. If it had not been for the Wyatt Rebellion she might have spared Jane herself, for she was well aware that the young girl had clearly had no wish to take the crown.

When the news of Wyatt's ill-fated rebellion came to us in Germany, there was great gloom in the family because the Princess Elizabeth herself seemed to be involved.

"This will be the end," groaned my father. "So far she has had the good fortune to escape her ill wishers . . . but how can she do so this time?"

He did not know her. She might be young but she was already skilled in the art of survival. Those frolics with Seymour which had ended in his journey to the scaffold had provided a lesson well learned. When they charged her with treason she had shown herself to be astute, and it was impossible for her judges to confute her. She parried their accusations with diplomatic dexterity so that none was able to prove the case against her.

Wyatt died by the ax, but Elizabeth escaped. She was imprisoned in the Tower of London for a while at the same time as Robert Dudley. What a bond that made between them I was to discover. We heard later that after many months she had been released from the menace of the Tower, whence she was taken to Richmond, and there confronted by her half sister the Queen and told of the latter's plan to marry her off to Emmanuel Philibert, Duke of Savoy.

"They want to get her out of England," cried my father. "That's clear enough, God knows."

Shrewd as ever, the young Princess declined the match and with great temerity told her sister that she could not marry. Elizabeth always knew just how far to go and in some way she succeeded in convincing Mary that marriage with any man would be distasteful to her.

When she was sent to Woodstock in the charge of Queen Mary's faithful Sir Henry Bedingfeld, the Knollys family breathed more easily, particularly as rumors of the Queen's bad state of health kept filtering in.

Terrible news came to us from England of the bitter persecution of Protestants. Cranmer, Ridley, and Latimer were all burned at the stake with three hundred other victims, and it was said that the smoke of the Smithfield Fires was like a black pall hanging over London.

How we applauded our father's wisdom! Who knew, had we stayed he might have been one of those destined for such a fate.

It could not continue, he told us. The people were weary of death and persecution. The whole country was ready to rise in revolt against the Queen and her Spanish adherents. However, when the news came that she was pregnant we were in despair. Her hopes—"God be praised," said my father—were soon proved to be without foundation. Poor sick Mary, she wanted a child so badly that she could delude herself into suffering all the signs of pregnancy when she was barren.

But we, who shamelessly longed for her death, had little sympathy to spare for her.

I remember well the misty November day when the messenger came with the news. It was the day we had been waiting for.

I was seventeen years old then, and I had never before seen my father so excited.

In the hall he cried: "Rejoice in this day. Queen Mary is dead. Elizabeth is proclaimed Queen of England by will of the people. Long live our Queen Elizabeth."

We knelt and gave thanks to God. Then we hastened to make our preparations for our return.

Royal Scandal

•=o•=o•=o•=o•=o•=o•=o•=o•=o•=o•=o•=o•=o•=o•=o•=o•=o•=o•=o•=o•=o•=o•=o•=o•=o•=o•=o

Much suspected—of me,
Nothing proved can be,
Quoth Elizabeth, prisoner.

> *Scratched with a diamond on a*
> *pane of glass in a window at*
> *Woodstock by Elizabeth before*
> *she became Queen.*

We arrived back in time to see her coronation. What a day that was with the people rejoicing and telling themselves that good times lay ahead. The smell of smoke from the Smithfield Fires still seemed to cling to the air but that only added to the jubilation. Bloody Mary was dead and Elizabeth the Good ruled our land.

I saw her leave for the Tower at two of the afternoon of that January day; she was dressed in the royal robes of a queen and she looked the part in her chariot, which was covered with crimson velvet over which was a canopy borne by her knights, one of whom was Sir John Perrot, a man of mighty girth who claimed to be the illegitimate son of Henry VIII and therefore brother to the Queen.

I could not take my eyes from her in her crimson velvet robe, ermine cape and cap to match her robe under which her fair hair showed, glinting red in the sparkling frosty air. Her tawny eyes were bright and eager, her complexion dazzlingly fair. I thought she was beautiful in that moment. She was all that our mother had told us. She was magnificent.

She was over medium height and very slender, which made her seem younger than she actually was. She was twenty-five at this time, and to a girl of seventeen that seemed quite old. I noticed her hands, for she called attention to them by displaying them as much as possible. They were white, elegant with long tapering fingers. Her face was oval and longish; her brows so fair that they were scarcely perceptible; her eyes were piercing—a golden yellow, but often later I thought they sometimes seemed quite dark. She was a little shortsighted and often when she was endeavoring to see she gave the impression of penetrating into the minds of those about her, which made them very uneasy. There was a quality about her which even then—young as I was and on such an occasion—I was able to perceive, and it thrilled me to watch her.

Then my attention was caught and held by someone

26

else as arresting as she was. This was Robert Dudley, her Master of Horse, who rode with her. I had never seen such a man. He was as outstanding in that assembly as the Queen herself. In the first place he was very tall and broad-shouldered and possessed one of the handsomest faces I had ever seen. He was stately, noble, and his dignity matched that of the Queen. There was nothing haughty about his expression; it was grave, and he had an air of extreme but quiet confidence.

My eager looks went from him to the young Queen and then back again.

I noticed that the Queen paused to speak to the most humble people, smiling and giving them her attention, brief as it must be. I learned in time that it was her policy never to offend the people. Her courtiers often felt the weight of her displeasure but to the common people she was always the benevolent Queen. When they cried: "God save Your Grace!" she answered: "God save you all!" reminding them that she was no less conscious of their well-being than they were of hers. Nosegays were offered to her and however humble the giver she took them as graciously as though they were rare gifts. It was said that one beggar gave her a branch of rosemary at the Fleet Bridge, and it was still in her carriage when she came to Westminster.

We rode with the procession—after all, were we not her kinsfolk?—so we saw the pageants of Cornhill and the Chepe, which was gay with banners and streamers which fluttered from every window.

The next day we were present at her coronation and saw her walk into the Abbey on the purple cloth which had been spread for her.

I was too bemused to pay much attention to the ceremony, but I thought she was beautiful when she was crowned first in the heavy crown of St. Edward and afterwards in the smaller one of pearls and diamonds. The pipes, the drums and the trumpet sounded as Elizabeth was crowned Queen of England.

"Life will be different for us now," said my father. And how right he was.

It was not long before the Queen sent for him. He was given an audience and came back to us full of enthusiasm and hope.

"She is wonderful," he told us. "She is all that a Queen should be. The people adore her and she is full of goodwill towards them. I thank God that he has preserved me to serve such a Queen, and so will I with my life."

She admitted him to her Council and intimated that she wished her good cousin, Catherine—my mother—to become a lady of her Privy Chamber.

We girls were jubilant. This would mean that we would go to Court at last. All those hours of musical tuition—madrigals, lute and harpischord—all the dancing, bowing and curtsying, everything we had endured that we might comport ourselves with grace, had been worthwhile. We chattered interminably; we lay awake at night discussing our future, for we could not sleep, so excited were we. I might have had some premonition that I was going to my destiny, so deeply did this wild exultation possess me.

The Queen expressed a desire to see us—not en bloc but singly.

"There will be places for you all," my mother told us excitedly. "And indeed you will have opportunities."

"Opportunities" meant good marriages and that was a matter which had deeply concerned our parents during our exile.

The day arrived when it was my turn to be presented to Her Majesty. Vividly I remember to this day every detail of the gown I wore. It was of deep blue silk, bombasted, and with a bell-shaped skirt and slashed sleeves. The bodice was tightly fitting and my mother gave me a girdle, which she greatly prized, to wear about my waist. It was set with small precious stones of varying colors and she told me it would bring me luck. Soon afterwards, I decided that it had. I had wanted to have my hair uncovered for, to tell the truth, I was extremely proud of it—but my mother said that one of the new French hoods would be more suitable. I was a little rebellious about this, for the veil which flowed out behind concealed my hair; but I had to give way this once, for my mother was very nervous as to the effect I might have on the Queen, and she stressed the point that if I displeased her I could spoil not only my chances but those of the others as well.

What struck me most forcibly at the first meeting was her aura of sovereignty, and at that moment—although neither of us knew it then—our lives became entwined. She was to play a more important part in my life than anyone else—except perhaps Robert—and my role in hers, in spite of all the momentous events of her reign, was not insignificant.

No doubt I was a little naïve at the time in spite of my attempts at worldliness. The German years had been stultifying but I was to realize at once that there was in her a quality which I had never seen in any other person. Her twenty-five years, I knew, had been filled with terrifying experiences, enough to break most people forever. She had come near to death and indeed lived under its shadow, as prisoner in the Tower of London, with the ax again and again ready to fall on that fragile neck. She had not been quite three years old when her mother had gone to her execution. Was she old enough to have remembered that? There was something about those big tawny eyes to suggest that she did and that she would learn quickly and remember what she had learned. She was notoriously precocious —a scholar in the nursery. Oh yes, she remembered! Perhaps that was why though Death had followed closely behind her through those precarious years it had never succeeded in catching up with her. She was regal—so briefly a Queen—and yet to be one minute in her company was to know that she wore her royalty effortlessly, as though she had been preparing for it all her life—which perhaps she had. She was very slender, straight-backed, and her fair skin had been inherited from her father. Her elegant mother had been dark-haired, olive-skinned. I, not Elizabeth, had inherited those dark eyes, which were also said to be like those of my grandmother Mary Boleyn, but my hair—abundant and curly—was the color of pale honey. It would be foolish to deny that this combination was very attractive, and I had quickly realized this. From what I had seen of Boleyn portraits Elizabeth had inherited nothing from her mother, except perhaps that indefinable brilliance, which I was sure her mother must have possessed to have so bewitched the King that he rid himself of his royal Spanish wife and broke with Rome itself for her sake.

Elizabeth's hair was like a golden halo with hints of red in it. I had heard that her father possessed a magnetism which drew people to him in spite of his cruelty, and she had that too; but in her case it was tempered with a feminine power to bewitch which must have come through her mother.

I felt in those first moments that she was all that I had pictured her to be and I immediately sensed that she had taken a fancy to me. My unusual coloring and my vivacity had meant that I had always been accepted as the beauty of our family and my good looks had attracted the Queen.

"You have a good deal of your grandmother in you," my mother had once said. "You will have to guard against your nature."

I knew what she meant. Men would find me attractive, as they had Mary Boleyn, and I should have to guard against granting favors where they could bring me no good. It was a prospect which delighted me and was one of the reasons why I was so pleased to have come to Court.

The Queen was seated on a large carved chair which was like a throne and my mother led me to her.

"Your Majesty, my daughter Letitia. We call her Lettice in the family."

I curtsied, keeping my eyes lowered as I had been told I must, conveying that I dared not raise them because of the dazzling brilliance of royalty.

"Then so shall I call her," said the Queen. "Lettice, stand up and come closer so that I can see you better."

Shortsightedness made her pupils seem very large. I was amazed by the delicate texture and whiteness of her skin; her light brows and lashes gave her a certain look of surprise.

"Why, Cat," she said to my mother, for it was a habit of hers to give people nicknames and my mother's being Catherine it was easy to see why she called her Cat, "you have a pretty daughter here."

In those days my good looks pleased her. She was always susceptible to good looks—particularly in men, of course, but she did like handsome women too . . . until the men she liked admired them also!

"Thank you, Your Majesty."

The Queen laughed. "You're a fertile wife, Cousin," she said. "Seven sons and four daughters, is it? I like to see large families. And, Lettice, give me your hand. We're cousins, you know. How like you England now you have returned to it?"

"England is a beautiful place since Your Majesty became its Queen."

"Ha!" she laughed. "I see you bring her up in the right fashion. That's Francis, I'll swear."

"Francis was always watchful of what was happening to his sons and daughters while we were away from home," said my mother. "When Your Majesty was in danger he was in despair . . . so indeed were we all."

She nodded gravely. "Well, now you are home and life

31

should go well for you. You'll have to find husbands for your girls, Cat. If they are all as handsome as Lettice that should not be difficult."

"It is such a joy to be home, Madam," said my mother. "I verily believe that neither I nor Francis can give thought to anything but that for a while."

"We shall see what can be done," said the Queen, her eyes on me. "Your Lettice has not much to say for herself," she commented.

"I had believed I must wait for Your Majesty's permission to speak," I said quietly.

"So you can speak up, then. I'm glad of that. I could never abide those who cannot give an account of themselves. A plausible rogue is more amusing than a silent saint. So what will you tell me of yourself?"

"I will say that I share my parents' delight in being here and seeing my royal kinswoman where we have always fervently believed she belonged."

"Well spoken. I can see that you have after all taught her to use her tongue, Cousin."

"That is something I taught myself, Madam," I retorted quickly.

My mother looked alarmed at my temerity, but the Queen's lips twitched in a manner which showed she was not displeased.

"What else did you teach yourself?" asked the Queen.

"To listen when I was incapable of taking part in discussion; and to throw myself into the center of it when I could."

The Queen laughed. "Then you have learned much wisdom. You will have need of it when you come to Court. Many prate but a few ever learn the art of listening and those who do are the wise men and women. And you . . . but seventeen, is it? . . . have learned this already. Come and sit near me. I would talk with you for a while."

My mother was looking well pleased and at the same

time flashed a warning glance at me, telling me not to let this initial success go to my head. She was right. I could be impulsive, and instinct warned me that the Queen could be as suddenly displeased as pleased.

My opportunity to walk on this dangerous ground was denied me, for at that moment the door opened unceremoniously and a man came into the room. My mother looked startled and I realized that he must have broken some strict rule of royal etiquette thus to burst in unannounced.

He was different from any man I had seen. There was an indefinable quality about him which was immediately apparent. To say that he was handsome—which he undoubtedly was—conveys little. There are many handsome men but I have never found one who was possessed of his outstanding quality. I had seen him before at the coronation. It may be thought that it was love which made me see Robert Dudley thus; it may be that he bemused and bewitched me as he did so many women—even Elizabeth herself—but I did not always love him, and when I look far back and remember what happened in our last days together I shudder even now. Loving or hating Robert Dudley, one would have to admit that charismatic quality. Charism is defined as a free gift of grace and I can think of nothing better with which to describe him. He was born with that free gift of grace, and he knew it well.

In the first place he was one of the tallest men I have ever seen and he emanated power. Power, I believe, is the very essence of attractiveness in men. At least it has always been so with me . . . until I grew older. When I discussed lovers with my sisters—and I did frequently because I knew they would play a big part in my life—I said my lover would be a man who would command others; he would be rich and others would fear his wrath—all except myself. He would fear mine. I realize that in describing the sort of lover I desired, I am in truth describing myself. I was always ambitious—not for temporal power. I never envied Elizabeth her crown, and I was glad that *she* had it because when the rivalry was strong between us I could prove that I could triumph over her without it. I wanted attention to be centered on me. I wanted to be irresistible to those who pleased me. I was at this time beginning to realize that I was a woman of deep sensual needs and that they would have to be satisfied.

Robert Dudley, then, was the most attractive man I had ever seen. He was very dark—almost to swarthiness, his hair growing thick and nearly black; his dark eyes were lively and gave the impression of seeing all; his nose was slightly hooked; his figure was that of an athlete, and he held himself like a king in the presence of a queen.

I sensed the change his arrival created in Elizabeth. Her pale skin was tinged with pink.

" 'Tis Rob," she said, "as we might have expected. So you come to us thus unannounced." The soft caress in her voice belied the sharpness of her words, and it was clear that the interruption was by no means unwelcome, clear too she had forgotten my mother and me.

She held out her beautiful white hand; he bowed as he took it and kissed it, keeping it while his eyes went to her face and by the smile they exchanged I could have sworn they were lovers.

"Dear lady," he said, "I made haste to come to you."

"Some calamity?" she replied. "Come, tell me."

"Nay," he replied, "only the desire to see you which would not be put aside."

My mother's hand was on my shoulder, turning me towards the door. I looked back at the Queen. I had supposed I should wait for permission to retire.

My mother shook her head as she inclined it towards the door. We went out together. The Queen had forgotten us; so had Robert Dudley.

When the door had shut behind us, my mother said:

"They say there would be a marriage between them but for the fact that he already has a wife."

I kept thinking about them. I could not forget the handsome, elegant Robert Dudley and the manner in which he had looked at the Queen. I was piqued that he had not cast even one glance in my direction, and I promised myself that if he had I should have made him take a second. I kept seeing him in his white starched ruff, his padded hips, his doublet, his bombasted breeches, the diamond in one ear. I remembered the perfect shape of his legs in their close-fitting hose; he had been garterless because of the symmetry of his legs, which allowed him to dispense with articles so necessary to men less well equipped.

The memory of that first meeting remained in my mind as something I had to avenge, because on that occasion when the triangle was formed neither of them gave a thought to Lettice Knollys whose mother, a short time before, had most humbly presented her to the Queen.

It was a beginning. After that I was often at Court. The Queen had a strong friendly feeling for her mother's family even though the name of Anne Boleyn was rarely mentioned. This was characteristic of Elizabeth. There were certain to be many people in the country who doubted her legitimacy. None would dare refer to it, of course, on pain of death, but she was too wise not to accept the fact that it was in their minds. Although Anne Boleyn's name was rarely mentioned, the Queen was constantly calling attention to her own resemblance to her father Henry VIII and in fact stressed the similarities whenever possible. As she undoubtedly had a look of him, this was not difficult. At the same time she was always ready to favor her mother's relations, as if in that way she might make amends to that forsaken lady. My sister Cecilia and I thus became maids of honor to the Queen and so within a few weeks we were ladies of the Court. Anne and Catharine were too young, but in due course their time would come.

Life was full of excitement. This is what we had dreamed of during the dull years in Germany and I was just of an age to enjoy it.

The Court was the center of the country—a magnet drawing to it the rich and ambitious. All the great families of the country circulated about the Queen, each vying with the other in magnificence. Elizabeth, at the very heart of it, loved display and extravagance—as long as she did not have to pay for it; she enjoyed pageantry, gaiety, balls and banquets—although I noticed that she was abstemious regarding both drinking and eating. But she was fond of music and was tireless where dancing was concerned, and although she danced mainly with Robert Dudley, she did take a fleeting delight in any handsome young man who could dance well. She fascinated me mainly because of the diversity of her character. To see her in some extravagantly glittering gown dancing—and often coquettishly—with Robert Dudley, so that the performance was like the titillating preliminary to an amorous climax, gave an impression of such lightness which in a queen would seem fatal to her future; then she could change suddenly; she would be acerbic, serious, asserting her authority and even then showing men of great talent like William Cecil that she had a complete grasp of a situation and it would be her will that would be done. As no one could be sure when her lighthearted mood would be over, everyone must tread cautiously. Robert Dudley was the only one who overstepped the mark; but I saw her, on more than one occasion, administer a playful slap on his cheek, familiarly affectionate and yet at the same time carrying with it a reminder that she was the Queen and he her subject. I saw Robert take the reproving hand and kiss it, which softened her mood. He was very sure of himself in those days.

It was soon clear that she had taken a liking to me. I

danced as well as she did, though none would have dared acknowledge this. At Court no one danced as well as the Queen; no woman's gown was as becoming as the Queen's; no one's beauty could possibly compare with hers; she was supreme in all things. I knew full well, however, that I was spoken of as one of the most beautiful women at Court; the Queen acknowledged this and called me "Cousin." I had a certain wit too, which I warily tried on the Queen. It did not displease her. She found that she could indulge her Boleyn relations from pleasure as well as duty to her dead mother, and there were frequent times when she kept me at her side. In those first days we, who were to confront each other in such bitterness and with such hatred in the years to come, then often laughed together, and she showed so clearly that she enjoyed my company. But she did not allow me—or any other of her pretty ladies—to be near her when Robert was with her in her private apartments. I often used to think that the reason she must constantly be told she was transcendingly beautiful was because she was unsure of it. How attractive would she be without royalty? I asked myself. But it was impossible to imagine her without it because it was so much a part of her. I would study my long lashes, my heavily marked brows, my luminous dark eyes and rather narrow face framed in masses of honey-yellow hair and exultantly compare my face with the pale one with its almost invisible lashes and brows, its imperious nose, its white, white skin which made her look almost delicate. I knew that any unprejudiced observer would admit that I was the beauty. But *her* royalty was there and with it the knowledge that she was the sun and the rest of us merely planets revolving around her, dependent on her for our light. In the days before she had become Queen she had been delicate and had suffered several illnesses during her hazardous youth and had, so we had heard, often been on the point of death. Now she was Queen she seemed to have thrown off these ailments; they had been the growing pains of royalty; but even when she had dispensed with them the pallor of her skin preserved the air of delicacy. When she painted her face, which she loved to do, she lost that look of fragility, but whatever she did, the royalty remained, and that was something with which no woman could compete.

She talked to me more frankly than she did to most of her ladies. I think it was due to the family connection. She enjoyed clothes inordinately and we often talked of them in a most frivolous fashion. She had so many gowns that even the wardrobe women could not be sure of the number; her figure was slender and the fashions which were so hard on plump women became her as well as they could any. She endured tight lacing and the uncomfortable whalebone busks we had to wear because they called attention to the tiny waist; and her ruffs were of gold and silver lace and frequently magnificently jeweled. Even in those days she sometimes wore what we called "dead-borrowed hair"—false pieces to give additional body to her red-gold locks.

I am writing of the days before the Amy Robsart scandal. She was never quite so lighthearted after that, never quite so carefree. In spite of her incessant demand for expressions of wonder at her perfections she was always ready to learn from experience. That was another of the many contrasts which made up her complex nature. She would never chatter so freely to anyone again as she did to me before the tragedy.

I think in those days she really might have married Robert if he had been free; but at the same time I sensed that she was not too unhappy about his previous attachment, which made her marriage to Robert impossible. This I was too naïve to realize at the time and I believed that the reason she was pleased he was married to Amy Robsart was solely because that marriage had saved him from an alliance with Lady Jane Grey. But that was too simple an explanation. It was obvious that I had a great deal to learn then about that devious mind.

She talked of him to me and I often smile to recall those conversations now. Even she, with all her power, could not see into the future. He was her "Sweet Robin." She called him fondly her "Eyes," because he was always on the watch for her well-being, she told me. She enjoyed giving pet names to the handsome men who surrounded her. None, though, could compare with her Eyes. We were all certain that she would have married him if he had had no wife, but when that encumbrance was removed she was too wily to step into the trap. Few women would have been as wise. Should I? I wondered. I doubted it.

"We were in the Tower together," she told me once, "I because of Wyatt's rebellion, Rob because of the Jane Grey matter. Poor Rob, he always said he had no great feeling for it and that he would have given all he had to see me on the throne." I saw the soft look come into her face which changed it completely. That rather hawklike expression completely disappeared, and she was soft and feminine suddenly. Not that she was not always feminine. That quality never failed to show itself in her sternest moments, and I always believed it was, in some measure, her strength, the very reason she was able to make men work for her as for no one else. Being a woman was a part of her genius. I never saw that look, though, for anyone but Robert. He was the love of her life—next to the crown, of course.

"His brother Guildford had married Jane," she went on. "That sly fox Northumberland had seen to that. It could have been Rob—imagine that. But Fate married him off so he was not available, and although it was a mésalliance, it is one for which we must be grateful. So there we were in the Beauchamp Tower. The Earl of Sussex came to me. I remember it clearly. Would not you, Cousin Lettice, if you thought that before long your body would be deprived of its head? I had made up my mind that it would be no ax for me. I would have a sword from France." Her expression was blank suddenly and I knew she was thinking of her mother. "But in fact I never intended to die. I determined that it must not come to that, and I stood firm against them all. Something within me said: 'Have patience. In a few years all this will have changed.' Yes, I swear it. I knew this would come to pass."

"It was the prayers of Your Majesty's subjects which you heard," I said.

She never saw through flattery, or perhaps she did and liked it so much that she gobbled it up like a gourmand who knows it is bad for him but finds it irresistible.

"That may be. But I was taken to the Traitor's Gate and for a moment—though only for a moment—my heart failed me. And as I alighted and stood in the water, because the fools had misjudged the tide, I cried out: 'Here lands as true a subject, being prisoner, as ever landed at these stairs. Before Thee, oh God, I speak it, having no other friend but Thee alone.' "

"I know it well, Your Majesty," I told her. "Your brave words were recorded. They were both brave and clever, for the Lord, put thus on His mettle, must prove that He was as good an ally as all your enemies put together."

She looked at me and laughed. "You amuse me, Cousin," she said. "You must stay with me."

Then she went on to explain: "It was all so romantic. But then anything concerned with Rob always is. He made friends with the warder's boy, who adored him. Even little boys are aware of Robin's charm. The boy brought him flowers and Robin sent them to me . . . by way of the child . . . and there was a note for me enclosed in them. Thus I knew he was in the Tower and where. He was always audacious. He might have got us straightway to the block, but then, as he said when I taunted him with this, we were both halfway there already. And he never visualized failure; that is a quality we share. When they allowed me to walk out for exercise in the precincts of the Tower I went past Robert's cell. Oh, they were afraid to be too harsh with me, those jailers. Wise men! There was a chance I remember . . . one day. And so should I. But I found Robin and saw him through the bars of his window and that encounter sweetened our prison stay for both of us."

Once she started talking of Robert she found it difficult to stop.

"He was the first to come to me, Lettice," she went on. "That was right and fitting. The Queen, my sister, was sick unto death. Poor Mary, my heart went out to her. I was ever her good and faithful subject as all should be to their sovereign. But the people were sickened by what had happened during her reign. They wanted an end to religious persecution. They wanted a Protestant queen."

Her eyes were slightly veiled. Yes, I thought, it was so, my Queen. And if they had wanted a Catholic queen would you have obliged? I had no doubt in my mind as to that. Her religion sat lightly on her; perhaps it was as well; the late Queen had been so heavily weighed down by hers that it had ruined her good name with her people and made them rejoice in her death.

"A queen must rule through the will of the people," said Elizabeth. "Praise God, it is a truth which is clear to me. When my sister was near to death, the road to Hatfield was crowded with those who would come to pay homage to Elizabeth, whose name, but a short while before, few of them dared mention. But Robert had always been for me, and it was meet and fitting that he should be the first to come to me. He stood before me, freshly arrived from France. He would have been with me before, he told me, but by so doing he would have put me in danger. And he brought gold with him . . . a token that should it be necessary to fight for my rights he would be beside me and

41

would raise money to support me . . . aye, and he would have done so."

"His loyalty did him credit," I said, and added slyly: "And brought him much good. Your Majesty's Master of Horse, no less."

"He has a way with horses, Lettice."

"And with women, Your Majesty."

I had gone too far. I realized that at once and a shiver ran through me.

"Why say you that?" she demanded.

"A man of such excellent parts, of such fine countenance and figure must surely enchant all that is female, Madam, walk they on two or four legs."

She was suspicious and although she allowed my comment to pass, my face was slapped none too gently a short while later because, she said, I handled one of her gowns clumsily. But I knew it was not for the gown but for Robert Dudley. Those beautifully shaped hands could deliver a sturdy blow, particularly when some jeweled ring cut into the skin. A gentle reminder that it would be unwise to displease the Queen.

I noticed that on the next occasion when Robert was present she watched him closely—and me. We did not look at each other and I think she was satisfied.

Robert was completely unaware of me in those days. He was firmly bent on one ambition from which nothing could make him swerve. At that time the determination to marry the Queen occupied him day and night.

I often wondered about his poor wife in the country and what she thought about the rumors. The fact that he never brought her to Court must have aroused her suspicion. I thought what fun it would be to bring her there. I imagined myself calling on Lady Amy and suggesting that she accompany me back to Court. I liked to picture myself presenting her. "Your Majesty, my good friend, Lady Dudley. You have shown such favor to my lord that passing Cumnor Place in Berkshire and meeting the lady, I was sure you would wish to give Lord Robert the pleasure of his wife's company." By which I betray that mischievous streak in my nature—also my annoyance because, I, Lettice Knollys, so much more attractive than Elizabeth Tudor, was ignored—not even seen at all—by the most handsome man at Court; and all because she possessed a crown and I had nothing but myself.

I would, of course, never have dared to bring Lady Dudley to Court. There would be more than a sharp slap on the cheek if I did. I could see myself returning to Rotherfield Greys never to emerge again.

I was amused when an old woman was arrested for having slandered the Queen. It amazed me that a woman of no fixed address who spent her life tramping the countryside, doing odd jobs for which she could get food and lodging, should think she knew more of what happened in the Queen's bedchamber than those of us who were in attendance on her.

However, it seemed that old Mother Dowe, while doing some mending for a lady, had heard that lady say that Lord Robert had given the Queen a petticoat for a gift. Later Mother Dowe offered the information that it was not a petticoat which Lord Robert had given the Queen, but a child.

If the story had been clearly conjecture and utterly incredible there would have been no need to take any notice of a mad old woman; but in view of the Queen's attitude towards Robert and his towards her, and the fact that they were undoubtedly often in each other's company unattended, the story could have been believed. Thus the old woman was arrested and the news of that arrest spread through the country at great speed.

Elizabeth showed her growing skill by dismissing the woman as mad and allowing her to go about her business, thus earning her undying gratitude, for the poor creature must have anticipated cruel death for spreading such rumors; and very soon the case of Mother Dowe was forgotten.

I often wonder whether it had some effect on the Queen's attitude to what happened soon after.

It was inevitable that, both at home and abroad, there should be speculation about her marriage. The country needed an heir; the recent troubles and dissensions which had beset us had been due to uncertainty about the succession. The Queen's ministers desired that she should choose a husband without delay and give the country what it wanted. She was not yet even middle-aged, neither was she so very young, though none would dare remind her of this.

Philip of Spain was making overtures. I heard her and Robert laughing about it because she had learned that the King had said that if he were persuaded to the match he would insist on Elizabeth's becoming a Catholic and he could not remain with her for long even if their brief encounter did not leave her pregnant. He could have said nothing more calculated to arouse her indignation. Become a Catholic!—when one of the main reasons for her popularity was her professed Protestantism and the cessation of the Smithfield Fires. And for any future husband to mention the fact that he wanted to escape from her as soon as possible was enough to bring about her haughty refusal.

But of course her ministers were eager for her to marry, and it seemed that, had it not been for the fact that Lord Robert was already married, some of them would have agreed to her union with him. There was a great deal of envy directed against Robert. My long life, much of which has been lived among ambitious people, leads me to the belief that envy is more prevalent than any other emotion and certainly the deadliest of the seven sins. Robert had the Queen's favor to such an extent that she could not hide her fondness for him and showered honors on him; and

44

those who would see that favor diminished found more suitable prospective husbands for her. The nephew of Philip of Spain—the Archduke Charles—was one of these suitors. The Duke of Saxony was another; then Prince Charles of Sweden was brought in. It was a case of the more the merrier as far as the Queen was concerned, and she delighted in teasing Robert by pretending to consider them, but she did not deceive many into thinking that she would accept any of them. The prospect of marriage always excited her—even when she was much older—but her attitude to it forever remained a mystery. Somewhere at the back of her mind she greatly feared it, yet at times, to consider it fascinated her as nothing else did. None of us ever understood that aspect of her character, which intensified as the years passed. At this time we were all unaware of it and everyone believed that she would marry sooner or later and that she would have taken one of her royal suitors if it had not been for Robert.

But Robert was there, always by her side, her Sweet Robin, her Eyes, her Master of Horse.

From Scotland came another offer. This time from the Earl of Arran but this was summarily dismissed by the Queen.

In the apartments of the Queen's women we used to whisper together. We speculated and I was often warned because of my boldness.

"You'll overstep the mark one day, Lettice Knollys," I was told. "Then the Queen will send you packing—Boleyn cousin though you may be."

I used to shiver at the thought of being sent back in disgrace to the boredom of Rotherfield Greys. I already had several admirers. Cecilia was sure I should have an offer of marriage before long, but I did not want to marry yet. I wanted time to make the right choice. I longed for a lover, although I was far too astute to take one before marriage. I had heard stories of girls who became pregnant and were dismissed from Court and married off to some country squire and doomed to spend the rest of their lives in the dullness of the country and endure their acquired husband's reproaches for their light behavior and the great good he had done them by marrying them. So I enjoyed my flirtations, going so far and no further, and exchanging accounts of adventures with girls of a like nature.

I used to let myself dream that Lord Robert looked my way and I wondered what would happen if he did. I could not regard him as a suitor because he already had a wife, and if he had not, doubtless he would have been the Queen's husband by this time. But there was no harm in allowing myself to imagine that he came courting *me* and how, in spite of the Queen, we met and laughed together because she was not the one he wanted. Wild fancies—premonitions, I thought later—for at that time they *were* but fancies. Robert would never allow his gaze to stray from the Queen.

I remember one occasion when she was in a thoughtful mood. Her temper had been none too good because she had heard that Philip of Spain was to marry Elizabeth of Valois, daughter of Henri Deux of France, and although she did not want a suitor she did not like anyone else to have him.

"She's a Catholic already," she commented, "so he'll not have to bother about that. And as she is of little importance she can leave her country and go to Spain. The poor thing won't have to worry about being left, pregnant or otherwise."

"Your Majesty knew well how to deal with such ungallant conduct," I said soothingly.

She snorted. She had some very unfeminine habits sometimes. She looked at me quizzically. "I wish him joy of her and her of him—though I fear she'll get little. What disturbs me is the alliance between two of my enemies."

"Since Your Majesty came to the throne your people have ceased to fear their enemies abroad."

"Then more fool they!" she snapped. "Philip is a powerful man and England must always be wary of him. As for France . . . it has a new king now and a new queen . . . two sad little people, I believe, though one of them is my own Scottish kinswoman of whose beauty poets prate."

"As they do of Your Majesty's."

She bowed her head but her eyes were fierce. "She dares to call herself Queen of England—that Scottish girl, who spends her time dancing and urging poets to write odes to her. They say her charm and beauty are unsurpassed."

"She is the Queen, Madam."

The fierce eyes were on me. I had slipped. If one queen's beauty was measured by her royalty, what of another?

"So you think that is why they praise her, then?"

I called in the helpful and anonymous "They." "They say, Madam, that Mary Stuart is light in her fancies and surrounds herself with lovers who curry favor by writing odes to her beauty." I was crafty. I must extricate myself from her displeasure. "They say, Madam, that she is by no means as beautiful as hearsay would have us believe. She is over tall, ungainly and suffers from spots."

"Is that so, then?"

I breathed more freely and tried to remember anything derogatory I had heard against the Queen of France and Scotland, and I could only recall praise.

So I said: "They say that Lord Robert's wife is sick of a fatal disease and that she cannot last the year."

She closed her eyes and I was not sure whether I dared go on. "They say!" They say!" she burst out suddenly. "Who says?"

She turned on me sharply and nipped my arm. I could

have cried out with pain, for those beautiful pointed fingers were capable of very sharp nips.

"I but repeat gossip, Madam, because I think it may amuse Your Majesty."

"I would hear what is said."

"So I thought."

"And what else say *They* of Lord Robert's wife?"

"That she lives quietly in the country and that she is unworthy of him and that it was ill luck that he should have married when he was but a boy."

She sat back nodding, and there was a smile about her lips.

It was not long after that when I heard that Lord Robert's wife was dead. She had been discovered at the bottom of a staircase at Cumnor Place with her neck broken.

The Court was agog. None dared talk of it in the presence of the Queen, but they could scarcely wait to do so out of her sight and hearing.

What had happened to Amy Dudley? Had she committed suicide? Was it an accident? Or had she been murdered?

In view of all the rumors which had persisted through the last months, in view of the fact that the Queen and Robert Dudley behaved like lovers, and Robert seemed to have a conviction that soon he would marry the Queen, the last suggestion did not seem an impossibility.

We whispered about it and forgot to watch our words. My parents sent for me and lectured me severely on the need for the utmost discretion. I could see that my father was worried.

"This could rob Elizabeth of her throne," I heard him tell my mother. Certainly he was worried, for the Knollys fortunes were as ever wrapped up in those of our royal kinswoman.

The rumors grew more and more unpleasant. I heard that the Spanish Ambassador had written to his master that the Queen had told him Lady Dudley was dead several days *before* she was found dead at the bottom of the stairs. This was completely damning, but I could hardly accept it as truth. If Elizabeth and Robert were planning to have Amy murdered, Elizabeth would never have told the Spanish ambassador that she was dead before she was. De Quadra was wily; it was in his country's interest to discredit the Queen. This was what he was trying to do. Being aware of the potent masculinity of Robert Dudley, I could imagine a woman's going to great lengths to get him. I put myself in Elizabeth's position and asked myself: Would I? And I could well picture our plotting together in the heat of our passion.

We all waited tensely for what would happen next.

I could not believe that the Queen would ever put her crown in jeopardy for any man, and that if Amy had been murdered, she would have allowed herself to become involved. Of course she was capable of indiscretion. One only had to remember the case of Thomas Seymour when she had allowed herself to be led into a very dangerous state of affairs. Ah, but the crown was not hers at that time and she had not then begun that passionate devotion to it.

The great point was that Robert was now free to marry her. The whole Court, the whole country, and, I suspected, the whole of Europe waited to see how she would respond. One thing was clear. On the day she married Robert Dudley she would be judged guilty, and that was what men like my father were afraid of.

The first thing she did was send Robert away from Court, which was wise. They must not be seen together so that people would in any way connect the Queen with the tragedy.

Robert, expressing great distress—feigned or otherwise (although perhaps he could have been distraught by what

49

had happened even if he had arranged it)—sent his cousin, Thomas Blount, to Cumnor Place to take charge of the proceedings, and there followed an inquest at which the verdict was Accidental Death.

How difficult Elizabeth was during the weeks which followed. It was so easy to offend her. She swore at us—she could curse like her royal father, it was said, and took a great pleasure in using his favorite oaths—and then would give us a nip or a slap. I believed she was undergoing torment. She wanted Robert and yet she knew that to marry him would be tantamount to an admission of guilt. She would know that in the streets of the cities people would suspect her; if she married Robert they would suspect her; if she married Robert they would not respect her again. A queen had to be above ordinary passions. They would see her as merely a weak and sinful woman; and she knew that if she were to keep her hold on the glittering crown she must retain her people's devotion.

At least that was what I surmised occupied her thoughts as she loured in her apartments. But later I began to think I was wrong.

Robert returned to Court—bold and boastful, certain that soon he would be the Queen's husband. After a while he grew sullen, and I, in common with the rest of the world, badly wanted to know what they said to each other when they were alone.

Now I believe that she had no hand in Amy's death, that in a way she had no real wish to marry Robert; she preferred to be unattainable as she had been while his wife lived. She wanted Robert to have a neglected wife not a dead one. Perhaps she did not want marriage because in a strange way she was afraid of it. She wanted romantic attachments; she wanted admirers pining for her love; but she wanted none of that climax which would be triumphant for them and so distasteful to her.

I wonder if that were indeed so.

Whatever the reason, she did not marry Robert. She was too wily for that.

And it was at this time that Walter Devereux came to my notice.

The First Encounter

. . . *herself [Elizabeth] helping to put on his robes, he sitting on his knees before her, and keeping a great gravity and discreet behaviour, but as for the Queen, she could not refrain from putting her hand in his neck to tickle him, smiling, the French Ambassador and I standing beside her.*

> The Scottish Ambassador, SIR JAMES
> MELVILLE, *on the occasion of Robert
> Dudley's being created
> Earl of Leicester.*

She [Elizabeth] said she was never minded to marry. . . . I said, "Madam, ye need not tell me that. I know your stately stomach. Ye think, gin ye were married, ye would be but Queen of England, and now ye are King and Queen baith—ye may not suffer a commander."

> SIR JAMES MELVILLE

God's death, my lord, I have wished you well, but my favour is not so locked up in you that others shall not participate thereof . . . I will have here but one mistress and no master.

> ELIZABETH *to* LEICESTER
> Fragmenta Regalia

I married Walter in the year 1561, when I was in my twenty-first year. My parents were pleased with the match, and the Queen readily gave it her nod of approval. Walter was the second Viscount of Hereford then, about the same age as myself, and because his family was one of standing, it was considered a good match. The Queen remarked that it was time I had a husband, which gave me some misgiving and I wondered if she had noticed that my eyes often wandered in Robert Dudley's direction.

I had come to the conclusion that Robert would never marry anybody but the Queen. Walter had asked me several times to be his wife. I was quite fond of him and my parents wanted the match. He was young and, as my father pointed out, appeared to have a good future ahead of him which would keep him at Court, so I chose him from several suitors and settled for married life.

It is not easy to remember in detail how I felt about Walter, all those years ago. The Queen had hinted that I was a girl who should be married—and she was right. I believe for a while I even thought I was in love with Walter and gave up dreaming of Robert Dudley.

After the ceremony, Walter and I went to his ancestral home, Chartley Castle, a rather impressive edifice rising from a fertile plain. From its high turrets it was possible to see some of the finest scenery in Staffordshire. It was about six miles southeast of the town of Stafford and situated halfway between Rugby and Stone.

Walter was proud of Chartley and I expressed great interest in it because it was to be my home. It had a circular keep and two round towers which were quite ancient, having been constructed as long ago as 1220. They had already stood up to more than three hundred years of wind and weather and looked ready to withstand three hundred more. The walls were twelve feet thick and the loopholes were built so that arrows could be shot horizontally, which made it a wonderful fortress.

There had been a building of some sort there in the days of the Conqueror before the castle was built and the present Chartley had been erected on that old site.

"It belonged to the Earls of Derby," Walter told me, "and it was during the reign of Henry VI that it came into the Devereux family, when one of the daughters of the house married a Walter Devereux, Earl of Essex. We've had it ever since."

I agreed that it was indeed a noble castle.

The first year of my marriage was happy enough. Walter was a devoted husband, deeply in love with me, and marriage and all it entailed agreed with my nature. I went occasionally to Court, where the Queen received me affectionately. I fancied she was more than mildly pleased that I was married, which showed that she had become aware of the pleasure I took in masculine society. She hated the attention of any man to stray from her even for a few moments, and perhaps she had noticed some of her favorites eye me with approval.

Walter had never been among those favored. He lacked that dashing gallantry which she so much admired. I think he was too innately honest to think up extravagant compliments which they were all expected to pay and which when considered were really rather absurd. He was for the Queen and the country; he would serve them with his life; but he simply could not dance attendance on her as those in her innermost circle must.

This meant of course that we were not so often at Court as I had previously been, but when we did go she never forgot her good cousin—myself—and invariably wanted to hear how I was enjoying married life.

Oddly enough, I was quite prepared in those early days of marriage to spend a certain amount of time in the country. I even developed a fondness for the life. I took an interest in my home. It was cold and drafty in the winter and I had great fires roaring in the grates; I made rules for the servants. They must be up at six in the summer and seven in the winter; the beds and fireplaces must be cleaned by eight and fires started for the day. I became interested in the herb gardens and made one of the servants who was especially interested in herbal art instruct me. I arranged flowers in bowls and set them about the house; I sat with the women and embroidered the new altar cloth they were working on. It seems scarcely possible now that I could have thrown myself so wholeheartedly into the country life.

When my family visited us or we had people from the Court to stay, I took a pride in showing what a good housewife I had become. I was proud of our Venetian glasses, which sparkled so delightfully in candlelight when they were filled with good muscatel, romney or malmsey; and I made the servants polish the silver and pewter until the whole scene was reflected in their shining glory. I was determined that our table should be admired for the good fare we offered our guests. I liked to see it laden with meat and fowl and fish, pies fashioned into fanciful shapes, which usually contrived to do some honor to the visitors; and we did the same with marchpane and gingerbread, so everything was much admired.

People marveled. "Lettice has become the best of all hostesses," they said.

It was another trait in my nature that I must always be the best and this was like a new game to me. I was satisfied with my home and my husband; and I gave myself wholeheartedly to that enjoyment.

I used to love to walk through the castle and imagine the days of the past. I had the rushes swept regularly so that our castle was less odoriferous than most. We suffered a good deal from the proximity of the privies—but what house did not?—and I made a rule that the emptying of ours should be done while we were at Court so that we should escape that unpleasantness.

Walter and I would ride round the estate and sometimes walk near the castle. I shall always remember the day he showed me the cows in Chartley Park. They were slightly different from cows I had seen elsewhere.

"They are our very own Stafford cows," said Walter.

I examined them closely, interested because they were ours. They were sand-white in color and there were smudges of black on their muzzles, ears and hoofs.

"We must hope that none of them produce a black calf," Walter told me, and when I wanted to know why he explained: "There's a legend in the family. If a black calf appears that means there will be a death in the family."

"What nonsense!" I cried. "How can the birth of a black calf affect us?"

"It's one of those stories which become attached to families like ours. It all started at the time of the Battle of Burton Bridge when the owner of the house was killed and the castle passed temporarily out of the family."

"But it came back to them."

"Yes, but it was a tragic time. A black calf was born at that time and so it was said that black calves meant disaster for the Devereux family."

"Then we must make sure that no more are born."

"How?"

"Get rid of the cows."

He laughed at me tenderly. "My dear Lettice, that would indeed be defying fate. I am sure the penalty for that would be greater than the birth of a black calf."

I looked at those large-eyed placid creatures and said: "Please, no black calves."

And Walter laughed at me and kissed me and told me how happy he was that I had, after much persuasion, agreed to marry him.

My daughter Penelope was born a year after my marriage.

I experienced the delights of motherhood and of course my daughter was more beautiful, more intelligent and better in every way than any child who had been born before. I was well content to stay at Chartley with her and could not bear to leave her for long. Walter believed at that time that he had found the ideal wife. Poor Walter, he was always a man of poor judgment.

However, while I was crooning over my daughter, I became pregnant again, but I did not experience quite the same ecstasy over this one. I had never remained absorbed for any length of time in any of my enthusiasms and I found the prenatal months irksome. Penelope was showing a spirit of her own, which made her not quite the docile child she had been; and I was beginning to think with increasing longing of the Court and to wonder what was happening there.

I heard the news from time to time and a great deal of it was about the Queen and Robert Dudley. I could imagine how irritated Robert must be by her continued refusal to marry him now that he was free. Oh, but she was wily. How could she marry him and escape the smears of scandal? She never could. For as long as she lived, if she did so, she would be suspected of complicity in the murder of Amy Dudley. People still talked of it—even in country places like Chartley. Some murmured that there was one law for the people and another for the Queen's favorites. There were few people in England who did not believe Robert at least guilty of his wife's murder.

Strangely enough, the effect it had on me was to make me more fascinated than ever. He was a strong man, a man who would have his way. I indulged in fantasies about him and was delighted because the Queen would not have him.

Walter continued to be a good husband, but that wonder he had found in my society—and which had endeared him to me—was no longer there. A man cannot go on being amazed at the sexual prowess of his wife, I suppose; I was certainly not enchanted by his, which had never seemed to me more than one might have expected from any man. It was only because I had been eager for such experiences that I had been so delighted by them. Now with a year-old daughter and another child clamoring to be born, I went through a period of disenchantment, and for the first time I began to be unfaithful . . . in thought.

I could not go to Court in my state but I was always eager to know what was going on there. Walter came back to Chartley with news that the Queen was ill and not expected to live.

I felt a terrible depression, cheated—which was strange, for I could not see into the future. Perhaps it was a blessing that I could not, though even if I could have foreseen I wonder if I should have acted differently. I doubt it.

Walter was gloomy and I guessed my parents too were wondering what would happen to the country if the Queen died. There was a possibility that Mary Queen of Scots, who had been forced to leave France on the death of her young husband François Deux, might be offered the throne.

"Why," said Walter, "two of the Pole brothers did their best to march on London, their object being to put Mary Stuart on the throne. Of course they declared they had no wish to do this and merely wanted the Queen to name Mary of Scotland as her successor."

"And bring back Catholicism!" I cried.

"That was their aim."

"And the Queen?"

"Sick unto death. She sent for Dudley. She would have him with her at the end, she said."

" 'Tis not the end yet," I put in quickly.

I looked at Walter and thought: If she dies, Robert will marry. And now I am married to Walter Devereux!

And I think it was in that moment that I began to dislike my husband.

"She sent for him," went on Walter, "and told him that if she had not been Queen she would have been his wife. Then she called her ministers to her bedside and told them that it was her dying wish that Robert Dudley be made Protector of the Realm."

I caught my breath. "She really does care for him," I said.

"Did you have any doubt of it?"

"She would not marry him."

"Nay, for he stands suspected of murdering his wife."

"I wonder . . ." I began; and I was picturing her carried to her grave, her brief reign over. And what would happen to the country? Some would try to put Mary of Scotland on the throne; and there would be others who wanted the Lady Catharine Grey. We could be plunged into civil war. But the question which plagued me most was: What will Robert do if she dies? And I was asking myself if I had hurried too quickly into marriage and whether it would have been better to have waited a while.

Then I gave birth to my second child—a daughter and I called her Dorothy.

The Queen recovered, which was what might have been expected of her. Moreover she had come through unscathed, which was rare. Robert's sister Mary, who was married to Henry Sidney, had been with the Queen night and day attending to all her needs, caught the smallpox from her and was severely disfigured. I heard that Lady Mary asked leave to retire from Court, permission which could scarcely be denied in the circumstances was given, and she went to her family estate at Penshurst, from where she never really wanted to emerge again. Her reward for nursing Elizabeth, who was not likely to forget it. One of the Queen's virtues was her loyalty to those who served her; besides, Mary Sidney was her beloved Robert's sister.

Walter said that people again believed that a marriage between the Queen and Robert might now take place.

"But why should it be acceptable now when it was not a short time ago?" I demanded.

"It's not such a short while," Walter reminded me, "and the people are so delighted to have her well again that they would be prepared to accept anything. They want her married. They want an heir to the throne. Her recent illness has shown how dangerous it could be if she died without heirs."

"*She* won't die until she wants to," I said grimly.

"That," retorted Walter coolly, "is in the hands of God."

So the Court was soon as it was before her illness. Robert was back in favor, always at her side, always hopeful, I had no doubt; and perhaps more so than ever now that it was being hinted that people would accept a marriage between them.

The Queen was in high spirits—happy to be well again. She pardoned the Pole brothers, a gesture which was typical of her. She wanted to show her people how merciful she was and that she bore no grudges to any. The Poles were exiled, though—and the Court was gay again.

But there was no announcement of her betrothal to Robert.

It was galling to receive the news through Walter and those who came to Chartley to visit us, because they never told me all I wanted to know. As soon as I had recovered from Dorothy's birth, I promised myself, I would go to Court again. The Queen would welcome me and I rehearsed how I would kneel before her with tears of joy in my eyes at her recovery. I knew how to produce those tears with the juice of certain plants. Then I would cajole her into giving me her version of events and I would tell her how a quiet life in the country was no worthy substitute for her royal apartments. She was always a little envious of babies—but perhaps not so much of girls.

She received me with a show of affection and I did my scene, implying thankfulness for her recovery, which I managed very well, and which I fancied touched her, for she kept me at her side and gave me some plum-colored velvet to have made into a gown and a lace ruff with a wire underpropper to go with it. It was a mark of her favor.

It was while I was at Court that news came that the Archduke Charles—that suitor whom she had declined—was now seeking the hand of Mary Queen of Scots. The intensity of Elizabeth's feelings towards that royal rival would not be disguised. She was inordinately interested in Mary. If she gleaned any information about her, she would be tense with concentration; and she never forgot any detail of what she had been told. She was jealous of Mary not because of the Scottish Queen's unquestionable legitimacy, nor because of her claim to the throne, but because Mary was reputed to be one of the most beautiful women in the world; and the fact that she was also a queen made comparison natural. That Mary was beautiful and talented, there was no doubt; but I felt sure she could not have possessed one hundredth part of the shrewd cunning and that heaven-sent cleverness of our own Lady Elizabeth.

I fell to thinking how different their lives had been. Mary, the petted darling of the French Court, fawned on, loved by her father-in-law and his mistress Diane de Poitiers, who was of far greater importance than Queen Catherine de' Medici, doted on by her young husband, beloved of the poets. And our Elizabeth, growing through her uneasy childhood and girlhood, never very far from death. I think it was probably this which had made her what she was; and in that case it was doubtless worthwhile.

It was amazing that one who was as clever as she was could not have seen fit to hide her jealous rage because the Archduke was seeking Mary's hand. Had she suffered it in private it would have been a different matter, but she sent for William Cecil, was abusive in her reference to that "Rake of Austria" and declared that she would never give her consent to a marriage between him and Mary, and she wished Mary to be advised that since she considered herself heiress to the crown of England, it behooved her to take heed of the opinion of England's Queen.

Cecil was afraid that the Queen's outburst would be ridiculed by the foreigners concerned and when the Emperor of Austria wrote to the effect that his son had been insulted and he had no intention of submitting himself to that indignity again, the Queen smirked and nodded.

Robert must have felt his chances were good at that time. I caught glimpses of him now and then and there was no doubt that he was very sure of himself. He was constantly with the Queen, alone in her apartments; so it was small wonder that people like Mrs. Dowe believed the rumors which were spread about them. But it seemed that Elizabeth was still thinking of the Amy Dudley affair and that was why she went on holding back.

When we heard that another of her suitors, Eric of Sweden, had fallen romantically in love, she could not stop herself repeating the story over and over again. He had seen a beautiful girl named Kate selling nuts outside the palace and had become so enamored of her that he had married her. It was like a fairy story, said Elizabeth. So touching. But what great stroke of good fortune for poor Kate that she had refused Eric! Indeed, she said, Kate should be as grateful to her as she was to her lover. But it was clear that a man who could marry a nut seller was no mate for the Queen of England.

She loved to discuss her suitors. She would often make me sit beside her while she went over details of the offers of marriage which had been made to her. "And here I am, still a virgin," she sighed.

"But not for long, Your Majesty," I said.

"Think you not so?"

"There are so many seeking the honor, Madam. You will, I doubt not, decide to accept one and make him the happiest man on earth."

The tawny eyes were half closed. I guessed she was thinking of her Sweet Robin.

Ever since she had heard that the Archduke Charles had offered himself as a husband for Mary Queen of Scots, she had made much of the Scottish Ambassador, Sir James Melville. She played the virginals for him—she performed with great skill on this instrument—she sang and above all she danced, for of all social activities, dancing was her favorite and, as I have said, the one at which she most excelled. She was so slender and she carried herself with such dignity that in a room of dancers she would always have been selected as the Queen.

She would demand of Melville how he had liked a performance and always there would be a request to know how it compared with that of his mistress, the Queen of Scots.

I, and other women of the Court, used to laugh at the manner in which poor Melville strove to give the right answer which would compliment Elizabeth without denigrating in one whit the accomplishments of Mary. Elizabeth would seek to trap him, and sometimes she would snap at him because she could not lure him into admitting her superiority.

It was astonishing how such a woman could be so concerned with the vanities of life; but of course she was vain. She and Robert were matched in that. They both believed themselves to be supreme: he, certain that in due course he would overcome her resistance—and when he married I reckoned that he promised himself he would be the master—and she determined always to call the tune. The crown glittered between them. She could not bear to share it with anyone, and he was so determined in his pursuit— of the woman or the crown? I thought I knew, but I wondered whether Elizabeth did.

One day she was clearly in a good mood. She was smiling to herself while we dressed her—for when I was at Court I was brought back to the bedchamber. I think she liked the occasional tart retort for which I was getting a reputation. After all, if I went too far I could always be given a black look, a blow, or one of those painful nips which she was so fond of administering as a warning to those who she considered had taken advantage of the favor she had shown them.

She was smiling and nodding to herself; and when I saw her with Robert I could tell by the manner in which she looked at him that whatever was in her mind concerned him.

When the secret was out none of us could believe it.

She had long had the welfare of her Scottish cousin close to her heart and she made it known that she believed she had found the perfect bridegroom for her. It was a man whom she prized above all others, one who had already proved himself her most faithful servant. The Queen of Scots would know how deeply she esteemed her when she offered her the finest man in her kingdom as a husband. None other than Robert Dudley.

I heard that Robert gave way to furious rage when he heard. It must have seemed like the death knell to all his hopes. He knew very well that Mary would never accept him, and the fact that Elizabeth offered him showed that she had no intention of accepting him herself.

There was a deep silence in the apartments that day. Everyone was afraid to speak. It was not long before Robert came striding in. He pushed everyone aside and went into her private chamber, and we heard their shouting as they talked together. I doubt there has ever been such a scene between Queen and subject, but of course Robert was no ordinary subject, and we could all understand his fury.

Suddenly they were quieter and we wondered what that meant. When Robert came out he looked at none of us but he had an air of confidence, and we all wondered what had happened between them to produce that.

We soon learned.

It could not be expected that a Queen could consider marrying the mere son of a duke. Lord Robert must be elevated. Elizabeth had therefore decided to bestow honors on him and he was to be made Earl of Leicester and Baron of Denbigh—a title which had never been used by anyone but a royal personage—and the estates of Kenilworth and Astel Grove were to be his.

Everyone was smirking behind their hands. Of course she was not going to relinquish her Sweet Robin. She wanted to do him honor and this seemed a good way of doing it while, at the same time, she insulted the Queen of Scots.

We at Court understood her motive, but the people would see it differently. She had suggested a match between the Queen of Scots and Robert Dudley. How wrong all the scandalous gossip had been about the murder of Dudley's wife! The Queen was certainly not involved, for she had not married him when she could and now she was offering him to the Queen of Scots!

Our clever Queen had achieved her purpose. Robin received his honors and people ceased to lay part of the blame for the murder of his wife at the door of the Queen.

I was present when the honors were bestowed on Robert. It was a very ceremonial occasion indeed which took place in Westminster Palace; and I had rarely seen the Queen in such a happy mood. Of course he looked magnificent in his glittering doublet, his satin bombasted breeches and his elegant ruff of silver lace. He held his head high; he would come out of that hall a much richer and more influential man than he had gone in. A short while ago he had thought all hope of marriage with the Queen was over since she had announced her determination to banish him to Scotland. But now he knew that she had no intention of doing this and it had just been a ruse in order that she could comfortably shower gifts on him— an assurance of her affection when he had feared her indifference.

Elizabeth entered the hall a scintillating figure, love for Robert softening her face, making her almost beautiful. Before her, carrying the sword of state, walked a very tall young man—little more than a boy—who, it was whispered to me, was Lord Darnley. I scarcely looked at him then, my attention being all for Robert, although I should have paid more attention to him if I had known what part he would play in the future.

All eyes, of course, were on that pair, the two principal actors in the scene; and I marveled as I had so often in the past—and was to do in the future—at the Queen's blatant exposure of her feelings for him.

Robert knelt before her while she fastened the mantle about his neck, and as she did so, to the amazement of all, she put her fingers inside the collar and tickled his neck as though she found the desire to touch him in this way irresistible.

I was not the only one who noticed. I saw Sir James Melville and the French Ambassador exchange glances, and I thought: This will be reported throughout Europe and in Scotland. The Queen of Scots had already professed herself to have been insulted by the suggested match and referred to Robert as the Queen's Horse Master.

Elizabeth did not seem to care. She turned to Melville,

for she must have seen the look he exchanged with the Frenchman. There was very little she missed.

"Well," she cried, "what think you of my Lord Leicester, eh? Methinks you like better yon lang lad." She nodded towards Lord Darnley and I saw Melville flinch a little. I did not understand then, but later I realized she was letting him know that she was aware of the supposedly secret negotiations which were in progress to marry Mary of Scotland to Lord Darnley. It was characteristic of her that while she tickled Robert's neck she was considering the outcome of a marriage between Mary and the tall young man.

Later she pretended to be against it while at the same time doing everything she could to bring it about. She had summed up Darnley—not yet twenty years old, very slender so that he looked even taller than he in fact was, a pretty boy with round, rather prominent blue eyes and soft skin as delicately colored as a peach. The effect was charming enough for anyone who liked pretty boys. He had a veneer of pleasant manners, too, but there was something peevish and even cruel about those slack lips. He played the lute well and danced charmingly, and of course he had a flimsy claim to the succession, for his mother was the daughter of Margaret Tudor, Henry VIII's sister.

To compare him with Robert was to call attention to his weakness. I could see that the Queen reveled in the comparison and was as determined as Melville that secretly nothing should be placed in the way of Darnley's going to Scotland while outwardly she would pretend to be against it.

After the ceremony, when she retired to her private apartments, Robert—now Earl of Leicester and on the way to becoming the most powerful man in the kingdom—visited her.

I sat in the women's chambers while everyone talked of the ceremony and how fine the Earl of Leicester had looked and how proud the Queen had been of him. Had we noticed how she tickled his neck? She doted on him so much that she could not hide her love for him at a public ceremony before officials and ambassadors. What must she be like in private?

We giggled together. "It won't be long now," declared someone. Many of them were ready to wager that this was to prepare the way. It would be easier for a queen to marry the Earl of Leicester than it would to have taken Lord Robert Dudley. When Elizabeth had suggested he was a fit bridegroom for a queen, she had not meant Mary of Scotland but Elizabeth of England.

I was alone with her later. She asked me what I had thought of the ceremony, and I replied that it had seemed very impressive.

"The Earl of Leicester looked very handsome, did he not?"

"Exceedingly so, Madam."

"I never saw a more handsome man, did you? Nay, do not answer me that. As a virtuous wife you would not think he compared with Walter Devereux."

She was looking at me sharply and I wondered whether I had betrayed my interest in Robert.

"They are two very admirable men, Your Majesty."

She laughed and gave me a playful pinch. "To be truthful," she said, "there is not a man at Court who can compare with the Earl of Leicester. But you see Walter as his equal and that pleases me. I like not unfaithful wives."

I felt a twinge of uneasiness. But how could she know the effect Robert had on me? I had never betrayed it surely, and he had never glanced my way. Perhaps she thought that all women must desire him.

She went on: "I offered him to the Queen of Scotland. She did not think him worthy of her. She had never seen him or she would have changed her mind. I paid her the greatest compliment I could pay anyone. I offered her the Earl of Leicester, and I will tell you something: If I had not decided to die unmarried and in the virgin state the only man I would have married would have been Robert Dudley."

"I know of Your Majesty's affection for him and his for Your Majesty."

"I have told this to the Scottish Ambassador, and do you know what he replied, Lettice?"

I waited respectfully to hear and she went on: "He said, 'Madam, you need not tell me. I know your stately stomach. You think that if you married you would be but Queen of England and now you are both King and Queen. You will not suffer a commander.' "

"And did Your Majesty agree with him?"

She gave me a little push. "I think you know full well."

"I know," I said, "that I count myself fortunate to be connected by blood with your royalty and to serve such a noble lady."

She nodded. "There are burdens I must accept," she said. "When I saw him standing there before me today, I could have found it in my heart to throw aside my resolutions."

Our eyes met. Those large pupils were searching lamps which looked into my mind. They made me apprehensive then as they were to so often in the future.

"I should always be guided by my destiny," she said. "We must needs accept it . . . Robert and I."

I felt that she was warning me in a way and I wondered what had been said of me. My attractions had not been impaired by childbearing; in fact I believe they had been enhanced. I had been aware of men's eyes following me, and I had heard it said that I was a very desirable woman.

"I will show you something," she said, and she rose and went to a drawer. She took from it a small package wrapped in paper and on the outside was written in her handwriting: "My Lord's Picture."

She undid it and there was a miniature. Robert's face looked out at me.

" 'Tis a very fair likeness," she said. "Think you not so?"

"None could think it other than my Lord Leicester."

"I showed it to Melville and he thought it a good likeness too. He wished to take it to his mistress, for he felt that once she looked on that face she would never be able to refuse him." She laughed slyly. "I would not allow him to have it. It is the only one I have of him, I told Melville, so I could not spare it. I think he understood."

She had handed it to me and now she snatched it rather sharply. She carefully wrapped it up. It was symbolic of her feelings for him. She would never let him go.

There was no doubt that Robert had believed that, having been so honored by the Queen, the next step would be marriage, and I too believed that this was really what she intended, despite her insistence on her determination to remain in the virgin state. He was very rich now—one of the richest men in England—and he immediately set about improving the castle of Kenilworth. It was only to be expected that he gave himself airs, and he was certainly on very familiar terms with the Queen. Her bedchamber was in some ways a state chamber, and after the custom of ages she had received ministers in it, but Robert continued to enter unannounced and unbidden. Once he snatched the shift from the lady whose duty it was to hand it to her and gave it to her himself; he had been seen to kiss her while she was in bed.

I was reminded of what I had heard of Elizabeth's past with Thomas Seymour when he had made free in her bedchamber; but I was growing more and more convinced that there had been no physical lovemaking between them. Elizabeth was always greatly amused by the titillation of the senses—hers and those of her admirers—and some said this was how she intended her relationships to remain.

There were a great many rumors about her and naturally these strayed far from the truth; but her matrimonial cavortings were the wonder of the world. There could never have been a queen who had been wooed so often and never won; and while this provided the utmost and enjoyable entertainment for the Queen, it was decidedly embarrassing and unflattering for her suitors.

Robert, at the head of these, was beginning to be exasperated. They were both of an age which was no longer young and surely if the Queen was going to get a healthy heir it was time she married.

As a queen she knew the importance of this and yet she dallied. When her hand had been sought by foreign princes it had been thought that she declined them because she wanted Robert Dudley; but now that time was passing and she showed no inclination to marry, all but Robert's most bitter enemies would have preferred to see her married to him since she certainly appeared to be in love with him.

However, she held back, and then people began to wonder if there was some other reason why she refused to marry. It was whispered that there was something about her which was different from other women. She could never bear children, it was hinted and, knowing this, it seemed pointless for her to marry a man merely to let him share her throne. It was whispered that her laundresses had let out the secret that she had so few monthly periods that the implication was that she could not bear children. I was of the opinion though that not one of her laundresses would have dared betray such a secret. It was a mystery, for if ever a woman was in love Elizabeth was in love at that time with Robert Dudley; and the odd thing was that she made no effort to conceal it.

I used to wonder whether her upbringing had had some effect on her. She had been a baby of three when her mother had died, but she was old enough—being exceptionally precocious—to have missed her. It seemed hardly likely that her gay and clever mother spent a great deal of time with her daughter, but I imagined the visits she did pay would have been memorable to the child. Anne Boleyn had been noted for her elegant taste and I had heard that she took a delight in dressing her daughter in beautiful garments. Then suddenly she would have disappeared. I could picture the quick-witted little girl asking questions and not being satisfied with the answers. The lovely clothes came no more and instead her governess had had to send special pleas to the King for a few necessary garments of which his daughter was in urgent need. A father would be formidable who had beheaded two wives. One stepmother had died in childbirth, another had been despised and divorced; and lastly there had been Katharine Parr, the kind and lovely Dowager Queen whose husband she had philandered with to such an extent that she had been dismissed from their home. Then had followed a life spent in and out of prisons with the executioner's ax suspended precariously over her head. And at last to come to the throne. No wonder she was determined to keep it. No wonder, with such a father, she distrusted the passions of men. Could this be the reason why she was not going to surrender one small part of her power . . . even to her beloved Robert?

But he was growing very restive as the months passed and we often overheard sharp words between them. Once we heard her reminding him that she was the Queen and he had better take care. After that he would go away sullenly and she would fret for him, and he would come back and they would be friends again.

There was a great deal of talk about what was happening in Scotland.

Mary had married Darnley, much to Elizabeth's secret amusement although she pretended to be incensed about it. She used to laugh about Mary with Robert. "She'll sup sorrow with a long spoon," she said, "and to think that she might have had you, Robert."

I believed she wanted to punish Mary for not taking Robert although she, Elizabeth, had no intention that she should.

She was now winning the true respect of the wily politicians around her. Men like William Cecil, Chancellor Nicholas Bacon and the Earl of Sussex began to see in her an astute politician. Her position in the beginning had been an uneasy one. How could she feel safe when the slur of illegitimacy could be flung at her at any time? There could never have been a ruler in a more vulnerable position than Elizabeth. She was about thirty-three years of age at this time and somehow she had managed to find a place in her people's hearts which rivaled that which her father had held. In spite of everything he had done he had never lost the people's favor; he might squander the country's wealth on ventures such as the Field of the Cloth of Gold; he might take six wives and murder two of them; but he was still their hero and their King and there had never been a serious attempt to depose him. Elizabeth was his daughter in looks and in manner; her voice resembled his; she swore as he had done; everywhere she went it was said: "There goes great Harry's daughter," and she knew that this was one of the greatest advantages she possessed. No one could deny the fact that she was Henry's daughter and that there had been a time when he had accepted her as legitimate.

But she must be wary and she was. Mary Queen of Scots was a claimant to the throne. Therefore what better than to marry her to a weak dissolute youth who would help to bring Scotland low and disgust those who might be inclined to favor Mary. Catharine and Mary Grey—Lady Jane's sisters—were both in the Tower, having married without the Queen's consent. Thus she had arranged that those in England who might be considered to have a

74

greater claim to the throne than she had were safely under lock and key.

News came that the Queen of Scots was pregnant. This was disconcerting. If Mary showed herself fruitful by bearing a son, people would begin comparing her with the Queen of England. She was downcast until news came of that fateful supper in Holyrood House in Edinburgh when, before the eyes of the heavily pregnant Queen, her Italian secretary Rizzio had been murdered. She pretended to be shocked and angry when the suggestion that Rizzio was Mary's lover was mentioned, but she was secretly pleased. At the same time she was wistful. Oh, she was an enigma, this Queen of ours.

The Court was at Greenwich—a favorite palace of the Queen's because she had been born there. The presence chamber here was very fine, hung with rich tapestry, and she always enjoyed showing newcomers the room in which she was born. She would stand in that room, a strange expression in her eyes, and I wondered whether she was thinking of her mother's lying there, exhausted, with her beautiful black hair spread on the pillow. Was she thinking of the agony of Anne Boleyn when she was told: "It is a girl" when a boy would have made all the difference to her future. There would be a fierce determination in her face sometimes as though she were telling herself she would prove better than any boy.

Well, there we were on this occasion—she in one of her magnificent dresses from her overfull wardrobe, white and crimson satin sewn all over with pearls the size of birds' eggs, and a ruff in which tiny diamonds glittered like dewdrops.

She was dancing with Thomas Heneage, a very handsome man to whom she was beginning to show a great deal of favor, when William Cecil entered. There was that about his demeanor which suggested that he had important news to impart, and the Queen signed to him to come to her at once. He whispered to her and I saw her turn pale. I was near her, dancing with Christopher Hatton, one of the finest dancers at Court.

"Your Majesty is unwell?" I whispered.

Several of her women gathered round, and she looked at us mournfully saying: "The Queen of Scots is lighter of a fair son and I am but a barren stock."

Her mouth was drawn down and she looked sad and pale. Cecil whispered something to her and she nodded.

"Send Melville to me," she said, "that I may tell him of my pleasure."

When the Scottish Ambassador was brought to her all vestige of sadness left her. She gaily told him that she had heard the news and rejoiced in it. "My sister of Scotland is indeed blessed," she said.

"It is a miracle of God that the child has been safely delivered," replied Melville.

"Ah yes. Such strife there has been in Scotland, but this fine boy will be her comfort."

When Melville asked if she would be godmother to the Prince she replied: "Right gladly."

Later I saw her eyes follow Robert, and I thought: She can't go on like this. A son born to the Queen of Scots has brought home to her so clearly her need to give an heir to England. She'll take Robert Dudley now, for surely she always intended to have him in the end.

I was in such high favor with the Queen that New Year that she gave me thirteen yards of black velvet to be made into a gown, which was a costly present.

We were at Greenwich for the Twelfth Night festivities. I was in a mood of excitement because I believed that during the last few weeks Robert Dudley had become aware of me. Often in a crowded room I would look up suddenly and find his eyes on me. A look would pass between us and we would smile.

There was no doubt that Robert was not only the most handsome but the richest and most powerful man at Court. There was a virility about him which was immediately recognizable. I was never quite sure whether he attracted me so forcibly originally because of these qualities or because the Queen was so enamored of him, and to become too friendly with him would mean incurring her wrath. Any meeting between us would have to be conducted with the utmost secrecy, and if it ever came to the Queen's ears there would be a violent storm which could be the end of both Robert's favor and my own. Therefore the prospect was one of intense excitement. I had always enjoyed taking risks.

I was not so foolish as not to know that if the Queen had summoned him he would immediately forget me. Robert's first love was the crown and he was a single-minded man. What he wanted he wanted fiercely and he did all in his power to get. Unfortunately for him there was only one way of sharing that crown. Elizabeth alone could give it to him, and as each day passed she was showing herself more reluctant to give him what he wanted.

He was growing visibly angry now. One could observe the change in him. So many times she had raised his hopes and procrastination followed. He must be realizing at last that there was a great possibility of her never marrying him at all. He had taken to staying away from the Court for a few days, and this always angered her. Whenever she went into a room where people were gathered together, she always looked round for him and if he were absent she would be irritable and when she retired one of us would most certainly receive a blow for our incompetence, which was really due to Robert's absence.

Sometimes she sent for him and demanded to know why he had dared absent himself. Then he would reply that it seemed to him that his presence was no longer necessary to her. They would quarrel; we used to listen to them as

77

they shouted at each other and we marveled at Robert's temerity. Sometimes he would stalk out of the apartments and she would shout after him that she was glad to be rid of him. But then she would send for him and there would be reconciliations and he would be her Sweet Robin for a while. But never would she give way on the all-important question.

I guessed, though, that he was beginning to lose hope and to realize that she had no intention of marrying him. I saw her pat him, caress him, stroke his hair and kiss him —but it stopped at that. She would never allow lovemaking to reach a natural climax. I was beginning to think there was something abnormal about her in this respect.

Then came the occasion for which it seemed to me at the time I had been waiting all my life. There was no doubt that I had become obsessed by Robert. Perhaps it was seeing them together so much that made me more and more impatient with them because they played at being lovers—or at least she did—in a manner which I thought foolish. Perhaps I wanted revenge for those painful nips and slaps I had suffered. Perhaps I wanted to show her that in a certain field I could compete even with a queen and be the victor. It was irksome to a nature like mine continually to appear humble and grateful for her favor.

This occasion stands out clearly in my memory.

I was present with her tiring women while we prepared her for the evening. She was seated before her mirror in her chemise and linen petticoat looking at her reflection. A smile played about her lips, and she was obviously contemplating something which amused her. I imagined she was thinking of bestowing the title of King of the Bean on Robert. This was part of the Twelfth Night revelries and the chosen man was allowed to act as he liked throughout the evening. He could ask anyone present to do what he asked and they must obey.

She was almost certain to bestow this honor on Robert

as she had in the past, and I imagined she was thinking of this while we dressed her. She looked at the Nuremberg egg watch in its crystal case and said: "Come, you are slow. What are we waiting for?"

One of the tiring women came to her with a tray on which were pieces of false hair. She selected one and her hair was eventually dressed to her satisfaction.

The next operation was to get her into her privy coat of bone and buckram. Nobody wanted to do this, for she had to be tight-laced and was apt to be irritable if she was too tightly laced and equally so if her waist did not appear as small as she liked it. But this night she was absent-minded and we went through the procedure with no comment from her.

I helped to fix the whalebone hips and we put on her petticoats. Then she sat down while a selection of ruffs was brought to her. She chose one of the new picadillie style with elaborate folds of pointed lace, but before it was put on her overgown was donned. It was very elaborate on this night, and she glittered and sparkled in the light of the cressets and candles.

I brought her girdle to her and fixed it about her waist. She watched me attentively while I made sure that her fan, pomander and looking glass were attached to it.

I tried to read the meaning behind her penetrating gaze. I knew that I was especially attractive that night and that my dress—conspicuous by its very simplicity—was more becoming to me than hers, for all its brilliance, was to her. The color of my undergown was a deep midnight blue and the seamstress had had the clever idea of decorating it with stars worked in silver thread. My upper gown was of a lighter shade of blue and toned exquisitely, while my puffed sleeves were the same color as the undergown. The material was cut away at the neck and I wore a solitary diamond on a golden chain; above this was my ruff of the most delicate lace which, like my undergown, was lightened by starry silver knots.

The Queen's eyes narrowed a little. I looked too attractive to please her. Inwardly I laughed with triumph. She could not scold me for overdressing as she did some of her ladies.

She said: "I see you wear the new virago sleeves, Cousin. *I* find they add little to a gown."

I lowered my eyes that she might not see the mischief in them. "Yes, Your Majesty," I said demurely.

"Come, then. Let us be on."

I was with her when she joined the company, I walking discreetly several paces behind her. Such occasions always impressed me deeply, for I was still new enough to Court life to be overawed by them. There was immediate silence when she appeared and people parted to make a path for her, which, I had once said to Walter, reminded me of Moses when he parted the Red Sea. If she glanced at a man he fell to his knees, and of course a woman would curtsy to the floor, her eyes lowered until the Queen passed on or bade her rise if she wished to speak to her.

I saw Robert at once and that look passed between us. I knew that I was exceptionally beautiful that night. I was twenty-four, not exactly unhappily married, but dissatisfied; and this dissatisfaction was something the Earl of Leicester shared with me. I was eager for an adventure which would enliven the monotony of my days. I was weary of domesticity in the country. I was not meant to be a faithful wife, I was beginning to fear, and I was obsessed by Robert.

He was about ten years older than I, in his prime at this time. But Robert seemed to be the sort of man whose prime would last throughout his life—or almost. At least he would always be attractive to women.

There were two men on whom the Queen had begun to bestow her smiles; one of them was Thomas Heneage and the other Christopher Hatton. Both of them were extremely handsome. One could pick out those who would find this special favor with the Queen. They were always good-looking and had some particular social grace and they must all dance well. This may imply that she was a lighthearted coquette, for she flirted with these gallants in a manner which was most unqueenly; but she had other favorites in a different category. She relied on men like Cecil and Bacon; she recognized their worth and was a loyal and devoted friend to them. Their positions were in fact more firm than those of the good-looking favorites who could be displaced by an equally good-looking newcomer. Robert was the leading favorite in this field and I often thought that she encouraged the others primarily to discountenance him.

At this time she considered he had taken too much for granted. He had become overbearing since she had bestowed great honors on him, and she wanted to impress on him yet again that it was she who called the tune.

She seated herself and sat smiling at the three men of the moment—Robert, Heneage and Hatton.

One of the pages came in with the Bean on a silver platter and presented it to the Queen. She took it and smiled at the young men ranged about her. Robert was looking at her and was on the point of taking the Bean when the Queen said: "I appoint Sir Thomas Heneage King of the Bean."

It was a tense moment. Sir Thomas, flushed with pleasure, was kneeling before her. Glancing at Robert, I saw his face turn pale and his lips tighten. Then he held his head high and smiled because he knew that everyone would be watching him. Had she not previously delighted to make him her King of the Bean every Twelfth Night since her accession?

There would be gossip. "The Queen has fallen out of

love with Leicester," people would say. "She will never marry him now."

I felt almost sorry for Robert, but I was exultant, too— for this was all part of the night's adventure.

Sir Thomas was claiming as his first privilege the right to kiss the Queen's hand. She gave it to him, declaring that no choice was left to her but to obey. But she smiled dotingly on him and I knew she was doing it to anger Robert.

That night I danced with Robert; the pressure of his fingers was firm on mine and the glances we gave each other were full of meaning.

"I have long noticed you at Court," he told me.

"Is that so, my lord?" I answered. "I had been unaware of it, thinking you had only eyes for the Queen."

"It would have been impossible not to see the most beautiful lady of the Court."

"Hush!" I cried mockingly. "You speak treason."

I laughed at him, but as the evening passed he grew ardent. His intentions became so clear that I reminded him that I was a married woman and he as good as a married man. He answered that there were some emotions which were too strong to be denied no matter what bonds attempted to deter them.

Robert was not a witty man; he was not given to flowery language or quick retorts. He was direct, strong, determined and he made no secret of the reason for his pursuit of me. I was not displeased. My ardor matched his, for instinctively I knew that with Robert I could reach a fulfillment I had never attained before. I had been a virgin when I married Walter and thus far had strayed from the paths of marital virtue only in my thoughts. But I wanted this man with a fierceness which matched his desire for me. I could tell myself that he would take me out of pique, but I was determined to prove to him that, having tried me, he would not be able to do without me.

I thought of the Queen's louring expression when she quarreled with Robert. I knew too that if she could see and hear me now she would be ready to kill me. That was one of the reasons why I had to go on.

He said that we must meet in secret. I knew what that meant, and I didn't care. I abandoned caution and conscience. I only cared that he should become my lover.

The Queen danced with Christopher Hatton—the best of all dancers. They had the floor to themselves and this was what she loved. When they had finished everyone applauded with great verve and declared that even the Queen had surpassed herself.

Thomas Heneage, King of the Bean, said that as they had seen dancing such as had never before been equaled, he was going to forbid anyone else to take the floor for a while because it would be sacrilege even to tread on that ground where the royal feet had trod.

I smirked inwardly. This fulsome flattery always amazed me. I should have thought that a woman as astute as Elizabeth undoubtedly was would have laughed it to scorn; but she never did and took it as though it were obvious fact.

Instead of dancing, said our King of the Bean, we should have a game called Question and Answer and he would ask the questions and select those who were to answer them.

When a man who has been great is seen to slip a little way, his enemies can scarcely wait to glory over his downfall. They reminded me of crows sitting on a tree by a gallows where a man is dying. Robert had been openly shown to be enjoying less favor than usual, and therefore everyone, it seemed, was eager to humiliate him further. Rarely had a man engendered such envy, for I doubted that any reigning sovereign had ever shown such favor to a subject as the Queen had to Robert Dudley.

It was inevitable that Heneage should have a question for Robert, and the assembly waited breathlessly for it.

"My Lord Leicester," said Heneage, "I command you to ask a question of Her Majesty."

Robert bowed his head and waited for it.

"Which is the more difficult to erase from the mind, an evil opinion created by a wicked informer or jealousy?"

I watched Robert's face, for I was standing near to him. The manner in which he concealed his anger was really rather commendable.

He turned to the Queen. His voice was cool. "Your Majesty hears the command of King Bean, and he being your chosen King of the Night, I can do nothing but obey. So I ask you, in your wisdom, to give us an answer."

When he had repeated the question the Queen looked grave and, smiling affectionately at him, answered: "My lord, I would say that they are both hard to be rid of, but that jealousy is the harder."

Robert was so angry to be publicly held up to ridicule, and the fact that the Queen seemed to have allied herself with Heneage was doubly infuriating.

He did not go to the Queen again that night. When many people were dancing, he took my hand and drew me out of the chamber and away to a small room of which he knew. He pulled me in and shut the door.

"My lord," I said, and I could hear the trill of excitement in my voice, "we must have been seen."

He seized me roughly then. His lips were near my own. "And if they have seen us," he said, "I should not care. I care for nothing . . . but this."

He had taken the ruff from my neck and thrown it from him. His hands were on my shoulders, forcing my dress from them.

"My lord, would you have me stand naked before you?" I asked.

"Aye," he cried. "Aye, that I would. So have I seen you many times in my dreams."

I was as eager for him as he was for me and there was no hiding it.

"You are beautiful . . . beautiful as I knew you would be," he murmured. "You are all that I want, Lettice. . . ."

He, too, was all that I had dreamed he would be. It was an experience such as I had never known before. I could not help being aware that on his side it was made up of anger as well as desire, and this infuriated me while at the same time it did nothing to stem my passion. I was determined to show him that never could he know such a mistress as I would be. I was going to make him as reckless as I was. He should be as ready to risk losing the Queen's favor as I was to break my marriage vows.

I think I succeeded temporarily. I sensed the wonder in him, the delight, the knowledge that we two were made for each other.

I knew that he could not tear himself away although it was obvious that he would be missed. I exulted in this; it seemed to me that nature had endowed me with special powers to attract men and bind them to me. And I was born to make love with this man and he with me.

We were enthralled by each other, and I felt that our discovery must be obvious for all to see, and I confess that, when eventually we did return to the ballroom, I began to feel uneasy.

The Queen must have missed Robert. Had she noticed, too, that I had been absent? I should soon discover, I was sure. A cold fear touched me. What if I should be dismissed from Court?

She gave no sign during the days which followed. Robert did not come to Court, and I knew that she missed him. She became very irritable and volunteered the remark that some people imagined they could absent themselves without leave and would have to be taught otherwise.

I was with her when news came that there was trouble between the Earl of Leicester and Sir Thomas Heneage. Leicester had sent word to Heneage that he would visit him with a stick as he had a lesson to administer, to which Heneage replied that he would be welcome and a sword would be awaiting him.

Elizabeth was furious, and there was fear in her fury. She was afraid that Robert would fight a duel and be killed, and she had no intention of allowing her favorite men to behave so foolishly. She sent for Heneage and we heard her shouting at him. Did he think he could defy her? It was dangerous to talk of swordplay, she told him. If he behaved so foolishly again someone else might be talking of an ax.

I think she boxed his ears, for when he came out those appendages looked very red and he was completely subdued.

Then it was Robert's turn. I could not resist listening.

She was very angry with him—more so than with Heneage.

"God's death," she cried, "I have wished you well but my favor is not so locked up in you that others may not have a share of it. I have other servants besides you. Remember there is one mistress here and no master. Those whom I have raised up can as easily be lowered. And this shall happen to those who become impudent through my favor."

I heard him say quietly: "Your Majesty, I beg leave to retire."

"It's yours," she shouted.

And as he came from her chamber he saw me and looked at me. It was an invitation to follow him and as soon as I could I slipped away and found him in that chamber which had previously been the scene of our passion.

He seized me and held me, laughing aloud.

"As you see," he said, "I am out of favor with the Queen."

"But not with me," I said.

"Then I am not unhappy."

He locked the door and it was as though a frenzy seized him. He was mad with desire for me and so was I for him, and although I knew that his anger with the Queen mingled with his need for me, I did not care. I wanted this man. He had haunted my thoughts from the first moment I had seen him riding beside the Queen at her accession; and if his desire for me was in some measure due to her treatment of him, she was part of my need of him too. Even in our moments of extreme ecstasy it was as though she was there with us.

We lay together, knowing full well that it was a dangerous thing to do. Were we to be discovered we could both be ruined, and we did not care; and because our need for each other transcended our fear of the consequences, it heightened our passion, intensified those sensations which I at least—and I think the same applied to him—believed could come to me through no other.

What was this emotion between us? The recognition of two like natures? It was overwhelming desire and passion and not least of our emotions was the awareness of danger. The fact that each of us could risk our future for this encounter carried our ecstasy to even greater heights.

We lay exhausted, yet triumphant in some way. We should neither of us ever forget this experience. We were bound together by it for the rest of our lives and whatever should happen to us we should never forget.

"I shall see you again ere long," he said soberly.

"Yes," I answered.

"This is a fair meeting place."

"Until we are discovered."

"Are you afraid of that?"

"If I were I should count it worthwhile."

I had known he was the man for me as soon as I had seen him.

"You're looking smug, Lettice," said the Queen. "What has happened to make you thus?"

"I could not say that anything has, Your Majesty."

"I thought you might be with child again."

"God forbid," I cried in real fear.

"Come, you have but two . . . and girls. Walter wants a boy, I know."

"*I* want a little rest from childbearing, Madam."

She gave me one of her little taps on the arm. "And you're a wife who gets what she wants, I'll warrant."

She was watching me closely. Could she possibly suspect? If she did I should be drummed out of the Court.

Robert remained aloof from her, and although this sometimes angered her, I was sure that she was determined to teach him a lesson. As she had said, her favor was not so locked up in any man that he could dare take advantage of her fondness. Sometimes I thought she was afraid of that potent attractiveness—of which I had first-hand knowledge—and she liked to whip herself into a fury against him to prevent herself falling completely victim to his desires.

I did not see him as often as I should have liked. He did come once or twice unobtrusively to Court and we met and made passionate love in the private room. But I could sense that frustration in him and I knew that what he wanted above all things was not a woman but a crown.

He went to Kenilworth, which he was turning into one of the most magnificent castles in the country. He said that he wished I could go with him and that if I had had no husband we could have married. But I wondered whether he would have talked of marriage if it had not been safe to do so, for I knew that he had not given up hope of marrying the Queen.

At Court his enemies were starting to plot against him. They clearly thought he was in decline. The Duke of Norfolk—a man I found excessively dull—was a particular enemy. Norfolk was a man of little ability. He had strong principles and was weighed down by his admiration for his own ancestry, which he believed and I suppose he was right in this—was more noble than the Queen's, for the Tudors had sneaked to the throne in a very backdoor manner. Vitally brilliantly clever people they might be, but some of the ancient nobility were deeply conscious of their own families' superiority and none more than Norfolk. Elizabeth was well aware of this and, like her father, ready to nip it in the bud when it appeared, but she could not stop the blossoms flowering in secret. Poor Norfolk, he was a man with a sense of duty and tried always to do the right thing, but it invariably seemed the wrong thing . . . for Norfolk.

For such a man it was galling to see the rise of Robert to the premier position in the country, which he felt because of his birth belonged to him, and there had been one occasion not very long before this when a quarrel had flared up between Norfolk and Leicester.

There was nothing Elizabeth liked better than to see her favorite men jousting or playing games, which called attention not only to their skill but to their physical perfections. She would sit for hours watching and admiring their handsome bodies; and there was none she had liked to see in action more than Robert.

On this occasion there had been an indoor tennis match and Robert had drawn Norfolk as a partner. Robert was winning, for he had exceptional skill in all sports. I was sitting with the Queen in that lower gallery which Henry

VIII had had built for spectators, for he too had excelled at the game and enjoyed being watched.

The Queen had leaned forward. Her eyes had never left Robert, and when he scored a point she had called out "Bravo" while during Norfolk's less frequent successes she was silent, which must have been very depressing for England's premier duke.

The game was so fast that the contestants had become very hot. The Queen seemed to suffer with them, so immersed was she in the play, and she lifted a mockinder—or handkerchief—to wipe her brow. As there was a slight pause in the game and Robert was sweating profusely, he snatched the mockinder from the Queen and mopped his brow with it. It was a natural gesture between people who were very familiar with each other. It was actions like this which gave rise to the stories of their being lovers.

Norfolk, incensed by this act of lese-majesty—and perhaps because he was losing the game and was aware of the royal pleasure in his defeat—lost his temper and shouted: "You impudent dog, sir. How dare you insult the Queen!"

Robert had looked surprised when Norfolk had suddenly lifted his racket as though he would strike him. Robert had caught his arm and twisted it so that Norfolk had called out in pain and dropped the racket.

The Queen had been furious. "How dare you brawl before me?" she had demanded. "My Lord Norfolk must look to it or it may not be only his temper which is lost. How dare you, Sir Norfolk, conduct yourself in such a manner before me?"

Norfolk had bowed and asked leave to retire.

"Retire," the Queen had shouted. "Pray do, and don't come back until I send for you. Methinks you give yourself airs above your station."

It is a dig at his overweening family pride, which she resented as a slur on the Tudors.

"Come, sit beside me, Rob," she had said, "for my Lord Norfolk, knowing himself the loser, has no longer stomach for the game."

Robert, still holding the mockinder, had seated himself beside her, well pleased to have scored over Norfolk, and she took the mockinder from him and smiling had attached it once more to her girdle, implying that the fact that he had used it in no way displeased her.

So it was not to be wondered at that now, when Robert was thought to be in decline, Norfolk headed the long list of his enemies, and it was clear that they were going to exploit the situation to the full.

Attack came from an unexpected quarter and a very unsavory one.

There was a tense atmosphere at Court. The Queen was never happy when Robert was not with her. There could not be any doubt that she loved him; all her emotions concerning him went deep. It had even been obvious in their quarrels how much she was affected by him. I knew that she wanted to call him back to Court, but she was so beleaguered by the marriage question and Robert was growing more and more insistent, that she had to hold him off. If she sent for him it would be a victory for him and she had to make him understand that she called the tune.

I had begun to accept the fact that she was afraid of marriage, although of course the Scottish ambassador had been right when he had declared she wanted to be supreme ruler and share with none.

I felt drawn to her in a way because my thoughts were as full of Robert as hers were and I was watching for his return as hopefully as she was.

Sometimes when I was alone at night I used to contemplate what would happen if we were discovered. Walter would be furious, of course. To hell with Walter! I cared nothing for him. He might divorce me. My parents would be deeply shocked, especially my father. I should be in disgrace. They might even take the children from me. I saw little of them when I was at Court, but they were growing into real people and were beginning to interest me. But chiefly I should have to face the Queen. I used to lie in bed shivering—not only with fear but with a kind of delicious delight. I should like to look into those big tawny eyes and cry: "He has been my lover but never yours. You have a crown and we know he wants that more than anything. I have nothing but myself—yet next to the crown, he wants me. The fact that he has become my lover is a measure of his love for me, for he has dared risk a great deal to do so."

When I was with her I felt less brave. There was that in her which could strike terror into the boldest heart. When I contemplated her fury if we were discovered I wondered what her punishment would be. She would blame me as the seductress, the Jezebel. I had noticed that she always made excuses for Robert.

It was into this atmosphere that the scandal burst. It was like the reopening of an old wound. It touched the Queen almost as surely as it did Robert, and it showed clearly how wise she had been not to marry him, though of course if she had, this man, John Appleyard, would never have dared raise his voice.

The fact was that Amy Robsart's half-brother, John Appleyard, had for some time been spreading the scandal that when Robert Dudley had arranged for his wife to be murdered, he had helped cover up the crime and that, his conscience now worrying him, he felt he should confess his guilt.

Robert's enemies, headed by the Duke of Norfolk, were quick to make the most of this. They took up the case and declared that John Appleyard must tell his story in a court of law.

There was a campaign of persecution and everyone was saying that Leicester's brief glory was over.

Elizabeth talked to me about the scandal. She always watched me closely when Robert's name was mentioned and I wondered if I had betrayed anything.

"What think you, Cousin Lettice, of this matter?" she asked. "Norfolk and some of his friends seem to think that Robert should be made to answer these charges against him."

"I think they are like vultures, Madam," I said.

"Vultures indeed! You speak as though the Earl of Leicester were a rotting corpse."

"He is without your favor now, Madam, and though his body may appear to be in good health, it is his spirit which is dying."

"He's not food for the vultures yet, I promise you. Was he concerned in this murder, do you think?"

"Your Majesty's knowledge of the matter would, as in all others, be greater than my own."

I often marveled at my own temerity. One of these days my tongue would carry me into disaster. Fortunately she had not seen the significance behind that remark or if she did ignored it.

"We must be watchful of our enemies, Lettice," she said, "and I think Robin's are gathering around him fast."

"I fear so, but he is strong and will confute them, I doubt not."

"We miss Robert Dudley at our Court," she said wistfully. "What think you, Lettice?"

"I think Your Majesty does indeed miss him."

"And some of my women miss him too, doubtless."

That piercing look—what did it mean? What did she know? How would she act if she discovered we had been lovers? She would brook no rivals. And I had lain with him behind locked doors and broken my marriage vows. The Queen's wrath would be terrible.

She did not pursue the subject, but I knew she went on thinking of Robert.

He was in danger now. If Appleyard swore in a court of justice that Robert Dudley had bribed him to cover up the murder of his wife, he would be finished. Even the Queen could not condone a murder.

It was like her to act precisely at the right moment.

She sent for him to come to Court.

He came, looking pale and not quite his arrogant self. I was there with other women in the tiring chamber when he was announced. The change in her was miraculous. It made my heart sink, for it was clear that she was as much in love with him as ever.

He was to be brought to her, she said.

She sat admiring her reflection in the mirror, considering for a moment whether she would choose a different dress; but that would mean delay and she was extravagantly clad enough as it was. She took the rouge pad and applied a little to her cheek. The color seemed to add a sparkle to her eyes, but perhaps that was due to the prospect of seeing Robert.

Then she went to the chamber in which she would receive him.

I heard her say: "So you have come to me, at last, you rogue. I want an account of this desertion. Think not I'll brook such treatment."

But her voice was soft and shaken with emotion; and he came forward and, taking her hands, kissed them fervently.

I heard her whisper: "My Eyes . . . my Sweet Robin . . ."

She noticed me then.

"Leave us!" she snapped.

I had to go, but I went angry, hurt and humiliated. He had not as much as glanced at me.

He was back, and in greater favor than ever. She

wanted an account of this scoundrel Appleyard. He had taken gifts from the Earl of Leicester, it seemed, and had made no complaint at the time. It was finally drawn from him that he had been offered bribes to circulate these stories and, said the Queen, for such criminal action he deserved to be punished.

This was one of those occasions when Elizabeth showed her wisdom. John Appleyard had been guilty of lying and trying to incriminate the Earl of Leicester; but she had no wish to pursue the matter. John Appleyard should be given a warning that it would go hard for him if he were ever caught in such conduct again. Now he must thank the Queen for her clemency and his God for his good fortune, for the matter was to be dropped, and no one was to hear more about the death of the Earl's wife.

This was certainly high favor. Robert was always at her side. He gave me a few helpless glances as though to say: I feel the same towards you as ever, but what can I do? The Queen keeps me with her.

The fact was that he had so much to lose now if he was discovered in a liaison, and he was not prepared to risk it. That was the difference in our natures. I was. I became fretful and dissatisfied, and I had many a slap from the Queen because, as she said, she would have no glowering creature about her.

She was worried. Robert's experiences had had their effect on his health, and, having caught a chill, he was confined to his bed.

How anxious we were—both of us. And how frustrated I was, for she could visit him and I could not. I schemed perpetually, trying to discover some way of reaching him —but it was no use.

She went to him, though, and came back complaining that his apartments were damp.

"We must select others," she said; and it struck me

that there was something ominous in the manner in which she addressed her remarks to me.

Those she chose were next to her own.

It became clear that she had noticed something between Robert and me because when he recovered a little she sent for me.

"I am going to send you back to Chartley," she said.

I must have looked stricken and shown that I felt sick with frustration.

"But, Madam," I protested, "he is often away from home on your service."

"When he comes back to Chartley he must find a warm bed waiting for him. I dareswear he thinks it is time you gave him a bonny son."

The shrewd eyes were studying me intently.

"It is not good for lusty partners in marriage to be separated for too long," she continued. "There could be mischief such as I do not care to see in my Court. Come, cheer up. Think of your home and your children."

"I shall miss Your Majesty."

"Your family must make up for *any*thing you miss at Court."

My mother was at Court and I went to tell her that I was to leave.

She nodded. "Yes, the Queen has spoken to me. She thinks you are of a nature to need marriage and that it is unwise for you to be kept from your husband for too long. She said that she had noticed lewd looks in the eyes of some people as they rested on you."

"Did she say whose eyes?"

My mother shook her head. "She mentioned no names."

So she knew something. She had seen, and she was dismissing me, for she would not tolerate a rival.

Sadly, angrily, I left for Chartley. Robert made no effort to say goodbye. He was clearly determined not to jeopardize his return to favor.

I began to wonder how far he had used me to arouse the Queen's jealousy. To a woman of my nature that was maddening. I was enraged that in so using me he had brought about my banishment from Court.

I should have hated him. I was nothing to him but a means of gratifying a temporary passion.

I had been a fool.

One day, I promised myself, I will make them both realize that I cannot be treated in this way.

So it was back to Chartley, and how depressed I was as I rode north! How I hated the sight of that stone fortress perched on the hill which was to be my home, for how long I could not say!

My parents had spoken to me before I left Court—and how I envied them for being able to stay there!—my father as Treasurer of the Royal Household and my mother as one of the bedchamber women.

"It is time you went back to Chartley, Lettice," said my father. "Too long a stay at Court is not good for young people if they are married."

"You must have missed Walter and the children," added my mother.

I retorted that I should not see a great deal of Walter at Chartley in any case.

"No, but he will be there whenever he can, and think of the joy of being with the little girls."

It was true that I should be glad to see the children, but they could not make up for the excitement of Court.

I was depressed for the first days thinking of Robert and wondering what was happening between him and the Queen. The recent estrangement had certainly not made her less fond, and I often wondered whether my deductions had been correct and her affections for him would, in the end, overcome her objections.

I began to ask myself whether she had mentioned me to

him. I could picture his denial of anything between us and, if it should be proved against him, assuring her that it was nothing but a temporary diversion because she continually denied him his heart's desire. I vowed that one day I would make him pay for his treatment of me. I would make him realize that I was not to be taken up and thrown aside at his convenience. But when my anger cooled I had to accept its futility. There was nothing I could do . . . at this time . . . so I sought solace with my family, and strangely enough I found it.

Penelope was in her sixth year—a beautiful child, bright and willful. I could see myself in her very clearly. Dorothy, a year younger, was quieter, but nonetheless determined to have her own way. They, at least, were delighted to see me; and my parents had been right when they said they would bring me consolation.

Walter came to Chartley. He had served with Ambrose Dudley, Earl of Warwick, with whom he had become very friendly. I was interested to hear of Warwick because he was Robert's elder brother and had been under sentence of death with him in the Tower of London for involvement in the attempt to put Lady Jane Grey on the throne.

Walter was as loving as he had been in the early days of our marriage, and as for myself I was nonetheless attractive for having extended my experience. But how different he was from Robert, and how I railed against fate for marrying me to Walter Devereux when there was a man like Robert Dudley in the world.

However, my nature being what it was, I was able to derive some pleasure from my relationship with Walter, and at least he was devoted to me.

It was not long before I was pregnant.

"This time," said Walter, "it will be a boy."

We went to one of Walter's country houses—Netherwood in Herefordshire—which he thought would be more healthy for me, and there on a dark November day my child was born. I must confess to a great exultation when I learned it was a boy. Walter was delighted and ready to indulge me for giving him that which, like most men, he most desired—a son and heir.

The question arose of what we should call him. Walter suggested that he should be named Richard after his father, or possibly Walter, after himself. But I said I should like to get away from family names, and I had a fancy for the name of Robert; and as Walter was ready to please me that became the boy's name.

I was delighted with him, for from the start he was a most handsome child, bright and clearly intelligent. Oddly enough—and I surprised myself in this—I became absorbed by him; he helped to soothe my hurt and, wonder of wonders, I ceased to fret for the Court.

Eight years passed before I saw Robert Dudley again, and a great deal had happened in the world during that time.

The Years of Banishment

My Lord of Leicester is very much with her Majesty, and she shows him the same great good affection she was wont. . . . There are two sisters now in the Court, that are very far in love with him, so they long have been—my Lady Sheffield and Frances Howard; they, striving who shall love him best, are at great wars with each other, and the Queen thinketh not well of them and not the better of him. For this reason there are spies set over him.

GILBERT TALBOT *to his father*
LORD SHREWSBURY

My son had changed the household. His sisters doted on him and all the servants adored him; his father was inordinately proud of him and, oddest of all, I wanted nothing more at that time than to care for him. I would not leave him to his nurses, because I could not bear that they might take his affection from me.

At this time, Walter had every reason to be very content with his marriage. I often thought of Robert Dudley with longing, but, being away from him, I was able to look the facts straight in the face. They were not very palatable for a woman of my pride.

Robert Dudley had made me his mistress temporarily because he was out of favor with the Queen, and as soon as she had beckoned him it was "Goodbye, Lettice. It would be unwise for us to meet again."

My pride was as strong as my physical needs. I was going to try to forget that episode. My family—and in particular my adored son—would help me to do so. I threw myself into the management of my household and for a time became a model wife. I spent some hours in my stillroom. I grew a variety of herbs which my servants used for flavoring dishes and I was constantly trying something new. I made perfumes from lavender, roses and hyacinths; I found new ways of mingling fragrant wild flowers with rushes and frequently used meadowsweet, which the Queen had made fashionable because she had once said it reminded her of the country. I sent for fine cloths—brocades, velvet and grogram—which made my servants goggle-eyed, accustomed as they were to fustian and kersey. My seamstresses were good but of course could not catch the stylish mode of the Court. Never mind! I was a queen in the country and people talked of me—of my elegance, of my table, of the wines I gave to my guests— muscatel, malmsey and those from Italy which I served with my own spices. When visitors came from Court I tried to impress them. I wanted them to return and talk to me that he might know that I could live very satisfactorily without him.

In this domestic atmosphere it was natural that I should become pregnant again. Two years after Robert's birth, I produced yet another son and this time I thought it only fair to name him after his father. So he became Walter.

Events of great moment had been happening in the outside world during those years. Darnley, the husband of Mary Queen of Scots, had died mysteriously in a house in Kirk o' Field just outside Edinburgh. This house had been blown up by gunpowder quite obviously in an attempt to remove Darnley, but the unfortunate man must have had warning of the explosion and had tried to escape. He did not get very far. He was found in the garden of the house—dead but untouched by the explosion, and as there was no sign of violence it was presumed that he had been suffocated by a damp cloth's being held over his mouth. So it was clearly a case of murder. Since Mary was deeply enamored of the Earl of Bothwell—and hated her husband Darnley—and Bothwell had divorced his wife, it seemed clear who was behind the murder.

I must confess that when the news came to Chartley of what had happened I felt a strong desire to be at Court so that I might acquire Elizabeth's reactions at firsthand. I could imagine the horror she would express and the delight she would hide at the predicament in which the Queen of Scots must find herself. At the same time she might be a little uneasy. People would surely be reminded of a similar dilemma in which she had been caught when Robert Dudley's wife had been found dead at the bottom of that staircase in Cumnor Place.

If the Queen of Scots married Bothwell, her throne would surely be in jeopardy. It would be assumed that she had been an accomplice in her husband's murder. Moreover, her position was by no means as strong as Elizabeth's. I could never prevent myself smiling when I remembered the chorus of adulation every time the Queen appeared, and even men like Cecil and Bacon seemed to think she was divine. I sometimes thought that she insisted on this partly because she could not forget the existence of the Queen of Scots, who, common sense told her, was more beautiful than she could ever be even with all her false hair, her chalk and rouge and extravagantly glittering garments.

Events followed quickly after that. At first I would not believe it when I heard that Mary had lost no time in marrying Bothwell. Foolish woman! Why had she not considered the example of our shrewd and wily Elizabeth at the time of *her* involvement? Mary could not have proclaimed her guilt more loudly to the world; and even if she had not been concerned in Darnley's murder, the stories about Bothwell's being her lover while Darnley lived now appeared to be true.

In a brief space of time there had followed the defeat at Carberry Hill. I felt so restive then. I wanted to be at Court, to see those large tawny eyes expressing so much while they hid so much more. She would be angry at the insult to royalty. Many people remembered that Catherine of Valois, widow of Henry the Fifth, had entered into a not very reputable liaison with Owen Tudor, a Welshman of obscure background and no fortune to speak of. Whether they had even married or not was uncertain; but by him she had three sons, the eldest of whom married Margaret Beaufort and became the Earl of Richmond; and these two were the parents of Henry the Seventh. A flimsy claim to the throne indeed, and so, because of her somewhat doubtful Tudor roots, she was always insistent that due honor be paid to the blood royal. She would deplore the fact that a queen had ridden through the streets of Edinburgh seated on a jennet wearing a tradeswoman's red petticoat while the mob shouted "whore and murderess" after her. Yet at the same time she would be remembering that Mary had dared call herself Queen of England and that there were some Catholics in the country who would be ready to risk a good deal—including their lives—to see Mary on the throne, and a return to Catholicism.

No, Elizabeth would never forget that this foolish woman above the Border was a very great threat to that crown, which was so essentially hers and which she would not share even with the man she loved.

And Robert? What would he be thinking? This was the woman to whom he had been offered in marriage, who had referred to him slightingly as "The Queen's Horse Master." I was sure that his pride was such that he could not but enjoy a certain satisfaction to see her brought so low.

There was defeat, capture and imprisonment at Lochleven, escape from Lochleven and yet another disastrous and final defeat at Langside and—folly of follies—Mary was so deluded as to think she might receive help from "Her dear sister of England."

I could imagine that dear sister's excitement at the prospect of having her greatest rival deliver herself, of her own free will, into her hands.

Soon after Mary had arrived in England we had a visit from my father. His mood was one of mingling apprehension and pride, and when I heard the reason for his visit I could well understand his mood.

The Queen and Sir William Cecil had sent for him and told him that they had a mission for him.

" 'It is a sign of my trust and faith in you, Cousin,' " he proudly told me the Queen had said to him; and he went on: "I am to be guardian of the Queen of Scots. I am going up to Carlisle Castle, where Lord Scrope will join me in this task."

Walter said it was one he would not welcome.

"Why not?" I demanded. "The Queen would only entrust it to one in whom she had complete trust."

"That's so," agreed Walter, "but it will be a dangerous task. Where Mary of Scotland is there is trouble."

"Not now she is in England," said my father, rather naïvely, I thought.

"But she will be your prisoner and you her jailer," Walter pointed out. "Just suppose that . . ."

He did not finish, but we knew what he meant. If ever Mary rallied enough forces to her banner and fought for the throne of England and won it, what of those who, on the instructions of her rival, had acted as her jailers? Moreover, what if she escaped? Walter was thinking that he would not care to be the one who might be held responsible for that calamity.

Oh yes, it was a considerable responsibility that my father had taken on.

But merely to mention the possibility of Elizabeth's being replaced was treason. All the same we couldn't help the thought being in our minds.

"We shall guard her carefully," said my father, "yet at the same time not let her know that she is a prisoner."

"You set yourself an impossible task, Father," I told him.

"I think that perhaps it is God's will," was his answer. "It may be that I have been selected to turn her thoughts from Catholicism, which I believe to be the root of all her troubles."

My father was a very innocent man, which may well have been due to his simple faith. With the passing of the years his devotion to Protestantism had increased, and it was bringing him to the belief that all those not of his faith were doomed to damnation.

I did not challenge him on this. He was a good man and I was fond of him, as I was of my mother; and I did not wish them to know how different was my outlook from theirs. I often wondered what they would have thought had they known of my brief liaison with Robert Dudley. That they would have been deeply shocked I was well aware.

My father had with him some clothes which he was taking from Elizabeth to Mary. I said I should like to see them and, rather to my surprise, my father allowed me to. I had expected some queenly garments—puffed and slashed and decorated with gems, lace ruffs, silken undergowns, linen petticoats and of course jeweled and embroidered overgowns. All I found were some shoes, very well worn, a piece of black velvet to be made into a dress and some undergarments which were clearly not new.

And this was the gift of the Queen of England to Mary, who was noted throughout France and Scotland for her elegance! Such garments would be scorned by her maids.

I was sorry for Mary, and once again I felt the urge to be at the center of events, to know firsthand and not rely on visitors who came riding to Chartley and would tell us what had happened weeks after it had taken place. I was not of a nature to enjoy standing aside and merely looking on.

Soon after my son Walter was born, two events took place.

The Queen of Scots had been moved from Carlisle Castle to that of Bolton. My father was a little fascinated by her, as most men were who came into contact with her; but in my father's case the effect of this was to make him want to save her soul rather than enjoy her body; and I heard that he was attempting to convert her to our faith. She had by this time realized how foolish she had been to put her trust in Elizabeth and walk straight into her enemy's camp. It was true she might have done no better if she had gone to France, but who could be sure of that? She had not exactly endeared herself to Catherine de' Medici, the Queen Mother, and there was a woman as wily as our own Elizabeth and certainly more lethal. Poor Mary—there she was with three countries to choose from: Scotland, from which she had fled; France, where she might have had a fair reception from her Guise relations—and England, which she chose.

She had made an attempt to escape by the romantic but often not very practical method of sliding down the walls by means of knotted sheets, and had been caught by Lord Scrope, and naturally after that her jailers had been obliged to increase security. Lady Scrope, who was with her husband, was the sister of the Duke of Norfolk, and she it was who talked so glowingly of the attractions of her brother to the Queen of Scots that Mary became interested in Norfolk, and thus the foolish man was drawn into a web of intrigue which was to result in his downfall.

In due course there came the rebellion of the Northern Lords and my husband was called to his duty. He joined the Earl of Warwick's forces and became Marshal of the Field.

My mother had been ill for some time, and she wrote telling us of the Queen's great sympathy for her. "No one could have been kinder than Her Majesty," wrote my mother. "How lucky we are in our sovereign lady."

It was true that Elizabeth was loyal to her friends. She had given poor Lady Mary Sidney an apartment in Hampton Court, where she came sometimes to stay in retirement because she hated to show her pockmarked face; and Elizabeth visited her regularly and would sit for a long time chatting with her. She made it clear that she did not forget that Lady Sidney had acquired her scars while nursing her.

Then I received a message.

I was to return to Court.

My excitement was intense. Why had I ever thought my

simple country pleasures would compensate me for the excitement of the Court? And when I say "Court" I mean of course those two who were so often in my thoughts. The very prospect of returning set my nerves tingling.

I could scarcely wait to get there.

I went straight to the Queen, who had given orders that I should be brought to her. I was unprepared for her greeting. As I would have knelt she took me in her arms and kissed me. I was astonished but I soon learned the reason.

"I am stricken with grief, Lettice," she said. "Your mother is very ill indeed." The large eyes were glazed a little. "I greatly fear . . ." She shook her head. "You must go to her at once."

I had hated her. She had deprived me of what I most wanted in life. But in that moment I almost loved her. Perhaps it was because of that capacity in her for friendship and loyalty to those whom she loved. And she loved my mother.

"Tell her," she said, "that she is in my thoughts. Tell her that, Lettice."

She put her arm through mine and walked with me to the door. It was as though she had forgiven me for anything of which she might have suspected me because she shared my grief.

With my brothers and sisters I was at my mother's bedside when she died. I knelt by her bed and gave her the Queen's message. I knew by the expression which flitted across her face that she had understood.

"Serve God . . . and the Queen," she murmured. "Oh, my children, remember . . ."

And that was all.

Elizabeth was certainly deeply moved. She insisted that my mother be buried at her expense in St. Edmund's Chapel. She sent for me and told me how deeply she had loved her cousin and that her loss would be sincerely felt. She meant it, I know, and she was tender to us all . . .

temporarily. I believe at this time she even forgave me for catching Robert's eye.

After the funeral she called me to her and talked about my parents—how she had loved my mother, how she esteemed my father.

"There was a family bond between your mother and me," she said, "and she was a good and gentle soul. I hope you will follow her example."

I told her wistfully that I missed serving her and she answered: "Ah, but you have compensations. How many is it now . . . four?"

"Yes, Madam, two girls and two boys."

"You are fortunate."

"I count myself so, Madam."

"That is well. There was a time when I thought you had a roving eye."

"Madam!"

She gave me a slap on the arm. "It seemed so. I esteem Walter Devereux. He is a man who deserves nothing but good."

"He will be overwhelmed with joy to hear that he has Your Majesty's good opinion."

"A lucky man. He has his heir. What have you called him?"

"Robert, Madam."

She looked at me sharply. Then she said: "A good name. A favorite of mine."

"Of mine now, Your Majesty."

"I shall reward your husband for his services to us. Lord Warwick has spoken of him most warmly, and I have decided one way in which I will show my appreciation."

"May I be allowed to ask what that is, Your Majesty?"

"Certainly. I am sending his wife back to Chartley, so that when he returns to his home he will find her there."

"He is at this moment busily engaged in the North."

"'Tis so. But we have got the better of these rebels, and should he return I would not have him disappointed and missing his wife."

It was dismissal. The friendliness she had felt in our mutual grief was over. I was not to be forgiven for Robert's brief interest in me.

My children were growing up. Penelope was nearly ten and Robert five. The domestic life, however, could never satisfy me. I was certainly not in love with my husband and felt little excitement during his visits. I was growing more and more restive because life was so dull. I was fond of my children—and in particular young Robert—but a child of five could not compensate a woman of my nature and provide the stimulus she needs.

When visitors came to Chartley I heard scraps of news —very often about the Earl of Leicester, who continued to dominate life at Court, and to these I listened avidly. He was still in high favor with the Queen, and the years were passing. It seemed unlikely now that Elizabeth would ever marry. She had recently flirted with the idea of taking the Duc d'Anjou, but like all her previous proposed matches, it came to nothing; and she would soon be forty, which was a little old for childbearing. Robert was still her favorite man, but no nearer to marrying her than he had ever been. And with each passing year the possibility must be becoming more and more remote.

There were uneasy rumors about certain amours of his. It was hardly to be expected that a man like Leicester would be prepared to be dangled on a string forever. I heard that two ladies of the Court (one of these was Douglass, wife of the Earl of Sheffield, and the other her sister, Lady Frances Howard) were both enamored of him and vied with each other for his attention.

"He likes them both well enough," said my informant, a visitor from Court who stayed a night or two at Chartley on his way North, and he added with a sly smile: "But the Queen has noted their follies and she likes them not."

Certainly she would not like it if they were involved with Leicester. I expected their dismissal would soon come as mine had. I was surprised to discover that I could still be jealous. I remembered hearing it said that there was something fascinating about the Howard women. Anne Boleyn was a Howard through her mother; Catherine Howard, who had been Henry VIII's fifth wife, had possessed that same attraction. Poor girl, it had cost her her head, though if she had been a little more subtle she might have saved it. They were not subtle, though, these Howards. They were attractive to men because they had need of them; but they were not calculating enough to take advantage of their assets.

I was now avid for news, and I asked myself how I could ever have thought I had ceased to be concerned with Robert Dudley. I knew very well that I only had to meet him again and I should be as eager for him as I ever was.

I asked my visitor what he knew about the Douglass Sheffield and Frances Howard matter.

"Oh," he told me, "rumor has it that Lady Sheffield became Leicester's mistress when they were both staying at Belvoir Castle."

I could picture it. The affair would progress rapidly as mine had, for Robert was a very impatient man and as the equivocation of the Queen drove him to distraction he would not want to endure similar frustration from other quarters.

"The story goes," went on our visitor, "that Leicester had written a love letter to Douglass in which he recklessly said he deplored the existence of her husband, thus implying that he would have married her if she had not already been a wife. Then, they say, came the hint that Sheffield might not long be there to plague them."

I gasped in horror. "Surely he could not have meant . . ."

"After the death of his wife there have been rumors about him. The silly Douglass—but perhaps she was not so silly and intended it to happen—dropped the letter on her return home, and it was found by her sister-in-law—who had little love for her—and promptly showed it to the cuckolded husband. They parted beds that night and Sheffield went off to London to arrange a divorce. He had the letter, you see, with what might be construed as a threat against his life . . . considering the direction it came from."

"All men in the public eye are envied and slandered." I found myself fervently defending Robert. "And surely there never was one more so than the Earl of Leicester."

"Well, you see, he has this Italian physician."

"You mean Dr. Julio."

"So he is called. He is in truth Giulio Borgherini, but people find difficulty in pronouncing his name. He is said to have great knowledge of poisons and to use them in the service of his master."

"You believe this?"

He shrugged his shoulders. "There was the death of his wife. People will never forget that. They will always remember it when something like this arises."

When he had left us I thought a good deal about Robert. I was bitterly hurt that he should want to marry Douglass Sheffield.

Walter came back. He was puffed up with pride because of the Queen's approval and had some wild scheme in his head about colonizing Ulster. The Queen had made him a Knight of the Garter and Earl of Essex—a title which had formerly been in his family through a marriage with the Mandevilles. That it was restored to him was a sign of the Queen's great favor.

I was a countess now and should have liked to accompany Walter to Court, but the Queen's invitation was clearly for him alone, so I was obliged to remain behind.

When he returned he was full of the latest scandal. As I might have expected it involved Robert Dudley.

"They say," he told me, "that the Earl of Sheffield, having discovered that his wife had betrayed him with Leicester, decided to seek a divorce. Imagine the scandal that would have meant. I doubt it would have pleased Her Majesty."

"Is she still as enamored of him as ever?"

"Clearly so. She is peevish when he is not at her side and it is a marvel—the manner in which her eyes follow him around."

"Tell me about the Sheffield scandal."

"Unnecessary now. He died."

"Died!"

"Oh yes, just at the right moment to avoid the scandal. It's not difficult to imagine the Queen's wrath if she had known Leicester was philandering with Lady Sheffield."

"How did he die?"

"They say poison."

"*They* always say these things."

"Well, he is dead and that means that Leicester will sleep easy at night."

"And Lady Sheffield . . . has he married her?"

"I've heard nothing of marriage."

"What is Lady Sheffield like?"

Walter shrugged his shoulders. He never noticed what a woman looked like. He was more interested in politics than private lives, and it was only due to Leicester's position in the country that he considered his love affairs for a moment; they were only important because they might alienate him from the Queen.

Walter was more concerned with a plot to marry Norfolk to the Queen of Scots, which Lady Scrope had possibly set in motion when she was with her husband at the time he was guarding Mary with my father.

Norfolk had always been a fool. He had already been married three times and all his wives had died. He was in his thirties, and no doubt the reputation of the Queen of Scots enthralled him. She was reckoned, after all, to be one of the most fascinating women of the day, and she had had three husbands to match Norfolk's three wives. Doubtless the foolish fellow thought it would be rather intriguing to be a queen's consort. So the plot went on. Norfolk professed to be a Protestant, but at heart he was a Catholic. I expect that he imagined he could one day be King of England in all but name. He could never forget that his family was of higher rank than the Tudors.

It was not a secret plan, and when it reached the Queen's ears she sent for Norfolk, and those present at the meeting read in it a stern warning to Norfolk.

The Queen had said that it had come to her ears that Norfolk was eager to change his title of Duke for King.

Norfolk must have been so shaken with those big tawny eyes on him that he denied this. He stammered that the Queen of Scots was an adulteress and suspected of murder, and he was a man who liked to sleep on a safe pillow. When the Queen replied that some men might be ready to take risks for the sake of a crown, Norfolk replied that he was as good a prince in his bowling alley in Norfolk as she was in the heart of Scotland. A rather dangerous remark for the same might have been said of Elizabeth at Greenwich. He then plunged further into danger when he said that he could not marry the Queen of Scots knowing that she pretended to the crown of England, and that if he did so Queen Elizabeth might charge him with seeking the crown of England.

The Queen retorted tartly that she might well do so.

Poor foolish Norfolk! He must have signed his death warrant in that moment.

It was surprising to hear—again through visitors from the Court—that the Earl of Leicester had oddly enough forgotten the enmity between himself and Norfolk and placed himself on the Duke's side. Heaven knew what was in Robert's mind, but I grew to discover that he could be as devious as Elizabeth herself. I believe now that he was afraid Elizabeth would die—she was often ill and on several occasions since her accession her life had been believed to be in danger—and if she did, Mary Stuart would come to the throne.

Robert was a man who could appear courteous and gentle outwardly while he was planning murder. Always to the forefront of his mind would be his own advantage. While he decided to support Norfolk he told him that he would arrange a meeting with Elizabeth so that he could present the case to her.

In view of his previous conversation with the Queen, Norfolk should have known better. Elizabeth, no doubt primed by Robert, for it would be characteristic of him to place one foot in each camp, nipped Norfolk's proposition in the bud, before he was able to begin to explain the advantages of a match between himself and Mary, taking his ear between her thumb and forefinger and pinching it so hard that he flinched.

"I would wish you," she said, "to take good heed of your pillow."

She was reminding him of his observation that he liked to sleep on a safe one and telling him as clearly as she could that the one he was proposing to take would lead him to another kind of pillow—a block of wood on which he might rest his head until the ax descended to sever it from his body.

Norfolk's heart must have quailed, for he fell on his knees, vowing that he had no desire for marriage, only to serve her.

Unfortunately for him he was not speaking the truth,

and as it came out afterwards when he received secret communications from the Queen of Scots, he was soon once again deep in the intrigue to marry her and rescue her from captivity.

Walter was immersed in his plans for Ulster, but when he went to Court he did hear a little of what was happening in those circles. He was disturbed because the Catholic threat to England was growing and the Queen's refusal to marry complicated it. While she lived, the country was safe for Protestantism, but if she died it would be plunged into war. He told me that ministers were constantly discussing the seriousness of a situation in which the succession was insecure, a fact which left England very vulnerable, particularly with the Queen of Scots actually in captivity in the country. Walter secretly agreed with this and told me that even Leicester had joined those who supported the plan for Norfolk to marry Mary Queen of Scots, so that she could be assured of an English husband. He could then make a Protestant of her, and if Elizabeth were to die and Mary inherit the throne, the religion of England would not change.

William Cecil was against such a marriage, but there were many influential men in the country who would have been pleased to see Cecil deposed. As Leicester had joined the plotters he was chosen to explain to the Queen the danger in which Cecil was placing the country. His present policy was alienating those influential Catholic countries, France and Spain, and to placate them it might be necessary to send Cecil to the block.

I heard from several sources what had happened at that meeting of the Council and never had the Queen shown her true nature so openly as she did on that occasion. I could picture her clearly. Her greatness must have been evident as she faced those schemers. The ax for Cecil! She broke out into a torrent of abuse for all those round that table who had dared suggest such a thing.

She reminded them that these were not the days of her father when ministers were sent to the block to make way for others. Cecil was against the marriage of Mary of Scotland and Norfolk, was he? They should know that Cecil's mistress agreed with him, and they should be well advised to watch their actions, lest they find themselves in that position into which they were trying to hustle Cecil. She would like them to inform their friend, the Queen of Scots, that if she did not take better care of them, some of her friends might find themselves shorter by a head.

When Walter discussed this with me, I said that I supposed they would drop their plan to remove Cecil now, but he shook his head and hinted that they might be conspiring against him in secret.

I was a little afraid then because I knew that Robert was involved, and I wondered what would happen if the Queen discovered that *he* was working against her. His treachery would be a thousand times worse than that of anyone else. I could not understand myself. I had wanted revenge on him for what he had done to me. I had often, overwhelmed by my young bitterness, declared—to myself, of course—that I should like to see *him* dismissed from Court as I had been. And now, here I was, worried because he was in acute danger.

But even though he was deeply involved with the conspirators, I might have known he would find a way out. I heard the story in snatches: How news had come to the Queen that Robert was dying and how she left everything to go to his bedside. She loved him. There was no doubt of that and I think that hers was a more abiding passion than that which Mary of Scotland ever had for Bothwell. With Mary it had been that irresistible physical attraction which had overwhelmed her so that she had bartered her crown for it; but she never had for him that enduring devotion which Elizabeth felt for Robert. Elizabeth simply wanted her throne more than she wanted Robert. But she loved him all the same.

He was relying on that affection to extricate him from a very dangerous situation—and it worked.

I could well imagine that pathetic bedside scene, with Robert lying there enacting the deathbed scene with great panache. All her love would have flowed to the surface. She could be so loyal to those whom she loved, just as she could never forgive those whom she hated.

I could picture Robert's account of his devotion to her. How he feared for her and had been led to believe that it was best for Elizabeth that Mary should marry Norfolk. And that was the reason why he had given his support to the plan . . . solely out of love for her . . . and now he could not forgive himself for acting without her knowledge, although he had done it out of his concern for her. He was clever with women. He knew how to give just the right amount of flattery; he was very artful with the artless comment. It was small wonder that so many women loved him—and Elizabeth was one of the many.

She had wept. Her Sweet Robin must not fret. She commanded him to get well, for she could not lose him. I could imagine the looks which would pass between them. Of course he would live. Hadn't he always obeyed her commands?

How typical it was of our sovereign lady that she should forgive Robert while at the same time she sent for Norfolk.

The Duke was arrested and sent to the Tower.

We all believed that Norfolk would lose his head, but the Queen seemed reluctant to sign the death warrant. Following her usual line in such cases, she prevaricated and in due course Norfolk was released, though he must live in restraint on his estates. But he was a man who seemed determined on self-destruction. It had been said that the very name of the Queen of Scots exerted a terrible fascination. Perhaps it was so, for Norfolk had not seen her. Perhaps he was intrigued by a queen who had committed adultery and was suspected of murder. It was difficult to say, but the fact remained that Norfolk was soon involved in the Ridolfi plot.

Ridolfi was a Florentine banker who had a plan to capture Elizabeth, set Mary on the throne after marrying her to Norfolk, and bring Catholicism back to England. The plot was doomed to fail. Several agents were caught and tortured, and in a short time Norfolk's involvement was revealed. There was no hope for him then. William Cecil, now Lord Burleigh, pointed out to the Queen that Norfolk could no longer be allowed to live; and in this he was supported by the Privy Council and the House of Commons.

Once again the Queen shrank from signing the death warrant. She was so distressed that she became ill with one of her mysterious disorders which resulted in what she called heavy and vehement pains. These pains could have been attributed to poison and, in view of the fact that the Ridolfi plot had just been uncovered, there was fear that the Queen's life might be in danger. But it turned out to be merely another of those illnesses which attacked her when something unpleasant had to be done. I used to wonder whether, when a death warrant was presented to her, she thought of her mother and the memory upset her. The fact remained that she was reluctant to kill, even when she herself had been put in danger.

Her ministers thought that here was a good case for ridding herself of Mary Queen of Scots, who was implicated in the plot; but this she refused to consider.

Eventually, however, the Duke of Norfolk's death warrant was signed, and a special scaffold was erected on

Tower Hill, for since the Queen's accession there had been no beheadings there and a new one was required.

All this happened during the years of my exile.

Walter had gone to Ireland full of plans for colonizing Ulster, but in less than a year he was having to confess to failure. He did not give up, however, and after returning to England for a while to consult with the Queen and her ministers he went back to try again.

He would have liked me to accompany him, but I pleaded that the children needed me. I had no intention of going to that wild country and enduring all kinds of discomfort. I was almost certain, too, that the expedition would be a failure, as most things Walter undertook would in time prove to be.

I was glad that I had stood firmly against going, for it was while Walter was in Ireland that the Queen intimated that I might return to Court.

I was filled with a wild excitement. My son Robert was eight at the time and Walter six; the girls were growing up but still not of an age to make it necessary to find husbands for them.

A spell at Court was just what I needed.

So I found myself at the Kenilworth revels and at the beginning of a new and exciting life. I was no longer young, being in my thirty-fourth year, and at Chartley I had begun to feel that life was passing me by.

Perhaps that was why I plunged so recklessly into the richness which fate threw at me during the following years, with little thought of where it would lead me. My banishment had lasted too long, but it had at least shown me that I could never forget Robert Dudley and that my relationship with the Queen added to the flavor of my life without which it would have been insipid.

There were two things I wanted—my passionate life with Robert and my battle for superiority with the Queen

—and I wanted them desperately. Having them once, I could not be satisfied to live without them and I was ready to face any consequences to get them. I had to prove to myself and to Robert—and perhaps one day to the Queen herself—that my physical attractions were irresistible to him—far more so than the Queen's royalty.

I was heading for a dangerous road. I did not care. I was reckless, eager for life, and was convinced I knew how to find what I wanted.

Kenilworth

Kenilworth where he [Leicester] lodged the Queen and her ladies, forty earls and seventy other principal milords, all under the roof of his own castle, for the space of twelve days. . . .

DE LA MOTHE FENELON, *the French Ambassador*

. . . the clok bell sank not a note all the while her Highness waz thear; the clok stood also withal, the hands of both the tablz stood firm and fast, always pointing at two o'clock. . . .

The fireworks were a . . . blaze of burning darts, flying to and fro . . . streams and hails of fiery sparks, lightening of wildfire a' water and a' land.

ROBERT LANEHAM *on the revels at Kenilworth*

I was to join the Queen at Greenwich and as my barge carried me along the river I was overwhelmed by the excitement and bustle of London life and the fact that I was coming back to it. The river was, as ever, the busiest of the country's thoroughfares. Craft of all description was sailing along in the direction of the palace. The Lord Mayor's gilded barge was among them, escorted by the less glorious vessels of his officials. The watermen in their livery and silver badges rowed skillfully among the more cumbersome barges, whistling and singing, calling pleasantries to each other. In one was a girl who might have been a boatman's daughter; she was strumming at a lute and singing, " 'Row thy boat, Norman' "—a song which had been sung for more than a hundred years—in a powerful but somehow raucous voice to the delight of the occupants of passing boats. It was a scene typical of London's river.

I felt in turns exultant and apprehensive. Whatever happened, I warned myself, I must not be banished again. I must guard my tongue—but not too much perhaps, for the Queen liked the occasional caustic remark. I would be watched with regard to her favorite men—people like Heneage, Hatton and the Earl of Oxford—and most of all the Earl of Leicester.

I was telling myself I must have changed in eight years, but I fancied it was not for the worse. I was more mature naturally. I had borne several children, but I knew that men found me more attractive than ever. One thing I was determined on. I should not allow myself to be picked up and dropped as I had been before. Of course, I kept reminding myself, he would only have behaved as he did because of the Queen. There was not another woman who could have displaced me for herself alone. Still, my feminine vanity had been wounded and in future—if there was a future with Robert—I would let him know that I had no intention of allowing it to happen again.

It was spring and the Queen had come to Greenwich, which she liked to do at this time of the year to enjoy the delightful situation there. Everything had been freshened for her arrival; and in the quarters of the ladies attendant on her I was greeted by Kate Carey, Lady Howard of Effingham; Anne, Lady Warwick; and Catharine, Countess of Huntingdon. Kate was my mother's sister and cousin to the Queen; Anne was the wife of Robert's brother Ambrose; and Catharine was Robert's sister.

Aunt Kate embraced me, told me I was looking in good health and that she was glad to see me back at Court.

"You have escaped so long," said Anne with a little grimace.

"She has been with her family and now has a goodly one to show for those years away from Court," said Aunt Kate.

"The Queen talked of you now and then," put in Catharine. "Did she not, Anne?"

" 'Tis true that she did. She once said that as a young girl you were one of the prettiest she had ever had at her Court. She likes good-looking people about her."

"She liked me so well that she dispensed with me for eight years," I reminded them.

"She thought your husband had need of you and she did not wish to deprive him."

"So now she sends him to Ireland?"

"You should have gone with him, Lettice," said my aunt. "It's not good to let husbands rove too far away."

"Oh, Walter is welcome to his diversions."

Catharine laughed, but the other two looked grave.

"Lettice my dear," said Kate, very much the wise aunt, "do not let Her Majesty hear you talk like that. She dislikes flippancy regarding the married state."

"It is strange having such a respect for it that she is so reluctant to enter into it herself."

"There are matters beyond our knowledge," said my

aunt primly. "She will see you tomorrow at supper when you will be one of the lady tasters. I doubt not that she will have a word with you during the meal. You know how she is ever ready to dispense with ceremony at the table."

I knew my aunt was warning me to take care. I had been banished from the Court for a number of years, which meant that I had without doubt offended the Queen in some way, for she was notoriously lenient with her relatives—particularly those on the Boleyn side. She would be a little sterner with the Tudor ones because she had to be watchful of them, but the Boleyns, having no claim in the throne, were grateful to her for raising them up, and she loved to honor them.

I could scarcely sleep that night, so excited was I to be back at Court. I knew that sooner or later I was going to come face to face with Robert. As soon as we met I should know whether I still attracted him, and then it would be my joy to discover how much and whether he was prepared to take further risks for me. On one thing I had made up my mind: No more quick embraces and then goodbye because the Queen would not tolerate his affection for another woman.

"It will have to be something better this time, Robert," I murmured to myself. "Always supposing that you still find me desirable . . . and of course that I feel the same irresistible urge to take you as my lover."

Although it was a sleepless night, what joy it was to lie on my pallet and contemplate the future. How had I endured those barren years . . . oh, but not quite barren. I had the children . . . my own adorable Robert. I could leave him without compunction, for he was well cared for, and boys, when they passed out of babyhood, became impatient of a fond and doting mother beside them. He would always be there, my beloved boy, and when he grew older he could count on his mother as his very good friend.

As it was Sunday there was a great attendance at the palace. The Archbishop of Canterbury, the Bishop of London, the Chancellor, officers of the crown and other gentlemen had all come to pay their respects to the Queen. She would receive them in the Presence Chamber, which was hung with rich tapestry, and the floor would have been covered with fresh rushes.

People had assembled to watch the procession, which was really impressive. The Queen liked them to be given freedom to see all the pomp. Having come to her present high eminence by cautiously considering the will of the people, she was always especially eager to please them; when she rode among them she would speak even to the humblest; she wanted them to realize that although she was a glorious being, a divinity on earth, she loved the people and was in a way their servant. It was one of the secrets of her great popularity.

I watched the earls, Knights of the Garter and barons enter, and then came the Chancellor walking between two guards, one of whom carried the royal scepter and the other the sword of state in a red scabbard which was studded with fleurs-de-lis. The Queen followed immediately afterwards, but I could not stay to see her as I had to be at my duties.

The preparation of the table always amused me. No sacred rite could have been performed with more reverence. I and a young countess were the tasters on this morning, for it was a tradition that one taster must be unmarried and the other married—and both of high rank.

First a gentleman appeared holding a rod and behind him came a man carrying the tablecloth; following him came others with the saltcellar, platter and bread. I could scarcely repress a smile as they knelt before the empty table before placing these things on it.

Then it was our turn. We approached the table, I carrying the tasting knife. We both took bread and salt and rubbed it into the plates to make sure they were clean; and when we had finished these tasks the dishes were brought in. I took the knife and cut portions which I gave to several of the guards who had been standing looking on. They ate what I gave them. This ceremony was to safeguard the Queen from poison.

When they had finished eating, the trumpets were sounded, the two men with kettledrums came in and played their instruments to let it be known that the meal was ready.

The Queen would not sit in the main hall but would take her food in a small adjoining chamber. I presumed that she would summon me to her side while she was eating.

I was right. In due course she arrived. We took the food she wanted into a small chamber, and there she bade me welcome back to Court and told me that I might sit beside her.

I expressed myself overwhelmed by the honor and she looked at me searchingly. I longed to examine more closely what the years had done to her, but for that I must wait.

"Ha," she said. "The country does good to you, and so does childbearing. Two sons, I believe, I shall see them one day, I trust."

"Your Majesty has but to express the command," I replied, stating the obvious.

She nodded. "Much has happened since you were at Court. I miss my dear cousin, your mother, sadly."

"Your Majesty was always good to her. Often she told me so."

Was it really a tear I saw in the tawny eyes? It might be, for she was sentimental about those who she believed had been her true friends, and my mother had undoubtedly been one of them.

"She was too young to die." It was almost a reproach.

To my mother for leaving her? To God for taking her and causing sorrow to the Queen? "Catherine Knollys, how dare you leave your sovereign, who had need of you!" "Lord, why did You have to take this good servant from me?" I almost gave voice to these thoughts. Guard your tongue, I warned myself. But it was not my tongue which had brought about my exile. Indeed, Her Majesty, who spent her life among sycophants, had on occasions liked it.

"I rejoice to see Your Majesty in good health and recovered from your sickness," I said.

"Oh, they believed me to be near to death and I confess there were times when I fancied it myself."

"No, Madam, you are immortal. So must you be, for your people have need of you."

She nodded and said: "Well, Lettice. I like to see you with us. You still have some beauty left. Essex will have to do without you for a while. He is making a fair hash of things in Ireland. His judgment is not good, I fancy, but his heart is. I trust he will meet with better fortune over there. We shall be leaving Greenwich ere long."

"Your Majesty tires of the place?"

"Nay. 'Twas always a favorite. I suppose one would feel thus about one's birthplace. But I have to humor my Lord Leicester. He is in a fever of impatience to show us Kenilworth. I hear he has made it into one of the finest residences in the country. He will give me no rest until he has shown it to me."

I suddenly bent forward and, taking that most beautiful white hand in mine, I kissed it. If Robert was in a fever of excitement to show the Queen Kenilworth, I was in like state to see him.

I looked up and tried to express fear at my forwardness, but Elizabeth was in a sentimental mood and after all I was a member of the family.

"Madam," I said, "I am presumptuous. I was overcome by my pleasure to be back with you."

The hard eyes softened momentarily. She believed me.

"It pleases me to have you here, Lettice," she said. "Make your preparations for Kenilworth. I doubt not you will wish to have some new dresses for the event. You will have your seamstress with you. There is some scarlet velvet . . . enough for a gown. Tell them I have said you may have it." Her mouth turned up at the corners. "We shall all have to look very fine for my Lord Leicester, I trow."

She loved him. I could hear it in her voice when she said his name; and I wondered whether I was setting out on a dangerous road. Even to think of him made my pulse race. I knew that if he had changed I was still going to want him.

If he looked my way, if he showed in the smallest manner that he was ready to revive his desire for me, I would not hesitate to become the Queen's rival.

"I will take a little of the Alicante wine," she said.

I mixed it with water as she liked it. She always ate and drank very sparingly and rarely took wine, preferring a light ale; and when she did take it, it was liberally mixed with water. Sometimes she would grow impatient of food and on informal occasions would rise before the rest of the company was finished. We deplored this because it meant that we had to leave the table, for none of us could stay when she had left; and as we were served after she was, it often meant a hurried meal—so we were not very anxious to eat with the Queen.

But on this occasion she lingered, and all were able to have their fill.

Sipping the wine, she smiled softly—thinking of Robert, I knew.

It was July when we set out for Kenilworth, which is between the towns of Warwick and Coventry and about five miles from each, so it was a far distance from London and we were to take a leisurely journey.

It was a brilliant and large cavalcade which set out, comprising thirty-one of the leading men of the country, and all her ladies, of whom I was one, and four hundred servants. The Queen planned to stay at Kenilworth for more than two weeks.

People came out to watch us pass and there were the usual cheers for the Queen and those pleasant little exchanges between her and the people which she would not have missed for anything.

We had not gone far when we saw riding towards us a party of horsemen. Even from a distance I recognized him at their head. My heart beat faster. I knew how I should feel even before he reached us. How well he sat his horse. He had qualified for the role of Queen's Horse Master in every way. He was older yes—a little more corpulent than he had been eight years before; his face was a shade more ruddy and there was a touch of white in the hair at his temples. In his blue velvet doublet with slashings arranged in a pattern of stars after the new German fashion, and the feather in his hat of the same tone as the doublet, though of a paler shade, he looked magnificent, and I saw at once that the old magnetism was still there. I doubted Elizabeth loved the middle-aged Robert less than she had the young man. I could see it would be the same with me.

He pulled up within a very small distance of our party, and I noticed the faint color beneath the Queen's white skin which indicated her pleasure.

"Why," she said, "it is my Lord Leicester."

He was at her side. He took her hand and kissed it, and as I saw their eyes meet as he raised her hand, the wildest pangs of jealousy overwhelmed me. I could only control this by consoling myself that he was merely paying tribute to the crown. If she were not the Queen he would have eyes for no one but me.

He brought his horse close beside hers.

"What do you mean by coming thus unannounced, you rogue?" she demanded. The rogue, as I had heard it before, was a term of endearment said in that manner.

"I could not allow any but myself to conduct you to Kenilworth," he said ardently.

"Well, since we are eager to see this magic castle of yours, we'll forgive you. You look in good health, Rob."

"Never better," he answered. "And that may be due to the fact that I am beside my lady."

I felt sick with fury, for he had not so much as glanced my way.

"Well, we will go on," said the Queen, "or we'll take weeks to reach Kenilworth."

We dined at Itchingworth, where we were lavishly entertained, and as there was a forest the Queen expressed her desire to hunt.

I watched her ride off side by side with Robert. She made no attempt to hide her doting fondness. As for him, I could not be sure how much was real affection, how much ambition. Surely he was not still hoping for marriage—but even if he were not, he needed to keep her favor. There was not a man in England more detested than Robert Dudley. He had come up by such leaps and bounds through the Queen's especial interest and had engendered so much envy in doing so that there were thousands who hoped for his downfall, many who knew him and many who did not—such was human nature.

I was beginning to understand Robert, and looking back much was clear to me which had not been in the days of our intimacy. He had a courteous way with any who approached him, be they ever so humble, and in fact his manner sometimes belied the calculating strength which lay behind it. He had a temper which could be violent when it was roused; there were many dark secrets in his life; but those who approached him in the normal way received nothing but pleasantness from him. But of course he must tread warily, even with the Queen. If she had memories which had affected her attitude to love, so had he. His grandfather, financial adviser to King Henry VII, had been beheaded—thrown to the wolves, it was said, to placate the people who were dissatisfied with the taxes imposed by the King and collected by Dudley and Empson; Robert's father had lost his head after trying to put Lady Jane Grey and his son Guildford on the throne. So it was only natural that Robert should make an extreme effort to keep his own head on his shoulders. I think he was safe enough. Elizabeth hated signing death warrants even for her enemies. It was hardly likely that, in any circumstances, she would ever sign one for this beloved man.

But of course he could fall from favor, and naturally he was making a supreme effort not to do so.

He still had not noticed me when we reached Grafton, where the Queen had her own house. Elizabeth was in excellent spirits. In fact her demeanor had remained the same from the moment Robert arrived. They rode side by side, and often her laughter rang out as they exchanged secret jokes.

The weather was unusually hot and when we came to Grafton we were very thirsty. We went into the hall, Robert and the Queen leading the way, and Robert called out to the servants to bring the light ale which the Queen liked to drink.

There was a bustle and scurrying about and in due course the ale was brought, but when the Queen tried it she spat it out.

"I cannot drink that stuff," she cried indignantly. "It's too strong for me."

Robert tried it and declared it was stronger than malmsey and made him feel so heavy with drink that he would not trust his temper. He ordered the servants to find the light ale which Her Majesty wanted.

But this was not easily done, for there was none in the house, and the thirstier the Queen grew the more angry she became.

"What servants are these," she cried, "that they know not how to serve me my good ale! Is there naught to drink in this place?"

Robert said he dared not let them bring water, for he could not trust it to be uncontaminated. The closeness of the privies to the house was always a menace and particularly in weather like this.

He was not a man to sit down and lament in a crisis; he sent his servants into the village and before long some light ale was discovered and when Robert brought it to the Queen she expressed herself well pleased with the drink and the bearer.

It was while we were at Grafton that Robert noticed me. I saw him start, look and look again.

He came to me and, bowing, said: "Lettice, it does me good to see you."

"And I am pleased to see you, my Lord Leicester."

"It was Lettice and Robert when we last met."

"That is a long time ago."

"Eight years."

"You remember then?"

"There are some things one never forgets."

The adventure was there. I saw it in his eyes. I believe, as with me, that danger was a fillip to his zest. We stood there looking at each other, and I knew he was remembering—as I was—intimate moments which had taken place behind the locked doors of that secret chamber where we had made love.

"We must meet again . . . alone," he said.

I replied: "The Queen will not wish it."

" 'Tis true," he answered. "But if she does not know

she cannot be displeased. Let me say that it pleases *me* that you will be with us at Kenilworth."

He left me. He was very anxious that the Queen should not be aware of our interest in each other. I persuaded myself that it might be because he feared I should be sent away again.

What excited me was that it was still the same between us. I missed nothing of that magnetism. It had increased with age. I hoped my attraction had for him. We only had to be near each other to know that we both had much to give.

This time, though, it would not be given so freely on my part. He would have to know that I wanted a relationship on a firmer basis. I thought of marrying him. How could I when I had a husband? That was right out of the question. But I would not be picked up and dropped at the Queen's command. I should make that clear to him from the start.

Now the days were full of excitement. We looked for each other and the glances which passed between us were significant. When the opportunity came we should be prepared to take it.

I think the tantalizing position added to our desire.

It would be easier when we were at Kenilworth.

It was the ninth of July when we reached the castle. There was a shout as it came into view and I saw Robert glance at the Queen, begging for her admiration. It was truly a magnificent sight. Those castellated towers and mighty keep proclaimed a fortress in very truth; and on the southwest side was a beautiful lake shimmering in the sunshine. This was spanned by a graceful bridge which Robert had recently had built; and beyond the castle the verdant forest was visible, promising the Queen good hunting.

"It has the look of a royal residence," said the Queen.

"Designed with the sole purpose of pleasing a queen," replied Robert.

"You'll put Greenwich and Hampton to shame," she retorted.

"Nay," replied Robert, always the courtier. "It is only your presence which gives these places their royalty. Without you they are but piles of stones."

I felt a desire to laugh. You lay it on too thickly, Robert, I thought; but she evidently did not think so, for she was giving him a loving, well-pleased look.

We were approaching the keep and ten girls dressed in palls of white silk to represent the sybils stood in a row barring our way. Then one of them stepped forward and spoke a rhyme extolling the perfections of the Queen and predicting a long and happy reign for her which would bring prosperity to her people.

I was watching her as the recitation went on. She loved every word. It was the kind of charade which had so appealed to her father and her love of it was one of the chief characteristics she had inherited from him. Robert watched her with deep satisfaction. How well he must know her! He must care for her in a way. How she must have frustrated him, holding the glittering crown out to him and then, just as he thought he might take it, drawing it back. If the prize had not been so great, if she did not hold his future in her hands, how long would he have allowed himself to be so treated?

We went on to the next little farce and I realized that this was a foretaste of what the next days would be like.

Robert led the Queen into the tiltyard, where they were met by a ferocious-looking man as tall as Robert himself; he wore a silk robe and brandished a club which he waved threateningly. Some of the ladies squealed in mock horror.

"What do you here?" he cried in a voice of thunder. "Know you not that this is the domain of the mighty Earl of Leicester?"

136

Robert answered: "Good servant, see you not who is among us?"

The giant opened his eyes in amazement as he turned to the Queen and shaded them as though blinded by such brilliance. Then he fell to his knees and when the Queen bade him to rise he offered her the club and the keys of the castle.

"Open the gates," he cried. "This is a day which will long be remembered at Kenilworth."

The gates were opened and we went through. On the walls of the courtyard stood six trumpeters in long silken robes; they were very impressive, for their trumpets were five feet long. They blew a welcome on these which made the Queen clap her hands in pleasure.

As we progressed the scene grew more spectacular. In the middle of the lake an island had been made and on this was a beautiful woman. Two nymphs lay at her feet and about them were a company of ladies and gentlemen holding high blazing torches.

The lady of the lake spoke a panegyric similar to those we had heard before. The Queen cried out that it was beautiful. Then she was led to the base court where was assembled a company dressed to represent the gods: Sylvanus of the woods offered her leaves and flowers, Ceres was there with corn, Bacchus with grapes, Mars with arms, and Apollo with musical instruments to sing a song of the nation's love for the Queen.

She received them all with gracious words, complimenting them on their skill and beauty.

Leicester told her that there was much more for her to see but he believed that she must now be weary and wished to rest. She must be thirsty too and he could promise her that she would find the ale at Kenilworth to her taste.

"I have made certain that nothing shall displease Your Majesty as it did at Grafton, by testing the ale, and, finding it harsh, I brought down ale makers from London so that we shall not offend you here."

"I can trust my dear Eyes to care for my comfort," said the Queen with emotion.

In the inner court a salute of guns was fired, and as she was about to pass into the castle, Robert drew her attention to the clock on that tower which was called Caesar's. Its face was of a delicate shade of blue and the numbers and hands were of pure gold. It could be seen all round the neighborhood. He begged her to watch it for a moment, for if she did she would see the gold hands stop.

"This signifies that while Your Majesty honors Kenilworth with her presence, time stands still," he told her.

She was clearly happy. How she loved this pomp and ceremony! How she loved this adulation and, above all, how she loved Robert!

There was some speculation among her entourage that surely on this visit she would announce her intention to marry him. It seemed certain that this was what Robert was hoping for.

Those days at Kenilworth will never be forgotten—not only by me, which is understandable, as they made a turning point in my life, but by all those present.

I think it is safe to say that there never was, nor ever will be, such entertainment as Robert devised for his Queen's pleasure.

There were displays of fireworks, Italian tumblers, bull- and bear-baiting, and of course tilting and tournaments. Wherever the Queen was, there must be dancing, and she would stay up far into the early hours of morning to dance and never seemed to tire of it.

In the first days at Kenilworth, Robert scarcely left her side, and in fact later he must never absent himself too long. On the rare occasions when he partnered others in the dance I saw her watch him closely and with impatience. I heard her say once: "I trust you enjoyed the dance, my Lord Leicester." She was very cold and very haughty until he leaned towards her and whispered something which made her smile and restored her good humor.

It was hardly possible to believe that they were not lovers.

I might have felt that I was dreaming of the impossible except for the fact that on several occasions I would see his eyes stray round the room and I knew they were looking for me; and when they found me something flashed between us. We were going to meet, but I knew that it was imperative that we take the utmost care.

I was schooling myself. When the moment came I wanted to be ready. No quick tumble behind locked doors this time, Robert. No "Let it be tonight if the Queen can spare me." He would be plausible. He was the most plausible man on earth, but I should be wary. I was wiser now.

It amused me to think that Elizabeth and I were rivals. She was a worthy adversary indeed with her weapons of power and promises of greatness . . . and her threats, of course. "Do not think my favor is so locked up in you . . ." Her father all over again. "I brought you up. I could as easily throw you down." Henry VIII had said that to his favorites . . . men and women who had worked for him and given him of their best: Cardinal Wolsey, Thomas Cromwell, Catherine of Aragon, Anne Boleyn, poor little Catherine Howard—and Katharine Parr would have been another if he had not died in time. Henry had once loved Anne Boleyn as passionately as Elizabeth loved Robert, but that had not saved her. These thoughts must occur now and then to Robert.

If I displeased her what would happen to me? Such was my nature that contemplation of my danger did not deter me; in some ways it added to my eagerness.

At last there came the moment when we were alone together. He took my hand and looked into my eyes.

"What do you want of me, my lord?" I asked.

"You know," he replied fervently.

"There are many women here," I said. "And I have a husband."

"There is only one I want."

"Take care," I teased. "That's treason. Your mistress would be very displeased with you if she heard you utter such words."

"I care for nothing but that you and I should be together."

I shook my head.

"There is a room—right at the top of the west tower. It is never visited," he persisted.

I turned away but he had caught my hand and I was immediately shaking with that desire which he alone could arouse in me.

"I shall be there at midnight . . . waiting."

I said: "You may wait, my lord."

Someone was mounting the stairs and he quickly went off. Afraid to be seen, I thought angrily.

I did not go to that room in the tower, though it was difficult to prevent myself doing so. I found a good deal of pleasure, though, imagining his striding up and down waiting impatiently.

He was reproachful and a little more reckless next time we met. We were not alone and although he appeared to be exchanging pleasantries with a guest he was saying: "I must speak to you. There is much I have to say to you."

"Then just for a talk perhaps," I said.

And I went to the room.

He seized me and attempted to kiss me into submission but I noticed that first he had carefully locked the door.

"No," I protested. "Not yet."

"Yes," he said. "Now! I have waited too long. I will not wait a second longer."

I knew I was weak. My resolutions slipped away. He

had only to touch me—and I had always known my need of him matched his for me. It was useless to resist. We would talk afterwards.

He laughed triumphantly. I was triumphant too, because I knew this was a temporary surrender. I should have my way in the end.

Afterwards he said complacently: "Oh, Lettice, how we need each other!"

"I have got along very well without you for eight years," I reminded him.

"Eight wasted years!" he sighed.

"Wasted! Oh no, my lord, you advanced far in royal favor during that time."

"Any time not spent with you is wasted time."

"You sound as though you are talking to the Queen."

"Oh, come, Lettice, be reasonable."

"That is exactly what I intend to be."

"You are married. I am in this position . . ."

"Hoping to marry. They say: 'Hope deferred maketh the heart sick.' Is that how it is with you? Are you so sick with waiting that you look elsewhere for what you imagine can be a few secret meetings with someone who finds you too handsome to resist?"

"You know it is not so, but you also know my position."

"I know that she has been dangling you these many years and still there is little hope. Or do you go on hoping?"

"The Queen's temper is uncertain."

"Do I not know that! You forget I was banished from the Court for eight years. And do you know why?"

He drew me closer to him.

"You should have a care," I warned him. "She noticed once."

"Do you think she did?"

"For what other reason should I have been kept from Court?"

He laughed. A little complacently, I thought, so sure that he could do what he would with the women who interested him.

I held back and he was immediately the pleading lover.

"Lettice, I love you . . . you only . . ."

"Then let us go and tell the Queen."

"You've forgotten Essex."

"He is your safeguard."

"If he were not there I would marry you and prove to you the true state of my feelings."

"But he *is* there and you may say 'if' with the greatest complacency. You know full well you dare not tell the Queen what has happened tonight."

"I would not tell her, no. But if I could marry you I would do so and in time break the news to her."

"As a woman cannot have two husbands, there can be no marriage. And if the Queen were to discover that you and I had been together, we know what would happen. I should be sent away from Court. You would be in disgrace for a while and then taken back into favor. That is one of your greatest accomplishments, I believe. The fact is I came here to talk . . ."

"And then you found that our love overwhelmed us both."

"I found that I enjoy my pleasures and that in some respects you suit me well. But I will not be picked up and dropped when it is expedient to do so as though I were some serving wench."

"That you could never be mistaken for."

"I hope not. But it would seem you imagined I could be treated like one. It shall not happen again, my lord."

"Lettice, you must understand. More than anything, I want to marry you, and I tell you this. . . . One day I am going to."

"When?"

"Ere long."

"And Essex?"

"Leave him to me."

"What do you mean by that?"

"I mean who can know what will happen? Be patient. You and I were meant for each other. I knew it when we first met. But you were married to Essex, so what could I do? Ah, Lettice, if you had not married him, how different it would have been. But you have come back to me. Don't think I am ever going to let you go again."

"You should let me go now or I shall be missed, and if I am, and if I am being spied on, and it comes to the Queen's ears, I would not be in your shoes, Robert Dudley. And I fancy mine would not be very comfortable either."

He unlocked the door. Then he held me in an embrace so fierce that I thought the whole thing was going to start all over again; but he realized the sense of my warning and let me go.

I crept back to my apartment. My absence had been noticed by some of the others. I wondered whether any of them thought I had been with a lover, and I amused myself by imagining their shocked wonder if I told them I had and who it was.

The weather grew less hot; there had been a few refreshing showers and the entire company seemed to be in excellent spirits. I saw nothing of Robert in private, but frequently, of course, in the company of others, for he was constantly at the Queen's side. They hunted a great deal together, spending the hours until twilight in the forest; and when they returned to Kenilworth there was invariably some welcoming pageant for Elizabeth. There was no end to Robert's inventiveness, but all the time he had to be wary, for the pleasure he had given the Queen could be quickly forgotten and all his efforts in vain if in some way he should manage to offend her.

On this particular day a water pageant had been devised to welcome her on her return to the castle, for Robert made good use of the lake, which was always its most effective by night when the lighted torches gave a magic touch to the scene. On this occasion a mermaid greeted her and beside her was an enormous dolphin, on whose back sat a man in a mask who was meant to represent Arion. As soon as he saw the Queen he began to recite verses extolling her virtues and the joy of Kenilworth because she did it the honor of staying within its walls.

This incident put the Queen in high good humor because Arion, after having delivered the first few lines of his oration, could not remember the rest of the piece. He fumbled and began again and then in a burst of rage he tore off his mask so that his red sweating face was exposed.

"I am no Arion," he cried aloud. "I am but honest Harry Goldingham, Your Majesty's most loyal subject."

There was silence. Robert glared at the offender, but the Queen burst into loud laughter and cried: "Good Harry Goldingham, you have amused me well, and I do declare that I liked your performance best of anybody's."

So Harry Goldingham left his dolphin and was as pleased with himself as he could be. He had won the Queen's special praise for his performance and no doubt he reckoned it would give him good standing with his lord and master, the Earl of Leicester.

During the evening the Queen referred again and again to the incident, and she told Robert that she would never forget the pleasure she had enjoyed at Kenilworth.

I was piqued by the Queen's absolute devotion to Robert. It meant that he was never free of her. It was only during the time when she was at her toilet that he could get away, and then I had my duties. It was very frustrating for us both and, thus tantalized, our desire for each other was intensified.

Once when I thought there was an opportunity for a few words I saw him in close conversation with another woman. I knew her by sight and had had a special interest in her. She was that Douglass Sheffield whose name had been coupled with Robert's at one time. I remembered the rumors I had heard about them.

I did not believe the story that he had had her husband murdered. What was the point of murdering the Earl of Sheffield? Douglass was much more desirable to Robert with a husband—as I was. The real proof of Robert's love would be marriage. That would mean that he wanted his bride more than the Queen's favor. I did not need a visit to Kenilworth to remind me of what her wrath would be like if he did marry. It would be fierce and terrible, and I doubted even Robert would be able to restore himself to her favor after such an event.

I had not attached a great deal of importance to the Douglass Sheffield scandal until now, because incredible stories had always been circulated about Robert. He was the most envied man in the realm; no one had more enemies; he stood so high with the Queen that thousands—at Court and throughout the country—longed, as envious people will, to see him brought low; and it is a sad commentary on human nature that even those who would gain nothing by it, yet wanted to see it.

Of course there had been the murky scandal of Amy Robsart's death and the scars of that would remain with him throughout his life. Had he murdered her? Who could say? She had certainly seemed to stand between him and ambition, and he greatly desired a marriage which had been impossible while she lived. There were too many dark secrets in Cumnor Place; and there was no doubt that the incident of Amy's death had given the envious the ammunition they needed.

Dr. Julio, Robert's physician, being an Italian, was becoming known as Leicester's poisoner, so it was small wonder that it had been said at the time of the Earl of Sheffield's death that Robert had had him removed. But why, when he had no wish to marry his widow? Except, of course, that Sheffield was at the time threatening divorce—having discovered that Douglass had committed adultery with Robert. That would have created a scandal which Robert would want to avoid at all costs, for if it came to the Queen's ears he would be in great trouble.

That Robert was of a dark and devious nature mattered not to me. I wanted a man who could challenge me. I wanted no mild, ineffectual creature like my husband. I was heartily tired of Walter, and I was as deeply enamored of Robert Dudley as any woman could be. That was why when I saw him talking earnestly to Douglass Sheffield, I was filled with uneasiness.

It was a Sunday. The Queen had attended church in the morning, and as the weather was warm and pleasant, it was decided that some players from Coventry should do *Hock Tide,* a play about Danes, for her entertainment.

I was mildly amused to see these rustics in their improvised costumes and their local accents portraying men of whom they could have had no conception. The Queen was delighted with them; she enjoyed being among the simple country folk, and to bring home to them the fact that, glittering and glorious as she was, she had a great respect and love for them. Again and again on our progress we must stop by the road if any humble person approached her; and she never failed to have a kind word or reassurance to offer. There must have been many people in the country who would cherish an encounter with her throughout their lives and serve her with the utmost loyalty because she had never been too proud to speak to them.

So now she gave as close an attention to the Coventry players as she would have done to any of the Court actors, and sat in her chair laughing when laughter was expected and applauding only when applause was looked for.

The play was about the coming of the Danes, their insolence, violence and the outrages they inflicted on the English countryside. The chief character was Hunna, King Ethelred's general, and of course the play ended in the defeat of the Danes. As a tribute to her sex, the captive Danes were led onto the stage by women, at which the Queen loudly applauded.

When it was over, she insisted that the players be presented to her that she might tell them how much she had enjoyed their play.

"Good men of Coventry," she said, "you have given me much pleasure and shall be rewarded. Yesterday's hunting brought us several good bucks and I shall order that you be given two of the finest, and in addition you shall have five marks in money."

The good men of Coventry fell on their knees and declared they would never forget the day they had had the honor of playing before the Queen. They were loyal men, and after this day there would not be one of them who would not willingly give his life for her.

She thanked them and, watching her, I noticed how she preserved that rare and royal gift in that she could lose none of her dignity and yet at the same time be completely at ease with them and make them so with her. She could lift them up without descending from her royalty. I was aware of her greatness as never before; that we should be rivals for the same man filled me with an intense excitement and the fact that he was ready to risk so much for the fulfillment of his passion for me was an indication of its depth.

This emotion between us was something which must not be denied. We were bold adventurers, both of us, and

I could be sure that the danger was as irresistible to him as it was to me.

It was that very day that I found an opportunity of speaking to Douglass Sheffield.

The play being over and still some hours left before twilight, the Queen, riding side by side with Robert and followed by certain of the ladies and gentlemen, had left for the forest, when I saw Douglass Sheffield walking alone in the gardens and I went to her.

I came up with her near the lake as if by chance and called a greeting.

"It is Lady Essex, is it not?" she asked, and I answered that it was, and that I believed she was Lady Sheffield.

"We should know each other," I went on, "there is a family connection through the Howard family." She was one of the Effingham Howards and it was my great-grandmother, wife of Sir Thomas Boleyn, who was of the family.

"So we are distant cousins," I added.

I studied her intently. I could understand what Robert had found attractive. She had the quality which many of the Howard women had. My grandmother Mary Boleyn and Catherine Howard must have been somewhat similar. Anne Boleyn had something more—this immense physical attractiveness plus a calculating streak which made her ambitious. Anne had miscalculated—of course she had had a very fickle man to deal with—and she had ended up headless, but with a little dexterous handling of her affairs and aided by the birth of a son, it need not have happened as it did.

Douglass then was the soft and yielding type, sensuous and making no demands in return for what she gave. Her sort immediately attracted the opposite sex, but very often it was not durable.

I said: "The Queen grows more and more enamored of my Lord Leicester."

Her mouth drooped and she looked rather sad. I thought: There *is* something, then.

"Do you think she will marry him?" I went on.

"No," said Douglass vehemently. "He cannot do that."

"*I* cannot see why. He wants it and at times it seems she is as eager as he is."

"But he could not do it."

I began to feel uneasy. "Why not, Lady Sheffield?"

"Because . . ." She hesitated. "No, I must not say. It would be dangerous. He would never forgive me."

"You mean the Earl of Leicester would not?"

She looked perplexed and tears came into her eyes.

"Is there anything I can do?" I asked soothingly.

"Oh no, no. I must go in. I don't know what I'm saying. I have been unwell. I have my duties, so . . ."

"I thought you looked sad of late," I said, determined to detain her. "I sensed there was something and that I must speak to you. There is a bond between those whose blood is linked, I believe."

She looked a little startled and said: "It may be so."

"Sometimes it is helpful to talk to a sympathetic listener."

"I don't really want to discuss anything. There is nothing to be said. I shouldn't have come. I should be with my son."

"You have a son?"

She nodded.

"I have four children, Penelope, Dorothy, Robert and Walter. I miss them very much."

"So you have a Robert too?"

I was alert. "That is *your* son's name?"

She nodded.

"Well," I went on, "it's a good name. That of our Queen's husband . . . if she ever decided to marry."

"She could not," said Douglass, falling into the trap.

"You seem vehement."

"It is when you talk of their marrying . . ."

"It is what *he* is hoping for. Everybody knows it."

"If she had wanted to marry him she would have done so long ago."

"After the mysterious death of his wife," I whispered. "How could she?"

She shivered. "I often think about Amy Dudley. I have nightmares about her. Sometimes I dream I am in that house and that someone creeps into my room . . ."

"*You* dream that you are his wife . . . and he wants to be rid of you. How strange!"

"No . . ."

"I believe you are afraid of something."

"How men change," she said wistfully. "They are so ardent and then it is someone else who claims their attention."

"And their ardor," I said lightly.

"It can be . . . rather frightening."

"It would be with a man like the Earl . . . after what happened at Cumnor Place. But how do we know *what* happened there. It's a dark secret. Tell me about your little boy. How old is he?"

"He is two years old."

I was silent, calculating. When had the Earl of Sheffield died? Was it not in '71 that I had heard how the Howard sisters were pursuing Robert? It was in that year—or perhaps the next—that Lord Sheffield had died and yet in the year '75 Douglass Sheffield had a two-year-old son called Robert.

I was determined to discover what this meant.

I could scarcely expect her to pour out her secrets on this occasion even though there was a relationship between us. I had learned far more than I could have hoped from the rather foolish woman. But I would make a determined effort to discover the truth.

I tried to be sympathetic and friendly when she said she

was suffering from a headache. I took her back to her apartment and gave her a soothing potion. Then I made her lie down and told her I would let her know if the Queen returned.

Later that day she told me that she had been feeling very unwell when we had met in the gardens and she was afraid she had talked a lot of nonsense. I reassured her and said we had merely had a friendly chat and how pleasant it was to meet a cousin. My potion had done her so much good and she wondered if I would give her the recipe. Of course I would, I told her. I understood perfectly these feelings of depression. After all, I had children of my own and longed to be with them.

"We'll have another chat . . . soon," I said.

I was determined to get to the bottom of the Douglass Sheffield affair.

The next day the Queen was entertained in the afternoon by a farce called *A Country Bridal*. This was, in a manner, poking fun at rustics, and I wondered that the Queen did not feel it was an insult to some of her people. The bridegroom, who was well over thirty, wore his father's worsted jacket of a tawny color, a pair of harvest gloves on his hands, and a pen and inkhorn strapped to his back. He hobbled onto the grass. A great deal of football was played in the country and often players were injured during the game, so the hobble was meant to imply that he had broken a leg at play.

With him were the mummers and Robin Hood with Maid Marian. The Queen's foot tapped as she watched the dancing, and I expected at any time that she would join in.

The bride in her worsted gown came next; she had made her face excessively ugly and wore a wig of hair sticking out in all directions. The spectators roared with laughter at the sight of her, and there were many of them, for the Queen had especially asked that any of those around the neighborhood should be allowed to see the show. So they had come in their hundreds—not so much to see the country wedding as to be in the company of the Queen. She herself—at her best as she always was when the people were present—smiled graciously, reserving her ill humor for her attendants later on. The bridesmaids were in their mid-thirties and, like the bride, quite ugly.

People rolled about in ecstasies of mirth to see the married couple stagger off, and I could not help thinking that this was rather a dangerous show to have put before our unmarried Queen, and the fact that the bride and groom made a great effort to tell us their ages could have been considered as touching Elizabeth. Perhaps that was what Robert had intended. Perhaps he wanted to show her that she was waiting too long. Of course anyone less like the ugly clumsy bride there could not be. She sat there, supreme in her power and her glory—glittering with jewels, her exquisite ruff about her neck, her head held high, looking beautiful, and young too, if one did not look too closely at her face, for her body was as slender as a young girl's and her skin was so delicate and white. She must have seemed like a goddess to these country folk, even apart from her jeweled garments. She was always fastidious and took regular baths, and those of us who attended on her must do the same, for she could not abide evil smells. When she visited country houses the cleaning of them had to begin weeks before her arrival. Ill-smelling rushes made her turn away in disgust, and of course there was the ever-present problem of the privies. I had often seen that somewhat curved nose quiver with distaste on more than one occasion and some sharp remark would be made about the ill preparation for her visit.

Considerable inconvenience was caused, when we traveled, by the Queen's bath, without which she could not manage. Few country houses could provide her with one.

In Windsor Castle there were two rooms set aside for her bath, and the ceilings of these were of glass so that she could see the whiteness of her body while she bathed.

Only among the humble people would she accept uncleanliness, and she never showed by a twitch of her nostrils that she noticed their odors. She certainly had the art of queenship at her fingertips.

On this occasion she received the ugly bride and groom and told them how much they had made her laugh, and they, like the Coventry players, were overcome by her graciousness and I knew would give her their utmost loyalty forever.

I was deeply concerned with my own problems. When Douglass Sheffield had mentioned her son Robert, I had become very suspicious. My first impulse was to waylay Robert and demand the truth about Douglass and her son. Could I do that? After all, he was not exactly responsible to me for his actions—particularly those which had occurred some time ago. True, he had said he would marry me . . . if I were free. That meant little. I was *not* free. I wondered if at some time he had said the same to Douglass, and then by a strange coincidence—or was it coincidence?—she became free soon after he had talked of marrying her.

No. I would not tackle him. Douglass was a fool. I could overcome her scruples with a little delicate handling, and perhaps I should be more likely to get the true story from her than from Robert. Moreover, it would not have been easy to talk with him, for he had to dance continual attendance on the Queen. We could perhaps escape to the room in the tower, but there was a possibility that there my desire might overcome my common sense. I must be firm with myself. If Robert gave me his version of the story how could I be sure it was the truth? I doubted not he would have some plausible story to tell, whereas Douglass would not have the wit to make one up.

During the next days I cultivated Douglass. She was easy prey. There was no doubt that she was worried about her future; and that she was madly in love with Robert there was no doubt either.

In a few days of revels in which she was obliged—as I was—to see Robert in continuous attendance on the Queen, I had brought her to a state when she was eager to confide in someone, and who should that be but kind and sympathetic Cousin Lettice?

At last it came.

"I will tell you exactly what happened, Cousin, only you must swear not to breathe a word to anyone. It would be the end of him and of me. The Queen's wrath can be terrible as you know. That is what he is always telling me."

"You must not tell me if it will make you uneasy to do so," I said artfully, "but if it would ease your mind . . . or you think I might have some advice to offer. . . ."

"You are so sympathetic, Lettice. I am sure you can understand as few people would."

I nodded. She was probably right about that.

"It happened four years ago," she told me. "John and I were happily married, and I had never thought of another man. He was a good husband, a little stern . . . and not very romantic . . . if you know what I mean."

"I do," I assured her.

"The Queen was on one of her progresses through the country, the Earl of Leicester traveling with her, and my husband and I joined her entourage at Belvoir Castle, the Earl of Rutland's place. I can't explain what happened to me. I had been a faithful wife until then, but I had never seen anyone like Robert. . . ."

"The Earl of Leicester," I murmured.

She nodded. "He was the most attractive man I had ever seen. I could not understand myself because he was the most powerful man in the assembly, and was so firmly in the Queen's favor. Everyone was saying that she would marry him soon."

"They have been saying that since she came to the throne."

"I know. But at this time it seemed as though there was a secret understanding between them. It gave him something . . . which I can't describe. If he spoke to any of us, or smiled at us, we were so proud. My sister and I quarreled about him, because he was so charming to us both. Frankly, we were jealous. It was strange because before I had never so much as glanced at another man. I accepted John Sheffield as my husband and he was good to me . . . and then . . . this happened."

"What happened?" I asked.

"We met in secret. Oh, I am so ashamed. I never should have. I can't think what came over me."

"You became his mistress," I said, and I could not disguise the cold note which crept into my voice.

"I know it sounds unforgivable. But you can't imagine what it was like. . . ."

Oh yes, Douglass, indeed I do! I thought. It seems I was as gullible as you.

"So he seduced you," I said.

She nodded. "I held out for a long time," she excused herself, "but you can't know how relentless he can be. He was determined that I should submit, he told me afterwards, and my refusal was a challenge. I protested that I did not believe such things should be done outside marriage and he asked how he could marry me since I had a husband already. Then he talked of how different it would be if I had not had a husband, and he talked so persuasively that I almost believed John was going to die and I should marry Robert. He wrote a note which he impressed on me I should destroy as soon as I had read it. In it he said that he would marry me when my husband died, which he could promise me would not be long, and then we could legally enjoy the ecstasies together which we had already tasted."

"He wrote that!" I cried.

"Yes." She looked at me almost pleadingly. "How could I destroy such a note?" she asked. "I kept it. I used to read it every day and sleep with it under my pillow. I saw Robert several times at Belvoir. We used to meet in an empty chamber there and sometimes in the wood. He said it was very dangerous and if the Queen knew it would be the end of him. But he was doing it all because he was so madly in love with me."

"I understand perfectly," I said bitterly. "And when your husband died. . . ."

"Something dreadful happened before that. I lost Robert's letter. I was in a panic. He had commanded me to destroy it, but I couldn't. Every time I read it, it brought him back so clearly. He had said in that letter that he would marry me when my husband died. . . . You see. . . ."

"Yes, I do see," I assured her.

"My sister-in-law found the letter. She had never liked me, and I was frantic. I summoned all my women one by one. I questioned them, I threatened them, but they declared they had not seen it. Then I asked Eleanor—my husband's sister. She had found it and read it and taken it to my husband. There was such a scene. He made me confess everything. He was absolutely shocked and he hated me. He locked me out of our bedroom and told me to go to the Queen's lapdog, who had already murdered his wife. He said terrible things about Robert and that he was going to ruin him and me, and that the whole country would know what had happened at Belvoir and that Robert Dudley planned to murder him as he had murdered his wife. I sobbed all night and in the morning he had gone away. My sister-in-law told me that he was going to

London to arrange a divorce and that very soon everyone would know me for the harlot I was."

"And what happened then?"

"John died before he could make any of this known."

"How did he die?"

"It was some sort of dysentery."

"And you think that Leicester arranged it . . . ?"

"Oh no, no. He did not. It just happened that way."

"It was very convenient for Leicester, wasn't it? Had your husband suffered before from this . . . dysentery?"

"I never knew that he did."

"Well, then there was no obstacle to your marriage."

She looked forlorn. "It would have been the end of everything for him, he said. He used to tell me how much he wanted to marry me, but you see the Queen was so jealous and she had such a fondness for him."

"Which we understand."

"Oh yes, anyone who knew Robert would understand. You see, there were people who knew. There are always some people who know. There was John's family. They were angry. They blamed Robert for John's death and me too of course."

"They accused him of murdering your husband so that you would be free, and yet when you were free he didn't marry you."

"So you see how rumor lied," she said.

I thought: Well, John Sheffield *was* about to make trouble for him, trouble which would have put him in danger of losing the Queen's regard as a marriage would. I could imagine Elizabeth's fury if she had known of the secret meetings at Belvoir Castle and that Robert had talked of marriage with Douglass. And if Robert had in fact married Douglass he would have been involved in a matter as unsavory as that of the death of his own wife.

I was learning more and more about this man who was

dominating my life—as he did the Queen's and Douglass Sheffield's.

"And your son?" I persisted.

She hesitated and then she said: "He was born in wedlock. Robert is not a bastard."

"You mean that you are Leicester's wife?"

She nodded.

"I can't believe it," I burst out.

" 'Tis true," she answered firmly. "When John died, Robert contracted to marry me in a house in Cannon Row, Westminster, and afterwards he said he could not go through with it because of the Queen's fury. But I was frantic. I was dishonored and this gave me a great deal of anxiety. At length he gave way and we were married."

"When?" I demanded. "And where?"

I was desperately trying to prove that she was lying. I was half convinced that she was, but whether that was because I so badly wanted to believe it, I was not sure.

She answered promptly: "In one of his places—at Esher in Surrey."

"Were there witnesses?"

"Oh yes, Sir Edward Horsey was present and so was Robert's physician, Dr. Julio. Robert gave me a ring with five pointed diamonds and one table diamond. It had been given him by the Earl of Pembroke, who had asked him to give it only to his wife."

"And you have this ring?"

"It is carefully hidden away in safety."

"Why do you not proclaim yourself as his wife?"

"I'm afraid of him."

"I thought you were madly in love with him."

"I am. It is possible to be both in love and afraid."

"And your child?"

"Robert was delighted when he was born. He comes to see him whenever possible. He loves the boy. He always wanted a son. He wrote to me when he was born, thanking God for him and saying that the boy would be a comfort to us in our old age."

"It would seem that your cup should be full of bliss."

She looked straight at me and shook her head. "I am so much afraid."

"Of discovery?"

"No. I would welcome it. I should not care if the Queen dismissed him from Court."

"But *he* would," I reminded her grimly.

"I should be happy to live quietly away from Court."

"Then you would have to live without this ambitious man you call your husband."

"He *is* my husband."

"Then what are you afraid of?"

Again she gave me that steady look. "Amy Robsart was found at the bottom of a staircase with her neck broken," she said simply.

She did not go on. There was no need to.

As for myself, I could not believe her. My senses were crying out against this story. It could not be true. Yet she told it guilelessly, and I did not think she was capable of much invention.

Of one thing I was sure. Douglass Sheffield was a very frightened woman.

I had to speak to him. But how difficult it was! I was determined though to discover the truth even if it meant betraying Douglass. If he had in fact married her, it must have meant that he was really in love with her. The very thought enraged me. Had I not often imagined myself married to him, and consoled myself with the assurance that he would never have married anyone but me, and the only reason he had not done so before I had married Essex was because he was dazzled by the Queen's favor and feared an end of his career at Court if ever he turned to anyone else? Not even for me could he afford to risk the

Queen's displeasure, and I had understood what disaster there would be for him if he did. Yet he had risked it for silly little Douglass Sheffield. That was if there was any truth in this story of a marriage.

So I must know because I should have no peace until I did.

On the day following that one when I had received Douglass's revelations, one of the servants came to tell me that Lady Mary Sidney wished to speak to me in her apartments. Lady Mary, Robert's sister, who was married to Sir Henry Sidney, was always given the utmost consideration by the Queen because of the smallpox she had developed while nursing her and which had disfigured her. She came to Court now and then to please the Queen, though I knew she would rather have remained in retirement at Penshurst. Elizabeth always made sure that very special apartments were allotted to her. Another reason why Elizabeth was fond of her was because she was Robert's sister. Her affection for him overflowed to the rest of the family.

Carefully veiled and keeping her face in shadow, she greeted me. Her apartments were magnificent, as everything was at Kenilworth, but I imagined that these rooms were of the best. On the floor were fine carpets from Turkey such as I had rarely seen before. Robert was one of the first to make use of carpets to a large degree. There were no rushes on the floors at Kenilworth. I glimpsed the four-poster bed in the next room with its hangings of scarlet velvet. I knew that the sheets would be embroidered with the letter L in a coronet. The pewter pans of the night stools were set in cases covered with quilted velvet to match the colors of the room. How Robert loved extravagance—but it was so tasteful. I let myself imagine a home we would share together one day.

Lady Mary had a gentle voice and she received me with affection.

"Come and sit down, Lady Essex," she said. "My brother has asked me to speak to you."

My heart was racing fast. I was all impatience to hear.

"We cannot tarry much longer at Kenilworth," she said. "It will soon be time for the Queen to continue with her progress. As you know, she rarely stays so long in one place. She made an exception in the case of Kenilworth as a mark of her affection for my brother."

It was true, of course. The visit to the castle had been made during one of her progresses through the country which she frequently undertook. It was part of her wisdom that she did so because these progresses kept her in touch with the humblest of her subjects and her gracious and careful treatment of them continued to be the reason for her popularity in every town and hamlet throughout the land. It meant, too, that there was scarcely a large country house in which she had not stayed for a night at least, and those which lay on her route must be prepared to entertain her in a royal manner. If she were displeased with the hospitality she received, she would not hesitate to make this known. It was only with the humble folk that she remained gracious.

"My brother has been planning the Queen's route with her. They have decided that she will be passing close to Chartley."

I was exultant. He had arranged this and persuaded the Queen to stay at Chartley because it was my home. Then my heart sank as I thought of the inconveniences of Chartley, which, compared with Kenilworth, was poor indeed.

I said: "My husband is in Ireland."

"The Queen knows this, but she thinks you can very well play the hostess. You look dismayed. It has been suggested that you leave us and go to Chartley in advance that you may make arrangements for the visit."

"I fear she will find Chartley most uncomfortable . . . after this."

161

"She does not expect to find a Kenilworth wherever she goes. She has said that she believes there is no place like it. Do your best. Make sure that the place is clean. That is of the greatest importance. Fresh rushes everywhere and the servants in fresh clean livery, of course. Then all will be well. Let your musicians practice the tunes she likes best and if you give her plenty of dancing and music, she will enjoy her stay. I trow she loves that better than anything."

There was a knock on the door and a young man entered. I knew him. He was Philip Sidney, Mary's son and therefore Robert's nephew. I had taken an interest in him because I had heard that Robert loved this young man dearly and looked upon him as a son. He was a very noble-looking boy; he must have been about twenty years of age at this time. He had a very special quality—as Robert had—yet how different was that of this young man. There was something truly gentle about him, although this did not denote a lack of strength. It was a rare quality; I had never known anyone like him then, nor have I since. He was very courteous to his mother, and it was clear to me that she doted on him.

"I have been telling Lady Essex about the Queen's proposed stay at Chartley," said Mary. "I think she is a little disturbed."

He turned his radiant smile on me and I said: "I think she will find Chartley such a poor place compared with Kenilworth."

"Her Majesty realizes that most homes must seem so after this, and I think mayhap she prefers it so because it pleases her to know that my uncle has the finest estate in the country. So cast aside your qualms, Lady Essex. I have no doubt the Queen will enjoy a short stay at Chartley."

"My husband, as you know, is in Ireland on the Queen's business."

"You will prove a most charming hostess," he assured me.

"I have been away from Court so long," I explained. "I only rejoined Her Majesty shortly before we began this progress."

"If I can be of any use to you I shall be at your service," said Philip, and Lady Sidney smiled.

"It was for that reason that I asked you to come to me," she said. "When Robert told us that the Queen proposed visiting Chartley, I reminded him that the Earl of Essex was not in the country. He said that he was sure Lady Essex would do the honors with charm and grace, and suggested that if you needed help, Philip should accompany you back to Chartley and do anything you wished him to."

Philip Sidney smiled at me and I knew at once that I could rely on him.

We would leave together for Chartley, and there would set about making the castle fit and ready to receive the Queen.

Robert would be with her. I should have a chance of talking to him at last, on my own ground, and this I was determined to do.

Disclosure

As the thing is publicly talked of in the streets, there can be no harm in writing openly about the great enmity between the Earl of Leicester and the Earl of Essex, in consequence, it is said, of the fact that while Essex was in Ireland, his wife had two children by Leicester.

The Spanish Commissioner,
ANTOINE DE GUARAS

The next day I left for Chartley with a few of my servants, accompanied by Philip and his retinue. I found him a most agreeable companion. The journey was less irksome than I had believed it would be, for I was naturally not pleased to leave Robert behind with those two who were clearly besottedly in love with him—the Queen and Douglass Sheffield. I could laugh to compare them—our imperious, demanding, all-powerful Lady Elizabeth, and poor shrinking Douglass, who was afraid, as they say, of her own shadow. Perhaps in the latter case it was the warning ghost of Amy Robsart. Poor girl! I could understand it, though. I could well picture her nightmares about Amy, for she could be in a similar position to that unfortunate lady—if her story was true.

In due course we arrived at Chartley. This time I was not depressed to see it as I had been on the last occasion when I had returned to it from Court, for very soon Robert would actually be within these walls.

I had managed to send a messenger ahead of us to proclaim our arrival, and the children were waiting at the gates to greet us.

I felt proud, for my little darlings were a handsome quartet. Penelope had grown; she was going to be a beauty, and now she was like a lovely bud on the point of bursting in flower. Her skin was smooth and childlike, and she had beautiful thick fair hair and the dark attractive Boleyn eyes—her coloring inherited from me. She would develop early and the signs of womanhood were already showing themselves. Then Dorothy—less noticeable perhaps, but only when seen side by side with her more flamboyant sister. And my darling of them all—my Robert, eight years old now—quite a man, adored by his younger brother Walter and tolerated by his sisters. I embraced them all with fervor, demanding to know whether they had missed me and, being assured they had, was gratified.

"Is it true, my lady," asked Penelope, "that the Queen is coming here?"

"It's true indeed, and we have to make ready. There is much to be done and you will all have to be on your best behavior."

Little Robert bowed low to show us how grandly he would greet the Queen and commented that if he liked her he would show her his best falcon.

I laughed at that and told him that it would not be a matter of whether he liked her but whether she liked him. If she did, I told him, "she might graciously inspect your falcon."

"I doubt she has ever seen such a falcon," cried Robert hotly.

"I doubt she has *not*," I told him. "I don't think you realize that it is the *Queen* who is coming. Now, children, this is Mr. Philip Sidney, who will stay with us and show us how we must prepare to entertain the Queen."

Philip had a word with each of the children and when I saw him talk to Penelope it occurred to me that he would make a very suitable husband for her. She was too young as yet, for the disparity in their ages was too wide at this stage—he being a young man ready for marriage and she but a child—but when they were a few years older it would not seem so. I would tell Walter that while Leicester remained in such high favor it would be an excellent idea to marry our daughter to his nephew and link ourselves with that family. I was sure my husband would agree with this.

My servants had already started to work on the castle. The privies had been emptied and I noticed with relief were not evident by their odor. The rushes were swept out each day and a large quantity of hay and straw had been laid in so that on the day of the Queen's arrival everything could be renewed. Wormwood seed was mingled with the

167

rushes, for it was well known that fleas could not live with it; and sweet-smelling herbs were used to scent the air.

Beef, mutton, veal and pork were being prepared in the kitchen. Pies, decorated with royal symbols, full of meats seasoned with the best of our herbs, were being baked in the ovens. Our table would be loaded with dishes, otherwise it would be considered a repast unworthy of royalty —although the Queen herself would, I knew from past experience, eat sparingly. I had already ordered that the best of our wines be brought out; Walter was proud of his cellars, where he kept the products from Italy and the Levant. I was not going to let anyone say I did not know how to entertain the Queen.

Through the days of preparation the musicians practiced those songs and tunes which I knew to be Elizabeth's favorites. It was rarely that there had been such excitement in Chartley Castle.

Philip Sidney was an ideal guest. His easy manners and charm had quickly made him a favorite with the children; and the servants were eager to do some service for him.

He read the children some of his poems, which I feared might bore the boys, but even young Walter was content to sit and listen, and I noticed how they all watched him intently while he read.

Over meals, he told them of his life, which, to my children, seemed very adventurous; days at Shrewsbury School and Christ Church, Oxford, and how his father had sent him out to complete his education by three years' travel on the Continent. Penelope rested her elbows on the table and watched him as though she were in a trance; and I thought: Yes, I should like this very attractive young man as her husband. I will certainly talk to Walter when he returns and perhaps we can make a match of it.

Some of Philip's adventures had been lighthearted, others somber. He had been in Paris staying at the house of the English Ambassador on that fateful August night of '72, the Eve of St. Bartholomew; he had heard the tocsins sound in the early hours of the morning and, looking from his window, he had seen the terrible sights of bloodshed and massacre when the Catholics had risen against the Huguenots and slaughtered so many of them. He did not enlarge on this although young Robert urged him to.

"That night," he said, "was a blot on the history of France, and is one which will never be forgotten." Then he turned the occasion into a gentle lesson on the need for tolerance of the opinions of others, to which the children listened with an attention which astonished me.

Then he told them of the festivities at Kenilworth, which had been enacted on the lake at midnight; he spoke of the mummers and the dancers, the plays and the pageants; and it was like seeing it all over again.

He spoke often and affectionately of his uncle, the great Earl of Leicester, of whom the children had of course heard often. Robert's name was known everywhere. I hoped they had not heard the whispers of scandal attached to it or, if they had, they would have the sense not to speak of it before Philip. It was clear that the young man regarded his uncle as some sort of god; and it pleased me that such a clearly virtuous person should have an entirely different picture of Robert from that of the envious scandalmongers who longed to believe the worst.

He told us how clever his uncle was with horses.

"He is the Queen's Horse Master, you know, and has been from the day of her accession."

"When I grow up," announced my son Robert, "*I* am going to be the Queen's Horse Master."

"Then you cannot do better than follow in the footsteps of my uncle Leicester," said Philip Sidney.

He explained to us all the art of manège, which Leicester had mastered, and that there were certain tricks which were practiced by the French to perfection. After

169

the St. Bartholomew massacre, he went on to tell us, Leicester had sounded out Frenchmen who had worked in the stables of murdered noblemen and who he thought might be seeking employment, but they all had too high an opinion of their skills and the payment demanded was excessive.

"In time," Philip said, "my uncle decided to go to Italy for his horsemen. They had not such high ideas of what they were worth as the French. In any case, there is little any man alive can teach my uncle about horses."

"Is the Queen going to marry your uncle?" asked Penelope.

There was a brief silence while Philip looked at me. I said: "Whoever told you she might?"

"Oh, my lady," said Dorothy reproachfully, "*everybody* is talking about them."

"There will always be gossip about people in high places. The best thing is to shut one's ears to it."

"I thought we were to learn all we could and never shut our ears and eyes to anything," insisted Penelope.

"Ears and eyes should be open to the truth," said Philip.

Then he started to talk again about his adventures in foreign places, and as usual he fascinated them.

Later I saw him in the gardens with Penelope, and noted afresh how they seemed to like each other's company in spite of the fact that he was a young man of twenty-one or two and she but a girl of thirteen.

On the day of the Queen's expected arrival, I was on the lookout. As soon as the cavalcade was sighted—and there would be scouts who would give me some warning—I must ride out with a little party to welcome her to Chartley.

I received the warning in good time. I was dressed in a very fine coat of mulberry-colored velvet and a hat of the same shade with a cream-colored feather which curled down at one side. I knew that I looked beautiful, not only because of my elegant well-chosen clothes but because of the faint color in my cheeks and the sparkle in my eyes which the prospect of seeing Robert had put there. I had dressed my fair hair simply with a love lock falling over my shoulder—a fashion from the French which I much fancied because it called attention to the natural beauty of my hair, which was one of my greatest assets. This would contrast with the Queen's frizzed, puffed style which had to be augmented by false hair. I promised myself I must look far younger and much more beautiful in spite of her splendor—and that should not be difficult because I was.

I met them halfway from the castle. He was riding beside her and in the brief time since I had seen him I had miscalculated that overwhelming magnetism which swept away every desire I had except to be alone with him and make love.

His Italian-style doublet in which rubies had been set, his jornet about his shoulders of the same deep red wine color, his hat with the white feather—all these were of matchless elegance; and I scarcely noticed the glittering figure at his side who was smiling benevolently at me.

"Welcome to Chartley, Your Majesty," I said. "I'm afraid you will find it somewhat humble after Kenilworth, but we shall do our best to entertain you in a manner which I fear cannot be worthy of you."

"Come, Cousin," she said, riding beside me. "You look in good spirits, does she not, my Lord Leicester?"

My Lord Leicester's eyes met mine, earnestly pleading, conveying one word: "When?"

He said: "Lady Essex does indeed look in good health."

"The entertainments at Kenilworth were such as to excite us all and revive our youth," I replied.

The Queen frowned. She did not want it to be said that her youth needed reviving. She must be seen as the

171

perpetually youthful. It was about such matters as this that she was pettishly foolish. I could never understand that trait in her character. But I was sure she thought that if she behaved as though she were perpetually young and the most beautiful woman in the world—kept so by some divine alchemy—everyone would believe it.

I could see that I must be careful, but being in Robert's company went to my head like strong wine and I felt reckless.

We rode at the head of the cavalcade—Robert on one side of her, I on the other. In a way it seemed symbolic.

She asked about the countryside and the state of the land, and showed a rare knowledge and interest; she was gracious and declared that the castle was a fine sight with its towers and keep.

Her apartment satisfied her. It should have, for it was the best in the castle and the bedchamber which Walter and I occupied when he was at home. The bed hangings had been shaken and repaired where necessary and the rushes on the floor gave off the fragrance of sweet-smelling herbs.

She seemed well pleased and the food was excellent, the servants all being excited by her presence and eager to please and humor her. She treated them with her usual grace and had them ready to grovel if need be in her service; the musicians played her favorite tunes and I had made sure that the ale was not too strong for her taste.

She danced with Robert, and as the hostess it was fitting for me to take the floor with him—but briefly, of course. The Queen would not have him dance for long with anyone but herself.

The pressure of his fingers on my hand was full of meaning.

"I must see you alone," he said, turning his head and smiling at the Queen as he did so.

I answered, with a blank expression, that I had much to say to him.

"You must have someplace here where we could be alone to talk."

"There is a room in one of the two round towers. We scarcely use that tower now. It is the west one."

"I will be there . . . at midnight."

"Take care, my lord," I mocked. "You will be watched."

"I am accustomed to it."

"So many are interested in you. You are as talked of as the Queen herself . . . and so often your names are linked in the same snippet of gossip."

"Nevertheless I must see you."

He had to return to the Queen, who was tapping her foot impatiently. She wanted to dance, and with him, of course.

I could scarcely wait until midnight. I took off my gown and wrapped myself in a robe of lace and ribbons. I had much to say to him, but I did not think it would be possible to be alone with him without our passion overcoming all other needs. I wanted to be seductive as poor Douglass could rarely have been and Elizabeth never. I knew I had that in my power; it was my strength as the Queen's crown was hers. I had quickly ascertained that Douglass was not of the party and must have gone home to her son—hers and Robert's.

He was waiting for me. As soon as I entered I was in his arms and he was attempting to strip off the gown beneath which I was naked.

But I was determined that first we should speak.

He said: "Lettice, I am mad with my need for you."

"Methinks, my lord, it is not the first time you have been maddened by your need of a woman," I replied. "I have made the acquaintance of your wife."

"My wife! I have no wife now."

173

"I did not mean the one who died in Cumnor Place. That's past history. I mean Douglass Sheffield."

"She has been talking to you!"

"Indeed she has, and telling me an interesting tale. You married her."

"That's a lie."

"Is it so? She did not seem to lie. She has a ring you gave her . . . a ring which was to be given only to your wife. More important than a ring—she has a son—little Robert Dudley. Robert, you are sly. I wonder what Her Majesty will say when she hears."

He was silent for a few seconds, and my heart sank, for I desperately wanted him to tell me that Douglass's story was untrue.

He seemed to come to the conclusion that I knew too much for him to protest, for he said: "I have a son, yes—a son by Douglass Sheffield."

"So all she says was true?"

"I did not marry her. We met at the Rutlands' place and she became my mistress. Good God, Lettice, what am I supposed to do! I am kept dangling. . . ."

"By the Queen, who does not know whether she wants you or not."

"She wants me," he replied. "Have you not noticed?"

"She wants you in attendance—together with Heneage, Hatton and any handsome man. The point is does she want to marry you?"

"As her subject I have to be ready to obey her if she wishes me to."

"She'll never marry you, Robert Dudley. How can she when you are already married to Douglass Sheffield?"

"I swear I am not. I am not such a fool as to do that which would finish me with the Queen."

"If we were discovered here tonight that might finish you with the Queen."

"I am ready to risk that to be with you."

"As you were ready to risk marrying Douglass Sheffield to be with her?"

"I did not marry her, I tell you."

"She says you did. You have a child."

"He would not be the first to be born out of wedlock."

"What of her husband? Is it true that he threatened to divorce her on account of her liaison with you?"

"Nonsense!" he cried.

"I heard that a letter you wrote to her was discovered by him and that he had the evidence he needed to put you in a very uncomfortable position with the Queen. And he died just as he was about to do this."

"Good God, Lettice! Are you suggesting that *I* had him removed!"

"The whole Court found it strange that he should die so suddenly . . . and at such an opportune moment."

"Why should I want him dead?"

"Perhaps because he was going to disclose your relationship with his wife."

"It was not important. It was not as you have been led to believe."

"The Queen might have thought it important."

"She would have seen it for the trivial matter it was. Nay, *I* did not want Sheffield dead. It was better for him to be alive from my point of view."

"I see you have the same sentiments for Lord Sheffield as you have for the Earl of Essex. If you wish to make love to a woman, it is more convenient for her to be someone else's wife than a widow. Otherwise she might begin to think of marriage."

He had placed his hands on my shoulders and was pressing the robe from them. I felt the familiar excitement creeping over me.

"I am not Douglass Sheffield, my lord."

"Nay, you are my bewitching Lettice, and there is none to compare."

175

"I hope those words never reach the Queen's ears."

"The Queen is outside all this. And I would risk her knowing . . . for this."

"Robert," I insisted, "I am not a light of love to be taken up and cast aside."

"I know it well. I love you. I never ceased to think of you. Something is going to happen, but you must not believe evil tales of me."

"What is going to happen?"

"The day will come when you and I will marry. I know it."

"How? You are committed to the Queen. I have a husband."

"Life changes."

"You think the Queen will turn her favor in some other direction?"

"Nay, I shall keep it and have you too."

"You think she would agree to that?"

"In time. As she grows older."

"You are greedy, Robert. You want everything. You are not content with a share of life's good things. You want yours and everyone else's."

"I do not expect more than I know I can get."

"And you believe you can keep the Queen's favor and have me too?"

"Lettice, you want me. Do you think I don't know that?"

"I admit I find you personable enough."

"And what is your life with Walter Devereux? He's a failure. He's not your kind. Admit it."

"He has been a good husband to me."

"A good husband? What has your life been? The most beautiful woman of the Court moldering in the country!"

"I may come to Court providing I do not offend Her Majesty by attracting the attention of her favorite man."

"We must be careful, Lettice. But I tell you this: I am going to marry you."

"How and when?" I laughed at him. "I am no longer the young innocent I was. I shall never forget that when she sent for you, when she hinted that she *knew* you were not indifferent to me, you let me go. You behaved as though I meant nothing to you."

"I was a fool, Lettice."

"Oh, never that! You were a wise man. You knew where the advantage lay."

"She *is* the Queen, my dearest."

"*I* am not your dearest, Robert. She, with her crown, is that."

"You are wrong. She is a woman who will be obeyed, and we are her subjects. Therefore we have to placate her. That is why things are as they are and must be. Oh, Lettice, how can I make you understand? I never forgot you. I longed for you. All those years I was haunted by you . . . and now you have come back . . . lovelier than ever. This time there must be no parting."

He was beginning to win me over—although I only half believed him, but desperately I wanted to.

"What if she decrees otherwise?" I asked.

"We will outwit her."

The thought of our standing together against her intoxicated me. He understood very well my weaknesses as I understood his. There could be no doubt that we were meant for each other.

I laughed again. "I would she could hear you now," I said.

He laughed with me, for he knew he was winning. "We are going to be together. I promise you. I am going to marry you."

"How would that be possible?"

"I tell you I have made up my mind that it shall be."

"You do not always get your will, my lord. Remember

177

you once made up your mind to marry the Queen. . . ."

"The Queen is set against marriage." He sighed. "I have come to believe she will never take a husband. She plays with the idea. She likes to be surrounded by suitors. If she had ever married I should have been the chosen one. But in her heart she has decided never to marry at all."

"So for this reason you feel you may turn to me?"

"Let us face the truth, Lettice. If she would have had me I should have married her. Of course I would. Only a fool would not. I should have been a king in all but name. But that does not prevent my loving the most beautiful, the incomparable Lady Essex. Oh my God, Lettice, I want *you*. I want you to be my wife. I want to see our children . . . a son to carry on my name. Nothing but that will satisfy me. It is what I shall aim for and I know it will come to pass."

I was not sure whether I believed him, but how I wanted to! And when he talked he spoke with such conviction that I was carried along. He was the most plausible of men; he could talk himself out of any difficulty as he must have so many times with the Queen. Few could have lived so dangerously and yet preserved themselves as Robert had.

"One day, my dearest," he assured me, "it shall be as I plan."

I believed him. I refused to look at all the obstacles.

"And now," he said, "enough of talk."

We knew what we were risking, but we could not leave each other. The dawn was just appearing in the sky when we parted and went to our rooms.

The next day I was apprehensive, wondering whether the events of the previous night might be obvious, but none looked at me questioningly. I had reached my room without being detected and Robert evidently did too.

The children were excited by all that was happening in

their home, and, listening to their talk, I learned that they were already fascinated by Robert. In fact it was difficult to know whom they admired most—the Queen or the Earl of Leicester. The Queen was remote of course, but she had insisted that they be presented to her, and she asked them several questions, which I was proud to see they answered with intelligence. Clearly they had found favor with her as most children did.

There was an occasion when Leicester was missing and had been for some time. The Queen had asked for him and he was not to be found. I was with her at the time, and her growing impatience worried me. I wanted no display of the royal temper in my house which would make the visit a failure and all our efforts in vain. Moreover I was growing as suspicious as the Queen. Memories of our encounter were still strongly with me. I could not stop thinking of his protestations and imagining that we were indeed married and that this was our home. I thought then that I should have been quite content to stay in the country with Robert Dudley.

But where was he now? Douglass Sheffield was not here, but was there some other beauty whom he met in the night, to whom he had promised marriage, always supposing the Queen would permit him to marry and the prospective bride's existing husband be conveniently removed?

The Queen said she would look at the gardens. Quite clearly she suspected he was out there with someone and she was determined to catch him. I could guess what her fury would be like—it would match my own.

Then a strange thing happened. As we stepped into the grounds we saw him. There was no beautiful young woman with him. In his arms he carried my youngest, Walter. The other three children were with him. My Lord Leicester looked slightly less immaculate than usual.

There was a smudge of dirt on his cheek and another on one of his puffed sleeves.

I felt the Queen relax beside me and I heard her low chuckle.

She cried out: "So my Lord Leicester has become a stable lad."

Seeing us, Robert hurried forward, put down Walter and bowed first to the Queen, then to me.

"I trust Your Majesty did not need me," he said.

"We wondered what had become of you. You have absented yourself these last two hours."

How magnificent he was! He was facing his royal mistress and that other mistress with whom, shortly before, he had been passionately preoccupied, and none would have guessed the relationship between us.

My Robert ran up to the Queen and said: "That Robert . . ." pointing to the Earl of Leicester, "says he never saw a falcon to match mine. I want to show it to you."

She put out a hand and Robert took those white slender fingers into his grubby ones and started to pull her forward. "Come on. Let's show her, Leicester," he shouted.

I said: "Robert! You forget to whom you are speaking. Her Majesty . . ."

"Let be," interrupted the Queen, her voice soft, her eyes tender. She had always loved children, and they took to her immediately, probably for that reason. "I am about to be engaged on an important mission. Master Robert and I have a falcon to inspect."

"He will only obey me," young Robert told her with pride. Then he stood on tiptoe and she leaned down that he might whisper. "I'll tell him you are the Queen, then perhaps he will obey you. But I couldn't promise."

"We shall see," she replied conspiratorially.

Then there occurred this spectacle of our magnificent Queen's being dragged across the grass by my son and the rest of us following while Robert chatted about his horses and dogs, all of which he was going to show the Queen, Leicester having already seen them.

She was wonderful. I had to grant her that. She seemed but a girl herself among the children. She was a little wistful, and I guessed she was envying me my pleasant family. The girls, being older, were a little restrained. But they behaved rightly of course, for too much familiarity from them would have been frowned on. In any case it was my elder son who had caught the Queen's fancy.

He shouted and laughed and pulled at her gown to take her to another side of the stables.

I heard his high-pitched voice. "Leicester says this is one of the finest horses he ever saw and his opinion is worth something. He's the Queen's Horse Master, you know."

"I did know it," answered the Queen with a smile.

"So he must be good or she wouldn't have him."

"She certainly would not," said Elizabeth.

I stood back watching, Robert beside me.

He whispered: "Ah, Lettice, would to God this were my home, these my children. One day, though, I promise you, we shall have our home, our family. Nothing is going to stop us. I'm going to marry you, Lettice."

"Hush," I said.

My girls were not far off, and they were full of curiosity about everything.

When the Queen had made the required inspection we returned to the house and the children took their leave of her. She gave the girls her hand to kiss and when it was young Robert's turn, he took her hand and scrambled up onto her lap and kissed her. I saw by her soft expression that the gesture had found great favor with her. Robert examined the jewels on her gown and then looked searchingly into her face.

"Goodbye, Your Majesty," he said. "When will you come again?"

"Soon, young Robert," she said. "Never fear, you and I will meet again."

Looking back on my life, I think now that there are moments which are fraught with portent, yet how often do we recognize their significance when they come? I used to tell myself years later when I was suffering the bitterness and heartbreak of my great tragedy that the meeting between my son and the Queen was like a rehearsal for what happened afterwards and that on that occasion I was aware of something fateful in the air. But it was nonsense. It was nothing when it happened. The Queen had behaved as she would have done to any charming child who amused her. But for what happened later I might well have long forgotten that first meeting of theirs.

When there was dancing in the hall and the minstrels were playing her favorite tunes, Elizabeth called me to her and said: "Lettice, you are a fortunate woman. You have a fine family."

"Thank you, Madam," I said.

"Your little boy, Robert, bewitched me. I do not know when I have seen a more beautiful child."

"I know Your Majesty bewitched him," I answered. "I fear he forgot, in the excitement of your company, the fact that you were his Queen."

"I liked well his manner towards me, Lettice," she answered softly. "It is good sometimes to meet the simplicity of a child. There is no subterfuge there, no deceit. . . ."

I felt uneasy. Was she suspecting that other Robert?

There was a wistful longing in her eyes, and I guessed that she was regretting her obstinate attitude and wishing that long ago she had been brave enough to marry Robert Dudley. She might then have had a family like mine. But then, of course, she might have lost her crown.

When the visit was over and the Queen left Chartley I stayed behind for a while. My children could talk of noth-

182

ing else but the visit. I don't know whom they admired most—the Queen or the Earl of Leicester. I think perhaps the latter, because, in spite of the way in which the Queen had cast aside her royalty for them, Leicester seemed more human. Robert said that the Earl had promised him that he would teach him clever tricks with horses—turning, wheeling and jumping and how to be the finest horseman in the world.

"And when do you think you will see the Earl of Leicester again?" I asked. "Don't you know that he is at Court and must be in constant attendance on the Queen?"

"Oh, he said that he would be with me soon. He said that we were going to be great friends."

So he had said that to young Robert! There was no doubt about it—he had won the affection and admiration of my family already.

I should be going to Court again and it occurred to me that now Penelope and Dorothy were growing up they should not be left in the country. I would take them to London with me and we would live in Durham House, which was near enough to Windsor, Hampton, Greenwich or Nonsuch for me to be at Court and be now and then with my children. It would also mean that the girls would mingle in Court circles as they could not in the country.

Durham House was of especial interest to me because Robert had once occupied it. Now of course he lived in the much grander Leicester House, a very fine establishment, parallel with the river and close to Durham House, both houses being on the Strand, within a short distance of each other. I foresaw opportunities of meeting Robert, somewhat removed from the Queen's eagle eye.

The children were excited at the prospect, having had a taste of what closeness to the Court could mean, and no tears were shed when we left the inconveniences of Chartley for the London house.

Robert and I met frequently during the next month or

so. It was easy for him to take a boat from the privy stairs of Leicester House, sometimes dressed in the garments of one of his servants, and to come secretly to Durham House. What this revealed was that our passion for each other did not diminish but increased when we were able to see each other every day. Robert talked continually of marriage—as though Walter did not exist—and was always sighing for the home we would have with my children—whom he already loved—and our own.

We both of us dreamed of what, in my more realistic moments, seemed the impossible, but Robert was so sure that one day it would come to pass that I began to believe it too.

Philip Sidney was a frequent visitor to Durham House. We were all fond of him, and I continued to think of him as a match for Penelope. Sir Francis Walsingham came too. He was one of the Queen's most influential ministers, but although he was exceptionally skilled in the art of diplomacy he was not so proficient in that of flattery, so, while she appreciated his worth, he never became one of her favorite men. He had two daughters—Frances, who was quite a beauty with abundant dark hair and black eyes and older than Penelope by several years, and Mary, who was, in comparison with her sister, insignificant.

They were exciting days at Durham House with periods at Court and my finding it easy to slip from there to my own home and family. London life suited me. It excited me. I felt that I was part of the scene, and the people who came to the house were men and women closely associated with the Queen.

Robert and I had become reckless. We should not have been surprised when the inevitable happened. I became pregnant.

When I told Robert his feelings were mixed.

"Would that we were married," he said. "I want your son, Lettice."

"I know," I answered. "But what of this?"

I foresaw myself being hustled to the country, kept in seclusion, having my child taken out of my hands and brought up in secrecy. Oh no, that was not what I wanted.

Robert said he would find a way.

"But what way?" I demanded. "When Walter returns, which could be at any time, he will know. I can't possibly pretend it's his. What if the Queen hears? There will be trouble then."

"Trouble indeed," agreed Robert. "The Queen must never know."

"She would certainly not be very pleased with you if she knew you had fathered my child. What do you think would happen then?"

"God forbid that she should ever know. Leave this to me. Oh God, how I wish . . ."

"That you had never started this?"

"Nay. I could never wish that. I wish that Essex were out of the way. Then I'd marry you tomorrow, Lettice."

"Easy to say one would do that which one knows one cannot. It might be another story if I were free to marry."

At that he seized me in his arms and cried vehemently: "I'll show you, Lettice. By God, I'll show you."

His face was stern. He was like a man taking a vow.

"One thing I do know," he went on. "You are the woman for me and I am the man for you. Are you aware of that?"

"It had occurred to me that it might be so."

"Don't joke, Lettice. This is deadly serious. I have made up my mind that in spite of Essex on your side and the Queen on mine, you and I *shall* marry. We shall have children. I promise you. I promise you."

"It's a pleasant thought," I said, "but at the moment I have a husband and I am with child by you. If Walter were to return—and by the mess he is making in Ireland that could be at any time—we are going to be in trouble."

"I'll manage something."

"You don't know Walter Devereux. Ineffectual he certainly is and doomed to failure, but he is one who would consider his honor outraged, and he would care that the Queen would hate him for doing what he considered right. He would make such a noise about this that our conduct would be disclosed to the entire court."

"There is only one thing to do," said Robert. "Alas, I hate to do it, but it is necessary. We must get rid of the child."

"No!" I cried in dismay.

"I know how you feel. This is our child. Perhaps it is the son I long for . . . but the time is not yet ripe. There will be others . . . but not yet, not until I have made arrangements."

"So . . ."

"I will consult Dr. Julio."

I protested, but he persuaded me that there was no other way. If the child were born it would be impossible to keep the matter secret. The Queen would see that we never met again.

I was depressed. I was a worldly woman, deeply selfish and immoral, and yet I did love my children and if I could feel deeply about Walter's how much more so could I for Robert's.

But he was right, of course. He kept telling me that before long we were going to be married, and the next time I became pregnant there would be joyous preparations for the arrival of our child in our home.

Dr. Julio was a man of many skills, but abortion was dangerous and when I had taken his prescriptions I became very ill.

It is difficult to keep from servants the nature of one's sickness. A man such as Robert was spied on day and night and in the excess of our passion we had not always been as careful as we should have been. I had no doubt

186

that many of our household knew that the man who came up the privy stairs at night was Robert Dudley. One advantage was that few would dare gossip except in the utmost secrecy, for there was not a man or woman who would not fear the wrath of the Earl of Leicester—and that of the Queen—if any slander were directed against her favorite, even if it happened to be true.

But of course there were whispers.

There was one time when I was so ill that I thought I was about to die. Robert came openly to see me then, and I think that lifted my spirits to such an extent that I started to get well. He really did love me; it was not just that excessive physical excitement that he sought; he really cared for me. He was tender; he knelt by my bed and begged me to get well and he talked all the time of the life he and I would have together. I never saw a man more sure of anything.

And then Walter returned.

His mission in Ireland had been a failure, and the Queen was not very pleased with him. I was still weak and his concern for me disconcerted me while my conscience troubled me a good deal. I told him that I had been ill of a fever and would soon recover. The manner in which he accepted my word made me feel ashamed, particularly as he had aged considerably and seemed tired and listless. I had behaved so badly to him and had had nothing but kindness in return, yet I must keep comparing him with the incomparable Robert Dudley.

I had to face the fact that I was tired of Walter and I was irritated and frustrated because now that he had come home my meetings with Robert would be difficult to arrange, if they could occur at all. In any case after my recent experiences I should have to be more cautious in the future. I mourned the loss of the child and used to dream it was a little boy who looked like Robert. In the dream he would look at me sadly as though accusing me of robbing him of life.

I knew Robert would say: "We'll have more. Only let us marry and we shall have both sons and daughters to delight our old age." But that was small comfort at this time.

Walter declared his intention of never traveling again.

"I've had enough of it," he told me. "Nothing will ever come out of Ireland. From henceforth I shall stay at home. I shall live an untroubled life. We shall go back to Chartley."

Inwardly I decided we should not. I would not be buried in the country away from the delights of the town, the intrigues of the Court and the magic of Robert Dudley. Separation from him only enhanced my desire, and I knew that when we did meet I would be as reckless as ever—in spite of my conscience—living for the moment and meeting the consequences when the time came.

I grew stronger and felt capable of leading Walter where I wanted him to go.

"Chartley is inviting," I lied, "but have you noticed that our daughters are growing up?"

"Indeed I have. How old is Penelope?"

"You must remember the age of your daughter—and your firstborn at that. Penelope is fourteen."

"Over young for marriage."

"But not too young for us to find a suitable *parti* for her. I should like to see her well contracted."

Walter acceded that I was right.

"I have a particular fancy for Philip Sidney," I said. "He was with us when I entertained the Queen at Chartley and he and Penelope developed a liking for each other. It's a good thing when a girl knows her future husband before she is hustled into marriage with him."

Once more Walter agreed and said that Philip Sidney would be an excellent choice.

"As Leicester's nephew he would find some favor with the Queen," he commented. "She dotes on Dudley as much as she ever did, I understand."

"He is still in high favor."

"There is a consideration, though. If the Queen married some foreign prince, I doubt Leicester would be tolerated at Court, and then his relations would not be so comfortably placed."

"Do you think she will ever marry?"

"Her ministers are trying to persuade her. The lack of an heir to the throne becomes a more and more pressing problem. If she died there would be dissension, and that's never good. She should give the country an heir."

"She's a little old for childbearing, though none is allowed to say so within earshot of Her Majesty."

"She might just manage it."

I laughed aloud, suddenly wildly pleased because I was eight years younger than she.

"What's amusing?" asked Walter.

"You are. You'd be in the Tower for treason if she could hear you."

Oh, what a bore he was and how tired of him I was!

There were only snatched conversations with Robert.

"This is unendurable," he told me.

"I cannot escape from Walter, nor can you come to Durham House."

"I'll manage it somehow."

"My dear Robert, you can scarcely share our bed. Even Walter would then be aware that something unusual was afoot."

Frustrated as I was, I was exultant to see how Robert fretted against the situation.

"Well, Robert," I said, "you are a magician. I await the magic."

Something had to be done soon after that because I suppose what was again inevitable happened. Someone—

189

I never found out who—had whispered to Walter that Robert Dudley had been taking an undue interest in his wife.

Walter refused to believe it—not of Robert but of me. What a simpleton he was! I could have managed him, but Robert had some pernicious enemies whose motive was not so much to make trouble for the Essex family as to wrest from Robert his favor with the Queen.

Then there was that night when Walter came into our bedchamber, his face very serious. "I have heard the most wicked accusations," he said.

My heart started to beat fast, so guilty was I, but I managed to ask calmly: "What about?"

"About you and Leicester."

My eyes were wide open and I hoped looked innocent. "What can you mean, Walter?"

"I heard that you are his mistress."

"Whoever could have said such a thing?"

"I was only told after my promise to keep the informant's identity a secret."

"And you believe this secret informer?"

"I don't believe it of you, Lettice, but Dudley's reputation is far from savory."

"Even so you could hardly believe it of him if you didn't believe it of me." You fool! I thought to myself, and I decided that attack was the best form of defense. "And I must say that I take an ill view of your tattling about your wife to people in dark corners."

"I didn't really believe it of you, Lettice. It must be someone else he has been seen with."

"You suspected me, of course," I accused, whipping myself to anger. It was most effective. I had my poor Walter almost begging for pardon.

"Not truly so, but I did want you to tell me yourself how false it all was. I shall call out the man who dared mention it."

"Walter," I said, "you know this to be false. I know it to be false. If you make a great noise about it, it will come to the Queen's ears and she would blame you. You know how she will hear no ill of Robert Dudley."

He was silent, but I could see that my remarks had struck home.

"I'm sorry for any woman who becomes involved with him," he said.

"So should I be," I retorted meaningfully.

But I was worried. I had to see Robert to tell him what had happened. It was difficult for me. I had to seek an opportunity, and as Robert was always attempting to do the same, we did manage at last to have a few words together.

"This is driving me mad," said Robert.

I replied: "Here is something to drive you madder." And I told him.

"Someone must have talked," said Robert. "They will be saying now that your recent illness was due to ridding yourself of a child you had by me."

"Who could have done this?"

"My dear Lettice, we are watched and spied on by those we trust the most."

"If this gets to Walter's ear . . ." I began.

Robert put in wryly: "If it got to the Queen's we should then have good cause to worry."

"What can we do?"

"Leave it to me. You and I are going to marry. Rest assured of that. But there will be work to be done first."

I understood how hard he was working to bring this about when a summons came from the Queen for Walter to attend on her without delay. When he returned to Durham House I was eagerly awaiting him.

"Well, what happened?" I asked.

"It's madness," he retorted. "She does not understand. She has ordered me back to Ireland."

I tried not to show my relief. This was undoubtedly Robert's work.

"She is offering me the post of Earl Marshal of Ireland."

"That is a great honor, Walter."

"She expects me to think so. I tried to explain the position to her."

"And what did she say?"

"She waved me aside." He paused and looked at me searchingly. "Leicester was with her. He kept saying how important Ireland was, and how I was the man to become Earl Marshal. I think he has done a great deal to persuade the Queen."

I was silent, pretending to be perplexed.

"Oh yes. Leicester said what a great opportunity it was to retrieve my failure. They wouldn't listen to me when I tried to explain that they did not understand the Irish."

"And . . . the outcome?"

"The Queen made it clear that she expects me to go. I don't think you will like it out there, Lettice."

I had to go carefully now so I said: "Oh well, Walter, we must make the best of it."

That satisfied him. He was still doubtful about Leicester, and although Walter's code made him accept the word of his wife, I could see that the suspicions were still there.

I pretended to make some preparations to go to Ireland, although, of course, I had no intention of going at all.

The following day, I said to him: "Walter, I'm very worried about Penelope."

"Why so?" he asked surprised.

"I know she is young, but she is mature for her age. I fancy that she is not very discreet in her friendships with the opposite sex. Dorothy worries me too and I found Walter in tears and young Robert looking very glum trying to comfort him. Robert said he was going to ask the Queen not to let me go to Ireland. I shall be so worried about them if I go away."

"They have their governesses and nurses."

"They need more than that. Particularly Penelope. It's her age . . . and the boys are too young to be left. I have spoken to William Cecil. He will take Robert into his household before he goes to Cambridge, but he should not leave his home just yet. We cannot both abandon the children, Walter."

The children saved me. Walter was very depressed but he was fond of his family and he did not want them to suffer. I spent a good deal of time with him, listening to his account of the Irish question, and I made plans for the future when he would come home—which would not be long, I told him. He would then have good standing at Court as the Earl Marshal of Ireland, and perhaps if he went back later we could all go with him.

Finally he departed. He embraced me warmly before he left and begged my pardon for the slander which had been uttered against me. It would be as well, he told me, to take the children back to Chartley and as soon as he returned we would make our plans for the future. We would get the girls married and the boys educated.

I embraced him with real affection, for he looked so melancholy, and I felt, mingling with relief that he was going, pity for him and shame because of what I was doing.

I told him that we must endure this separation for the sake of the children, and although this may seem like the greatest hypocrisy, at that moment there were genuine tears in my eyes and I was glad that my obvious emotion seemed to give him some comfort.

In July he sailed for Ireland and I resumed my meetings with Robert Dudley. Robert told me that he had indeed advised the Queen that Walter's presence was needed in Ireland.

"You get what you want," I commented. "I see that."

"I get what I deserve," he retorted.

I pretended to be alarmed. "Then I fear for you, my Lord Leicester."

"Never fear, my Lady Leicester-to-be. If one would succeed, one must learn how to take what one wants boldly. It's the best way."

"And now?" I asked. "What next?"

"For that we must wait and see."

I waited only two months.

One of the servants from Chartley rode up to Durham House. I could see that the man was greatly disturbed.

"My lady," he said, when he was brought to me, "a terrible thing has happened. A black calf has been born and I thought you should know."

"You did well to come here," I answered. "But this is but a legend and we are all in good health."

"My lady, the country folk say that this has never failed. It has always meant death and disaster to the lord of the castle. My lord is in Ireland . . . a lawless place."

"It is true that he is there on the Queen's business," I said.

"He must be warned, my lady. He must come back."

"I fear the Queen would not be willing to stake her policy on the birth of a black calf at Chartley."

"But if your ladyship went to her . . . explained . . ."

I replied that all I could do was to write to the Earl of Essex and tell him what had happened. "You shall be rewarded for bringing the news to me," I added.

When he had gone I was thoughtful. Could it really be true? How strange it was that the calf should be born as it must have been on that occasion when the death of the lord of the castle had originally given rise to the legend.

Before I could dispatch a letter to my husband I received the news that Walter had died of dysentery in Dublin Castle.

The Countess of Leicester

A gentleman of the Queen's bedchamber reminded her that the Earl of Leicester was still free to marry at which she angrily retorted that "It would be unlike herself and unmindful of her royal majesty to prefer her servant, whom she herself had raised, before the greatest Princes in Christendom."

WILLIAM CAMDEN

So I was a widow. I cannot pretend to have been smitten by sorrow. I had never been in love with Walter, and since I had become Robert's mistress I had deeply regretted my marriage, but I had had some affection for him, I had borne his children, and I could not help feeling a certain melancholy at his death. I did not brood on this, for thoughts of what my freedom would mean filled me with an excitement which overwhelmed all other feelings.

I could hardly wait to see Robert. When he did come, he came in secret as before.

"We shall have to tread warily," he warned, and a cold fear gripped me. Is he trying to evade marriage now? I asked myself. And there was one question which kept coming into my mind: How was it Walter had died so fortuitously? Dysentery, it was said. Many had died of it and in such cases there were always suspicions. I lay awake asking myself if it really was an irony of fate or whether Robert had played some part in it. What would the outcome be? I was uneasy, but as eager for Robert as ever. No matter what he did, nothing could change that.

It was I who broke the news of their father's death to the children. I summoned them all to my apartments and, drawing young Rob to me, I said: "My son, you are the Earl of Essex now."

He looked at me with wide, bewildered eyes, and my love for him overwhelmed me. I held him close and said: "Robert, my dearest, your father is dead, and you are his heir because you are his eldest son."

Robert began to sob and I saw tears in Penelope's eyes. Dorothy was crying too and little Walter, seeing the distress of his brother and sisters, broke into loud lamentation.

I thought, in some amazement: So they truly loved him.

But why should they not? When had he ever been anything to them but a loving father?

"This will make a difference to us," I said.

"Shall we go back to Chartley?" asked Penelope.

"We cannot yet make any plans," I told her. "We must wait and see."

Robert looked at me apprehensively. "If I am the Earl now, what shall I have to do?"

"Nothing yet. For a time it will not be much different from what it would have been if your father were here. You have his title but you still have your education to complete. Don't be afraid, my darling. Everything will be all right."

"Everything will be all right!" The phrase kept ringing in my ears, mocking me. I might have known it would not be so.

The Queen sent for me. Always sympathetic to the grief of others, she received me warmly.

"My dear cousin," she said, embracing me, "this is a sad day for you. You have lost a good husband."

I kept my eyes lowered.

"And you have the welfare of your children to occupy you. So your young Robert is now the Earl of Essex. A charming little fellow. I hope he is not too miserable at this loss."

"He is heartbroken, Madam."

"Poor child! And Penelope and Dorothy and the young one?"

"They feel the loss of their father deeply."

"Doubtless you would wish to leave Court for a while."

"I am so uncertain, Madam. Sometimes I think I want the peace of the country in which to mourn and at others it seems unbearable. Everywhere I look there I am reminded of him."

She nodded sympathetically.

"Then it shall be left to you to do what suits you best."

It was she who sent Lord Burleigh to me.

There was something reassuring about William Cecil, now Lord Burleigh. He was a good man, by which I mean that he more often acted for the sake of what he considered right than out of hope of advancing himself—something which could be said of very few statesmen. Of medium height and somewhat thin, he gave the impression of being smaller than he was; he had a brown beard and rather large nose, but it was his eyes with their hint of kindliness which were reassuring.

"This is a very sad time for you, Lady Essex," he said, "and Her Majesty is much concerned for your welfare and that of your children. The Earl was very young to die and leave children who are still in need of his care. I know it was his wish and yours that his son Robert should come into my household, and, I shall be happy to receive him whenever you think it fitting to send him."

"Thank you. He will need a little time to recover from his father's death. Next May he is to go to Cambridge."

Lord Burleigh nodded approvingly. "I hear he is a clever boy."

"He is well versed in Latin and French and enjoys learning."

"Then he should do well."

So it was arranged, and I felt that this was best because I knew that even aside from his brilliance Lord Burleigh was a kind and indulgent father to his own children and —that rarity—a good and faithful husband.

I suppose it was inevitable that rumors would begin to circulate. Whoever had told Walter of my relationship with Robert would be rekindling that gossip now that my husband was dead.

Robert came to me in a state of some anxiety and insisted that we talk. He told me then that it was being suggested that Walter had been murdered.

"By whom?" I asked sharply.

"Need you ask?" replied Robert. "Whenever anyone dies unexpectedly and I am on terms of acquaintance with that person, I am suspected."

"So people are talking about us!" I whispered.

He nodded. "There are spies everywhere. It seems I can make no move without its being recorded. If this gets to the Queen's ears . . ."

"But if we marry she would have to know," I pointed out.

"I shall break it to her gently, but I would not like her to hear it through anyone but myself."

"Perhaps," I said sharply, "you would rather we said goodbye."

He turned on me almost angrily. "Don't dare say such a thing! I *am* going to marry you. Nothing else will satisfy me. But just now we have to be careful. God knows what Elizabeth would do if she knew I were contemplating this. Lettice, they are going to open Essex's body to look for poison."

I dared not look at him. I did not want to know the truth if it implicated Robert. I kept thinking of Amy Robsart at the bottom of that staircase in Cumnor Place and Douglass Sheffield's husband, who died just as he was about to divorce his wife. And now . . . Walter.

"Oh God," I said, and I was praying, "I trust nothing will be found in him."

"Nay," said Robert comfortingly, "nothing will be found. He died a natural death . . . of dysentery. Essex was never a strong man and Ireland did not suit him. However, I think it would be a good plan if you went back to Chartley for a while, Lettice. It might help to stop the gossip."

I could see that he was right and, after having received the Queen's permission, I left Court.

It was a great relief when I received the news that nothing had been found in Walter's body to suggest that he had been hastened to his death.

He was brought to England, and the funeral took place

at the end of November at Carmarthen. I would not allow young Robert to make the long journey, for he was suffering from a cold at the time and he was in such low spirits that I feared for his health.

Lord Burleigh wrote to him assuring him that he was now his guardian and would welcome the time when he could receive him into his household, where he would be prepared for Cambridge.

I said that he should go after the Christmas holidays and that seemed agreeable to him.

I was in a state of expectancy. Obviously I could not marry Robert until a certain time had elapsed, for to hurry into marriage would set the tongues wagging again, which was the last thing we wanted. It would be necessary for us to wait for a year, I supposed. But we could accept that, for we should see each other in the meantime, and as soon as my son had left for Lord Burleigh's establishment I intended to take up my position at Court.

How long and dreary those winter days seemed! All the time I was wondering about Robert and what was happening at Court; and immediately after the Christmas holidays were over, I and my family—with the exception of young Robert—set out for Durham House.

A few days after my arrival I received a call from a lady I should have preferred not to see. This was Douglass Sheffield, and the story she had to tell gave me great misgivings.

She had asked that she might speak to me in secret, as she had something of moment to tell me.

There was no doubt that she was a very attractive woman and this fact made her story alarmingly plausible.

"I felt I must speak to you, Lady Essex," she said, "because I think you are in urgent need of advice. So I have come to tell you what happened to me in the hope that, when you have heard, you will realize the need to be cautious in your dealings with a certain gentleman of the Court."

"No one can overhear us, Lady Sheffield," I said coldly, "so there is no need for you to speak anything but openly. To whom do you refer?"

"To Robert Dudley."

"Why should you wish to warn me against him?"

"Because I have heard rumors."

"What rumors?" I tried—I fear not very successfully—to look surprised.

"That you and he are intimate friends. It is impossible for such a man to have friendships without its being talked of . . . in view of his relationship with the Queen."

"Yes, yes," I said somewhat impatiently, "but why should I be warned?"

"Any lady should be warned whose name is coupled with his, and I should feel it my duty to tell her of what happened to me."

"You have already spoken of this to me."

"Yes, but I have not told you everything. The Earl of Leicester and I were contracted in '71 in a house in Cannon Row in Westminster, but he was reluctant to go through with the marriage for fear of the Queen's displeasure. When I became pregnant I urged him to marry me and he did at Esher at the end of '73."

"You have no witnesses of this," I said defiantly, seeing, if it were true, all my dreams of marriage evaporating.

"As I told you once before, Sir Edward Horsey gave me away and Dr. Julio, the Earl's physician, was present. Later my boy was born. He is Robert Dudley after his father. I can tell you that the Earl is proud of his son. His brother, the Earl of Warwick, is the boy's godfather and takes a great interest in him."

"If this is really true, why is his existence kept a secret?"

"You know full well the position with the Queen. She

hates any man of whom she is fond to marry—most of all Robert Dudley, the favorite of them all. It is solely on account of the Queen that my son's existence is kept a secret."

"But if he is so proud of his son, I should have thought . . ."

"Lady Essex, you understand full well. I have not come here to argue with you but to warn you, for it would seem to me that the Earl of Leicester has transferred his affection from me to you and now has come the time for us both to beware."

"Pray come to the point, Lady Sheffield."

"The Earl of Leicester has spoken to you of marriage, but how can he marry you when he is married to me? I have come to tell you that he has offered me seven hundred pounds a year if I will disavow the marriage, and if I do not accept this offer he will give me nothing and withdraw himself from me completely."

"And what was your answer?"

"I emphatically refused. We were married and my son is legitimate."

Even as she spoke her voice quivered and the tears came into her eyes. I was sure that Robert would always get the better of such a woman.

But what if her story were true? And I could not believe she had made it up, for she did not seem to have the wit for that.

I said to her: "Thank you for coming along to warn me, Lady Sheffield, but I must tell you that you should have no fear for me. I know the Earl of Leicester, it is true, but I am recently bereaved of a good husband, and I can think of nothing at this time but my loss and my family."

She bowed her head in sympathy. "Then you must forgive me. Forget what I have said. I had heard rumors and I felt it was my duty to tell you the truth."

"I appreciate your kindness, Lady Sheffield," I told her, and conducted her to the door.

When she had gone I could drop my display of indifference. I had to admit that the story seemed plausible. I kept reminding myself that Robert desperately wanted a son to bear his name. He was no longer young, for he must be forty-five years of age and if he was to get a family he must do so now. Yet he already had this son and disowned the boy's mother. This was for my sake. I must remember that.

I could not wait to see Robert and as soon as I had an opportunity I tackled him with what I had discovered.

"So she came here," he cried. "The fool!"

"Robert, how much truth is there in this?"

"There was no marriage," he said.

"But you were contracted to her. She says there were witnesses."

"I did promise her that we might marry," he admitted, "but the marriage never took place. The child was born and he is my child. He is in the guardianship of my brother Warwick and in due course he will go to Oxford."

"She said you offered her seven hundred pounds a year to deny the marriage."

"I offered her money to stop talking."

"If she is your wife, how can we be married?"

"I tell you she is not my wife."

"Only the mother of your son."

"Young Robert is my baseborn son. What am I expected to do? Live like a monk?"

"What indeed . . . kept dancing as you are by Her Majesty. 'I will . . .' 'I won't . . .' Poor Robert! How many years has it gone on?"

"A good many, but this is going to be the end of it. You and I are going to marry in spite of everything."

"In spite of the Queen and your wife Douglass. Poor Robert, you are indeed a shackled man!"

"Don't taunt me, Lettice. I shall defy the Queen. As for Douglass Sheffield, she deceives herself. I tell you, there is no obstacle from that quarter."

"So there is no just cause why you and I should not marry?"

"None whatever."

"Then for what do we wait?"

"Until this talk about Walter's death has died down."

I allowed myself to be persuaded, because I wanted to.

The Queen's manner towards me made me a little uneasy, and I wondered whether she had heard the rumors about Robert and me. I found her eyes on me at odd moments, rather speculatively. This could have meant that she was wondering how I was bearing up in my widowhood, for she did take a great interest in the emotional problems of those about her—particularly members of her own family.

"Robin is rather sad at this time," she told me. "He is a man much devoted to his family and I like that. It shows good feeling. As you know I have a fondness for the Sidneys, and I shall never forget dear Mary and the way in which she nursed me, and the terrible affliction which came to her because of it."

"Your Majesty has always shown her the utmost kindness."

"I owe it to her, Lettice. And now, poor woman, she has lost her eldest girl. Ambrosia died this February. Mary was stricken with grief, poor woman. She has her dear boy, Philip, though, and a comfort he must be. I rarely saw a more noble-looking creature than Philip Sidney. I shall tell them to send their youngest daughter— Mary, named after her mother—to me and I shall give her a place at Court and find a husband for her."

"She is but fourteen, Madam, I believe."

"I know, but in a year or two we might marry her.

There's Henry Herbert, now Earl of Pembroke. I have been thinking of a wife for him. I daresay he would please the Sidneys—and the young lady's uncle, the Earl of Leicester."

"I daresay," I said.

Very shortly after that Mary Sidney came to Court. She was a beautiful girl with amber-colored hair and an oval face. Everyone commented on her likeness to her brother, Philip, who was recognized to be one of the best-looking men at Court. It was true he lacked the lusty virility of men like Robert. His was a different kind of attractiveness—an almost ethereal beauty. Young Mary Sidney had this too and I did not think it would be difficult to find a husband for her.

The Queen made much of her and I was sure this brought about some consolation to the family. Towards me, Elizabeth kept up that special attention, but I continued to remain unsure of what lay behind it. Often she would mention the Earl of Leicester to me—sometimes with a teasing affection as though she were aware of certain frailties in his nature but loved him nonetheless because of them.

I was very close to her at this time, being in her bedchamber, and she would often talk to me about the garments she would wear. She liked me to take them out and hold them up against myself, so that she could get an idea of what they looked like.

"You are a handsome creature, Lettice," she told me. "You resemble the Boleyns."

She was thoughtful, and I guessed she was thinking of her mother.

"You will doubtless marry again in due course," she said once, "but it is early yet. But you'll soon grow out of your widowhood, I'll trow." I did not answer and she went on: "Every fashion is white on black now—or black on white. Do you think it is becoming, Lettice?"

"For some, Madam. Not for others."

"And on me?"

"Your Majesty is fortunate that you only have to put a garment on to transform it."

Too far? No, her courtiers had conditioned her to accept the grossest flattery.

"I want to show you the handkerchiefs my laundress worked for me. Get them out. There! Black Spanish work edged with bone lace of Venice gold. What do you think of that? And there are some tooth cloths—coarse Holland, which is the best for the purpose, decorated with black silk and edged with silver and black silk."

"Very good, Madam." I smiled at her, revealing my perfect teeth, of which I was very proud. She frowned slightly; her own were showing signs of decay.

"Mistress Twist is a good soul," she commented. "There is a great deal of work in those items. I like well when my servants labor for me with their own hands. Look at these sleeves which my silk-woman, Mrs. Montague, made for me and presented to me with great pride, I might tell you. See those exquisite buds and roses."

"Black on white again, Madam."

" 'Tis becoming, as you say, to some of us. Have you seen the smock Philip Sidney gave me this New Year?"

I took it out, as she bade me. It was of cambric worked with black silk and with it were a set of ruffs edged with gold and silver thread.

"Exquisite," I murmured.

"I have had some wonderful New Year's gifts," she said, "and I will show you my favorite of them all."

She was wearing it. It was a gold cross set with five flawless emeralds and beautiful pearls.

"That is superb, Madam."

She put her lips to it. "I admit to a special fondness for it. It was given to me by the one whose affection is more important to me than that of any other."

I nodded, knowing full well to whom she referred.

She smiled almost roguishly. "I fancy he is somewhat preoccupied at this time."

"You mean, Madam?"

"Robin . . . Leicester."

"Oh, is that so?"

"He has pretensions. He has always fancied himself as royal, you know. He inherited his father's ambitions from him. Well, I would not have him otherwise. I like a man to have a good conceit of himself. You know well my fondness for him, Lettice."

"It has seemed clear, Madam."

"Well, can you understand it?"

The tawny eyes were alert. What was this leading to? Warnings flashed in my mind. Have a care. You are on very dangerous ground.

"The Earl of Leicester is a handsome man," I said, "and I know, as all do, that he and Your Majesty have been friends since your childhood."

"Yes, it seems to me sometimes that he has always been part of my life. If I had married he would have been the one I should have chosen. Once I offered him to the Queen of Scots, you know. She, poor fool, refused him. But does it not show how I have his welfare at heart? If he had gone to her a light would have gone out of my Court."

"Your Majesty has many bright beacons to make up for the loss."

She gave me a sharp nip suddenly. "Nothing could compensate me for Robin Dudley and you know it."

I bowed my head in silence.

"So I have his good at heart," she went on, "and I am going to help him to make a good marriage."

I felt she must be aware of the violent beating of my heart. To what was she leading? I knew her devious ways, when she would say one thing which was the complete opposite of what she meant. This was part of her great-

209

ness; it had made her the wily diplomat she was; it had kept her suitors at bay for years; it had kept England at peace. But what did she mean now?

"Well?" she said sharply. "Well?"

"Your Majesty is good to all your subjects and mindful of their welfare," I said perfunctorily.

" 'Tis true, and Robert always had a fancy for a royal bride. The Princess Cecilia has lost her husband, the Margrave of Baden, and Robert sees no reason—providing I approve—why he should not ask her hand in marriage."

"And what does Your Majesty say to this suggestion?" I heard myself say.

"I have told you that I want the best for my dear friend. I have said he may make his proposal with my approval. We must wish the pair of them happiness, I suppose."

"Yes, Madam," I said quietly.

I could scarcely wait to get away. It must be true. She would not have said it otherwise. But why was she telling me, and was there really a hint of malicious triumph in her voice or had I imagined it?

What had she heard? What did she know? Was this mere gossip or was it her way of telling me that Robert was not for me?

I was angry and fearful. I must see Robert without delay and demand an explanation. To my intense dismay I learned that he had left Court. He had gone to Buxton, on the advice of his doctors, to take the baths. I knew that whenever he was in a difficult situation he feigned illness. He had done this several times when he was in danger with the Queen. It always had the effect of softening her, for she could never bear to think of his being seriously ill. I felt angry. I was almost certain that his departure was due to the fact that he could not face *me*.

So it was true, then, that he was hoping to marry the Princess Cecilia!

I knew that she had visited England at one time. She was the sister of King Eric of Sweden, who had been one of Elizabeth's suitors; and there had been a rumor at the time that if Robert Dudley would persuade the Queen to take Eric, his reward would be the hand of Eric's sister, Cecilia. It could not have been much of a dilemma for Robert, who at that time had been certain that the Queen's husband would be himself and it was hardly likely that he would consider Cecilia fair exchange for his royal mistress. Elizabeth had prevaricated with Eric as with all her suitors and in due course Cecilia had married the Margrave of Baden. They had visited England together, a country Cecilia declared she yearned to see, but it was suspected that her motive in bringing her bridegroom to pay his respects to the Queen was in fact to urge her to take Eric for her husband.

She had arrived in winter, heavily pregnant. With her extraordinarily long fair hair, which she wore loose, she was so appealing that she won immediate popularity. Her son was christened in the Chapel Royal at Whitehall and the Queen herself stood as godmother.

Unfortunately the happy parents stayed too long and, being under the impression that they were guests of the country, ran up debts which they could not pay. This meant that the Margrave was forced to make an attempt to evade his creditors, was caught and put in jail. A very odd experience for visiting royalty and when the news of what had happened was brought to the Queen, she immediately paid his debts.

But they no longer had a happy impression of England, particularly as, when Cecilia was about to sail for her home, more creditors boarded the ship and took her belongings away with them. It was an unfortunate episode and the Margrave and his wife must have wished they had never set foot in England.

But now that the Margrave was dead and Cecilia a widow, Robert wished to marry her.

I asked myself again and again why I loved him. I kept going over the story of Amy Robsart. Uneasily I thought again and again of the death of Lord Sheffield and my own Walter, and I asked myself: Could this really be coincidence? And if not . . . there was only one terrible conclusion to be drawn.

But my passion for Robert Dudley was not unlike the Queen's. Nothing that could be proved against him could alter it.

So now I was in a fury of impatience to see him. I was haunted by the fear that we should never marry, and that he was ready to throw me aside for a royal princess just as he had been ready to throw Douglass aside for me.

The Queen was in high good humor.

"Our gentleman is not acceptable, it seems," she told me. "Poor Robin and foolish Cecilia! I'd swear if she came here and he wooed her, she'd submit."

I was unable to stop myself: "Not all those who are wooed—even by Robert Dudley—submit."

She was not displeased.

" 'Tis true," she said. "But he is a man it is not easy to resist."

"I can believe it, Madam," I replied.

"Her brother, the King of Sweden, says he cannot believe she would wish to come to England after what happened on her last visit. So Robin is refused."

My relief was overwhelming. I felt as though I had been reborn. He would return now and I would hear from his own lips what had happened about the Swedish Princess.

Of course he had his answer.

"My God, Lettice, did you think I would marry anyone but you?"

"It would have been inconvenient for you if the Princess had said yes."

"Depend upon it I should have found a way out."

"It would not have been enough to go to Buxton to take the waters."

"Oh, Lettice, you know me well."

"Sometimes I fear too well, my lord."

"Oh come, come. The Queen decides I must offer Cecilia marriage. She does this kind of thing now and then to tease me, although both she and I know that nothing will come of it. What can I do but play along? Now, Lettice, you and I are going to marry. I am determined on that."

"I know the Princess has refused you but there are obstacles—the Queen and Douglass."

"Douglass is of no importance. She willingly became my mistress knowing full well that there would be no marrying. She has none but herself to blame."

"Herself and your devastating charms!"

"Am I to be taken to task for them?"

"For making promises that you have no intention of keeping you are."

"I assure you the position was always clear to Douglass."

"As you would doubtless say it was with me. But *we* have talked of marriage, my lord."

"Aye, and marriage there shall be . . . and that before long."

"There is still the Queen."

"Ay yes, we must indeed take care where she is concerned."

"She might even decide to marry you herself to prevent my doing so."

"She will never marry. She has a fear of that state. Do you think I have known her all this time without realizing that? Have patience, Lettice. Believe in me. You and I *shall* marry, but we must go carefully. The Queen must not know of it until it is a fact and it must not be a fact until some little time has elapsed since your husband's death. We know our minds . . . but we must be cautious."

Then he said we wasted time in talk, for we both knew each other's mind and needs; so we made love as I had begun to think only we could; and as usual I forgot my misgivings when I was with him.

Robert had acquired a house about six miles out of London and he had spent a great deal of time and money on enlarging it and making it splendid. It had been granted by Edward VI to Lord Rich, from whom Robert had bought it. It had a magnificent hall—fifty-three by forty-five—and a number of beautifully proportioned rooms. Robert had made it a fashion to lay handsome carpets on the floor and these were replacing the rushes in all his houses. The Queen was very interested and I went with the Court to Wanstead, where Robert put on one of his lavish entertainments.

We were able to meet now and then, but these meetings always must be conducted in the utmost secrecy and I was beginning to be irked by this. I could never be entirely sure of Robert and I believe this was one of the reasons why I was so infatuated with him. There was such an element of danger in our relationship that it inevitably added to the excitement.

"This will be one of our favorite houses," he told me. "Kenilworth always will be first because it was there that we declared our love."

I retorted that the one in which we were married would be my favorite because it had taken us so long to reach that state.

He was constantly soothing me, placating me. He had quite a gift for it. Robert was a smooth-spoken person, which belied his ruthlessness and was in itself a little sinister. He was almost always courteous—except when he lost his temper—and this could be very deceptive.

It was while we were at Wanstead that I again heard rumors about Douglass Sheffield.

"She is very ill," one of the Queen's women whispered to me. "I have heard her hair is falling out and her nails breaking off. It is expected that she will not last long."

"What illness is this she is suffering from?" I asked.

My informant looked over my shoulder and, bringing her lips to my ear, whispered: "Poison."

"Nonsense!" I said sharply. "Who would want to remove Douglass Sheffield?"

"Someone who must get her out of the way."

"And who might that be?"

The woman shut her lips tightly and shrugged her shoulders.

"It is said that she has had a child by a very important man. It could be that he is the one who finds her an encumbrance."

"It could indeed be so if this talk be true," I answered casually.

I waited for news of Douglass Sheffield's death, but it did not come.

Sometime later I heard that she had gone to the country to recover.

So Douglass lived on.

It was the New Year, time for giving gifts to the Queen.

She had been complaining about her hair, which was rarely dressed to her satisfaction, and I brought her two wigs for her to try—one black and one yellow, together with two ruffs trimmed with seed pearls.

She seized the wigs and, seated before the mirror, tried them on, demanding to know which suited her best; and as the Queen must look perfect on every occasion it was impossible to give her the truth.

I thought the black one made her look old, and as I knew it would displease her sooner or later and she would be reminded who gave it to her, I ventured: "Your Majesty's skin is so white and delicate that the black against it is too coarse."

"But does it not show the contrast?" she demanded.

"Yes, Madam, it does call attention to your flawless skin, but please may we try the golden one?"

She did and declared herself satisfied with it.

"But I shall try out the black," she told me.

Then she put on Robert's gift to her. It was a necklet of gold set with diamonds, opals and rubies.

"Is that not magnificent?" she demanded.

I said it was indeed.

She patted it tenderly. "He knows well my taste in jewels," she commented; and I thought how ironical it was to be called upon to applaud a lover's taste in the expensive gifts he gave to another woman.

She was perverse during the months which followed, and again the thought occurred to me that she knew something. I wondered whether she was remembering how Robert had persuaded her to send Walter back to Ireland and how he had died soon afterwards. She seemed watchful of me and kept me beside her.

I fancied Robert was aware of her attitude. He talked often to her of his swollen legs—he suffered from gout now—and hinted that his doctor was suggesting more visits to Buxton. I presumed he wanted to be ready for flight if the occasion should arise when it would be convenient for him to be out of the way.

She fussed about him and watched what he ate at table and told him with some asperity that he must eat and drink less.

"Look at me!" she cried. "I am neither too lean nor too

fat. And why is this? Because I do not stuff myself like a pig, nor drink until I'm stupid in the head."

Sometimes she would snatch the food from his platter and declare that if *he* would not take better care of his health *she* would.

Robert did not know whether to be pleased or anxious, for there was that undoubted touch of asperity in her attitude towards him. Yet when he did go to Buxton she wanted to know how he fared and became melancholy and irritable with us all.

Robert was at Buxton when I accompanied the Queen on one of her summer journeys round the country and in due course we arrived at Wanstead, where Robert's servants greeted us with all the display their master would have wished.

"But it is not the same, Lettice," said the Queen. "What would Kenilworth have been without him?"

Sometimes it occurred to me that she was thinking she would marry him after all; but I supposed that, as she grew older, those emotions which she might have experienced when she was young were less insistent; and she grew more and more in love with her crown and the power it brought her. Yet when Robert was not with her there was always a change in her. Christopher Hatton, for all his good looks and dancing skill, could never be to her what Robert was. I was sure that she used Hatton to arouse Robert's jealousy, for she must have known that there were women in Robert's life since she had never given him the satisfaction a normal man needs and she was determined to show him that it was only her passionate devotion to the preservation of virginity which prevented her having as many lovers as he had.

When I realized increasingly how much Robert meant to her I grew very uneasy.

Robert had had a room at Wanstead made into what was called the Queen's Chamber. Throughout the house he indulged his love of extravagant splendor, but the chamber set aside for the Queen must naturally surpass all others. The bed was gilded and the walls covered with tinsel cloth so that it shimmered as the light caught it; and, knowing her addiction to cleanliness, he had had a hothouse installed so that she could take baths when she was there.

" 'Tis a fine place, Lettice," she said, "but it cannot fail to be dull lacking the presence of its master."

She sent word to him that she was at Wanstead and his reply delighted her. She read it to me.

"Poor Robin," she declared, "he is beside himself with frustration. He cannot bear to think of my being here and he not at hand to get his players to work for my pleasure and to get off his fireworks. I tell you this: The sight of him would mean more to me than all the plays and fireworks in my kingdom. He says that had he known I was going there, my Eyes would have left Buxton whatever the doctors said. And so he would."

She folded the letter and tucked it into her bosom.

I fervently wished she were less devoted to him. I knew that when—or perhaps if—we married, there would be dire trouble; and there was something else which made me uneasy. I believed I was pregnant. I was not sure whether this was good or not, for I saw in it a chance of bringing matters to a conclusion.

I would not have another miscarriage if I could help it. The last had depressed me considerably, for there was a side to my nature which surprised me. I did love my children, and they meant more to me than I would have believed possible; and when I thought of those I would have by Robert, I was very happy. But if we were to have a family, now was the time to begin.

The Queen's ministers had never ceased to urge her to marry, for there was constant anxiety as to the succession. They reckoned that if she would marry immediately there might still be time for her to give the country an heir. She was forty-five. Yes, it was late in life to begin childbearing, but her body was in good state. She had never abused it by overdrinking and overeating; she had taken regular exercise; she tired most of us out with her dancing; she rode and walked and was full of energy, both physical and mental. So they believed there might just be time.

This was a delicate matter for them to discuss with her, for she would become very angry if it were suggested she were no longer youthful; so there was a great deal of secret activity and the ladies of her intimate bedchamber were asked some searching questions.

The negotiations with France began. The Duc d'Anjou had become Henri III and his younger brother who, as the Duc d'Alençon, had once been the Queen's suitor, had taken the title of Duc d'Anjou from his brother, who now had the greater one of King of France. The Duc was still unmarried and no doubt his mother, Catherine de' Medici, felt that a share in the crown of England would be a great advantage to her son and to France.

When he had plied his suit previously, Elizabeth had been thirty-nine and he seventeen and the difference in their ages had not displeased her. Would it do so now that the Duc was more mature and—I had heard—debauched —and she perhaps felt the need for a little haste?

It always amazed me to see the excitement talk of marriage could arouse in her. It was an extraordinary side of her character that the fact that this little Frenchman, with the unsavory reputation and far from prepossessing appearance, who was considering marrying her—and she could have had many of the greatest princes in Europe or the most handsome man in England whom she loved— should have aroused such delight in her. She was as frivolous as a young girl, and indeed she acted like one. She became even more coquettish and demanded outrageous compliments about her appearance, talking of gowns and ruffs and ribbons as though they were matters of state. If one did not know her for the wily diplomat, the shrewd ruler, that she was, it would have seemed that the foolish creature was unworthy of her crown.

I had tried to understand her attitude. In my heart I knew she had no more intention of marrying Anjou than she had any other suitor. The only one she had ever seriously considered marrying was Robert Dudley. But she was fascinated by the subject of marriage; she may have imagined herself united with a man—with Robert, I supposed—but it had to be a fantasy; she would never face the reality. Somewhere in the dark recesses of her mind was this bogey of marriage. Perhaps this was because her mother, demanding it, had paid for it with her life. I would never really understand. It was like a child who is terrified of the dark and yet asks for bloodcurdling stories about it and listens fascinated, begging for more.

I wanted to see Robert to tell him that I was with child, for I was certain of it. If he had really meant that we should marry, now was the time to prove it. I could not stay at Court when my pregnancy was obvious. The Queen had sharp eyes and I believed that recently she had watched me even more closely.

However the negotiations for the French marriage took her mind off those about her. Although those of us who knew her well were sure she had no intention of marrying the Duc, there was a growing feeling in the country about the proposed marriage, and those who did not have to be so careful of what they said were hinting that she should stop deceiving herself. There could be no issue and the marriage would mean putting power in the hands of the hated French.

But of course she could be unpredictable and none could be absolutely certain of what she would do; and there was an opinion that if she really had decided to marry at last, it would be better for the country and herself to take an Englishman and one of whom she was fond. Everyone knew who that was and that she had proved her true feelings for him over many years; and since he was the most powerful man in England already, if he were raised to be husband of the Queen, it could not be so very different.

Astley, one of the gentlemen of the bedchamber, even went so far as to remind her that Leicester was unmarried. It can be imagined what apprehension this caused me, but the Queen's reply delighted me. She was very angry and I knew it was because she thought that this courtship from which she intended to extract the maximum enjoyment was going to be snatched from her.

She shouted so that many of us heard, not only in the Presence Chamber but beyond: "Would it not be unlike myself and unmindful of my royal Majesty to prefer my servant, whom I myself have raised, before the greatest princes in Christendom."

What an insult to Robert! His pride would be deeply wounded. I wanted to be with him when he heard what the Queen had said, because it would show him that he had no hope of marrying her after all.

I sent word to him that I must see him as I had urgent news for him.

He came to Durham House and as the Queen was busy with the marriage negotiations he was freer than he usually was.

He embraced me with no lessening of his fervor and I said to him: "I am with your child, Robert, and something must be done about it."

He nodded, and I went on: "It will soon be obvious and then there will be difficulties. I have the Queen's permission to retire from the Court because I am concerned about the children. I also pleaded sickness. If we are ever going to be married, the time is now. The Queen won't have you. She has stated that clearly enough, and if she won't, then she can raise no objections to your marrying someone else."

"That's true," said Robert. "I will arrange it. Come to Kenilworth and the ceremony shall take place there. There will be no more delay."

He meant it this time. He was furious with the Queen for her excitement over the French suitor, and of course what she had said of him had been reported to him. He was not going to allow himself to be so humiliated before the whole Court and dance attendance on her while she archly prepared herself for her meeting with the Duc d'Anjou, who seemed likely to succeed where he had failed.

Fate was favoring me. This was my triumph. I had won. I knew her so well. She would not marry Anjou—she had no intention of doing so. She enjoyed pretending because it infuriated Robert and showed everyone how desperately he wanted to become her husband.

"It is the crown he wants, Cousin," I said to myself, and how I should have loved to say it to her!

How I should enjoy standing before her and telling her that I was the one he loved. "See," I would maliciously point out. "He has even risked your displeasure to marry me."

I made the journey to Kenilworth and there we went through a ceremony of marriage.

"As yet," said Robert, "we must preserve the utmost secrecy. I must choose the right moment to break it to the Queen."

I knew he was right about this so I agreed.

I was happy. I had achieved my purpose. I was the Countess of Leicester, Robert's wife.

Back at Durham House my father came to see me. He had always kept a sharp eye on us and I think I gave him more anxiety than any of my brothers and sisters, although when I had married Walter he had believed I had settled for a life of domesticity.

After Walter's death he had begun to visit me more frequently and I have no doubt that he had heard rumors about Walter's suspicious end.

Francis Knollys was a very good and pious man and I was proud that he was my father, but he had grown even more puritanical as the years passed. He watched over my children and was very concerned about their religious upbringing; as none of them was inclined to religion, they found this rather tiresome, and I had to admit that I agreed with them.

Now he called unexpectedly and it was impossible to hide my condition from him. He was alarmed and after embracing me he held me at arm's length and looked at me searchingly.

"Yes, Father," I said, "I am with child."

He stared at me in horror.

"But Walter . . ."

"I was not in love with Walter, Father. We were separated so much. We had not a great many shared interests."

"That is no way for a wife to talk of her husband."

"I must be truthful to you, Father. Walter was a good husband, but he is dead and I am too young to remain a widow for the rest of my life. I have found a man whom I love dearly. . . ."

"And you are with child by him!"

"He is my husband and in due course our marriage will be taken out of secrecy."

"Secrecy! What is this? And you already with child!" He looked at me in horror. "I have heard a name mentioned with yours and this shocks me. The Earl of Leicester . . ."

"He is my husband," I said.

"Oh God in heaven!" cried my father, and he was praying aloud, for he was not a man to use oaths. "Do not let this be true."

I said patiently: "It *is* true. Robert and I are married. What's wrong with that? You were glad enough to marry me to Walter Devereux. Robert Dudley is a far greater man than Walter could ever be."

"He is a far more ambitious man."

"What's wrong with ambition?"

"Stop wrangling," said my father sternly. "I want to know what this is all about."

"I am not a child, Father," I reminded him.

"You are my daughter. Let me know the worst."

"There is no worst. It is all the best of news. Robert and I love each other and because of this we are married and shall soon have a child."

"Yet you must hide yourself, hide your marriage. Lettice, have you no wisdom! His first wife died mysteriously. He has always hoped to marry the Queen. I have heard disturbing stories about Lady Sheffield."

"They are untrue."

"She was first his mistress and then his wife, some say."

"She was never his wife. That is a story circulated because she had a child by him."

"And you find this acceptable?"

"I would accept a great deal if Robert went with it."

"And now you have put yourself in a similar position to that of Lady Sheffield."

"Indeed I have not. I am married to Robert."

"So she thought. My child—for so you seem since you can be so easily deluded—it is clear that he went through a form of marriage with Lady Sheffield—a mock ceremony. Then when he wanted to, he could discard her. Don't you see he has put you in a similar position?"

"That's untrue!" I cried, but it was hard to prevent my voice trembling. It *had* been a secret ceremony, and Douglass Sheffield must have been deceived because she was clearly a woman who could not easily lie.

"I am going to see Leicester," said my father firmly. "I am going to find out exactly what this is all about, and I am going to see the ceremony performed before my eyes, and with witnesses. If you are to be Robert Dudley's wife, you must be so surely so that he cannot discard you when he wishes to turn his attention to someone else."

My father left me then and I wondered what the outcome would be.

I was soon to discover.

My father came to Durham House and with him were Robert's brother, the Earl of Warwick, and a close friend, the Earl of Pembroke.

"Prepare yourself to leave at once," said my father. "We are going to Wanstead. There you are to be married to the Earl of Leicester."

"Has Robert agreed to this second ceremony?" I asked.

"He is eager for it. He has convinced me that he is devoted to you and has no wish but that your union shall be legal."

By this time I was heavily pregnant but delighted to make the journey.

When we reached Wanstead, Robert was waiting there with Lord North, who had always been one of his greatest friends.

He embraced me and told me that my father was determined on this ceremony and he himself was nothing loath. He would not have any doubt his great desire to marry me and live with me as my husband.

The next morning we were joined by my brother, Richard, and one of Robert's chaplains, a Mr. Tindall, who was to perform the ceremony; and there in the gallery at Wanstead, my father gave me away to the Earl of Leicester, and the ceremony was conducted in such a manner and with such witnesses that it could never be denied that it had taken place.

My father said: "My daughter will soon give birth to your child. Then there will have to be an acknowledgment of the marriage in order to preserve her good name."

"You may safely leave that to me," Robert assured him, but my father was not so easily set aside.

"It must be known that she is truly married and the Countess of Leicester."

"My dear Sir Francis," replied my husband, "can you imagine what the Queen's wrath will be like when she knows I have married without her consent?"

"Then why did you not ask her consent?"

"Because it would never have been given. I must have time to break it to her . . . to choose my moment. If she were to announce her betrothal to the French Prince, then I should be justified in telling her I have a wife."

"Oh, Father," I said impatiently, "you must see the point of all this. Do you want us to be thrown into the Tower? As for you, what would your position be when it was known that you had actually attended the ceremony. You know full well her temper."

"I know it full well, as you say," replied my father, and Warwick joined with his brother and said that of course they must be discreet and leave it to Robert to make the decision because of his intimate knowledge of the Queen's moods.

So it was agreed and, that night, Robert and I were together in the Queen's chamber and I could not stop thinking of Elizabeth sleeping there, believing that the chamber was kept solely in readiness for her visits; and there was I, in this superb bed with my husband with whom I was madly in love and he with me, and I pictured what her fury would be like if she could see us now.

This was indeed the supreme victory.

I think Robert derived a great deal of satisfaction from

it too, for, in spite of his pleasure in me, he must have been smarting from those insulting words of hers. He could not have had a greater revenge.

How deeply involved we three were together. Even on our wedding night, it seemed that she was there with us.

But whatever the outcome, the fact remained that, without doubt, I was Robert's wife.

The next day there was disconcerting news. A messenger arrived from the Queen. She had heard that the Earl of Leicester was at his estate of Wanstead and she had decided that she would stay there for two nights on the last stages of her journey to Greenwich. As her Eyes had been so sad because last time she had visited Wanstead he had been at Buxton taking the baths, she was shortening her journey that she might spend two days in his company.

It was almost as though she knew. The thought occurred to us both that she did and that she had arranged this because of it. Robert was greatly disturbed, for, as he had pointed out to me, when the explanation came he must be the one to give it and he must choose the moment. It would never do for her to discover through someone else. It was most disconcerting that this should come on the day after our wedding, but at least there was a warning; and on consideration it seemed to us that if she had in fact known what had happened, she would never have given us the warning which enabled us to have time to cover up.

"We must act quickly," said Robert, and the others agreed with him. I should leave immediately and go back with my father to Durham House. Robert, with Warwick and North, should stay at Wanstead and prepare for the coming of the Queen.

I had to agree. My triumph in the Queen's bed was over.

Reluctantly and somewhat deflated I left Wanstead and went back to wait as patiently as I could for Robert to come to me.

I suppose the journeys to and fro and all the excitement proved too much for me in my condition; and perhaps because I had brought about the loss of a child before, life was punishing me. In any case I gave birth to a stillborn child and in as much secrecy as we could manage.

It was some little time before Robert could come to me, for the Queen was so pleased with his company at Wanstead that she insisted on his returning to Greenwich with her. When he came I had recovered from the worst of my misadventure and he comforted me by saying we would have a son before long. The Queen had shown no suspicion, so we had been unduly alarmed.

He was confident that when the time came he would be able to break the news to her gently and with the least disaster to ourselves. For the time being I could plead illness; and the fact that she was chattering continually about the proposed French marriage would make it all so much easier.

We were together for a while at Durham House, but I did wish that we could declare our marriage openly.

"All in due course," soothed Robert. He was so ebullient. After all, he had come through a great number of upsets with the Queen and survived. I was not so sure of myself. I remembered that I had once before been exiled from the Court for a very long time.

Still, life was exciting. I was Robert's wife—firmly married to him in a ceremony witnessed by my father; and my nature did revel in playing this dangerous game with the Queen.

Betrayal

Leicester considered his own ambitious hopes at an end, and privately married the widowed Countess of Essex, of whom he was deeply enamoured. Simier, having penetrated this secret, gave immediate information of it to the Queen, as he suspected that her regard for Leicester was the principal obstacle to her marriage with Anjou.

AGNES STRICKLAND

There followed months of subterfuge. I returned to Court, and whenever we could be, Robert and I were together. The Queen kept him a great deal with her, and I had to witness my husband making verbal love to my rival, which I have to confess caused me no small jealousy.

I knew of course that Elizabeth would never take a real lover and that in this respect she lived in a world of make-believe which had no substance in reality; and Robert tried to make up for my irritation with all this. We would exchange glances daringly in the Queen's presence; I would suddenly feel the pressure of his body against mine and the spark of desire would flare up between us even in the Presence Chamber. I warned him: "You will betray us one day." And I would be pleased that he risked so much. He shrugged his shoulders and pretended not to care, but I knew all the time that he was very eager to keep our secret in spite of the risks he took.

I gave the Queen an amber necklace decorated with pearls and gold for the New Year's gift and she declared herself delighted with it. She commented, though, that I looked a little pale, and she wondered whether I had recovered from my illness.

Robert had thought he should be especially lavish with his gifts just in case she thought he was not paying her as much attention as usual, and I helped him choose a beautiful clock set with rubies and diamonds, and some ruby and diamond buttons with bodkins to match for use in her hair. I knew she would delight in wearing them because he had given them to her.

I often saw her looking at them fondly and caressing them when they were in her hair; and she kept the clock beside her bed.

It was a bleak cold January day when Jehan de Simier arrived in London. He was a voluble gentleman with great charm of manners which delighted the Queen, particularly when he made a show of being overwhelmed by her beauty—and indeed she was a glittering figure when she received the Frenchman. She told how delighted she was that his master had renewed his courtship. She had thought of him constantly and it would appear that, this time, nothing would prevent their marriage.

She danced with him and played the virginals for his pleasure. She was so anxious that he should carry a good report of her to the Duc. She said that she was glad that she had not taken his brother—who as the Duc of Anjou had once courted her. *He* had been unfaithful and married someone else and she was delighted with the prospect of marriage with dear Alençon, as he had been, and Anjou, as he was now.

She looked at least ten years younger; dressing sessions were longer and she was very meticulous, scolding us if we did not dress her hair as she wished. Attending her was an ordeal but at the same time amusing. She was not irritable but gave to sharp little bursts of anger if she thought we did not do our best and we often had a slap or a pinch for our pains. I was amazed by her—though she had never looked her age because of her youthful figure and that amazingly white skin which she took such care to preserve. She could behave like a young girl in love for the first time. Yet she was deluding even herself, for she had no intention of marrying this French Prince.

She kept Simier at her side and made sure of his comfort. She asked him many questions about the Duc. How did he compare with his brother? she wanted to know.

"He is not quite as tall as his brother," was the answer.

"I hear that the King of France is indeed handsome and surrounds himself with almost as handsome young men."

"The Duc d'Anjou is not quite so fair as his brother," was the answer.

"I believe the King to be a trifle vain."

Simier offered no answer to that, for naturally he did

not want it reported that he had uttered treason against his King.

"Is the young Duc d'Anjou eager for this match?" asked the Queen.

"He has sworn to win Your Majesty," was the answer.

"It is not easy to marry a man whom one has not seen," she said.

Simier replied eagerly: "Madam, if you will but sign his passport, he will lose no time in coming to you."

Now her true feelings began to emerge, for there was always some excuse why the passport should not be signed.

Robert was amused.

"She will never make the French marriage," he said.

"If she doesn't, what will she do when she hears about us?" I asked.

"It will make no difference. She cannot expect me to remain unmarried any more than she intends not to marry herself."

She made it clear that she liked to have Simier dance attendance on her; she wanted to receive charming letters from her suitor; she declared herself longing for a glimpse of him, but the passport remained unsigned.

Catherine de' Medici, the prospective bridegroom's mother, was clearly getting restive. Wily as Elizabeth herself, she would realize that this matrimonial adventure was going the way of all the others; and there was no doubt that the Queen of England was a glittering prize for her young son, who had only distinguished himself by being exceptionally undistinguished.

Catherine de' Medici and the King of France sent a secret letter to Robert which he showed me, and in which they suggested that when the Duc d'Anjou came to England, Robert should be his adviser and help to show him the ways of the country; they were most eager to impress on him that the marriage would in no way endanger his position.

Robert was amused and gratified because it meant that his power was realized even in France.

"She will never take Anjou," he said. "I hear he is an ugly little creature."

"And she has always had such a fancy for handsome men," I added.

"'Tis true," replied Robert. "Her interest is immediately aroused by a handsome face. I am warning her to keep playing along with the French, and you see she has not granted him his passport, as I have advised her."

"What does she say when you are alone with her?" I asked. "How does she explain this coquettish attitude towards the French Prince?"

"Oh, she has always been the same. When I criticize him, she tells me I am jealous, and that pleases her, of course."

"I have always wondered how she, who is so clever, can so successfully play the fool."

"Never be deceived by her, Lettice. Sometimes I think that everything she does has some ulterior motive. She keeps peace between England and France while she pretends there will be an alliance. I have seen her do it again and again. She believes firmly in peace, and who can say she is not right? England has prospered since she came to the throne."

"At least if you confessed to her now she could not be angry."

"Could she not! Her rage would be terrible."

"But why—since she herself is contemplating marriage with this French Prince?"

"Never ask her why. She would be furious. She may marry, but not I. I am to be her devoted slave all the days of my life."

"She is going to discover her mistake sooner or later."

"I tremble to think of it."

"You tremble! You have always been able to manage her."

"I have never had to face her with such an event before."

I slipped my arm through his. "You'll do it, Robert," I said. "Just bring out that charm which none of us can resist."

But perhaps he did not understand the Queen as well as he thought he did.

It was impossible to keep my marriage secret from my daughters.

Penelope was vivacious and so much like me in looks that the relationship was immediately obvious to observers, except that many of them declared—and as I don't believe in false modesty, I will say they were right—that we looked like sisters. Dorothy was quieter but attractive in her own way; and they were both of an age when they were interested in what was going on around them, particularly if it involved a man.

The Earl of Leicester was a frequent visitor to the house and as they were aware of his secret comings and goings they found this intriguing.

When Penelope asked me if I was having a love affair with the Earl of Leicester, I told her the truth, which I thought was the best answer.

The girls were both excited and delighted.

"But he is the most fascinating man at Court!" cried Penelope.

"Well, why should that prevent his marrying me?"

"I have heard it said there is not a lady at Court to rival you for beauty," said Dorothy.

"Perhaps they said that to you knowing you were my daughter."

"Oh no. It is so. You look so young in spite of being the mother of us all. And after all, if you are rather old, so is the Earl of Leicester."

I laughed but protested: "I am not old, Dorothy. Age is determined by one's spirit and mine is as young as yours. I have made up my mind never to grow old."

"I shall do the same," Penelope assured me. "But, Mother, do tell us about our stepfather."

"What is there to tell you? He is the most fascinating man in the world, as you know. I have been determined to marry him for some time. Now I have done so."

Dorothy looked a little anxious. Rumors evidently reached the schoolroom nowadays, I thought, and wondered uneasily if they had heard of the Douglass Sheffield scandal.

"It's a perfectly legal marriage," I said. "Your grandfather was present. That speaks for itself."

Dorothy looked relieved, and I drew her to me and kissed her on the cheek.

"Never fear, dear child. All will be well. Robert has talked to me a great deal about you girls. He is going to make brilliant marriages for you."

They listened with shining eyes while I explained that their stepfather's position was such that the highest families in the land would be honored to be allied with his.

"And you, my daughters, are now related to him, because he has become your stepfather. Now you are going to start to live. But you must remember that, just as yet, our marriage is a secret."

"Oh yes," cried Penelope. "The Queen loves him and couldn't bear him to marry anyone else."

"That's true," I agreed. "So remember it, and not a word."

The girls nodded vigorously, clearly delighted with the situation.

I was wondering whether we should pursue the proposed match between Robert's nephew, Philip Sidney, and Penelope, which Walter and I had thought might be advantageous, but before I had time to broach this matter with Robert I received a message from him to say that he had left Court for Wanstead and he wanted me to join him there without delay.

The journey was only six miles so I set out immediately wondering what had made him leave Court so abruptly.

When I arrived at Wanstead he was waiting for me in a state of anger. He told me that in spite of his advice the Queen had granted Simier the passport he had been clamoring for.

"This means that Anjou will now come here," he said.

"But she has never seen any of her suitors before . . . except Philip of Spain, if he could be called one, and he never came wooing her."

"I cannot understand it. All I know is that she is deliberately flouting me. I have told her again and again what folly it is to bring him here. When she sends him back it will create bad feeling in France. While she pretends to consider and coquettes by letter, it is a different matter—though dangerous as I have repeatedly told her. But to bring him here . . . that's madness."

"What has made her do this?"

"She seems to have lost her senses. The thought of marriage has had this effect on her before, but she has never yet gone so far."

I knew what Robert was thinking, and he may have been right. He was the man she loved, and if she had an inkling that he had married someone else she would indeed be furious. That outburst of hers about not demeaning herself by marrying a servant whom she had raised up could well have been the outward sign of an inner wound. She wanted Robert to herself exclusively. She herself could flirt and frolic, but he should know that it was never serious. He was the one. Now Robert was wondering whether she had heard rumors concerning us, because it was becoming increasingly difficult to keep our secret.

"When I heard what she had done," he told me, "I went to her and before some of her attendants she demanded to know how I dared come without first asking permission to do so. I reminded her that I had done it frequently without reproof, and she told me to take care. She was in a strange mood. I said I would remove myself from Court as she seemed to wish that, to which she replied that if she wished it she would not have hesitated to say so, but now I had suggested it, she thought it a good idea. So I bowed and was about to leave when she asked why had I come bursting thus unceremoniously into her apartments. I indicated that I did not wish to speak before her attendants and she dismissed them.

"Then I said: 'Madam, I think it is a mistake to bring the Frenchman here.'

" 'Why so?' she cried. 'Do you expect me to marry a man I have never seen?'

"I replied: 'No, Madam, I do earnestly hope and pray that you will not marry outside this country.'

"Then she laughed and let out a stream of oaths. She said she understood that well for I had always had high pretensions. I had allowed myself to believe that because she had shown me some favor I might share the crown with her.

"I kept my temper and answered that no one would be so foolish as to hope to share her crown. All he could wish for was to serve her and if there was a chance of his doing so in an intimate capacity he would be fortunate.

"She then accused me of doing everything I could to impede Simier, who himself had complained to her of my lack of friendship towards him. I gave myself airs. I seemed to think I was of especial importance to her. I would have to lower my fancies, for when she married

237

she doubted her husband would tolerate that. At which I asked her leave to retire from Court.

"She shouted at me: 'It is granted. Go, and stay away. There has been a little too much of the pride and glory of my Lord Leicester at our Court of late.'

"So I came to Wanstead and here I am."

"Do you really think this French marriage will take place?"

"I cannot believe it. It's monstrous. She will never get an heir, and what other reason could there be? He is twenty-three and she is forty-six. She is not serious. She cannot be."

"I'll swear she feels this is the last chance to play her little courtship game. That's the answer."

He shook his head, and I went on: "Perhaps now that you are out of favor it would be a good time to make our marriage publicly known. After all, she has rejected you, why should you not seek consolation elsewhere?"

"In her present mood it could be disastrous. No, Lettice. God help us, we must still wait a while."

He was in such a state of anger against the Queen that I decided not to pursue the matter. He talked a great deal about what the withdrawal of the Queen's favor could mean to us, as though it had to be explained to me how disastrous that could be. A man who had enjoyed such favors had naturally incurred a great deal of rancor. Envy was the prevailing passion in the world and Elizabeth's Court was no exception. Robert was one of the richest and most powerful men in the country—made so by the Queen's gifts. He had the magnificent Leicester house in the Strand, the incomparable Kenilworth, Wanstead, lands in the North, South and Midlands, all of which brought in considerable revenues. Men came to him when they sought the Queen's favor, for it was well known that there had been times when she could deny him nothing he asked;

moreover, in the wholeheartedness of her affection she wanted all to know how she regarded him.

But she was a despot; her resemblance to her royal father was apparent in so many of her actions. How often had *he* warned a subject: "I have raised you up. I can as easily cast you down." Her vanity was great and an assault on it would never be forgiven.

Yes, Robert was right when he said we must tread warily.

All that day and far into the night we talked of our future, and although Robert could not believe she would marry the Duc d'Anjou even if she brought him to England, he was very uneasy.

The next day a summons came from the Queen. Robert was to return to Court without delay.

We discussed it together.

"I don't like it," said Robert. "I fear that when I come humbly back, she will want to show me how much I depend on her. I shall not go."

"Disobey the Queen!"

"I'll use the tactics she so successfully used in her youth. I'll pretend to be ill."

So Robert made a feint of preparing to leave but before he had time to do so he complained of the pain in his legs and he said the swelling was great. His doctors' remedy was to retire to bed at such times, so to bed he went and sent a message to the Queen acknowledging her summons but craving her indulgence for a few weeks as he was too ill to travel and must take to his bed at Wanstead.

It seemed advisable for him to stay in his apartments because we had to be careful that those who wished us ill did not carry tales to the Court; and how could we be sure who our friends were?

I was, thankfully, in the house when a party was seen approaching. The royal standard fluttered in the breeze heralding one of the Queen's journeys. In horror I realized that she was on her way to the invalid at Wanstead.

There was just time to make sure that Robert was looking wan in bed and to remove from the bedchamber all signs which might indicate that a woman shared it with him.

Then the trumpets sounded. The Queen had arrived at Wanstead.

I heard her voice; she was demanding to be taken to the Earl without delay. She wanted to assure herself of his condition, for she had suffered much anxiety on his account.

I had shut myself in one of the smaller rooms, listening intently to what was happening, feeling alarmed at what this visit could mean, and angry because I, the mistress of the house, dared not show myself.

I did have some servants whom I believed I could trust, and one of these brought me news of what was happening.

The Queen was with the Earl of Leicester, expressing great concern about his illness. She was not going to trust any of the nursing of her dear friend to anyone. She would remain in the sickroom, and the chamber which was kept for her at Wanstead must be made ready for her when she should need it.

I was dismayed. So it was not to be a brief visit!

What a situation! There was I, in my own house, with, it seemed, no right to be there.

Servants were scurrying up and down to the sickroom. I could hear the Queen as she shouted orders. Robert would not have to feign sickness; he would be ill with anxiety wondering what was happening to me and whether my presence was going to be discovered.

I thanked God for Robert's power and the fear in which many went of him, for just as the Queen could cast him down, so he could wreak vengeance on any who displeased him. Moreover, he had a reputation for dark deeds. People still remembered Amy Robsart and the

Earls of Sheffield and Essex. It was whispered that those who were enemies of the Earl of Leicester should take care not to dine at his table.

So I was not unduly afraid of betrayal.

Yet I was faced with a problem. If I left and were seen leaving, there would indeed be a storm. And yet was it safe for me to stay hidden in the house?

I decided on the latter course and prayed that Elizabeth's sojourn would be a brief one. I often laugh now to think of that time, although then it was far from a laughing matter. Food was smuggled up to me. I could not go out. I had to keep my faithful maid continually on the watch.

Elizabeth remained at Wanstead for two days and nights and it was not until—from the window of a small top room—I had seen the cavalcade disappear that I dared to emerge.

Robert was still in bed and in excellent spirits. The Queen had been attentive; she had insisted on nursing him herself, had scolded him for not taking better care of his health and had implied that she was as fond of him as ever.

He was certain that she would not make the French marriage and that his position at Court would be as firm as it ever had been.

I did point out to him that she might be incensed when she heard that he had married, since she appeared to have lost none of her affection for him. But Robert was so pleased because he was back in favor that he refused to be depressed.

How we laughed over the adventure now that the danger was past! But the problem of disclosure lay ahead of us. One day she would have to know.

Robert was still at Wanstead when we heard that there

had been an accident at Greenwich which could have cost the Queen her life.

It appeared that Simier was conducting her to her barge when one of the guards fired a shot. The Queen's bargeman, who was standing only six feet from her, was wounded in both arms and fell bleeding to the ground.

The man who had fired was seized immediately and the Queen turned her attention to the bargeman who lay at her feet.

When she had satisfied herself that he was not fatally wounded, she took off her scarf and bade those who were attending him to bind him up and stop the flow of blood, while she bent over him and begged him to be of good cheer, for he and his family should never want. The bullet had been meant for her, she was sure.

The man who had fired the shot—a certain Thomas Appletree—was dragged away, and the Queen went on to her barge, talking as she did so to Monsieur de Simier.

The incident was discussed throughout the country; and when Thomas Appletree was put on trial he declared that he had had no intention of shooting and that the firearm had gone off by accident.

The Queen, gracious as she always liked to be to her humble subjects, saw the man himself, and declared herself convinced of his honesty and that he was speaking the truth. He fell to his knees and told her with tears in his eyes that he had only ever had one wish and that was to serve her.

"I believe him," she cried. "It was an accident. I shall tell your master, my good Thomas, to take you back into his service."

Then she declared that the man who had been shot was to be well looked after and, as it turned out that he had not been badly hurt, the incident appeared to have been forgotten.

But this was not so. Many knew that the Earl of Leicester had quarreled with the Queen over the granting of the passport to the Duc d'Anjou. Simier complained that Leicester had done his best to make the mission a failure; and in view of Robert's reputation it was soon being hinted that he had arranged for the guard to shoot Simier.

Simier himself believed this and he was determined to have his revenge. We discovered in what manner when the Earl of Sussex came riding to Wanstead.

Thomas Radcliffe, third Earl of Sussex, was not a great friend of Robert's. In fact there was a fierce rivalry between them, and Robert was well aware that Sussex deplored the favors which the Queen had lavished on her favorite. Sussex was ambitious like the rest of those men who circulated about the Queen, but it was his boast that his only motive was to serve her and this he would do even if by so acting he offended her. He had little imagination or charm and was certainly not one of Elizabeth's favorite men, but she kept him for his honesty much as she kept Burleigh for his wisdom; and although she would berate them and vent her anger on them, she would always listen to them and often took their advice; she would never have dispensed with either of them.

Sussex was looking stern, I noticed, and not without a certain self-satisfaction, for the news he brought was that Simier, infuriated by what he believed to be an attack on his life by Leicester, had told the Queen what so many people already knew although it had been kept from her, that Robert and I were married.

Robert asked me to join them, for there was no purpose now in keeping my presence a secret.

"You are in deep trouble, Leicester," said Sussex. "You may well look dismayed. I have never seen the Queen in such a fury."

"What said she?" asked Robert quietly.

"At first she would not believe it. She screamed out that it was lies. She kept saying 'Robert would never do

243

it. He would never dare.' Then she called you a traitor and said you had betrayed her."

Robert protested: "She has spurned me. She is at this time contemplating marriage. Why should my marriage be of such moment to her?"

"She would not listen to reason. She kept saying that she would send you to the Tower. She said you could rot in the Tower and she would be glad of it."

"She is ill," said Robert. "Only a sick woman could behave so. Why, she offered me to the Queen of Scots and was willing for me to marry the Princess Cecilia."

"My Lord Leicester, it is said that she would never have allowed those marriages to take place and if she had they would have been political marriages. It was when she heard *whom* you had married that her fury increased." He turned to me apologetically. "I will not, Madam, insult your ears by telling you the names the Queen called you. Indeed, it would seem her fury is more violent against you than against the Earl."

I could believe it. She would know of the passion between us. I had not been mistaken when I had seen her watching me so closely. She knew that there was a power in me to attract men, which for all her glory she lacked. She would picture Robert and me together and she would know that what we shared was something which, by her very nature, she could never enjoy. And she hated me for it.

"No, never before have I seen the Queen in such a passion," went on Sussex. "Indeed, I felt she was on the verge of madness. She kept declaring she would make you regret your actions—both of you. You, Leicester, she really wanted to send to the Tower. It was with the greatest difficulty that I restrained her from giving the order."

"Then I have to thank you, Sussex, for that."

Sussex gave Robert a look of dislike. "I saw at once that the Queen would harm herself by giving such an
244

order. She would be allowing her emotions to override her good sense. I pointed out to her that it was no criminal act to enter into honorable marriage, and that if she showed her subjects how deeply enraged she was, they might put all manner of constructions on her conduct which would be detrimental to her. So, in due course, she relented, but she made it clear that she did not want to see you and that you should stay out of her way. You are to go to the Tower Mireflore in Greenwich Park and stay there. She has not said that you shall be guarded, but you are to consider yourself a prisoner."

"And I am to accompany my husband?" I asked.

"No, Madam, he is to go alone."

"And the Queen gave no orders for me?"

"She said she never wished to see you again, nor to hear your name spoken. And I must tell you, Madam, that when your name is mentioned she flies into such a passion that were you there she would be ready to send you straight to the block."

So the worst had happened. And we now had to face the consequences.

Robert lost no time in obeying the Queen's order and going to Mireflore. I went to my family at Durham House.

It was clear that we were all in disgrace, although after a few days the Queen relented somewhat and sent word to Robert that he could leave Mireflore and return to Wanstead, where I joined him.

Lady Mary Sidney came to visit us on her way to Penshurst. She felt it necessary to leave Court, for the Queen was so vituperative against her brother Robert, and particularly against me, that she found it distressing; and when she mentioned to the Queen that she was sure the Dudley family no longer enjoyed her favor and asked leave to retire to the country, this was granted. Elizabeth had said that she had been so badly treated by the very member of that family on whom she had lavished great favor, that it would be easier if she were not reminded of him. She would never forget what Lady Mary had done for her, but she was ready to allow her to retire to Penshurst for a while.

We would sit quietly with Lady Mary and talk of the future. I was pregnant and so longed for a son that I could let this storm pass over me. I was well aware that I should never again be welcome at Court and that the Queen was my enemy for life, for whatever she did—even if she married the Duc d'Anjou, which secretly I knew she never would—she would not forget that I had taken the man she loved, and would never forgive me for having made him so much in love with me that he had risked his future by marrying me. In spite of her self-deception over her charms, she knew very well that had it been a choice between two women, I would have been the chosen one. That knowledge would always be between us and she would hate me for it.

But I had married Robert; I was to bear his child; and just now I could snap my fingers at the Queen.

Lady Mary thought that this would be the end of the family's favor at Court, and it seemed very likely that the Queen would marry the Duc d'Anjou out of pique.

I did not agree with this. I knew her well, and I think that this rivalry between us had given me a rather special understanding of her. In so many superficial ways she was a hysterical, illogical woman, but beneath this she was as strong as steel. I did not think she would ever commit an act which did not seem to her politically wise. It was true she had given the passport which would bring Anjou to England. But the people were against an alliance with the French; the only reason for marriage could be to get an heir, and her age made that very uncertain; moreover, she would make herself ridiculous if she married this young boy. Yet, because she wanted the fun of courtship, because she wanted to create the illusion that she was nubile, and perhaps, too, because she was deeply hurt that Robert had married me she would continue with this farce.

Was this the act of a sensible, reasonable woman? Hardly. And yet, beneath it all was the iron hand of the shrewd ruler, the woman who knew how to make the cleverest men of her realm bow down before her and give the best of their talents in her service.

Never to be close to the Court again would create an emptiness in my life; but as long as we lived there would be a tie between us—the Queen and myself. It might even be strengthened by hatred. I had at last proved my own importance to her. I had scored the greatest victory of our campaign when I had so enslaved Leicester that he was prepared to flout her in order to marry me. There could have been nothing more revealing in the relationship between the three of us than that. And she would be fully aware of it. I had proved without question that I was by no means the insignificant third in our triangle.

Mary left for Penshurst, and soon after she had gone Robert received a summons from the Queen. He was to present himself.

Full of foreboding, he departed and in due course came back to Wanstead with mixed emotions.

She had belabored him, called him traitor and ungrateful man; she had enumerated all she had done for him, reminding him that she had raised him up and could as easily cast him down.

He had protested that she had made it clear over many years that she had no intention of marrying him and that he believed he had a right to family life and sons to follow him. He was ready to serve his Queen with his life, he had told her, but he had believed that he might enjoy the comforts of family life without impairing his service to his Queen and country.

She had listened grimly and then she had told him to

beware. "I'll tell you this, Robert Dudley," she had shouted, "you have married a she-wolf and you will discover this to your cost."

So I became the She-Wolf. It was a habit of hers to bestow nicknames on those about her. Robert had always been her Eyes, Burleigh her Spirit, and Hatton her Mutton. I could see that forever after I should be the She-Wolf—the picture of me in her mind being that of a wild animal, seeking victims to satisfy my violent passions.

"She seems determined to have Anjou," said Robert.

"I'll swear she won't."

"In her present mood she is capable of anything. She was shouting and swearing at me in a voice which could have been heard throughout the palace."

"Nevertheless," I said, "I doubt she will take Anjou."

The Frog Prince

How the hearts of your people will be galled, if not aliened, when they shall see you take a husband, a Frenchman and a papist, in whom the very common people know this, that he is the son of the Jezabel of our age—that his brother made oblation of his own sister's marriage, the easier to make massacre of our brethren in religion. As long as he is Monsieur in might, and a papist in profession, he neither can nor will greatly shield you, and if he grow to be a king, his defence will be like Ajaz's shield, which rather weighed down than defended, those that bare it.

PHILIP SIDNEY

. . . . England is like to be Swallowed by another French marriage, if the Lord forbid not the Banes by letting Her Majestie see the sin and punishment thereof.

JOHN STUBBS

Another crisis had arisen in my family. There had been a tacit understanding between Penelope and Philip Sidney that they would marry. Walter had dearly wished that this marriage should take place and he had mentioned it on his deathbed in Dublin.

Philip Sidney was an unusual man. He seemed almost ethereal and by no means eager for marriage and it might have been for this reason that the engagement drifted on.

I received a call from Francis Hastings, the Earl of Huntingdon, who had been appointed the guardian of my daughters. Huntingdon was a man of great importance, largely because, on his mother's side, he was of royal descent, her ancestor beind Edward's IV's brother, the Duke of Clarence; and because of this he had a claim to the throne and maintained he came before the Queen of Scots and Catharine Grey.

He was forceful and a strong Protestant, and there was a possibility that since Elizabeth seemed unlikely to provide the country with heirs, he could one day take the crown.

His wife, Catharine, was Robert's sister; they had been married at that time when Robert's father had been eagerly marrying his children into the most influential families in the land.

Now he came to see me and tell me that he considered it was time husbands were found for my daughters and he had an offer for Penelope. I pointed out that she had an understanding with Philip Sidney, but at this he shook his head.

"Leicester is out of favor and likely to remain so. An alliance with a member of the family is not the best for Penelope. Robert Rich has become enamored of her and offers for her."

"His father has just died, has he not?"

"Yes, and Robert has inherited the title and a very considerable estate. His name describes him well."

"I will test her feelings in the matter."

Huntingdon looked impatient. "My dear lady, this is a brilliant match. Your daughter should seize it gratefully."

"I doubt she will do that."

"She will, for she shall be made to. Let us be frank. She is your daughter and you do not stand high with the Queen. Whether Leicester will come back into favor we do not know, but the Queen has vowed she will never receive you. In these circumstances it would be well for your daughters to be safely married."

I saw the point of this and said I would broach the matter to Penelope.

Lord Huntingdon shrugged his shoulders impatiently, implying that consultation with the prospective bride was unnecessary. It was a good match, the best Penelope could hope for now that her mother was in disgrace, and it should be arranged without delay.

But I knew Penelope. She was no weak girl and would have decided views of her own.

When I told her of Lord Huntingdon's visit and its purpose she was stubborn.

"Lord Rich!" she cried. "I know of him and I do not want to marry him no matter what my Lord Huntingdon decrees. You know I am betrothed to Philip."

"You are of a marriageable age, and he has expressed no eagerness for it. Huntingdon points out that my disgrace will reflect on you and you should therefore be very ready to consider a good match while you can get one."

"I have considered it," said Penelope firmly. "I do not want to marry Robert Rich."

I did not pursue the matter, for I knew that would only increase her stubbornness. Perhaps when she grew accustomed to the idea it might not prove so repulsive to her.

There was great excitement throughout the country

251

when the Duc d'Anjou came to Court. He arrived in a manner calculated to win the Queen's heart, for he came secretly to England accompanied by only two servants and presented himself at Greenwich, where he asked permission to throw himself at the Queen's feet.

Nothing could have delighted her more and her infatuation—assumed though it must have been—amazed everyone. There could have been few men as unattractive as this French Prince. He was very short—almost a dwarf—and when he was a child had suffered from a violent attack of smallpox which had left his skin badly scarred and discolored. The end of his nose had become enlarged and had split in two, which gave him a very odd appearance. In spite of this, being a Prince, a life of debauchery had been possible for him and he had indulged himself freely. He had refused to learn, so his education had been scanty; he was completely unprincipled and irreligious, ready to become a Protestant or a Catholic to fit the moment. What he did have was a certain charm of manner and an ability to flatter and insinuate his passion—and this appealed to the Queen. When he was seated low in a chair he resembled nothing so much as a frog, which the Queen was quick to notice, and with her passion for nicknames he soon became her Little Frog.

I was disappointed not to be at Court to see the farce of these two together—the little French Prince in his early twenties, repulsively ugly, playing the ardent lover, and the dignified Queen in her forties, languishing under his passionate gaze and utterances. It must have been quite comic, but the implications were far from that, and there was not a man who had the interests of the Queen and the country at heart who was not dismayed. I reckoned that even Robert's greatest enemies felt it was a pity she had not married him and by this time given the country an heir.

Robert was obliged to attend Court, although he was in

disfavor, and I sometimes wondered whether she put on this nauseating display to anger him. I heard that she had had an ornament made in the shape of a frog—it was of flawless diamonds—and she carried it with her everywhere.

For a few days the Duc rarely left her side and they walked in the gardens, laughing and chatting, holding hands and even embracing in public; and when the Prince returned to France it was with the certainty that the marriage would take place.

It was the beginning of October when she summoned her council to debate on her marriage and as Robert was still a member of that council he was present, so I had an account of what took place.

"As she was not there," Robert told me, "I was able to discuss the matter with freedom, and as a purely political venture. It seemed she had gone so far with the Prince that it might be difficult to draw back, and for that reason the marriage might be necessary. We all knew the Queen's age and it seemed hardly likely that she could have an heir; and if by some chance she did, she would endanger her life by doing so. The Queen was old enough to be the Duc's mother, said Sir Ralph Sadler, and, of course, that was something with which we all had to agree. However, knowing her temper, we thought it advisable to suggest the project be dropped, but compromised by asking to be informed of her pleasure and assuring her that we would endeavor to make ourselves conformable to it."

"She did not like that, I'll swear," I put in. "She wanted you to beg her to marry and give the country an heir, keeping up the illusion that she was still a young woman."

"You're right. She looked daggers at us all when we told her—and at me in particular—and said that some were ready to marry themselves but wished to deny that pleasure to others. She said we had talked for years as though the only surety for her was to marry and get an heir. She had expected us to *petition* her to proceed with the marriage, and she had been foolish to have asked us to deliberate on her behalf, for it was a matter too delicate for us. Now we had aroused doubts in her mind, and she would break up the meeting that she might be alone."

She had been in an evil mood that day, abusing everyone; and those whose duties brought them close to her person, I had no doubt, bore the worst of the brunt.

Burleigh called the council together and said that as she seemed so set on marriage perhaps they should agree to it, for her temper was such that whether they advised it or not, she would follow her own inclination.

Even then *I* could not believe she would marry the Duc. The people were against it, and she had always considered the people.

Robert said he had rarely seen her in such a mood. It seemed that the Frog had cast some spell on her. He must be a magician, for an uglier man few had ever seen. It would be ludicrous if she accepted him. The English hated the French in any case. Wasn't it the French who had supported Mary Queen of Scots and given her grandiose ideas about her claim to the throne? Elizabeth would be playing right into the hands of the French if she married. There could be a revolt in the country. It was true that Anjou was a Protestant . . . at the moment. He was, everyone knew, like a weathercock. Fine today, raining tomorrow—only in his case it would be Catholic and Protestant. He turned with the wind.

We went to Penshurst to consult with the Sidneys what was best to be done.

There was a great welcome for us there. I had always been struck by the family loyalty of the Dudleys. Robert was greeted even more warmly now that he was in disgrace than he had been at the height of his popularity.

I remembered that Mary had left Court because she could no longer bear to hear her brother abused, and

254

Philip had come to Penshurst for the same reason. He was a special favorite of the Queen. She had made him her cupbearer. But she had willingly given him leave of absence, for she had declared that he looked so sullen every time she let it be known how enraged she was at the conduct of that uncle of his that she wanted to box his ears.

Philip was beautiful rather than handsome. The Queen liked him for his looks and his learning, for his honesty and goodness; but of course the type of men who excited her were of a different kind.

Philip was deeply concerned about the marriage, for he said it would cause disaster if it took place, and it was decided that as he had the gift of words, it might be a good idea if he wrote his objections in a letter to the Queen.

So those days at Penshurst were spent in discussion. Robert and I would walk in the park with Philip and discuss the dangers of the Queen's marriage, and although I was firm in my insistence that she would never marry, they wavered in their opinions. Robert might be said to know her better than any—indeed he had been close to her—but I felt I knew the woman in her.

Philip shut himself in his study and at last produced the letter which was read by us all, commented on and, as we thought, toned down. In the end it read:

How the hearts of your people will be galled, if not aliened, when they shall see you take a husband, a Frenchman and a papist, in whom the very common people know this, that he is the son of the Jezabel of our age—that his brother made oblation of his own sister's marriage, the easier to make massacre of our brethren in religion. . . .

He was referring to Catherine de' Medici, who was known throughout France as Queen Jezabel, so hated was she; and to the Massacre of the St. Bartholomew, which had taken place when Paris was full of Huguenots for the marriage of Anjou's sister Marguerite to Huguenot Henri of Navarre.

As long as he is Monsieur in might, and a papist in profession, he neither can nor will greatly shield you, and if he grow to be king, his defence will be like that of Ajax's shield, which rather weighed down than defended, those that bare it.

The letter was delivered and we waited at Penshurst with trepidation.

However, another incident occurred which no doubt made Philip's letter less significant than it might have been.

John Stubbs flared into prominence.

Stubbs was a Puritan who had graduated from Cambridge and took an interest in literary pursuits. His hatred of Catholicism had led him into danger. He was so violently opposed to the French marriage that he published a pamphlet entitled: *"The Discoverie of a gaping gulf whereinto England is like to be Swallowed by another French marriage, if the Lord forbid not the Banes by letting Her Majestie see the sin and punishment thereof."*

There was nothing in the pamphlet disloyal to the Queen, whose humble servant Stubbs declared himself to be, but when I saw a copy of it I knew that it would infuriate her—not for its political and religious views but because John Stubbs had pointed out that the Queen's age would prevent the marriage's being fruitful.

So enraged was the Queen—as I had guessed—that she ordered the pamphlet to be suppressed and the men involved—the writer Stubbs and the publisher and printer—to be tried at Westminster. The three men were sentenced to have their right hands cut off, and although the printer was later pardoned and the cruel sentences carried out on the other two, it was Stubbs who distinguished himself by speaking to the assembled crowd and telling them that the loss of his hand would in no way change his loyalty to the Queen. Then the right hands of both men were cut off by a blow—from a butcher's knife with a mallet—struck through the wrist. As Stubb's right hand fell off, he lifted his left and cried: "God save the Queen!" before he fell down in a faint.

That scene, when reported to her, must have shaken her; and, although at the time, I sometimes marveled with the rest at her seeming folly, when I look back I see the devious purpose of it.

While she dallied with Anjou—and she did so for a year or two—she was in fact playing a game of politics with Philip of Spain, whom she greatly feared; and it was to be seen with good reason. What she wanted most was to avoid an alliance between her two enemies, and how could France ally herself with Spain when one of her sons was about to become the consort of the Queen of England.

It was clever politics and those men about her could not see it until later; but then hindsight makes so much clear.

Moreover, during that time when she dallied with her Frog Prince and earned certain unpopularity with her people, she was sowing discord between the King of France and his brother; she was planning already—as was proved later—to send the erstwhile Protestant Prince to Holland, there to fight the battle against Spain for her.

This was for later. In the meantime she flirted and coquetted with the little Prince and neither he nor her courtiers and ministers understood her motive just then.

It was a wonderful day for Robert and me when our son was born. We called him Robert and made great plans for him.

I was contented for a while just to be with him, and I

was delighted when I heard that Douglass Sheffield had married Sir Edward Stafford, who was the Queen's ambassador in Paris. It was Edward Stafford who had carried out the negotiations for the proposed marriage between Elizabeth and Anjou and his handling of these matters had won the Queen's approval.

He had for some time been in love with Douglass, but her insistence that a marriage had taken place between her and Leicester had made it impossible for them to marry. Now that *my* marriage with Robert was common knowledge, Douglass—acting in a manner which was typical of her—married Edward Stafford, thereby tacitly admitting that there could never have been a binding marriage between herself and Robert.

This was deeply gratifying, and as I sat with my baby in my lap I promised myself that all would be well and in due course I should even regain the Queen's favor.

I wondered what Elizabeth would feel when she knew that Robert and I had a son, for I was sure that she longed for a son even more than she did for a husband.

I heard from friends at Court that she had received the news in silence, which had been followed by a bout of ill temper, so I guessed the effect it had had on her; but it was a shock to learn of what action she intended to take.

It was Sussex again—that harbinger of ill tidings—who brought the news to us.

"I fear there is trouble ahead," he told Robert, not without some satisfaction. "The Queen is asking questions about Douglass Sheffield. It has come to her ears that she has a son named Robert Dudley and that she declared he was the legitimate son of the Earl of Leicester."

"If that were so," I demanded, "how can she call herself the wife of Sir Edward Stafford?"

"The Queen declares it is a mystery which she is now determined to clear up. She says that Douglass is the daughter of a great house and she cannot allow it to be said that she has committed bigamy in her marriage with her ambassador."

Robert said firmly: "There was on my part no marriage with Douglass Sheffield."

"The Queen thinks it maybe otherwise and she is determined to have the matter sifted for the truth."

"She may sift but she will find nothing."

Was he braving it out? I was not sure. He certainly seemed shaken.

"Her Majesty says that she is of the mind that there was such a marriage, in which case your present marriage is none at all. She says that if indeed you married Douglass Sheffield, you will live with her as your wife or rot in the Tower."

I knew what this meant. If it were possible she was going to wrest my triumph from me. She wanted to prove that my marriage was no marriage and my son a bastard.

Oh, those were anxious days for me. Even now I tremble with rage when I recall them. Robert assured me that she could not prove that a marriage had taken place, for it had not, but I could not entirely believe him. I knew him well and that the overweening emotion of his life was ambition; but he was more virile than most men and when he desired a woman that desire could, temporarily, override ambition. Douglass was the sort of woman who would cling to her virtue—although she had become his mistress —and it may have been because of the child she was to have that she had successfully pleaded with him to marry her.

But now *we* had a son—our own young Robert—and I told myself that his father, who was adept at removing obstacles from his path, would surely be able to eliminate evidence of a marriage, if such there had been. No son of mine should be branded a bastard. I would not stand aside and allow the Queen that satisfaction. I was going to confound her malice, prove her wrong and let this be another victory for her She-Wolf.

Sussex informed us that the Queen had commissioned him to get to the truth of the matter. She was determined to know whether, in fact, a marriage had taken place. We had a good ally in Sir Edward Stafford, who was deeply enamored of Douglass and was as earnestly concerned in proving there had been no marriage between Douglass and Robert as we were.

Douglass, it seemed, wanted to defend what she called "her honor"; and of course she was fighting for her son. That was a point in our favor. Leicester, as a family man wanting legitimate sons, was, it was said, hardly likely to disclaim one as bright and intelligent as Douglass's Robert.

We waited in trepidation for the result of the inquiry. Douglass was questioned by Sussex, and it was disconcerting to remember how much Sussex disliked Robert, for we were sure that he would be delighted if he could bring a case against us.

Douglass insisted, under cross-examination, that there had been a ceremony when she and Leicester had plighted their troth in a manner which she considered binding. Then, it was said, she must have some document; there must have been some settlement. No, said silly little Douglass, there was nothing. She had relied on the Earl of Leicester and had trusted him completely. She wept hysterically and begged to be left alone. She was now happily married to Sir Edward Stafford, and the Earl of Leicester and Lady Essex had a fine boy.

Then, it would seem, Sussex was forced to declare that what had taken place between Lady Sheffield and the Earl of· Leicester was no true marriage and in that case Leicester had been free to marry Lady Essex when he did.

When the news was brought to me I was overcome with joy. I had been terrified on account of my son. Now there was no doubt that the little boy in the cradle was the Earl of Leicester's legitimate son and heir.

While I was rejoicing in my good fortune I could also enjoy the Queen's discomfiture. It was reported to me that when she heard the news she stormed and raged, called Douglass a fool, Leicester a rogue, and me a ravening she-wolf who roamed the world seeking for men whom it could destroy.

"My Lord Leicester will rue the day he ever took up with Lettice Knollys," she declared. "This is not an end of that affair. In time he will have recovered from his besotted folly and feel the She-Wolf's poisonous fangs."

I might have trembled to realize the hatred I had aroused in our all-powerful lady, but somehow I found it stimulating, especially now that I knew I had got the better of her again. I could picture her fury, and that it was mainly directed against me exhilarated me. My marriage was secure. My son's future was protected. And the mighty Queen of England—although she had exerted all her power to do so—could not take that from me.

Once again I was the victor.

I could come out into the open now that there was no need to skulk behind secrecy, and I turned my attention to my husband's magnificent residences and determined to make them even more grand. They should all exceed the splendor of the Queen's places and castles.

I refurbished my bedchamber in Leicester House, installing a walnut bed, the hangings of which were of such grandeur that no one could look at them without gasping. I was determined that *my* bedchamber must be more splendid than that set aside for the Queen when she came visiting the house. I remembered that when she came I should have to disappear—either that or she would refuse to come at all. And if she came I knew her curiosity would impel her to see my bedchamber, so I spared nothing in making it beautiful. The hangings were of red velvet, decorated with gold and silver thread and lace; everything in the room was covered in velvet, silver and gold cloth; my night stool was like a throne. I knew she would be furious if she saw it all. And she would certainly hear about it. There would be plenty of malicious hands ready to stoke up the fires of her hatred against me. All the bed linen was decorated with Leicester's crest, and very fine it was; we had rich carpets on the floors and walls, and what a joy it was to dispense with the rushes which in a short time became ill-smelling and full of lice.

Robert and I were happy. We could laugh together behind the elaborate curtains of our bed at the clever way in which he had married me in spite of all the obstacles against us. I referred to the Queen when we were alone together as That Vixen. After all she was as cunning as a fox; and the female of the species was more wily than the male. As she called me the She-Wolf I called Robert My Wolf, and he retaliated by naming me his Lamb, for he said that if the lion could lie down with that sweet creature so could the wolf. There was little that was lamblike about me, I reminded him, and he said that was true as far as the rest of the world was concerned. The joke persisted, and whenever we used these nicknames the Queen was never far from our thoughts.

Our little son was a joy to us both and I began to revel in my family, not only because I was devoted to them but because the Queen, for all her splendor, must feel the lack of sons and daughters.

There was, however, a certain sadness in the house which was brought about by Penelope. She had stormed and raged for a time, declaring her opposition to the marriage with Lord Rich. Lord Huntington would have had her beaten into submission, but I would not allow this. Penelope was very like myself—beautiful and high-spirited; in any case to have beaten her would have strengthened her resistance.

I reasoned with her. I pointed out that this marriage with Lord Rich was the best thing that could happen to her at this time. The family was in disgrace—particularly myself—and my daughter would never be received at Court, but if she became Lady Rich and the wife of such a man, that would be a different matter. She might feel that she would prefer a life in the country to marriage with a man she did not love, but she would change her mind when the boredom set in.

"I cannot say that I was wildly in love with your father when I married him," I confessed, "but it was not an unsuccessful marriage, and I have you children through it."

"And you were very friendly with Robert during that marriage," she reminded me.

"There is no harm in having friends," I retorted.

That made her somewhat thoughtful, and when Lord Huntingdon came once more to talk sternly to her, she relented.

She was married to Lord Rich, poor child. I was sorry for her and for Philip Sidney, although he had been somewhat lackadaisical and prepared to drift along without coming to any conclusion. Now he seemed stunned and I heard that he referred to Lord Rich as a coarse illiterate fellow. The marriage certainly brought him out of his lethargy and his relationship with Penelope changed from that time. He started to write verses to her and about her and according to them Penelope was the love of his life.

However, most people said how fortunate she was in view of the fact that her mother was in dire disgrace and the Queen still put out with her stepfather, who, many believed, would never regain his old footing with her.

At that time I believed that the Queen might in time relent towards me, for she certainly did towards Robert. After a few months he gradually began working his way back into favor. Her affection for him never ceased to astonish me. I think she still cherished romantic dreams about him, and when she looked at him she still saw the handsome youth who had been with her in the Tower instead of the aging man he was becoming, for he was putting on weight rather alarmingly, his face was too ruddy, and his hair seemed to whiten a little each week.

One of Elizabeth's greatest virtues was her fidelity to old friends. I knew she would never forget Mary Sidney's nursing, and every time she saw that sad pockmarked face, pity and gratitude welled up within her. She had arranged a marriage for young Mary Sidney with Henry Herbert, the Earl of Pembroke, and although he was twenty-seven years older than his bride, it was considered a very worthy match by all.

Robert was one who would always have a place in her heart, and if there were occasions when he was ousted there would always come the time when he would be reinstated. The truth was, she loved Robert, and she always would. Thus it was no great surprise that before six months had passed he was back in favor.

Alas, the same did not apply to me. I heard that the very mention of my name was enough to send her scarlet with rage and made her again swear in anger against the She-Wolf.

The vainest woman in the country could not forgive me for being more physically attractive than she was and for marrying the man who, in her heart, she had always wanted for herself. There were times when her anger flared up against him—this was largely due to his preference for me—but he was never really perturbed, for he knew that if her affection could survive his marriage it would outlast anything.

It is difficult to convey this charm of Robert's. It was a magnetism, and it was as potent now that he was aging as it had been in his youth. No one could be absolutely sure of him; he was an enigma. His manner was so charming and courtly, and he was always gracious to servants or those in a menial position, and yet that sinister reputation had clung to him since the death of Amy Robsart. There was a sense of power about him, and it may be that this was the essence of his attraction.

He was adored by his own family, and it was a fact that, as soon as my children knew him as their stepfather, they accepted him wholeheartedly. They were at greater ease with him than they had ever been with Walter.

It amazed me that he, who was so ambitious and full of determination to take up every advantage, should have so much time for the affairs of his family.

At this period Penelope was most unhappy. She often visited us at Leicester House and would pour out her wretchedness on the failure of her marriage. Lord Rich was coarse and sensual; she could never love him; she was most unhappy and longed to come home.

She was able to talk to Robert, who was so kind and understanding. He told her that whenever she felt so inclined she must regard his home as hers; and he forthwith suggested that she have one of the rooms decorated to her taste. It was to be known throughout the house as Lady Rich's Chamber and whenever she felt the need for refuge it was waiting for her.

She recovered a little of her spirits when she was with Robert and chose patterns for the hangings in her room and took an interest in the making of them. I was grateful to Robert for being a father to my unhappy daughter.

Dorothy loved him too. She had watched what had happened in Penelope's case and told Robert that she would never let it happen to her. She was going to choose her own husband.

He said: "I'll help you in it and we'll make a grand marriage for you—but only if you approve it."

She believed him, and both the girls looked forward to the times when he was with us.

Walter was fond of him, and it was Robert who made plans for my son to go to Oxford when he was older, which would be in a few years' time.

There was one member of the family whom I greatly missed. This was my favorite among all my children—my son Robert Devereux, Earl of Essex. How I wished that he could be with us, and how I deplored the custom of taking sons from their homes, particularly those who, through the death of their father, had inherited great titles. It was hard to think of my darling as the Earl of Essex— he would always be little Rob to me. I was certain that the other Robert, my husband, would have had a special interest in Essex, but alas, the boy was at Cambridge now, where he was to take his Master's degree. I had good reports of him from time to time.

As for yet another Robert—our baby son—Leicester doted on him and was already making plans for his future. I said jocularly that it would be difficult to find a place for him at Court because his father thought nothing was good enough for him. "Nothing but a royal princess will be suitable to be his bride," I commented.

"We must find one for him," said Robert, and I did not realize then how serious he was.

Leicester was as popular with my family as he was with his own brothers and sisters; it was comforting, particularly in view of the Queen's obsessional hatred towards me, to feel myself in the midst of an affectionate family.

Because I was out of Court—though Robert was fast creeping back to his old position—the family rallied round me even more than usual, and Robert's nephew, Philip Sidney, became a very frequent visitor.

He walked in the gardens of Leicester House in the

company of Penelope, and it occurred to me that there had been a change in their friendship. He had, after all, at one time been betrothed to her, but he had never seemed eager for marriage, and I had often thought it had been a mistake to mention it when he was twenty-two and Penelope but a child of fourteen. Now she appeared before him as a woman—and a tragic one at that—which made her seem attractive to a man of his nature. Her dislike of her husband was growing into hatred, and she was ready to turn to the handsome, elegant, brilliant young man whom she might so easily have married.

It could seem as though a dangerous situation was brewing, but when I mentioned it to Robert, he said that Philip was not a man to indulge in lusty passion, but to dream of romantic love. He would doubtless write verses to her and that would be where his devotion would lead him, so we need have no fear of Penelope's breaking her marriage vows. Lord Rich would be incensed if she did, and Philip would know this. He was certainly not a violent man; he consorted with people like the poet Spenser, for whom he had a great regard; he loved the play and took a special interest in the company of players, known as Leicester's Players, who, in the days before Robert's decline, performed regularly for the pleasure of the Queen.

The fact was that, having lost Penelope to Lord Rich, Philip did conceive a great passion for her and began to write poems to her in which he referred to himself as Astrophel and Penelope as Stella; but everyone knew of whom he wrote.

It was a situation which could be dangerous but I saw what it meant to Penelope. She blossomed again, and life became tolerable to her. She resembled me and I think that no matter what befell us, if we could find ourselves at the center of dramatic events, the excitement would carry us along.

So while she shared her husband's bed—and she told

me that he was a demanding husband in the bedchamber —she indulged in this romantic attachment with Philip Sidney, and she grew more beautiful every day. I could not help but be proud of my daughter, who was known as one of the most beautiful women at Court.

The Queen regarded her as Lady Rich rather than Penelope Devereux, that "She-Wolf's Cub," and she was causing a stir wherever she went. She was able to report to me what was happening at Court and how her stepfather was doing everything he could to further her advancement.

I must confess that I grew irked as time passed. It was a sadness for me to be outside the magic circle; but I was still told that whenever my name was mentioned, the Queen would fly into a rage, so it seemed unlikely that I could get back just yet. Even Robert had to tread very cautiously, and many a warning look was flashed at him from the tawny eyes. It was a time to take care.

The Duc d'Anjou came back to England to renew his courtship. Robert was worried because when Elizabeth was walking in the gallery at Greenwich with the Duc, before the French Ambassador, she said that they should marry.

"It was very disturbing," Robert told me, "and if it had been anyone but Elizabeth it would seem that she had in truth accepted him. Of course she had been fussing over him and caressing him in public. It is as though some spell has been cast upon her and she cannot see what others do. The little man is uglier than ever, for it is hardly to be expected that time would add to his beauty. He is more like an odious little frog than ever, yet she pretends to see great beauty in him. It is repulsive to see them together. She towers above him."

"She wants people to compare them and see how much more beautiful she is in spite of her age and his youth."

"It is a ludicrous sight—like a farcical play. The Country Wedding is not half as comic as the Queen and her French suitor together. But there in the gallery she actually kissed him and put a ring on his finger and told the French Ambassador that she would marry him!"

"Then surely she is committed."

"You don't know her. I had a meeting with her, and I demanded to know whether she was his mistress already. She replied that she was the mistress of us all, and I asked bluntly if she was still a virgin. She laughed at me and gave me a push—but a friendly one—and said: 'I am still a virgin, Robert, in spite of many attempts by men to induce me to change that happy state.' And she pressed my arm in a strange way and said: 'My Eyes should have no fear.' And I took it that she meant that she would not marry him after all. I believe she will now begin to extricate herself from this dilemma into which she has placed herself."

Of course that was what she did; and while she was confiding to her ministers that it had been necessary to gain time and keep the French and the Spaniards guessing, she would, with their help, evade the issue; but in the meantime, for the sake of appearance, they might start drawing up the marriage contracts.

I was so piqued because I could not watch her close at hand. I should have loved to have seen her frolicking with her Frog, declaring the happiest moment of her life would be on their wedding day, when all the time her sly, quick mind was seeking the most effective exit. She wanted the people to believe that Anjou was madly in love with her—not for what she could bring him but because of her enchanting person. It was strange that while so occupied with the political side of the issue, she could have such thoughts; but those who believed this impossible did not know Elizabeth.

Robert was delighted. He genuinely deplored the French match, but at the same time he could not have borne it if she had married someone else after refusing him. It amused me to see how the personal element was always present in these two, who were, I supposed, the most important people in my life. I watched myself with the same dissecting calm, I hoped, and I usually found more than one motive behind my own actions.

Robert reported that the Queen had sent a message to Anjou to the effect that she was afraid of marriage because she believed that if she entered into that state she would not have long to live, and she was sure that her death was the last thing he wanted.

"The little man was confounded," said Robert. "I think he is at last realizing that it will be no different with him than with the others who have sought her. He broke into furious lamentations when he heard this and taking off the ring she gave him, threw it away. Then he forced his way into her presence and said that he saw she was determined to deceive him and had never meant to marry him, at which she showed great concern, sighing deeply, declaring that if only these matters could be left to the heart, how much more pleasant life would be. He replied that he would rather they both died if he could not have her, and she then accused him of threatening her, which made him burst into tears like the silly little man he is. He blubbered that he could not endure that the world should know she had jilted him."

"And what did she do then?"

"She merely gave him her handkerchief with which to wipe his eyes. Ah, it is clear, Lettice, that she has no intention of ever marrying him and never had. But she has let us in for a fine bit of trouble, for now we have to placate the French, which will not be an easy task."

How right he was. The ambassadors of the King of France had already arrived in England to congratulate the couple and make the final arrangements for the marriage. When the true state of affairs was realized, the French Ambassador threw the Council into a state of panic by declaring that since the Duc d'Anjou had been insulted by the English, the French would ally themselves with Spain and that would not be a very pleasant prospect for the English.

Robert told me that the ministers had conferred together and the general opinion was that the matter had gone too far for them to draw back now. The Queen received them and demanded to know whether they were telling her that she had no alternative but to marry the Duc.

She had played with fire and if they were not careful a few fingers were going to be severely burned. She said there must be a way out of the situation, and she would find it. The marriage terms were discussed and the French showed themselves eager to comply with her demands, and in desperation she suddenly made the announcement that there was one clause which was vital to her agreement and that was that Calais should be returned to the English crown.

This was—and she knew it—outrageous. Calais—which her sister Mary had lost—had been the last stronghold possessed by the English, and in no circumstances would the French allow the English to get a foothold in France again. They must have realized at last that she was playing with them; and the situation then became fraught with danger.

She knew it better than anyone and she found an answer. The Spaniards were a menace. The little Duc was in one of his Protestant phases at the time and there would eventually have to be a confrontation with the Spaniards. The Queen firmly believed that such an encounter could more happily take place *outside* her realm; and as the Netherlands had sent out repeated calls for help, it might be a way out of a difficult situation to kill two birds with one stone by giving the Duc d'Anjou a sum of money to go to the Netherlands and conduct a campaign against the Spaniards there.

Nothing could be calculated to annoy Henri III of France and Philip of Spain more than that, and it would keep the little Prince's mind from matrimonial matters.

Languishing, as he said, with love for her, Anjou at length allowed himself to be persuaded to go to the Netherlands. Proudly she showed him her dockyard at Chatham, and the sight of so many fine ships impressed him greatly, but no doubt increased his desire to be her husband and master of them; and as she continued to show great affection for him he must have felt that this was still not an impossibility.

Robert came to me and told me what had happened. It deeply concerned him, he said, for she had told the Duc that as a mark of her great esteem, she was going to send with him, to escort him to Antwerp, a man whose presence at Court had always been more important to her than that of any other.

"You, Robert!" I cried.

He nodded.

I sensed the excitement in him, and I think my feelings for him began to change in that moment. He was back in favor; and I knew then that the ruling passion of his life— now as ever—was ambition. She, my royal rival, could give him what he craved. I was not a woman lightly to take second place.

He was glad to go to the Netherlands, even though it meant leaving me, because he saw opportunities there, and the fact that the Queen was sending him to be close to Anjou showed that she trusted him.

They were together again—my husband and his royal mistress. I might be the one his senses sought, but she was the one his head told him to follow, and even greater than his physical need was his ambition.

He did not notice that certain coldness in my manner.

He went on excitedly: "You see what she has been doing? She has been holding off the French all this time and now she has succeeded in getting Anjou to fight her battles for her."

His eyes were shining. She was a great woman, a great Queen. Moreover, all the tenderness she had shown to her Little Frog was devious politics. There was only one man whom she had ever loved enough to make her temporarily forget expediency and that was Robert Dudley.

He was hers to command. She had forgiven him for his marriage and was going to keep him with her. The marriage was unimportant. *She* did not want to marry him, in any case. But she was going to take my husband from me whenever she could. He was going to be reinstated as her favorite man and his wife was going to be denied the Court. This was her revenge on me.

I felt the cold anger rise within me. No, I was not a woman to be set aside lightly.

Of course he was passionately loving and assured me that he was going to hate leaving me, but already in his thoughts he was in the Netherlands, seizing what advantages he could there.

It was February when he left England. The Queen accompanied the party as far as Canterbury. I could not go because my presence would be repulsive to her.

I heard, though, that she took a fond farewell of my Robert, and talked to him very sharply because she feared he might eat or drink more than was good for him and not take enough care of himself. He caused her great anxiety by his thoughtlessness, she was heard to say; and she would recall him and put him into dire disgrace if she heard reports of ill health caused through lack of care.

Oh yes, she was still in love with him; and although she announced that she would give a million pounds to have her Little Frog swimming in the Thames, it was Robert of whom she was thinking.

"Leicester's Commonwealth"

His Lordship (Leicester) changeth wives and minions by killing the one, denying the other. . . .

Children of adulterers shall be consumed and the seed of a wicked bed shall be rooted out.

Leicester's Commonwealth

When Robert returned from the Netherlands, I was at Leicester House with Dorothy and my young son Robert. My elder son, Robert Devereux, Earl of Essex, had by this time taken his Master's degree at Cambridge and had expressed a desire for a quiet life, so Lord Burleigh, his guardian, had thought it an excellent idea for him to retire to one of his properties at Llanfydd in Pembrokeshire, where he could live the life of a country squire and devote himself to his books. I saw him only infrequently at this point, which did not please me, for, of all my children, he was my favorite.

Leicester had aged perceptibly. There was much more gray in his hair and his ruddy looks had intensified. The Queen was right to chide him for overindulgence at table. He had completely lost that mild depression which had been there after the disclosure of our wedding when he had thought, briefly, that he was out of favor forever. Now he was bursting with confidence.

He came into the house where I was waiting to greet him and swept me into his arms declaring that I was more beautiful than ever. He made love with the urgent need of a man who has abstained from the practice for a long time; but I sensed an absentmindedness, and I knew that my rival was Ambition.

I was faintly irritated that before coming to me he had been to the Queen. I knew this was necessary, but my jealousy made me irrational.

He could not stop talking of the future, which was going to be brilliant.

"She received me with great affection and berated me for staying away too long. She said she thought I had formed such an affection for the Low Countries that I had forgotten that of my birth and my gracious Queen."

"And perhaps," I put in, "your ever-patient wife."

"She did not mention you."

That made me laugh. "It was kind of her not to assault your ears with abuse of me."

"Oh, she'll get over that. I'll swear, Lettice, that in a few months' time she will be receiving you at Court."

"I'm ready to swear otherwise."

"I shall work for it."

"You'll waste your efforts."

"Nay, I know her better than you do."

"The only way you could obtain her forgiveness for me would be to leave me or rid yourself of me in some way. But no matter. She has taken you back into her loving circle, it seems."

"There is no doubt of it. And, Lettice, I believe there is a great future for me in the Netherlands. I was received with such courtesy. I believe they would be ready to make me Governor of the Provinces. They are a desperate country and they seem to look upon me as a savior."

"So, if you had the chance you would desert your royal mistress? I wonder what she would have to say to that!"

"I should have to persuade her."

"You have a big notion of your persuasive powers, my lord."

"How would you like to be Governor's lady?"

"Very well—since I am not accepted here as Leicester's Lady."

"It is only at Court."

"Only at Court! Where else is there to be recognized?"

He took my hands and his eyes were alight with that passion which ambition could kindle.

"I am going to see that our family is conveniently placed," he said.

"Haven't you done that? You seem to have set your relations and adherents in the right places throughout the country."

"I have always sought to secure my position."

277

"Yet you see how easily a frown from the Queen can unseat you."

"'Tis true. That is why I have to make sure that I strengthen my hold. There is young Essex. It is time he stopped skulking in Wales and came to Court. I could find a place for him."

"My son seems to like the country according to his letters to me and to Lord Burleigh."

"Nonsense. I have a fine stepson. I want to make his acquaintance again and bring him forward."

"I will write and tell him so."

"And our own little Robert . . . I have plans for him."

"He is but a baby."

"It is never too soon to plan their future, I assure you."

I frowned. I was anxious about our son. He was delicate, which seemed ironical when I considered his father and myself. My children by Walter Devereux were strong and healthy; it seemed a strange trick of fate that Leicester's boy should be a weakling. He had had difficulty in walking and I had discovered one of his legs to be a trifle shorter than the other, and when he eventually did walk it had been with a slight limp. I loved him the more for his deformity. I felt I wanted to care for him and protect him; and the thought of his making a great marriage made me uneasy.

"Whom do you propose for Robert?" I asked.

"Arabella Stuart," replied Robert.

I was aghast, seeing what he was thinking of. Arabella Stuart had a claim to the throne because she was the daughter of Charles Stuart, Earl of Lennox, the younger brother of the Earl of Darnley, who had married Mary Queen of Scots. Through his mother, the Earl of Lennox was the grandson of Henry VIII's sister, Margaret Tudor.

I said quickly: "You think she has a chance of the throne. How could she? Mary of Scotland's James comes before her."

278

"She was born on English soil," said Robert. "James is a Scot. The people would favor an English queen."

"Your ambition runs away with your good sense," I said tartly, and added: "You are like your father. He saw himself as the kingmaker, and he ended up without his head."

"I see no reason why there should not be a betrothal."

"And you think the Queen would allow it?"

"I think if I put it to her . . ."

"In cozy fashion," I suggested.

"What's the matter with you, Lettice? You must not be put out because Elizabeth will not receive you. I tell you I will soon have that changed."

"It seems you have come back from the Netherlands a conquering hero, sweeping all before you."

"You wait," he said. "I have other plans. What of Dorothy?"

"Dorothy! Have you a royal husband for her?"

"That's exactly what I have."

"I can't wait to hear whom you have found for her."

"Young James of Scotland."

"Robert, you can't be serious. My daughter Dorothy to marry the son of the Queen of Scots."

"Why should she not?"

"I should like to hear his mother's comments on the proposed match."

"Whatever they were they would be of no account. The Queen of Scots is but a prisoner."

"*And* those of your royal mistress."

"I believe Elizabeth could be persuaded. If James were to swear to remain a Protestant, she would be ready to accept him as her heir."

"And you, my lord, as his good father, would rule the kingdom. And if he should fail to reach the throne there is always Arabella. Have a care, Robert."

"I display the utmost care."

"You are indeed like your father. Remember him. He tried to make your brother Guildford King through Lady Jane Grey. Again let me remind you that it cost him his head. It's dangerous to dabble with crowns."

"Life is a dangerous gamble, Lettice, so one might as well play for high stakes."

"Poor Robert. You have worked hard. You almost reached the crown through Elizabeth. That was a bitter blow and shameful was the manner in which she kept you dangling all those years. Then it was: 'Robert, my Eyes, my Sweet Robin' and then just as you thought you had your hands on it, it was snatched away. At last you know how the game is played, but you don't give up, do you? You'll achieve your ambition secondhand, as it were. You'll place the power in your puppets' hands and you'll jerk the strings. Robert, you are the most outrageously ambitious man I have ever known."

"Would you have me otherwise?"

"You know full well I would not have you otherwise than you are, but at the same time I would say, Take Care. Elizabeth has received you back into favor, but she is unpredictable. You can be her Sweet Robin one day and That Traitor Leicester the next."

"But you see how she forgives me always. There could never have been a greater blow to her than our marriage, and if you could have seen her tenderness towards me when I was leaving for the Netherlands and on my return . . ."

"I was mercifully spared that."

"You must not be jealous, Lettice. My relationship with her is not to be compared with mine and yours."

"No, because she has refused you! It would have been a different matter if she had taken you, would it not? All I say is Take Care. Do not think because she had patted you on the cheek and said you eat too much that you may take

280

liberties with our gracious lady—or you will soon find that she is far from gracious."

"My dear Lettice, I think I know her better than anyone."

"You should. It has been a long acquaintance. But methinks the adulation you have received in the Netherlands may have made you see yourself a little more glorious than in truth you are. You are on dangerous ground, Robert, and I repeat that all I, as your humble wife, am doing is asking you to be careful."

He was not pleased. He had wanted me to applaud his schemes and to display a blind belief in his power to get what he wanted. He did not realize that I was changing towards him or how deeply I resented my expulsion from Court while he was received there with honors and seemed content that this should be so.

But even his new favor at Court did not save him from the Queen's wrath when she heard of his proposals. She sent for him and berated him soundly. I had his account of this—and that of others. She made it clear that both suggested marriages were anathema to her . . . simply because both of the participants were my children.

"Think not," she had screamed, so that many could hear, "that I would allow that She-Wolf to glory in her cubs."

So it was clear that I was not to be forgiven. I was no nearer to being received at Court.

Robert was downcast for a while and then as optimistic as ever. "It will pass," he said. "I promise you that ere long she will receive you."

But I doubted this, as the very mention of my name could throw her into such a fury.

She kept Robert at her side as much as possible. She was determined to show me, I was sure, that although I had scored a temporary victory in marrying him, the ultimate triumph would be hers.

If I was not to be received at Court, I was determined that, throughout the country, I would make my presence known. I began by introducing such magnificence into all our houses that people began to say that the Court was poor in comparison. I set seamstresses to work on the most beautiful materials available, and my gowns were as grand as any in the Queen's extensive wardrobe. I dressed my footmen in black velvet with silver boars embroidered on them, and I rode through London in a coach drawn by four white horses. When I moved out I was accompanied by attendants numbering fifty or more; and there was always a company of gentlemen to ride ahead and clear the way for my coach. People used to run out of their houses to see the cavalcade, convinced that it must be the Queen who was passing by.

I would smile on them as graciously as though I were indeed the Queen, and they would gape at me in wonder.

Sometimes I would hear the awestruck whisper: "It is the Countess of Leicester."

I enjoyed these excursions. I had only one regret and that was that the Queen could not see me. But I consoled myself with the knowledge that news of me made its way very quickly to my rival.

The Queen had knighted Philip Sidney in January, which showed that the family was in favor again. Absurdly enough, I was the only member of it who must remain in the cold. And my resentment grew.

Robert told me that Sir Francis Walsingham wanted to marry his daughter to Philip. He thought it was an excellent idea, for it was time Philip married. He was still writing poems extolling Penelope's beauty and his hopeless passion for her, but as Robert pointed out to me—and I agreed with him in this—Philip was not a passionate man who needed physical fulfillment. He was a poet, a lover of the arts, and to him a love affair conducted in verses would be more satisfactory and romantic than one which came to a natural conclusion. Penelope naturally enjoyed being adored in verse, but at the same time she was living with Lord Rich, and although it could not be said to be a happy marriage, at least she was bearing him children.

So the families thought that a union between Frances Walsingham and Philip was a good thing. Frances was a beautiful girl, and if Philip was temporarily lukewarm, they were sure he would change when he married.

Rather to my surprise Philip allowed the arrangements to go on and settlements were drawn up.

When Dorothy had heard of Robert's suggestion that she should marry James of Scotland, she had been a little upset. She told me that nothing on earth would have induced her to, even if the Queen had agreed to it.

"I believe him to be a most unpleasant person," she said. "Dirty and overbearing. Your husband is a little too ambitious, my lady."

"There is no need to upset yourself," I retorted. "The marriage will certainly not take place. The Queen would have you, me, and your stepfather in the Tower if we got as far as that!"

She laughed. "She *hates* you, my lady. I understand why."

"So do I," I answered.

She looked at me with admiration. "You never grow old," she told me.

I was delighted, for to hear such words from a young and critical daughter was praise indeed.

"I suppose it's because you live excitingly."

"Is my life so exciting?" I pondered.

"Of course it is. You married my father and then you took Robert and he was supposed to be married to Douglass Sheffield, and now the Queen hates you and you just snap your fingers and ride out looking as royal as she does."

"Nobody could do that."

"Well, you look more beautiful anyway."

"Not many would agree with you."

"*Everyone* would agree with me . . . though they might not admit it. I intend to live as you do. I shall snap my fingers at fate, and if your husband brings the King of France or Spain to marry me, I shall answer him by eloping with the man of my choice."

"As both these kings are married, and if they were not would certainly not marry *you*, that is a situation we need not worry about."

She kissed me and said life was exciting and how marvelous it must be to be Penelope—married to an ogre with the most beautiful young man at Court writing love odes to her, which everyone read and said were works of art and which would immortalize her. "I believe that the way to enjoy life is to make it merry."

"There may be something in that," I agreed.

I should have been warned, I suppose. Dorothy was seventeen and romantic, but I still thought of her as a child. Moreover, I was so immersed in my own affairs that it never occurred to me to look into those of my daughter.

When Sir Henry Cock and his wife invited her to spend a few weeks with them at Broxbourne it seemed a good idea for her to go, and she went off in high spirits.

Soon after she had left, Robert came to Leicester House from Greenwich, and it was clear from his demeanor that something unpleasant had happened. The Queen was in a rage. She had discovered that Philip Sidney was betrothed to Frances Walsingham and her permission had not been asked. She was very annoyed with all parties concerned, and as Philip was Robert's nephew, and Robert was known to take a great interest in family affairs, it occurred to the Queen that he had deliberately withheld the knowledge from her.

Robert had explained that he thought the matter not important enough to worry her with.

"Not important enough!" she had screamed. "Have I not shown favor to that young man! It is only this year that I made him a knight, and he sees fit to betroth himself to Walsingham's girl and say nothing to me!"

Walsingham had arrived, humbly enough, and when the Queen's rage had subsided he was allowed to explain that he also did not think his family of sufficient importance to warrant her interest.

"Of insufficient importance!" cried the Queen, "You should know that all my subjects are of importance to me, you, my Moor, as well as any." The very nickname used was a reproach, for, with her passion for nicknames, she called him her Moor on account of his dark brows. "You know full well that I am concerned for your family, and you sought to deceive me. I feel it in me to refuse permission for these two to marry."

She showed her displeasure for a few days before she relented and finally gave way, called the young couple to her, gave them her blessing and promised to be a godmother to their first child.

About this time one of Robert's most dangerous enemies died. This was Thomas Radcliffe, the Earl of Sussex. He had been ailing for a long time, which, to Robert's gratification, had meant his long absences from Court. Sussex had served the Queen wholeheartedly, he always claimed, and would let nothing—even her displeasure—stand in the way of his devotion. He had never recovered from the exposure he had endured during the Northern rebellion when he had helped put down her enemies. He was well aware of Robert's ambition and, I believe, genuinely disturbed as to where it would lead him and the Queen. He and Robert had almost come to blows one day in the Queen's presence and called each other traitors to Her Majesty. She hated to see those she loved at war with each other; she was always afraid that some harm would be done to them; so she had ordered that they be removed by the guards and stay in their chambers until their tempers cooled.

Yet it was Sussex who had warned her not to send Robert to the Tower when our marriage had been disclosed to her. In her rage she would have done so, but Sussex had realized the harm such an action would have done to her. As Robert had said, Sussex would have been delighted to see him a prisoner in the Tower, so it seemed there was some truth in the Duke's claim that his first endeavor was to do what was best for the Queen.

Now he was on his deathbed, and Elizabeth went to see him at his home in Bermondsey, where she sat by his bed and was very tender to him; she wept at his passing, for she felt deeply the loss of those men she had bound deeply to her.

He was greatly concerned, he said, because he believed there was much he could still do for her. She told him to rest in peace. None could have served her better and she wanted him to know that when she had been sharp with him she had lost none of her affection for him because she had always known, even when he irked her most, that it was for her own good.

He said: "Madam, I fear to leave you."

At which she laughed and said he had a great conceit of himself, and so had she of herself, which was why she believed she could deal with any who worked against her. She knew that he was warning her against Robert, whose ambition, he had often said, would stop at nothing.

There were several at Sussex's deathbed to report what his last words to those present had been: "I am now passing into another world," he said, "and must leave you to your fortunes and the Queen's graces. But beware of the gypsy for he will be too hard for you all. You do not know the beast as I do."

Of course he was referring to Robert.

Elizabeth mourned Sussex and declared again and again that she had lost a good servant; but she did not heed the warning about "the gypsy."

One day Sir Henry Cock came to Leicester House in a state of great concern. I was immediately anxious, for I guessed that something had happened to my daughter.

I was right. It seemed that Thomas Perrot, the son of Sir John Perrot, was also at Broxbourne, and he and my daughter had formed a romantic attachment. The vicar of Broxbourne had come to Sir Henry with an unusual story. He said that two strange men came to him and asked for the keys of his church. Naturally he refused to give them; they went away and after a while he grew uneasy and went to the church to see if all was well. He found that the church door had been forced open and that a marriage was in progress. One of the two men who had previously asked him for the keys was acting as a minister. The vicar then told them that they could not perform a marriage ceremony in his church, as he alone was entitled to do that. One of the men, whom he realized later was Thomas Perrot, then asked him to marry him. This the vicar refused to do and the strange man proceeded with the ceremony.

"The fact was," said Sir Henry, "the young lady in question was her daughter, the Lady Dorothy Devereux, and she is now the wife of Thomas Perrot."

I was dumbfounded, but as this was the sort of adventure I should have indulged in myself I could scarcely blame my daughter. It must be that she was in love with Perrot and determined to marry him, so I thanked Sir Henry and said that if the marriage were a true one—and it would be of the utmost importance to make sure that it was—then there was nothing we could do about it.

When Robert heard what had happened, he was at first annoyed. Dorothy had seemed to him a good bargaining counter. Who knew what other glittering prizes he might have drawn out of his imagination for her? The fact that James of Scotland was not possible would not deter him; and now she had removed herself by marrying Perrot.

The marriage was proved to be legal, and very soon after Dorothy and her husband came to Leicester House. She was radiantly happy and so was her husband, and, of course, Robert was charming to them. He promised he would do all he could to advance them. Robert, as always, was the devoted family man.

It was the end of the old year 1583 and fortunately I had no idea then of the tragedy the new year would bring to us. Both Robert and I had always tried to hide our anxieties about our little son, by telling each other that lots of children were delicate in their infancy and grew out of it.

He was a bright little fellow, gentle in demeanor; he certainly did not take after either of his parents. He adored Robert, who, when he was at home, lost little time before paying a visit to the nursery. I have seen him carry the child on his shoulders while little Robert screamed with delighted terror as he was swung in the air, and, when put down, demanded more.

He loved us both. I think we seemed godlike to him. He liked to see me ride out in my chariot drawn by four white horses and my memory of him, his little hands stroking one of the ornaments on my dress, will stay with me forever.

Leicester was continually making plans for great marriages and he would not have given up the idea of Arabella Stuart even though the Queen had poured scorn on it.

After Sussex's death, Robert seemed more than ever with the Queen. I knew that one of her pleasures in keeping him constantly at her side came from the fact that she deprived me of his company. You may be his wife, she was telling me, but I am his Queen.

She was loving to him. He was her dear Eyes and Sweet Robin, and she became irritable if he stayed away from her for long. Sussex's warning had left her completely unmoved. They were saying at Court that no one would ever take his place with her, for if he could survive his marriage he could survive anything.

Alas her enmity towards me showed no sign of abating, and I was constantly hearing that it was unwise to mention my name in her presence and that on the occasions when she spoke of me it was always as that She-Wolf. She had evidently decided to accept my "cubs," though, for both Penelope and Dorothy were received at Court.

As the new year approached it was time to prepare the Queen's New Year's gifts. Robert had always endeavored to make each year's outstrip the previous one. I helped him to choose his gift, which was a large porringer of dark green stone with two magnificent gilt handles curled about it like golden snakes. It was most impressive. Then I discovered that he had another gift for her. It was a necklace made of diamonds. He had given jewels on many occasions, but never anything quite so extravagant as this. I felt myself go cold with rage when I saw that it was decorated with lovers' knots, and I believe I would have torn it apart if I could have done so.

He found me holding it in my hands.

"To placate Her Majesty," he said.

"You mean the lovers' knots?"

"That's just a design. I mean the diamonds."

"It's what I call a rather bold design, but I am sure the Queen will approve of it."

"She will be delighted with it."

"And no doubt ask you to clasp it round her neck?"

"I shall claim that honor." He must have sensed my mood, for he added quickly: "Perhaps if she is softened enough I might ask the all-important question."

"And that is?"

"That she will receive you at Court."

"You would not please her by begging such a favor."

"Nevertheless I intend to do my utmost to bring it about."

I looked at him cynically and said: "If I were there, your position would be difficult, Robert. You would have to play the lover to two women—and both of them of uncertain temper."

"Now, Lettice, let us be sensible. You know I have to placate her. You know I have to be in attendance. It makes no difference to us."

"It makes a great deal of difference. It means I have a husband whom I rarely see because he is constantly dancing attendance on another woman."

"She'll come round."

"I see no sign of it."

"Leave it to me."

He was jaunty and confident as he went off to put the lovers' knots round the royal neck, while I asked myself how long I was expected to endure this. There had been a time when I had been reckoned to be the most beautiful woman at Court; and the reason I was not now known as such was not due to a fading of my charms, but simply because I was not there.

I asked him as soon as I had an opportunity how the Queen had liked the necklace. He smiled complacently.

"It pleased her mightily. She would wear it immediately and has scarce put it aside since."

"A clever choice, I see. And was she any more inclined to look with favor on the giver's wife?"

He shook his head gloomily. "You know her temper.

She became moody when I broached the subject and made it clear that she was not ready to consider it yet."

I knew that I was as far from being received at Court as ever.

It was true we entertained at Leicester House, Kenilworth, Wanstead and our other smaller residences and then I came into my own, but it seemed that whenever I was enjoying my role as wife to the most influential man in England, the Queen would decide that she would visit the Earl of Leicester and that meant that Leicester's wife must disappear.

My patience was beginning to run out. Robert was still my loving husband—when he was with me—and I made it my business to make sure that there was no other woman in his life—apart from the Queen. Whether this was due to a slackening of desire because of his increasing years, the satisfaction he derived from me, or fear of incurring the Queen's displeasure, I could not say; but whatever else Robert was he was the Queen's man, and that was something she was never going to allow him—or me—to forget.

He might be satisfied with his rising star but I was certainly not with my declining one.

In my frustration at being excluded I gave way to even wilder extravagance. I wore more glittering gowns when I rode out, and added to my retinue. As I passed through the streets people stood in greater awe than before and once I heard it whispered: "She's a grander lady than the Queen herself." And that gave me pleasure . . . but only temporarily.

Was I, Lettice, Countess of Leicester, going to allow myself to be pushed aside simply because another woman was so jealous of me that she could not bear to hear my name mentioned? It was not in my nature to accept that. Something was going to happen.

I was considerably younger than Leicester, considerably younger than the Queen. They might be satisfied with the state of affairs, but I was not.

I began to look around and found that in our own household there were some very attractive men. That I had lost none of my appeal I could see by the covert glances that came my way—though none, fearing Leicester's terrible wrath, would dare make their meaning clear.

Naturally this state of affairs could not go on indefinitely.

In May of that year news reached England of the death of Anjou. There was talk of his having been poisoned, as there always was when someone important died, and one suggestion was that Robert's spies had been responsible because he feared the Queen might marry Anjou. That was nonsense and even Robert's enemies gave little credence to the story. The fact was well known that the Queen's Little Frog Prince had been a poor specimen of manhood—stunted, pockmarked as he was, he had indulged his senses to excess and no doubt because of his frail physique had suffered through this.

The Queen went into deep mourning for him and bewailed her loss. He was the one man she would have married, she declared, but no one believed her. I was never quite sure whether she deluded herself into thinking she might have married him; it was certainly safe to think so now that he was dead. It was difficult to understand how she, so clearheaded in state matters, should have his strange obsession about marriage. I think that it might have soothed her in some way to let herself believe that had Anjou lived she might have married him. She now needed Leicester close to her, so that one lover could compensate her for the loss of the other.

Anjou's death was followed by that of the Prince of Orange, the hope of the Netherlands, who was assassinated by a fanatic incited by the Jesuits. There was deep gloom throughout the country and the Queen was constantly in conference with her ministers, which meant that I scarcely saw my husband at all.

When he did pay me a brief visit he told me that the Queen was not only concerned about what was happening in the Netherlands, but the success of the Spaniards there made her very much afraid of Mary Queen of Scots. Ever since that queen had been the prisoner of ours, there had been alarms. Plots were constantly formed to rescue her and set her on the throne. Robert told me that again and again Elizabeth had been advised to get rid of her, but she believed that royalty was divine and whatever annoyance Mary of Scotland caused her, she still remained royal and a crowned queen at that. There could be no doubt of her legitimacy and claim to royalty, which made her all the more deadly an enemy. Elizabeth once told Robert that she was prepared to die at any time because no one's life was more threatened than her own.

The Court was at Nonsuch and I was at Wanstead when my little son's health took a turn for the worst. I called in our physicians and the gravity of their comments threw me into deep despair.

My little son had been subject to fits which left him very weak after they occurred; and all that year I had feared to leave him to nurses. He seemed to find great comfort in my presence and looked so sorrowful when I even hinted at going away that I could not leave him.

The July heat was oppressive and as I sat by his bedside I thought about my love for his father—of which he was the fruit—and how important Robert had once been to me, dominating my life. I had thought then that the affection between us would last forever and even now I knew that I should never be quite free of it. If we could have lived together without the shadow of the Queen over us, I believe ours might have been the greatest love story of our times. Alas, though, she was there. There was a trio where there should have been two. The Queen and Robert were larger than life, I always thought; and perhaps I, too, had a little of that quality. Not one of the three of us would set aside our pride or ambition, our self-love, or whatever it was. If I could have been the meek, adoring wife which Douglass Sheffield might have been, it would have been easier. I could have been content to remain in the shadows and allow my husband to wait upon the Queen, to give her the adulation she demanded and accept this as necessary to his career.

I could never do that; and I knew that sooner or later I would make that clear.

And now our child was in danger and I felt that when he died—as I feared he would—the link which bound me to Robert Dudley would have grown a little weaker.

When I sent a messenger to Court to tell Robert of the condition of our son, his response was immediate.

As I greeted him in the hall I could not resist saying: "So you came. She spared you."

"I should have come had she not," he answered. "But she is most concerned. How is the boy?"

"Sadly sick, I fear."

Together we went to our child.

He lay in his bed looking small and wan in all that magnificence which I had made for him. We knelt by his bed and Robert held one hand and I the other and we assured him that we should stay with him as long as he wanted us.

That made him smile and the pressure of those hot little fingers on my hand filled me with such emotion as I could scarcely bear.

He died peacefully while we looked on and then our grief was so intense that we could only cling together and mingle our tears. We were not the ambitious Leicesters at that time—only two unhappy, bereaved parents.

We buried him in the Beauchamp Chapel at Warwick and we had a statue made of him lying on his tomb in a long gown; the description described him as the "Noble Impe" and stated who he was and the date of his death at Wanstead.

The Queen sent for Robert and declared that she was determined to comfort him. She wept for the dear lost child and said that Robert's sorrow was hers. Her sympathy, however, did not extend to the child's mother. Not a word did she send me. I was still the outcast.

That was a year of disaster, for it was not long after the death of my child that a most scurrilous pamphlet appeared.

I found this in my bedchamber at Leicester House so someone must have put it there intentionally for me to see. It was the first I heard of it but in a short time the whole Court, the whole country were to be talking of it.

The target was Leicester. How he was hated! There could never have been a man who aroused such envy. He was now once more high in the Queen's favor and it seemed that none could ever displace him. Her affection for him was as steadfast as her hold on the crown. Robert must have been the richest man in the country; he spent lavishly and was often embarrassed for money, but that only meant that he had temporarily spent more than he could afford. He was at the Queen's side when she made important decisions, and some said, he was King in all but name.

So they envied him and their hatred was venomous.

I looked at the small book which was entitled *The Copye of a Letter wryten by a Master of Arte at Cambridge.*

On the first page my husband's name caught my eyes. "You know the Bear's love which is all for his paunch. . . ." I read, and I was soon in no doubt that the Bear was Robert.

There followed an account of his relationship with the Queen. I wondered what she would say if she ever saw it. And then . . . his crimes. Naturally Amy Robsart's death was one of the highlights. According to the pamphlet, Robert had acquired a certain Sir Richard Verney to murder her and made the way clear for the Queen and him to marry.

Douglass Sheffield's husband was mentioned as having been poisoned by Leicester and was said to have died of an artificial catarrh which stopped his breath. I knew what was coming next, for I could not hope to escape the libel. There it was. Leicester had taken me in lust while my husband lived and when I was with child we destroyed the child and afterwards he had my husband murdered.

It seemed that any person who had died mysteriously had been poisoned by him. Even the Cardinal de Chatillon was alleged to have been a victim because he threatened to make it known that Leicester had prevented the marriage of Elizabeth with Anjou.

Robert's Dr. Julio was mentioned as the man whose expert knowledge of poisons had aided Leicester in his wicked work.

I was astonished. I read on and on. So much in this book could be true, but it defeated its end by the absurd exaggerations and accusations. On the other hand it was a blow at Leicester, and the manner in which his name had been coupled with that of the Queen would create a very unpleasant situation.

Within a few days the pamphlet, which had been printed in Antwerp, was circulated throughout London and the country. Everyone was talking about what they were calling *Leicester's Commonwealth*.

Philip Sidney came riding over to Leicester House. He

was furious and declared that he was going to write a reply in defense of his uncle. The Queen made an order of the Council that the book—which she declared to her knowledge was entirely false—should be suppressed; but that was not an easy thing to bring about. People were ready to risk a good deal to get their hands on *Leicester's Commonwealth*. It was more interesting, though, than Philip's beautifully written piece in which he asked the man who had written this scurrilous pamphlet to come forth, but he knew him to be a base and wretched tongue that dared not speak his own name. He added that on his father's side he belonged to a great and noble family, but his chief honor was to be a Dudley.

It was no use. *Leicester's Commonwealth* flourished; and all the evil stories, which in the past had been hinted and whispered, were now set down in print—and more calumnies added.

There could be no doubt that as that tragic year passed Robert was the most talked of man in England.

The Overseas Adventure

*The Delegation arrived at the great chamber and spoke
"an oration to me. . . . They came to offer me, with many
good wordes for Her Majestic's sake, the absolute government of the whole provinces. . . ."*

LEICESTER *to* BURLEIGH

*The Queen is so discontent with your acceptance of the
government there, before you had advertised and had Her
Majestie's opinion, that, although I, for my own part,
judge this action both honourable and profitable, yet Her
Majestie will not endure to hear my speech in defence
thereof.*

BURLEIGH *to* LEICESTER

*With great oaths and referring to the Countess of Leices-
ter as "the She Wolf", the Queen declared there should
be "no more courts under her obeisance than her own and
would revoke you from thence with all speed."*

THOMAS DUDDLEY *to his master*
the EARL OF LEICESTER

The circulation of *Leicester's Commonwealth* could not fail to have its effect, even on me. I began to wonder how much of it was true and to look at my husband through fresh eyes. It was indeed a strange coincidence that the people who had stood in his way had been removed at remarkably convenient moments. He was, of course, rarely on the scene of the crime, but then he had his spies and servants everywhere. I had always known that.

I was overcome by uneasiness. How much did I know of my husband? If there was even some truth in what I was reading, I had to admit my position must be a precarious one. What if the Queen after all decided she might marry him, what would he do? Would he find the prospect irresistible? Should I be found at the bottom of a staircase with a broken neck? It seemed a logical outcome.

I considered us all—the three who formed this unholy trio. We were all complicated people, and none of us overscrupulous. Both Robert and Elizabeth had lived dangerously all their lives. Elizabeth's mother and Robert's father had both died violent deaths on the scaffold, and they themselves had come within a few paces of a similar fate. As for myself, I had been required by the Queen to live more in the shadows; but I was married to a man who, according to *Leicester's Commonwealth*, wielded the poison cup and other lethal weapons without compunction. The mystery of Amy Robsart would never be cleared; all that was known was that she died at a time when her death could have brought Robert's elevation to the side of the Queen. I thought of Douglass Sheffield, who had at one time become an embarrassment to him. Her nails had started to disintegrate and her hair to fall out. She had not died, but had apparently come near to it. What did we know of the dangers through which she had passed? At least she was now the most contented of wives, for Edward Stafford adored her.

I was growing more and more dissatisfied. It seemed to me that the Queen would never relent towards me. If she had denied her presence to Robert, I should have been somewhat reconciled. He was rich, and even if he had had no more favors from the Queen, we could have lived in great style at Kenilworth, Wanstead, Cornbury, Leicester House—or one of his manors—and I should have been romantically regarded as the woman for whom he considered the Queen's favor well lost.

But it was not so and, being determined to punish me, she took a malicious delight in keeping him from my side. For what? For being preferred by him! She was anxious to show me—and the world—that he would desert me any day for her. And he did.

On his brief visits we made passionate love, but I wondered if he realized that even our old ardor was changing for me. I wondered if Elizabeth noticed the change in *him*. A man who had lived as Robert had could not expect to escape unscathed. He had lived too richly, indulged himself too freely in what people call the good things of life, and the result was periodic visits to Buxton, where he took the waters and lived on simpler fare and hoped his gout would subside. Being so tall, he was still an impressive figure, and the aura, which had made him stand out like a prince in a crowd, remained. He was a man who created his own destiny. The legends which were attached to him would always make people speak his name with awe. He remained the most discussed man in the country, a role he thoroughly enjoyed and sought. The Queen's devotion to him, which had lasted for nearly a lifetime, would never be forgotten. But he was an aging figure now, and when I saw him after absences I was always a little shocked by his appearance.

I took great care of myself, determined to appear

young as long as I could. Being denied the Court, I had time to experiment with herbs and lotions which kept my skin beautiful. I bathed in milk; I made special washes for my hair which helped to keep its shining color. I used paint and powder with a skill unrivaled by the Queen's women, and so I preserved a youthful look which denied my years. I thought of Elizabeth—older than I—and I took a distinct pleasure in studying myself in my mirror and examining my complexion, which appeared—aided by those adjuncts to beauty which I could apply with such skill—as fresh as a young girl's.

Robert always declared himself astonished when he saw me after being away for some time. "You have not changed since the day I first saw you," he said. An exaggeration but a welcome one; yet I did know that I had preserved a certain flowerlike freshness, which gave me a look of innocence so ill matched by my nature that it may have been this contrast which set me apart and was the secret of my appeal to men. In any case I was kept aware of my attractions on which Robert never failed to comment. He often compared our Vixen with his Lamb —to the detriment of the former course and this he did to put me in a good mood. He did not want the time we spent together wasted in recriminations. He desperately hoped that we should have another child; but I was not eager for that. I would never really get over the loss of my little Robert, which may sound false in a woman of my nature, but is nevertheless true. That I was selfish, I knew, sensual, looking for admiration, seeking pleasure. . . . I recognized all this. I had learned too that I was not overscrupulous in the manner in which I reached my desires—but in spite of this I was a good mother. I take pride in that even now. All my children loved me. To Penelope and Dorothy I was like a sister, and they confided their matrimonial secrets to me. Not that Dorothy had trials at this time; she was blissfully happy in her runaway match. It was different with Penelope. She told me in detail of the sadistic habits of Lord Rich, the husband she had never wanted, of his taunts because of Philip Sidney's passion for her, and of the lurid life of their bedchamber. Such was her nature—so similar to mine—that she was not entirely cast down by all this. Life was exciting to her: the long battles with her husband; the sublime devotion of Philip Sidney (I often wondered what his wife, Frances, thought of that); and the constant looking forward to what adventures the day would bring. So I had my girls.

As for my boys, I saw Robert, the Earl of Essex, now and then. I insisted because I could not endure the separation. He was living in his house at Llanfydd in Pembrokeshire, which I protested was too far away. He had grown into a very handsome young man. His temper was a little uncertain and, I had to admit, that there was a definite waywardness, an arrogance in his nature; but the mother in me quickly protested that this was overshadowed by his perfect manners and an innate courtesy which was very appealing. He was tall and slender, and I adored him.

I urged him to join the family but he shook his head and a stubborn look I well knew came into his eyes.

"Nay, dearest Mother," he said, "I was not meant to be a courtier."

"You look like one, my darling."

"Appearances often lie. Your husband would want me to go to Court, I believe, and I am happy in the country. *You* should come to me, Mother. We two were not meant to be apart. Your husband is, I hear, often in close attendance on the Queen, so he perhaps would not miss you."

I noticed the contemptuous curve of his lips. He was one who had great difficulty in concealing his feelings. He was not pleased by my marriage. I sometimes thought he resented Leicester because he knew how much I cared for him, and he wanted all my affection bestowed on him. And of course hearing how Leicester neglected me for the Queen would make him angry too. I knew my son.

Young Walter idealized his brother Robert and spent as much time as he could in his company. Walter was a dear boy—a pale shadow of Essex, I always thought. I loved him, but the feeling I had for any of my children could not approach the intensity of that I felt for Essex.

But those were happy days when I could gather my family around me and we could sit at the fireside and talk together. They recompensed me in many ways for the loss of my life at Court and the company of my husband who was often there.

Being content with the children I had, I did not want the inconvenience of bearing more. I reckoned I was too old for that. Childbirth would be an ordeal for me now and I had had my share of it.

I did remember how eager I had once been to have a child by Robert. Fate had given us our little angel, our "Noble Impe"; but with him had come great anxiety and sorrow. I should never forget his death and those nights I had spent at his bedside after one of his fits. And now he was gone, but while I mourned his loss deeply, a great anxiety was lifted from me. There was compensation in knowing that my little darling was suffering no more. Sometimes I would ask myself whether his death had been a punishment for my sins. I wondered whether Leicester felt the same.

No, I did not want more children and this might be a sign that I was falling out of love with Robert.

When I was at Leicester House, where I liked best to be because of its closeness to the Court—so near and yet so far for those excluded from it—I saw more of Robert because it was easier for him to slip away for brief periods. But we could not be together for more than a few days before the Queen's messenger would arrive to demand his return to Court.

On one occasion he came to me rather preoccupied. After his protestations of eternal fidelity to me and that consummation of our passion which I fancied he tried to endow with the eagerness we had both known when we had snatched our secret meetings, I realized what had brought him this day.

It was a man named Walter Raleigh who was causing him some disquiet.

I had heard of him, of course. His name was on everyone's lips. Penelope had met him and said he was undoubtedly handsome and possessed of great charm; the Queen had quickly brought him into her intimate circle. He had leaped into prominence, the story went, one wet day when the Queen was returning to the palace on foot and had paused before a muddy stretch of ground over which she had to cross. Raleigh had taken off his elaborate plush cloak and spread it over the dirty ground that she might walk on it. I could picture the scene: the graceful gesture, the expensive cloak, the glitter in those tawny eyes as she noticed the handsome looks of the young man; the speculation in those of the adventurer who no doubt counted the cost of an elaborate cloak well lost for the sake of rich benefits to come.

It had not been long after that incident that Raleigh was at the Queen's side, delighting her with his wit, his compliments, his adoration, and his accounts of past adventures. She had grown very fond of him and had knighted him that very year.

Penelope told me that at one of the palaces—Greenwich, I think—when he was in the company of the Queen, he had tested her affection for him by scratching on a windowpane with a diamond the words:

Fain would I climb
Yet fear I to fall.

as though asking her to assure him that he would have nothing to fear by trying to rise in her favor.

Characteristically she took the diamond from him and beneath his couplet scratched the words:

If thy heart fails thee
Climb not at all.

which was in a way stressing the fact that her favors must be sought at all times and that no one should believe he would be favored without merit.

Robert had believed, after he had been taken back into favor, that his position was secure. So it was, I was certain; whatever he did she would never forget the bond between them. At the same time he was anxious that no young man should rise too high in her favor, and it appeared that this was exactly what Raleigh was doing. It was galling to Robert to see a younger man constantly beside the Queen; ever present was the fear that someone younger would replace him in her favor. She knew this, of course, and loved to tease him. I was sure that she showed Raleigh more favor when Robert was near than she ever did in his absence.

"Raleigh is giving himself airs," he told me. "Soon he will be thinking himself the most important man at Court."

"He is very good-looking," I replied slyly. "He has the qualities, it seems, which appeal to Her Majesty."

"True enough, but he is inexperienced, and I will not have him giving himself such airs."

"How will you stop him?"

Robert was thoughtful. Then he said: "It is time for young Essex to come to Court."

"He is happy enough in Llanfydd."

"He cannot spend his life there. How old is he now?"

"He is but seventeen."

"Old enough to begin making a way for himself. He has great charm and should do well at Court."

"Don't forget that he is *my* son."

"That's one of the reasons why I wish to bring him to Court, my dearest. I want to do everything I can for him . . . because I know how fond you are of him."

"He is a son to be proud of," I said fondly.

"Would he were mine! But the next best thing is that he is yours. Let him come here. I promise you I will do everything possible for his advancement."

I looked at him shrewdly. I understood the way in which his mind worked. It was true that Leicester liked to advance members of his family, for it had always been a policy of his to put what he called "his own men" in high places.

"But the fact that Rob is *my* son is enough to make our Vixen chase him out of Court."

"I don't think she will . . . when she sees him. In any case it's worth a try."

I laughed. "You seem greatly put out by Raleigh."

"He is of little moment," he said abruptly. "I think young Essex will amuse the Queen."

I shrugged my shoulders. "I will ask my son to come to me, and then perhaps if your mistress will allow you to leave her for a short time, you can meet him here and assess him."

Robert said he would be delighted to see my son, and I could rest assured that he would do all in his power to bring him forward at Court.

When Robert had gone I continued to think about it. I pictured his presenting my son to the Queen. "My stepson, the Earl of Essex, Your Majesty."

Those tawny eyes would be alert. *Her* son! The She-Wolf's cub! What chance would he have? It was true he had been born before I had fallen from favor, before she knew of her darling Robin's passion for me. But she would never accept my son.

Of course he was extraordinarily handsome; he had a unique charm; he was the kind of young man the Queen liked to have about her—except for one thing: he would never flatter her.

It would be amusing to see what effect he had on her. I would do what Leicester wanted and attempt to persuade him to go to Court and see what happened.

How often have I wished that I had the gift of prophecy. If I could but have seen into the future! If I could have glimpsed the anguish to come—then I should never have allowed my darling to go to her.

But her life and mine were linked by some tragic caprice of fate. We were doomed to fix our love on the same object—and what bitter suffering that was to cause me! And I do not believe that she escaped unscathed.

"Raleigh?" said Penelope. "He is a dashing fellow. Tom Perrot was talking of him when I spent a few days with him and Dorothy on my way here. Tom says he is quick-tempered. An ill-chosen word directed against him can plunge him into violent rage. Tom himself had a fracas with him, and they both landed up in the Fleet and spent six days there before their release was brought about. He said that a short while after, Raleigh was in the Marshalsea following a fight on the tennis court with someone named Wingfield. He's an adventurer. He's like the Queen's darling, Francis Drake. You know how she loves such men."

"So she loves this one?"

"Oh, he is one of her admirers! How she can listen to such false compliments I can never understand."

"Few understand the Queen—nor does she intend them

to. Leicester wants to present Essex to her. How think you that will work?"

"Well, he's good-looking enough to please her and can be charming when he wishes. Has he agreed to come to Court?"

"Not yet. I am sending a messenger asking him to come to me. Leicester will then arrive to turn on the persuasive powers."

"I doubt he'll come. You know how stubborn he can be."

"Stubborn and impulsive," I agreed. "He has always acted without much thought. But he is over young. He'll change, I doubt not."

"He will have to change a great deal—and quickly," commented Penelope. "He will never be able to pay those extravagant false compliments which the Queen demands from her young men. You know, he always speaks his mind, Mother. He has been thus since he was a boy."

As Essex had spent a good deal of time with the Riches in recent years I could be sure his sister knew what she was talking about.

I said: "Well, I don't think the Queen will receive him, since he is my son."

"She received us," replied Penelope, "though I have to admit she gives us some odd looks now and then and snaps at us rather sharply. Dorothy said the same."

"She's thinking all the time that you are the She-Wolf's cubs, as she so elegantly calls you."

"Who knows, perhaps between them your husband and your son will be able to persuade her to have you back."

"I doubt Essex would be able to do what my Lord Leicester has failed to."

Although she wanted to cheer me, I could see that Penelope agreed. Even after all these years it was unlikely that the Queen would relent.

Then we talked of family matters and how she hated her husband, and how difficult life was with him.

"I could endure him more if he were not so religious," Penelope told me. "But it is maddening, the manner in which he kneels down and prays before getting into bed and then proceeds to . . . well, I will leave that to your imagination, for I would prefer not to remind myself of it. He is demanding my dowry now and says he has had little from the marriage. And I have already given him his sons Richard and Charles and—curse of curses—I am pregnant again."

"He should be delighted that you are so fruitful."

"I assure you I don't share his delight."

"Philip does not seem to find you any less delectable."

"It is pleasant of course to be honored in verse, but Philip seems content enough with that."

"What does Frances think of these poems to another woman?"

"She raises no objection. He pays some attention to her clearly, since she has been delivered of a daughter whom, most loyally, she has named after Elizabeth our Queen. Her Majesty has shown a certain interest in her namesake."

Thus we chatted, and the time I spent with my daughter passed merrily as always.

In due course, Essex obeyed my summons and came to Leicester House. How proud I was of him when I presented him to his stepfather!

He was indeed a son to be proud of. Every time I saw him I was astonished by his handsome looks because I always felt that I underestimated them in my thoughts. His coloring was similar to mine. He had abundant hair, though his was more auburn than mine, and the large dark Boleyn eyes. He was very tall and, I suppose because he so often had to look down to people, he stooped slightly.

He had delicate, beautiful hands, and the fact that he left them unadorned seemed to call attention to their elegance. His Venetian breeches—very full at the top and narrowing towards the knee—were in the finest velvet and slashed and puffed, but not in the height of fashion when compared with those in the French style, which Leicester, the courtier, was wearing. Essex's cloak was embroidered with gold lace, I remember—but what did it matter what he wore? He could never look anything but completely distinguished. He wore all his clothes with an indifference which accentuated his natural elegance; and I was fondly amused to notice his determination not to be impressed by the Queen's favorite. In fact, he was not going to hide his contempt for a man who allowed his wife to be disdainfully treated, even though it was by the Queen.

He was clearly suspicious of Leicester's intentions—and I was fully aware of them. I had previously found my husband's desire for friendship with my family endearing, but now under the influence of *Leicester's Commonwealth* I looked for other motives behind the affectionate interest. By entering his orbit they became his men and women and their function would be to further his ends.

I was a little resentful and uneasy. I did not want him to use my son. Perhaps after all I was at that time not without a little foreknowledge. Then I dismissed my fears. It would be amusing to see whether Leicester could persuade young Rob to do what he wanted, and even more so to learn how the Queen received him.

Before Leicester's arrival I had told my son that his stepfather had something to discuss with him. Essex had replied rather curtly that he was not interested in Court matters.

"You must please be courteous to members of my family," I reproved him.

"I do not like matters as they stand," retorted my son. "Leicester spends his days dancing attendance on the

Queen in spite of the fact that she will not receive you at Court."

"He has other duties besides dancing attendance. He holds many posts in the government."

Essex looked mulish. "If she won't receive you, he should refuse to see her."

"Rob! You are talking of the Queen."

"I don't care. Leicester should first be loyal to you. I hear talk and resent it. I always will to see you humiliated."

"Oh, Rob my darling, I love you for your folly. There is nothing else he can do. Please see that. The Queen hates me for marrying him. She is determined to keep him from me. You must understand it would be disastrous for him to disobey her."

"If I were in his place . . ." muttered Rob, clenching his fist in a manner which made me laugh tenderly and happily. It was wonderful to have such a champion.

"You have lived overlong in the country," I told him. "Leicester owes his fame and fortune to her . . . and so will you."

"I! You will never make a courtier of me. I prefer a life of dignity in the country. I learned that in Burleigh's household. To see a wise old statesman like that tremble at the command of a woman! No, it is not for me. I will keep my freedom, my independence. I will live my life my own way."

"I doubt not you will do that, my son. But you do understand, do you not, that your mother wants the best for you."

He turned to me then and embraced me. My love for him overwhelmed me.

Then Leicester arrived, all charm and bonhomie.

"What a pleasure it gives me to see you," he cried. "Why, you are indeed a man. I wish for us to grow better acquainted. You are my stepson now, remember, and families should cling together."

"I agree with that," said Essex sharply. "It is wrong that a husband should be at Court when his wife is not received there."

I was aghast. Essex, I knew well, had never been one to consider his words, but he must know something of Leicester's power and how unwise it was to offend him. Hadn't he read *Leicester's Commonwealth!* I did not believe he would harm my son, but no man should make an enemy of Leicester.

"You don't know the Queen's temper, Rob," I said quickly.

"Nor do I want to," he retorted.

I could see that it was not going to be easy to persuade him.

As always I had to admire Leicester's tact. It was obvious how he had managed to hold his place at Court. He smiled indulgently, giving no sign that this green boy, who was clearly ignorant of Court matters, irritated him. He was patient and gentle, and I believed Essex was a little bewildered by him. I could see his opinion changing as Leicester talked easily and affably, and then listened with rapt attention to my son's views. I admired him as much as I ever had and, as I watched the two of them together, I thought how fortunate I was to have two such men holding such a place in my life—Leicester, a name to inspire awe and respect throughout the country; and Essex . . . ? Perhaps one day his would be the same.

In that moment I could snap my fingers at the Queen. Leicester might dance to her tune, but only because she was the Queen. I was his wife. I was the woman he loved. And in addition I had this wonderful son. Leicester and Essex. What more could any woman ask?

I realized that Essex was asking himself where was the villain of *Leicester's Commonwealth* and, in his impulsive way, dismissing this work as nonsensical libel. Watching them, I thought how different they were . . . these two Earls of mine. Leicester so clever, so subtle, speaking usually with exceeding caution—and Essex, hotheaded, never pausing to think what effect his words and actions might have.

Knowing so well their natures, I did not find it surprising that, within a short time, Leicester had persuaded Essex to go to Court.

I was resentful, of course, that I should have been excluded from that first presentation. How I should have enjoyed watching those hawk's eyes studying my handsome son.

But I had to hear it secondhand.

Penelope, who was present, told me.

"Of course, we were all anxious because she would immediately think of his being *your* son."

"Oh, she still hates me as much as ever."

Penelope did not answer that. She meant that she did.

"There was a moment when it seemed that she was uncertain. 'Madam,' said Leicester, all charm and smiles, 'I wish to ask the favor of presenting my stepson, the Earl of Essex.' She looked at him sharply and for a moment did not speak. I thought she was going to burst into a tirade."

"Against the She-Wolf," I commented.

"Then Essex came forward. He is so tall and he has that haughty look . . . but that stoop of his is not without appeal. He has a way when meeting a woman—so courteous, gentle almost, I have seen it with the humblest serving wench. One thing we do know, my lady. He likes women. And the Queen is a woman. It was as though something flashed between them. I have seen it before with her and men she is going to favor. She held out her hand and he kissed it with great charm. Then she smiled

314

and said: 'Your father was a good servant. I regret his death. It was too soon. . . .' She had him sit beside her and she asked him questions about the country."

"And he? Was he gracious?"

"He was overcome by her. You know her well. You may hate and rail against her in private . . ."

"It must be in private," I commented ironically.

"Certainly, if one is wise. But even hating her, one cannot help but be aware of her greatness. Essex was aware of it. His haughtiness dropped from him. It was almost as though he was falling in love with her. It is what she expects from men and they all feign to be dazzled by her charm, but Essex would never pretend, would he, so with him it must have been genuine."

I said: "So your brother seems to have been taken into the intimate circle."

Penelope was thoughtful. "It might well be. He is very young, but the older she grows the more she likes the younger men."

"But this is strange indeed. The son of the woman she hates more than anyone else."

"He is handsome enough to overcome that obstacle," replied Penelope. "But perhaps it is part of the attraction."

I felt myself grow cold with sudden fear. She had taken to my son. Did she know how much I loved him? Sooner or later he would betray to her that there was a special bond between us. He would never stoop to subterfuge to keep her favor as Leicester had done. He would defend me if my name were mentioned. He would not allow her to insult me in his presence.

I was deeply apprehensive.

According to Leicester, Essex had made a good impression on the Queen; she was turning away from the upstart Raleigh towards my son. He amused her. He was different from the others—young, brash, outspoken.

Oh, my beloved son, I thought, have I allowed Leicester to lead you into her web?

Being immersed in my personal affairs and exiled from Court, I had allowed myself to become oblivious of many clouds which were beginning to form over the country.

For so many years I had heard talk of those menaces: The Queen of Scots—about whom there were constant plots to put her on the throne and depose Elizabeth—and the Spanish enemy. I had come to accept them as facts of life. I think this applied to a great many of my countrymen and women; but certainly in the minds of the Queen and Leicester they were ever present.

My exile from Court was like a canker in my heart, particularly now that Essex was there. It was not that I wanted smiles from the Queen; I merely wanted to be there—a firsthand observer. There was small satisfaction in riding through the streets, clad like a queen, and entertaining people in my splendid houses where I could only learn of Court matters through others. So I yearned to be there, and it seemed as though I never would. That was her revenge on me.

Leicester talked often of the Queen of Scots. He wavered between seeking her favor and eliminating her altogether. While she lived, he said, there would be little peace for him or Elizabeth. He feared that one day one of the many plots on her behalf might be successful; in which case those who had supported and adhered to Elizabeth would be most unpopular with the new Queen. And he would be at the head of those to be deposed from power. Stripped from his power and his riches, he would doubtless be sent to the Tower to emerge only to his execution.

Once when we lay in bed together, and he was languorous and not mindful of his words, he said he had advised the Queen to have Mary strangled, or better still poisoned.

"There are poisons," he said, "which leave little trace

. . . and in due course none at all. It would be a mercy
to the country and the Queen if Mary were not there.
While she is, there will always be danger. At any time one
of the many plots could succeed, despite all our efforts."

Poison! I thought. It leaves no trace . . . in due course.
There was time enough for those traces to have disappeared when the search was made for them.

Oh, I was haunted by *Leicester's Commonwealth*.

I wondered whether the Queen ever talked to him of
me when they were alone. I wondered if she ever said:
"You were too hasty, Robin. If you had waited, I might
have married you."

She was capable of that. She would be prepared to talk
longingly of marriage now with a man who was not free
to marry her. I could imagine her taunting him: "You lost
a crown when you married that She-Wolf, Robin. But for
her, I could marry you now. I might have made a king of
you. How well a crown would look on those graying
locks."

I could not stop thinking of Amy Robsart.

When I went to Cornbury in Oxfordshire, I passed
Cumnor Place. I did not go in, for that would have created
gossip. But I should have liked to see the staircase down
which Amy had fallen. It haunted me, that staircase; and
sometimes when I was about to descend a long flight of
stairs I would look furtively over my shoulder.

I was mentioning that we had the ever-present menace
of the Queen of Scots and the Spaniards. There was alarming talk at this time that Philip of Spain was building a
great fleet of ships with which he intended to attack us. We
were working feverishly in our dockyards; men like Drake,
Raleigh, Howard of Effingham, and Frobisher were buzz-
ing around the Queen like so many bees urging her to prepare for the Spaniards.

Leicester said she was anxious and afraid that one day
the Spaniards would come against her, and that was why

317

she felt a campaign in the Netherlands was so important.

I knew that after the deaths of Anjou and William of Orange, deputations had come from the Netherlands offering her their crown if she would protect them. This she had shrunk from taking. She had no wish to increase her responsibilities, and she could imagine what the reaction of Spain would be if she accepted this offer. They would consider it an act of war. But this did not mean that she would not send money and men to fight in the Lowland campaign against the invading Spanish.

One afternoon Robert came to Leicester House in a state of great excitement. I heard his horse's hoofs clatter into the courtyard and I hurried down to him. I knew as soon as I saw him that something of great importance had happened.

"The Queen is sending an army to fight for the States-General," he told me breathlessly. "She has decided that she must choose its commander with great care and send the man best suited to the task even though she would prefer to keep him at home."

"You are to lead the army, then," I replied sharply. My heart was filled with sudden anger. She would hate to lose him, but as, at the same time, she was taking him away from me, that was compensation to her. I could imagine her gloating. He is her husband but it is I who decide whether she shall be with him.

He nodded. "She was most affectionate and she even wept a little."

"Touching!" I said with a sarcasm he pretended not to notice.

"She has done me this honor. It is one of the greatest she could bestow on me."

"I am surprised that she lets you go. But at least she has the satisfaction of knowing that I, also, will be deprived of your company."

Leicester was not listening. Vain as he was, he must already be seeing himself winning honor and glory.

He did not stay long at Leicester House. She had implied that since he was soon to leave her, he was to spend as much time as possible with her before he left. With *her!* I thought bitterly. She was telling me that although I was his wife, she was the important woman in his life. She commanded and he obeyed and every hour he spent with her was an hour in which I could not share.

A few days later I heard that he was not to go to the Netherlands after all. The Queen was suffering from an indisposition and she felt that she had not long to live. She could not therefore allow the Earl of Leicester to leave her. They had been together too long for them to part with the thought that they might never meet again. So he must stay behind and she would consider the matter of whom to send to command the army in the Netherlands.

I was seething with rage. I was certain that all her actions were directed against me in order to humiliate me more than she had already. *She* said my husband must go to the Netherlands, so he prepared to go. *She* said he must remain and so he remained. He must be there at her command. She was so ill that she wanted him with her. If I had been ill he would have had to go. She wanted me to know that I was of little importance in his life. He would abandon me if she commanded it. How I hated her! My only consolation was that her hatred of me was equal to mine of her. And I knew that in her heart she knew that I would be the chosen one . . . were it not for her crown.

It was while I was in this mood that I became an unfaithful wife. I committed the act quite deliberately. I was tired of brief visits—stolen from the Queen—as though she were his wife and I his mistress. I had braved her wrath to marry him, knowing that wrath could be relentless; and, having done that, I was not prepared to be treated in this way.

Leicester was growing old and, as I had long noticed, there were some handsome young men in his service. The Queen liked handsome young men about her, to pander to her whims, to flatter her, to do her service—well, I also liked them. I had been thinking more and more of this since I saw so little of my husband. I was still young enough to enjoy those pleasures I could share with the opposite sex. Looking back, I think perhaps I hoped Leicester would find out and then he would know that others valued me enough to risk his revenge.

At one time it had seemed that Leicester alone could please me. I wanted to prove to myself that that was no longer the case.

There was a young man in my husband's retinue—a certain Christopher Blount, a son of Lord Mountjoy—whom Leicester had made his Master of Horse. He was tall, of excellent figure and extremely handsome, fair-haired, blue-eyed with an appealing look of innocence which pleased me. I had noticed him often and I knew that he was aware of me. I would always give him Good Morrow when I passed, and he would always stand at attention and regard me with something like awe, which I found gratifying.

I made a point of speaking to him whenever I saw him, and I soon realized that he put himself in the way of being spoken to.

After I had seen him I would go to my room and think about him. I would look in the mirror and study myself critically. It seemed incredible that in five years I should be fifty. I shuddered at the thought. I should not be chary of snatching at the good things of life, for before long I should be too old to enjoy them. Previously I had always congratulated myself that the Queen was eight years older than I and Robert slightly more. But now I was seeing myself in relation to Christopher Blount. He must be twenty years my junior. Well, not only queens could play at being young. I wanted to prove to myself that I still had the power to attract. Perhaps I wanted also to be assured that Leicester was not as important to me as he had once been. If he must always be at hand to amuse the Queen, I could find amusement elsewhere. I felt in some way that I was not only scoring over Leicester but, just as important to me, over the Queen as well.

A few days later I saw Christopher in the stables and dropped a kerchief. An old trick but ever a useful one. It gave him an opportunity, and I wondered whether he would have the courage to take it. If he did, he deserved a reward, for he would know something of Leicester, and I doubted not he had read the *Commonwealth*. Then he would know it could be dangerous to dally with Leicester's wife.

I knew he would come.

He was at the door of my chamber holding my kerchief in his hand. I went to him, smiling, and, taking his hand, drew him into the chamber, shutting the door on us.

It was exciting, for him no less than for me. It was that element of danger which had so appealed to me in my first days with Robert. It was exhilarating to be with a young man, to know that my body was still beautiful and that my age seemed to be an additional attraction because I was so much in command of the situation and my experience filled him with wonder and respect.

Afterwards I quickly sent him away saying that it must never happen again. I knew it would, of course, but that made it more precious and exciting. He looked very serious and tragic, but I knew he would have braved the wrath of Leicester again and again rather than to have missed it.

When he had gone I laughed at myself and thought of Leicester's dancing attendance on the Queen.

"Two can play at that game, my noble Earl," I said.

The Queen had changed her mind once more. She had recovered and no one but Leicester, she had again decided, was worthy to lead the armies in the Netherlands.

He was in a state of great excitement when he came to Leicester House. He saw a wonderful future opening out before him, he told me. The crown of the Netherlands had been offered to the Queen; she would not accept it, but he saw no reason why he should not.

"How would you like to be a queen, Lettice?" he asked; and I replied that I should not refuse a crown if it were offered to me.

"Let us hope she will not stop your leaving again," I said.

"She will not," he replied. "She is eager for victory there. We need it. I promise you this: I will drive the Spaniards out of the Netherlands." He looked at me suddenly and saw the coldness in my eyes, for I was thinking how absorbed he was in his coming glory and how little concerned to leave me. But then *she* had seen that we had so little time together that his separation made little difference to the life we had been living for so long. He took my hands and kissed them. "Lettice," he went on, "I'm going to make it up to you. Don't think I don't understand what it has been like. I couldn't help it. It has been against my will. Understand please, my dearest."

"I understand well enough," I replied. "You had to neglect me because she wished it."

"It's true. I would to God . . ."

He seized me and held me to him, but I sensed that his excitement stemmed not from his passion for me but from the contemplation of the glory that would come from the Netherlands.

Philip Sidney was going with him and he would find a place for Essex. "That will please our young Earl. You see how I care for my family."

It was going to be a triumphant march into the Netherlands. He was already planning that. Now he would see his Master of Horse, as he had much to discuss with him.

I was amused, wondering what Christopher Blount's reactions would be. There was something very innocent about Christopher, and since what I secretly referred to as "the incident" had occurred I had seen expression of many emotions on his face. There were guilt, excitement, hope, desire, shame and fear all mingling. He would be seeing himself as a villain for having seduced his master's wife. I wanted to tell him that it was I who had seduced him. He was very charming, and although I had been tempted to repeat the experience, I had not done so. I did not want to spoil it for Christopher by making it an entirely physical relationship.

However, I was interested to see how he behaved with Leicester, and whether he would betray anything. I was sure that he would make a tremendous effort not to. And since he was to leave for the Netherlands with Leicester, I told myself, there could be no immediate repetition of the incident. But I was wrong.

The Queen was determined that Leicester should not spend his last night in England with me. I thought at least he would do that and was expecting him to come to Leicester House. He did not come. Instead, a messenger arrived with the news that the Queen insisted he remain at Court as she had much to discuss with him. I knew, of course, that she was showing me that, although I was his wife, it was she who had first call on his services. I was angry and frustrated. I hated his going. I suppose in my heart I still loved him, still wanted him. I knew then that there could never be anyone in my life to take his place. I was sick with frustrated jealousy when I thought of those two together. She would doubtless dance into the early hours of the morning, and he would be there offering her those sickening compliments, telling her how wretched he was to leave *her*. And she would listen, her head on one side, her hawk's eyes soft . . . believing her Sweet Robin, her Eyes, the only man she could ever love.

It had been a cold December day but the weather could not be more wretched than my mood. I decided I was a fool. To hell with Elizabeth, I said to myself. To hell with Leicester. I ordered my servants to make a good fire in my bedroom and when it was warm and cozy I sent for Christopher.

He was so young, so naïve, so inexperienced. I knew he adored me and his adoration was salve to my wounded vanity. I could not bear that his opinion of me should change so I told him I had sent for him to assure him that he must feel no guilt for what had happened. It had come upon us spontaneously before we had had time to realize what we were doing. It must never happen again of course, and we must forget it had.

He said what I expected him to. He would do all I asked of him except forget. That was something he could never do. It had been the most wonderful experience of his life, and he would remember it always.

The young are so charming, I thought. I understood why the Queen was so fond of them. Their innocence refreshes us, renews our faith in life. Christopher's rapture brought him near to idolatry, and this did much to restore my belief in my power to attract, which, because of Leicester's eagerness to leave me for the glory of the Netherlands, I had begun to doubt.

I took my leave of Christopher—or pretended to, as I fully intended that he should stay the night. I placed my hands on his shoulders and kissed him on the lips. Of course that was the tinder to the flame.

He was charmingly full of apologies, believing that he was to blame, which was so appealing.

I sent him off before the dawn and he went saying that if he died in battle in the Netherlands, would I honor him by remembering that he could never have loved anyone but me if he had lived to be a hundred?

Dear Christopher! Death seemed glorious at that moment, I was sure. He saw himself dying for the Protestant faith with my name on his lips.

It was very romantic and charming, and I had enjoyed the episode. I wondered why I had denied myself so long.

They left the next day, Leicester taking his farewell of the Queen and placing himself at the head of the party which also contained my lover and my son.

I heard later that they were lavishly entertained at Colchester, and the following day went to Harwich, where a fleet of fifty sail was waiting to take them across to Flushing.

Robert wrote to me in great exultation, telling me of the tumultuous welcome he had received everywhere, for the people regarded him as their savior. At Rotterdam, where it was dark when the fleet arrived, Dutchmen lined the bank, every fourth man holding aloft a fiery cresset. The crowds cheered him and he was taken through the market place to his lodging, where a life-size statue of Erasmus had been erected. From Rotterdam he had gone to Delft, and there he lodged in the very house where the Prince of Orange had been murdered.

"The celebrations," he wrote, "grew more splendid as I passed through the country. Everywhere I was regarded as their savior."

The people, it seemed, had suffered greatly for their religion and, being in dread of defeat from the Spaniards, saw the coming of Leicester with money and men from the Queen of England as their great hope.

He had gone there to command an army, but there was no fighting at this stage. It was all celebration and what Leicester—and England—were going to do for the country. I had been somewhat surprised when the Queen had

325

chosen Leicester for this task as he was a politician not a soldier; he had a way with words not swords. I wondered what would happen when the fighting started.

But he had his triumph first. For several weeks the revelry continued, and then came the great moment of decision. He wrote to me at once, for this was something he could not keep to himself.

"It was on the first day of January when a deputation was making its way to my lodging. I was not dressed and while my toilet was being completed one of my men told me that the ministers had come to say something to me. They were going to offer me the Generalship of the United Provinces. I was uneasy, for the Queen had sent me to fight for them and with them, not to govern them; and attractive as such an offer was, I could not accept it without consideration."

I pictured him, his eyes gleaming. Was it not what he had wanted? He had been the Queen's man for so long. Like a little dog on a chain, I had once gibed. "My sweet little creature, let me pet you . . . and you may only go as far as the chain by which I hold you will allow you to."

What it must have meant to him to be offered the crown of the Netherlands!

I turned back to his letter.

"I made no answer and continued to consider the matter. You will be pleased to hear that I have made Essex General of the Horse. I spent much time listening to sermons and singing psalms, for these are a people who take their religion very seriously. Now I must tell you that I have discussed this matter with the Queen's secretary, Davison, who is here, and with Philip Sidney and they are both of the opinion that I must satisfy the people by accepting the offer. So, my dearest Lettice, I am now Governor of the United Provinces."

There was a later note.

"I have been installed at The Hague. I wish you could

have seen this impressive ceremony. I sat beneath the arms of the Netherlands and England, on a chair of state, and all about me were representatives from the principal states. Thanks were given to the Queen and to me, the Lieutenant General, now Governor of the United Provinces. I took the necessary oath and swore to protect them and work for their good and that of the church. How I wish you were here! You would have been proud of me.

"Now, my dear Lettice, I want you to join me. Remember you come here as a queen. You will know how to do that. We shall live here and you will no longer be in exile as you call it. I long to see you."

I read and reread that letter. I was to go as a queen. I should be royal as she was, and beautiful as she never could be. Life was going to be exciting. I was exultant. What would she say, what would she do, when she heard that I was going to the Netherlands as Leicester's Queen?

I lost no time in beginning my preparations.

I *would* go as a queen. I would be more splendid than Elizabeth had ever been.

So at last I was coming to my triumph. I was realizing what it meant to be Leicester's wife. I should be Queen with no one to command me, and if it must be at The Hague instead of Greenwich and Windsor, what cared I?

Merchants came to Leicester House with the finest materials that existed. I planned my wardrobe with frantic haste and the seamstresses were busy night and day. I ordered coaches with the arms of the Netherlands entwined with those of Robert. I designed rich ornaments for myself, my companions and even the horses. I had decided to take a company of ladies and gentlemen with me. The cavalcade which rode to Harwich would excite the people of the countryside because they would never have seen anything so splendid before. What I would show them would be a hundred times more rich, more luxurious than anything the Queen had ever possessed.

Those were exciting weeks. I longed to begin my journey.

One February day, when I was in the midst of these preparations, I heard that William Davison, the Queen's secretary, who had accompanied Robert to the Netherlands, had arrived at Court to give the Queen a full account of what had happened.

Robert Governor of the United Provinces! Accepting such an office without consulting her! Taking a post which meant his living out of England! Her rage was terrible, said those who saw it.

Someone—who must have liked to ferment trouble—mentioned that Robert's Countess was also preparing to join him with the state of a queen.

How she swore! They said that her father never surpassed her in that. She swore by God's blood that she would teach Leicester and his She-Wolf a lesson. So they were playing at King and Queen, were they? She would teach them that royalty was not something to be taken up by commoners, simply because they were misguided enough to think themselves—erroneously—worthy of it!

She sent Heneage off at once. He was to go to Leicester and tell him he must arrange another ceremony. And in this he would give up his governorship and tell the people of the Netherlands that he was but a servant of the Queen of England and was now in deep disgrace for having acted without her permission. Then he could come back and kick his heels in the Tower.

Poor Davison was berated and hardly allowed to speak, but after a while she listened and then when her rage had subsided a little she must have thought of the humiliation she was imposing on Robert and modified her judgment. He would, of course, give up the governorship, but it must be relinquished in a manner which would bring the least humiliation. But he must not think she was not furious.

She had declared publicly, so that foreign princes might know, that she was determined not to take the Governorship of the Netherlands, and now one of her subjects had snatched it, seeing in it a prize which he could enjoy. It would appear that she had given that permission—for none would believe that a *subject* could have dared presume so much—and it would be believed that she had broken her word.

"As for that She-Wolf," she cried, "she can unpack her jewels. She can lay aside her fine gowns. She can give up all thought of riding in glory to The Hague. Instead she can go humbly to the Tower and beseech the privilege of seeing the prisoner, making sure how she conducts herself, lest she find a long stay awaiting her in that place."

Poor Robert! How brief was his glory. Poor me, who had thought to come out of the shadows only to find myself back in them. And the hatred of the Queen grown even more intense towards me, for I knew that she would convince herself that I, not her beloved Robin, had planned and schemed to put myself upon a throne.

After that disastrous Netherlands adventure, none but Robert could have survived. I had always known he was no soldier. He would have been wonderfully impressive during those parades through the streets. I could picture him at the ceremonies; but it was a very different matter when it came to facing the experienced and ruthless Duke of Parma, who could not be expected to stand aside while Robert indulged himself and the people with great spectacles.

It was a great blow when Parma struck where it was least expected and took the town of Grave, which Robert had thought to be well fortified—and afterwards that of Venlo.

The wrath of the Queen added to his difficulties, for no money was coming from England for the soldiers' pay and the officers were quarreling among themselves. Robert told me much later of the nightmare he lived through and how he never wanted to see the Netherlands again.

The entire campaign was a disaster, and for us there was a personal tragedy.

I was very fond of the Sidney family, and Philip was the favorite of us all. Mary, his mother, and I had become friendly since we were both exiles from Court—she voluntarily and I most reluctantly. She still wore a fine veil over her face and rarely went to Court although the Queen continued to welcome her and respect her desire for privacy in her own apartment in the royal residences.

In May I had news from Mary that her husband's health was worsening. He had been ailing for some time and had refused to rest; so it was not surprising to hear soon after that he was dead. I went to Penshurst to be with her, and I was glad I did, for in August, Mary herself died. Her daughter, Mary, Countess of Pembroke, came to Penshurst to be with her mother at the end, and we deplored the fact that Philip was with the armies of the Netherlands and could not be present.

It seemed a blessing in a way that Mary Sidney should die before the great tragedy befell her, for I knew her feelings well enough to understand that what was about to happen would be the cruelest blow of her life.

It was September—a month after the death of Lady Sidney—when Leicester decided to attack Zutphen.

The story of what happened was pieced together afterwards, but it is one of recklessness and heroism, and I often think that if Philip had been more realistic and less knightly it need never have happened.

A series of incidents led to what followed. When he left his tent he fell in with Sir William Pelham, who had forgotten to put on his leg armor. Foolishly, Philip said that he must not have an advantage over a friend and discarded his own. It was a ridiculous gesture for which he paid a high price, for later, during the action, a bullet struck his left thigh. He was able to remain on horseback, but suffered greatly from loss of blood and, surrounded by his friends, he cried out that he was dying of thirst rather than loss of blood. A water bottle was thrust into his hands, but just as he was about to drink he saw a dying soldier on the ground who called feebly for water.

"Take it," said Philip in words which have become immortalized. "Thy necessity is greater than mine."

He was carried to Leicester's barge and taken down to Arnhem and lodged in a house there.

I called on his wife, Frances, and found her, although heavily pregnant, preparing to leave. She said she must go to him, for he would need careful nursing.

"In your condition, you are unfit," I told her; but she would not listen, and her father said that since she was of such a determined mind he would not stop her.

So Frances went to Arnhem. Poor girl, her life had not been such a happy one. She must have loved him, though. Who could help loving Philip Sidney? Perhaps Frances knew that the love poems he wrote to my daughter Penelope were not to be taken as a slight to herself. There were not many women who would have accepted such a situation but Frances was an unusual woman.

Philip suffered acute agony for twenty-six days before he died. I knew his death would be a great blow to Robert, who had looked upon him as a son. His gifts, his charm, everything about Philip had been of such a nature to win admiration, and he was not one to inspire envy as men such as Robert, Heneage, Hatton and Raleigh did, for Philip was not ambitious. He was a man possessed of rare qualities.

I heard that the Queen's grief was intense. She had lost her dear friend Mary Sidney, whom she had always loved, and now Philip, whom she had so much admired, was dead.

The Queen hated war. She declared it to be senseless and to bring no good to any. All her reign she had sought to elude it, and now she was thrown into depression because of the loss of her dear friends and the ever more closely encroaching threat from Spain, which this rash and foolish adventure in the Netherlands had done nothing to ward off.

Philip's body was embalmed and he was brought home on a ship the sails of which were black and which was therefore called the *Black Pinnance*; and in the following February there was a memorial service for him in St. Paul's Cathedral.

Poor Frances had already been delivered of a stillborn child, which perhaps was to be expected after all she had endured.

Leicester came back to England, for the winter was no time for military campaigns, and with him came my son Essex.

First Leicester went to Court. There would have been trouble if he had not, and his position was precarious. I could imagine his misgivings when he presented himself to his royal mistress. Essex came to me. He was very upset by the death of Philip Sidney, and he wept as he told me that he had been at his deathbed.

"A nobler man never lived," he cried, "and now he is dead. He was pleased that the Earl of Leicester was with him. There was a deep love between those two, and my stepfather was in great grief at his passing. Philip left me his best sword. I shall treasure it always and hope I shall be worthy of it."

He had seen poor Frances Sidney—a brave woman, he said, for she had been in no fit condition to cross the sea. He would do all he could to help her, for that was what Philip would have wished.

After reporting to the Queen, Leicester came to me. The latest adventure had aged him, and I was shocked by his appearance. He had had a return of the gout and was weighed down with depression by the manner in which the adventure had turned sour.

He talked to me earnestly: "God be praised the Queen has not withdrawn her favor from me. When I came to her and knelt, she made me rise and she looked at me earnestly with tears in her eyes. She saw that I had suffered much, and she said that I had been a traitor to her. But what hurt her most was that I had been a traitor to myself, for I had wantonly ignored my health when I knew that the care of that was the first command she gave me. Then I knew that everything was forgiven."

I looked at him—this poor parody of the once glorious Leicester, and I was amazed at the woman. He had defied her and believed he had found a way to wear a crown in the Netherlands which would have meant deserting her and, greatest blow of all, had planned to send for me to share it with him. Yet she forgave him.

By God's truth, I said to myself, she loves him. Indeed she does.

Victorious England

Now for your person, being the most sacred and dainty thing we have in this world to care for, a man must tremble when he thinks of it; specially finding Your Majesty to have that princely courage, to transport yourself to the utmost confines of your realm to meet your enemies and defend your subjects. I cannot, most dear Queen, consent to that; for upon your well doing consists all the safety of your whole kingdom; and therefore preserve that above all.

LEICESTER *to* ELIZABETH

Her presence and her words fortified the courage of the captains and soldier beyond belief.

― WILLIAM CAMDEN

The last episode of the tragic story of Mary of Scotland was about to break. She was imprisoned at that time at our own home of Chartley, which now belonged to my son, Essex. He had been very reluctant to allow it to be used as a prison for the Queen, and had protested that it was too small and inconvenient. However, his objections had been overruled, and in those chambers, so well known to me and my family, where I had played merry games with my children, the last dramatic scenes of the Scottish Queen's life took place. There she had become involved in the Babington Plot, which was to lead to her destruction; and the next phase of her sad journey was to the fateful castle of Fotheringay.

The entire country was talking of it—how those conspirators had met, how letters had passed between them, how the Queen of Scots was deeply involved in a plot, and on this occasion she was incriminated without doubt. Walsingham had all the evidence in his hands, and Mary was found guilty of trying to bring about the murder of Queen Elizabeth for the purpose of taking her place on the throne.

But even with the evidence before her, Elizabeth was reluctant to sign the death warrant.

Leicester was impatient with her, and I reminded him that not so long ago he had thought of making terms with the Queen of Scots when he thought there was a possibility of Elizabeth's dying and her coming to the throne.

He looked at me in amazement. He could not understand my lack of understanding of political expediency. Previously I should have been with him in what he suggested. Oh yes, indeed I was out of love.

"If she does not take care," he cried vehemently, "there will be an attempt to rescue Mary and it may succeed."

"You would not then be in an enviable position, my lord," I commented wryly. "I believe Her Majesty of Scotland is very fond of lapdogs, but she likes to choose her own, and would I am sure have no house room for those who once pleased the Queen of England."

"What has happened to you, Lettice?" he asked, bewildered.

I retorted: "I have become a neglected wife."

"You know full well there is only one reason why I cannot be with you."

"I know full well," I replied.

"Then enough. Let us ponder on serious matters."

But what was serious to him might not have been to me. That did not occur to him.

The people were restive, and still the Queen played that game of prevarication which she had practiced all her life. Often it had worked for her. But now her loyal subjects wanted to know when they could rejoice in the shedding of the Catholic Queen's blood.

Finally Secretary Davison brought the death warrant to her and she signed; and that scene of which we have heard so much was enacted in the hall of Fotheringay Castle.

The menace to the Queen of England was removed. But there was an even greater one: the Spaniards.

She suffered from remorse—that extraordinary woman. She, who was so clever, so subtle, was haunted by dreams. She had signed the death warrant which had caused the Queen to be taken to the block and her head cut off.

The King of France said it would have been better to have poisoned her, so that there could have been some doubt as to how she died. There were some excellent poisons available, and some of Elizabeth's subjects were evidently well practiced in the use of them. Was this a sly allusion to *Leicester's Commonwealth?* She might have been smothered by a pillow, which if skillfully done left little trace. But no! The Queen of Scots had been found guilty, and the Queen of England had signed her death warrant; and she had been taken to the hall of Fotheringay Castle and been beheaded. And while England was rejoicing that the Scottish Queen could trouble them no more, Elizabeth went on suffering intense remorse.

Leicester said he feared she might lose her reason. She raged against them all, calling them murderers, accusing them of inducing her to sign the warrant, when all the time they had known that she had not meant the deed to be carried out. They had acted too promptly, knowing well her wishes.

How like her that was! I pointed out to Leicester that she was trying to shift the blame. She was even talking of having Davison hanged. At first Leicester, Burleigh and those who rejoiced that the menace was removed were aghast until they realized that she had no intention of being foolish and was merely placating her enemies. She was afraid of war. She knew that the Spaniards were building an armada to come against her. She did not want the French to join them and attack her at the same time. The Scots had to be considered too. They had turned out their Queen and made it necessary for her to flee, but they would be ready to come against the Queen of England for beheading her. Besides, there was young James, her son.

The Queen's remorse began to be less vociferous. In her heart she must have accepted the truth that life would be more comfortable now that the Queen of Scots was no more—though a queen had been beheaded and that could be a precedent. Even after all these years the daughter of Anne Boleyn had moments when she felt her throne to be too insecure for her comfort. The thought of what had happened to one whose claim had never been disputed would, I knew, have made her apprehensive. She did not want the deposing of queens to become a habit.

But there were other matters to occupy her, and the greatest of these was the growing menace of the Spanish Armada.

Word came to me from Leicester's spies that the Queen was very taken with my son these days. Essex was maturing and was no less attractive because of this. His good looks were outstanding with that auburn hair and those flashing dark eyes bequeathed by me. I think he was like me in many ways. He was certainly vain—as I had been in my youth; and he gave the impression that he believed the world had been made for him and that everyone must share his view. One characteristic he did not get from me and which was the absolute opposite of Leicester's nature was his frankness. He never stopped to think what effect his words would have; if he meant something, he said it. God knows, this was no quality for a courtier, and one which I was sure would not find favor with the Queen, who since her youth had been surrounded by sycophants whose one idea had been to say what she wanted to hear.

I couldn't help comparing Leicester with Essex because they were both Elizabeth's favorites, and I am sure she never cared for any men as she cared for these two. It was ironical that she should have chosen *my* husband and son, in view of the relationship between herself and me. It gave me a new zest for life when I heard how her affection for Essex was growing. I wanted her to become more and more fond of him; it made her vulnerable as only affection could. I determined to do everything I could to help him hold that vacillating favor. Not that I could do much, except offer him advice. But I could say that I knew her well —her strength and her weakness had been revealed to me because of the rivalry between us—so I could perhaps be a little useful to him.

I often doubted whether Essex would keep her favor. One of Leicester's great assets had been his ability, as someone once said, "to put his passion in his pocket." Again and again he, ever her special Eyes, had offended and come to her and been forgiven. That was a lesson my son would have to learn—to put aside rancor and keep a rein on his tongue. Perhaps at first she found his graceful youth appealing; she was amused no doubt by his outspoken comments; I wondered whether she would go on being so.

When he came to me, he would talk of the Queen, and his eyes would shine with admiration.

"She is wonderful," he said. "There is no one like her. I know she is an old woman, but in her presence one forgets ages."

"So well it is disguised with rouge and powder and her wigs," I replied. "I had it from her silk-woman that she is at this time engaged on making twelve wigs for the Queen, who is most particular that the hair shall be of the color her own hair was when she was a young girl."

"I know not of these matters," replied Essex impatiently. "All I know is that when one is in her company it is like being with a goddess."

He must have meant that or he would not have said it. I felt a great wave of jealousy sweep over me for this woman who had the power to take from me first my husband and now my son.

As I have betrayed, I always had a special affection for my handsome son, but my feeling for Essex now grew more intense, which, in my heart, I knew was in some measure due to the Queen's affection for him.

She was nonetheless devoted to Leicester because of her interest in Essex. I sometimes thought that Leicester was to her as husband, Essex as a beloved young lover, but being the woman she was, of a most possessive nature, she could not endure that either of them should enjoy the company of another woman, much less their wife and mother, nor stray from her side lest she need them.

Those were days of growing tension when tempers ran high. The Spanish menace was creeping nearer and constantly in everyone's mind. The Low Countries were in difficulties and Leicester was sent over again—this time to tell them to come to terms with Spain, for with the threat to her own shores, the Queen could no longer afford to concern herself with them.

On this occasion she would not allow Essex to accompany his stepfather.

"I must have someone to divert me," she said; and she honored him by making him her Master of Horse, a post which she took from Leicester, making him the exchange of Lord Steward of her household. She would have Leicester know that there could only be one Eyes for her, and nothing could change that; but at the same time she liked to have his handsome stepson beside her.

Leicester must have realized at that time that when the Queen gave her love it was forever. Poor Leicester! now old and ailing. Where was the handsome dashing hero of her youth and mine? He was no more, being replaced by a man still of great stature but overheavy, overruddy of complexion where once there there had been a healthy glow, plagued by the gout and other ailments which were the result of a lifetime of overindulgence.

Yet she stood firmly for him all through his life. He had survived the mysterious death of his first wife, his marriage to me, his attempts at deceiving her, and finally the fiasco of the Netherlands. Truly she was a faithful mistress.

She was as fond of finery as ever and had taken to wearing white a great deal. She had always had a fondness for it since the days when black and white were the fashionable colors. White was becoming to her aging face, she fancied; and on the rare occasions when I glimpsed her at that time—always unseen by her, perhaps passing through the streets on her progress about the country—I had agreed with her. She had preserved her skin, and her abstemiousness from food and drink had kept her figure slender and youthful. She carried herself with the utmost grace—in fact I never saw anyone walk or sit more regally—and from a distance she could still look youthful; and the glitter and pomp with which she surrounded herself made her readily accepted as immortal.

Knowing Essex well, I realized that in a way he was enamored of her. He could not tear himself away from her side. All through the summer he was at Court, and she would sit playing cards with him until the early hours of the morning. The very fact that he was outspoken would have delighted her, for being the man he was—concealment of any emotion being alien to him—he would have made his admiration for her obvious; and coming from a young man more than thirty years younger than she, this must have been a compliment such as a woman of her nature would greatly cherish.

I could sympathize with her. I knew what admiration from a young and personable man could mean. I had resumed my friendship with Christopher Blount, who had returned from the Netherlands more sophisticated than he had been when he went away. He was more forceful, more demanding, a quality to which I was not averse. I allowed myself to be taken by him and we continued to conduct this interesting affair which had for me the merit of romance simply because we had to be so cautious.

I told him I feared for his life if Leicester discovered, and so did he. But that gave a fillip to our lovemaking.

Meanwhile Essex was arousing the envy of all other men at Court and in particular Walter Raleigh, who felt himself ousted by my son.

Raleigh was an older man than Essex and a good deal cleverer. He had a honeyed tongue when he wished, yet he could give the Queen some truths when he judged it the right moment to do so. In addition to those rather flamboyant good looks, which had immediately attracted the Queen, he was a man of great talent and discernment.

She called him her Water—perhaps because his name was Walter; perhaps because she found him refreshing; perhaps because she liked him to flow along beside her. However, the fact that he had one of her nicknames was an indication of her affection for him.

There were the aging favorites too. Poor Hatton, like Robert, was getting old, and so was Heneage; but because of her faithful nature—and the fact that they were useful to her—she kept them with her, and was almost as faithful to them in her fashion as she was to Leicester, only of course they knew—and everyone at Court knew—that no one could ever hold the place in her heart which belonged to Leicester, the lover of her youth, to whom she had been faithful all her life.

Essex and my daughters brought me little anecdotes from Court which I loved to hear. Penelope was delighted that her brother was in such favor with the Queen, and she assured me that before long he would insist on the Queen's receiving me.

"I doubt I would want to go on such terms," I said.

"My lady, you would be ready to go on any terms," retorted my daughter. "You are never going to be taken as lady of the bedchamber or some such post, but I don't see why you should not come to Court as becomes your position as Countess Leicester."

"I wonder she likes to proclaim her jealousy as she does."

"She thrives on it," said Penelope. "Hatton has sent her a bodkin and bucket wrought in gold as a charm, with the pointed message that she might need it as Water is sure to be close at hand—referring to Raleigh, of course. You would think she would tell Hatton not to be such a fool, but she replied in like manner and assured him that Water should never overflow her banks, for he knew how dear her sheep were to her. So old Bellwether was thanked for his jealous pains. She loves them to fight among themselves over her. It helps her to forget the crow's-feet and wrinkled skin which confront her in that cruel mirror which is not so comforting as her courtiers."

I asked her how she was getting on with her married life and she shrugged the question aside with the remark that no sooner was she delivered of one child than she was pregnant with another, and one day she would tell Lord Rich that she had given him enough children and would bear no more.

Her frequent pregnancies did not seem to impair her looks or health, for she was as vital and as beautiful as she ever was; and I was on the point of telling her about my own love affair with Christopher Blount.

She went on to tell me that the Queen was certainly taken with Raleigh, and he was perhaps the nearest rival Essex had. Essex should be warned, she believed, not to be too frank with the Queen, but to use his frankness only when it pleased her and when she clearly wanted a candid answer.

"You are asking him to go against his nature," I said. "I believe that is something he would never do."

We talked of him lovingly, for Penelope was almost as devoted to him as I was. We were both very proud of him.

"But Raleigh is clever," she said, "as our Robin never could be. Yet Raleigh is making demands on the Queen and when the other day she asked him when he would stop being a beggar, he retorted sharply that he would only do so when Her Majesty ceased to be a benefactress—which made her laugh heartily. You know how she likes that kind of wit. Robin could never give her that. One thing I am afraid of is that he might overestimate his power over her. If he did that, there could be trouble."

I replied that when her favorites overstepped the mark she frequently forgave them. Look at Leicester.

"But there will never be another Leicester," said Penelope soberly.

I knew it was true.

I was growing fond of Christopher. I found him interesting and amusing, once he had overcome his awe of me, which it was impossible to sustain now that he was learning that I wanted him as much as he wanted me.

He told me about his family, which was noble but impoverished. His grandfather, Lord Mountjoy, had spent unwisely and his father had squandered more of the family fortunes in an attempt to find the philosopher's stone. William, Christopher's elder brother, was a man who had no respect for money and lived extravagantly beyond his means, so it seemed unlikely that there would be much left of the family fortunes.

The hope was brother Charles, who was a few years older than Christopher and a few younger than William. Charles had declared his determination to come to Court and restore the family's wealth.

I was interested in this family saga because of Christopher of course, and when his brother Charles began to be mentioned as a rival to my son, my amused interest quickened.

The Blounts were possessed of handsome looks, and it seemed that Charles had his fair share of them. He was brought to Court and was among the company which sat down to dine with the Queen. This did not mean that she would speak to all present, but it presented an opportunity to attract her attention, which Charles's appearance did at once.

The Queen, I was told, asked her carver who the good-looking stranger was, and when the carver said he did not know she told him to find out.

Charles, seeing the Queen's eyes on him, blushed deeply, a fact which enchanted her, and when she heard that he was Lord Mountjoy's son she sent for him. She talked to the bashful young man for a few minutes and asked after his father. Then she said: "Fail you not to come to Court and I will bethink myself how to do you good."

Those about them smiled. Another handsome young man!

Of course he followed up that invitation and soon was a great favorite with the Queen, for he had other qualities besides his good looks, being well read, particularly in history, so that he could meet the Queen on an intellectual level which delighted her. As he remained somewhat retiring and did not spend extravagant—for indeed he was unable to—the Queen found this refreshing, and he was fast becoming a prominent member in her little band of favorites.

One day when he tilted she was there to watch him and made no secret of her pleasure in his victory, to celebrate which she gave him a chess queen of gold and very richly enameled. He was so proud of it that he ordered his servants to stitch it onto his sleeve, and carried his cloak over his arm so that all could see this mark of royal pleasure.

When this caught my son's eye, he wanted to know what it meant and he was told that the Queen had bestowed the favor on young Blount at the previous day's tilting. Another fault of my son's was his jealousy, and he thought of the Queen's admiring this young man filled him with rage.

"It seems every fool must have a favor," he said slightingly; and as these words were spoken in the hearing of several people, there was nothing Charles Blount could do but challenge him.

I was very upset when Christopher told me, and so was he. He came to me almost in tears. "My brother and your son are to fight a duel," he said; and it was then that I learned the reason.

Duels could end in death and that my son was in danger sent me frantic with anxiety. I sent a message to him at once to come to me without delay. He did so, but when he heard what I wanted he became impatient.

"My dearest Rob," I cried, "you could be killed." He shrugged his shoulders and I went on: "And what if *you* killed this young man?"

"It would be a small loss," he replied.

"You would deeply regret it."

"He is trying to creep into the Queen's favor."

"If you are going to fight with every man at Court who is doing that, I don't give much for your chances of survival. Rob, I beg of you be careful."

"If I promise to, will that satisfy you?"

"No," I cried vehemently. "I can only have one satisfaction from this affair and that is for you to call it off." I tried to be calm, to reason with him. "The Queen will be very displeased," I said.

"It is her fault for giving him the token."

"Why should she not? He pleased her at the tilt."

"Dear Mother, I have already accepted the challenge. That is enough."

"My darling, you must give up this madness."

He was tender suddenly. "It is too late now," he said gently. "Don't be afraid. He hasn't a chance against me."

"His young brother is our Master of Horse. Poor Christopher is so upset about it. Oh Rob, can't you see how I feel. If anything happened to you . . ."

He kissed me, and his expression was so tender that I was overwhelmed by my love for him, and my fears increased tenfold. It is so difficult to convey his charm, and it was always especially effective following his louring looks. He assured me that he loved me, that he always would; he would do anything in his power to make me happy, but the challenge had been made and accepted. He could not in honor stop it now.

I could see that there was nothing for me but to pray fervently that he would come through this unharmed.

Penelope came to see me.

"Rob is going to fight Mountjoy's son," she said. "He must be stopped."

"Can we stop him?" I cried. "I have tried to. Oh, Penelope, I am so frightened. I have begged him but he refuses to stop it."

"If you can't persuade him, no one can. But you must see his point. He has gone so far it would be hard to withdraw now. It's disastrous. Charles Blount is such a handsome man—as handsome as Rob, but in a different way. Rob should never have shown his jealousy so blatantly. The Queen hates duels and will be furious if either of her pretty young men is harmed."

"My dear, I know her better than you ever will. This is all her doing. She will gloat because they have fought over her favor." I clenched my fist. "If anything happens to Rob I shall blame her. I would be ready to kill her. . . ."

"Hush!" Penelope looked furtively over her shoulder. "Be careful, Mother. She hates you already. If anyone heard what you said heaven knows what might come of it."

I turned away. I could derive little comfort from Penelope, and I knew that it was no use pleading further with my son.

So there was nothing I could do to stop the duel and it took place in Marylebone Park. There was defeat for Essex, which was probably for the best, since Charles Blount had no intention of killing my son or dying himself—which would have meant the end of both their careers. There was a good deal of wisdom in Charles Blount. He was able to end the duel in the best possible way since Essex insisted on its taking place. He wounded my son slightly in the thigh and disarmed him. Charles Blount was unharmed.

Thus ended the duel in Marylebone Park, but it was to have far-reaching consequences.

It should have taught Essex a lesson, but alas, it did not.

When the Queen heard there had been a duel, she was angry and would reprimand both men, but knowing the temper of Essex and having had an account of what led up to the quarrel between them, she approved Charles Blount's behavior.

Her comment was: "By God's death, it is fitting that someone or other should take Essex down and teach him better manners, otherwise there would be no rule with him."

That was an indication that she was not pleased with his arrogance and that he should take heed and curb it. Of course he did not.

I tried to warn him, to make him see how dangerous it was to rely on her favor. She could change as quickly as the wind and one day she could be doting and fond and the next an implacable enemy.

"I know her," I cried. "In fact few know her as I do. I have lived close to her . . . and look at me now . . . banished, an exile. I have felt her malice and hatred as few have."

He retorted hotly that if I had been treated shamefully, it was Leicester who was to blame.

"By my faith, Mother," he said, "one day I will do for you what Leicester should have done. I will *make* her receive you and treat you with the respect you deserve."

I did not believe him but I liked to hear him champion me all the same.

Charles Blount came to inquire for him every day and sent him a doctor in whom he had great faith; and while my son's wounds were healing, the two, who had once been enemies, became friends.

Penelope, who went to nurse her brother, found the company of Charles Blount very stimulating, and through this incident Christopher and I were drawn closer together.

His love and admiration for his brother and his anxiety for me, because he understood my fears for my son, made a stronger bond between us. He seemed to grow up and cease to be a mere boy; and when the affair was over we shared our relief that it had turned out far better than we had dared hope.

The matter of the golden chessman was soon forgotten at Court, but, looking back, I can see that it was an important milestone in our lives.

The year dawned with the main preoccupation, the growing menace of Spain. The Queen, Leicester told me, was constantly trying to ward off the final confrontation which she had been successful in eluding for many years, and now it was undoubtedly at hand. Men like Drake had raided Spanish harbors and destroyed them in a manner which was called "singeing the beard of the King of Spain." That was all very well, but it was not going to destroy the Armada, which even our most optimistic people had to admit was the finest in the world. There was a good deal of gloom' throughout the country, for many of our sailors had been captured by the Spaniards, and some had become prisoners of the Inquisition. The tales they had had to tell of Spanish torture were so shocking that the whole country rose in fury. They knew that in those mighty galleons would come not only the weapons of war to destroy our ships and subdue our country, but the instruments of torture through which they vowed they would force us all to accept their faith.

We had made merry long enough. Now we had to face realities.

Robert was constantly with the Queen—restored to the highest favor again—all differences forgotten in the great fight to preserve their country and themselves. It was not to be wondered at that the stories about them, which had existed in their youth, should still be circulated.

At this time a man calling himself Arthur Dudley came into prominence. He was living in Spain helped by the Spanish King, who must either have thought the story was true or that the man's allegations could help to discredit the Queen.

Arthur Dudley was reported to be the son of the Queen and Leicester who had been born twenty-seven years before at Hampton Court. The story was that he had been put into the charge of a man named Southern, who had been warned on pain of death not to betray the secret of the child's birth. Arthur Dudley now alleged that he had discovered who he was, for Southern had confessed this to him.

This tale was circulated throughout the country but no one seriously believed it, and the Queen and Leicester ignored it. It certainly made no difference to the people's determination to keep off the Spaniards.

As the year progressed I saw even less of my husband than usual. The Queen made him Lieutenant General of the troops as a mark of her absolute confidence in him.

The fleet, commanded by Lord Howard of Effingham, assisted by Drake, Hawkins and Frobisher—all tried seamen of great courage and resource—was assembling at Plymouth, where the attack was expected. There was an army of eighty thousand men, all eager to hold the country against the enemy. There could not have been a man or woman in that country—save those Catholic traitors—who was not determined to do everything he—or she—could possibly do to save England from Spain and the Inquisition.

We glowed with pride and determination; a change seemed to come over us all; we had that unselfish pride. It was not ourselves we were anxious to advance, but our country which we wanted to preserve. This astonished me, who am by nature a self-centered woman, but even I would have died at that time to save England.

On the rare occasions when I saw Leicester, we talked glowingly of victory. We should succeed. We must succeed; it must be the Queen's England for as long as God gave her life.

It was dangerous time, but it was a glorious time. There was with us an almost divine determination to save our country; some spiritual force told every one of us that while we had the faith we could not fail.

Elizabeth was magnificent and never so beloved by her people as at that time. The City of London's response was typical. Having been told that the City must provide five thousand men and fifteen ships as a contribution to victory, its answer was that it would not provide five thousand but ten thousand men, not fifteen but thirty ships.

It was a mingling of fear of the Spaniards and pride in England; and the latter was so strong that we knew— every one of us—that it would suppress the other.

Leicester spoke of Elizabeth in exulting terms and strangely enough I felt no jealousy.

"She is magnificent," he cried. "Invincible. I would you could see her. She expressed her wish to go to the coast so that if Parma's men set foot on her land, she would be there to meet them. I told her I would forbid it. I said she might go to Tilbury and there speak to the troops. I reminded her that she had made me her Lieutenant General and as such I forbade her to go to the coast."

"And she is to obey you?" I asked.

"Others lent their voices to mine," he answered.

Oddly enough I was glad they were together at this time. Perhaps because at this hour of her glory, when she showed herself to her people and her enemies as the great Queen she was, I ceased to see her as a woman—my rival for the man we both loved more than we could any other—and she could only be Elizabeth the Magnificent, the mother of her people; and even I must revere her.

What happened is well known, how she went to Tilbury, and made that speech which has been remembered ever since, how she rode among them in a steel corselet with her page riding beside her carrying a helmet decorated with white plumes, how she told them she had the body of a weak woman but the heart and stomach of a king and a King of England.

Truly she was great then. I had to grant her that. She loved England—perhaps it was her only true love. For England she had given up the marriage she might have had with Robert, and I cannot but believe that that was what she had longed for in the days of her youth. She was a faithful woman; true affection was there behind the royal dignity just as the brilliant statesman lurked ever watchful beside the frivolous coquette.

The story of that glorious victory is well known—how our little English ships, being so agile on account of their size, were able to dart among the mighty but unwieldy galleons and wreak havoc among them; how the English sent fireships among the great vessels, and the great Armada, called by the Spaniards The Invincible, was routed and defeated off our coasts; how the unfortunate Spaniards were drowned or cast ashore where scant hospitality was afforded them; and how some returned in disgrace and shame to their Spanish master.

What glorious rejoicing followed! There were bonfires everywhere with singing, dancing and self-congratulations.

England was safe for the Queen. How like her to strike those medals *Venit, Vidit, Fugit* as a play on the motto of Julius Caesar, who came and saw and conquered while the Spaniards came and saw and fled. That was very popular; but I think some of her sailors might have taken exception to the other medal in which she declared that the enterprise had been conducted by a woman—*Dux Femina*

Facti. England would never forget what it owed to Drake, Hawkins, Frobisher, Raleigh, Howard of Effingham, as well as Burleigh and even Leicester. However, she was the figurehead—Gloriana, as the poet Spenser had called her.

It was her victory. She was England.

The Passing of Leicester

First of all, and above all persons, it is my duty to remember my most dear and gracious princess, whose creature under God I have been, and who hath been a most bountiful and princely mistress to me.

LEICESTER'S WILL

I was at Wanstead when Leicester came home. I did not at first realize how ill he was. He was bolstered up with his glory. Never had he been in such favor. The Queen could not bear him to leave her for long, but she sent him away at this time because she feared for his health.

He did not usually go to Buxton at this time of the year, but she had decided that he must do so without delay.

I looked at him afresh. How old he was, divested of his glittering garments. He had put on weight again and left his youth far behind. I could not help comparing him with Christopher and I knew that I no longer wanted this old man in my bed even though he was the Earl of Leicester.

The Queen had seemed as though she could not honor him enough. She had promised to make him Lord Lieutenant of England and Ireland. This would bring him greater power than any subject of hers had ever known before. It was almost as though she decided that she wanted no more juggling for power between them; if she were not offering him a share in her crown this was something very near it.

There were others who realized this, and he was incensed because Burleigh, Walsingham and Hatton had persuaded her not to act rashly.

"But it will come," Robert told me, those eyes of his once so fine and flashing, now puffy and bloodshot. "You wait. It will come."

Then suddenly he knew.

Perhaps it was because he had ceased to think so much of matters of state. Perhaps his sickness—for he was very sick, more so than he had been during those bouts of gout and fever which had beset him over the last years—had made him especially perceptive. Perhaps there was an aura about me which women get when they are in love, for I was in love with Christopher Blount. Not as I had been with Leicester. I knew there would never be anything like that in my life again. But it was like an Indian summer of love. I was not yet too old to love. I was young for my forty-eight years. I had a lover twenty years my junior, yet I felt that we were of an age. I realized anew how young I was when I was face to face with Leicester. He was a sick and aging man and I lacked the Queen's gift of dedicated fidelity. After all I had been grossly neglected for her sake. I marveled that she could look upon what he had become and still love him. It was yet another facet of her extraordinary nature.

He had seen me with Christopher. I cannot say what it was. Perhaps the manner in which we looked at each other. It may have been that our hands had touched. He may have seen something kindle between us—or he could have heard whispers. There were always enemies to carry tales about us—of me no less than of him.

In our bedchamber at Wanstead he said to me: "You have a fondness for my Master of Horse."

I was not sure then what he knew, and to gain time I said: "Oh . . . Christopher Blount?"

"Who else? Have you a fancy for each other?"

"Christopher Blount," I repeated, feeling my way. "He is very good with horses. . . ."

"And women, it seems."

"Is that so? You would have heard that his brother and Essex fought their duel. It was over a woman. A queen from the chessboard, in gold and enamel."

"I am not speaking of his brother, but of him. You had better admit, for I know."

"What do you know?"

"That he is your lover."

I shrugged my shoulders and retorted that if he admired me and showed it, was I to blame?

"If you let him into your bed, you are."

"You have been listening to tales."

"Which I believe to be true."

His grip was painful on my wrist, but I did not flinch. I

faced him defiantly. "My lord, should you not look to your own life before you peer too closely into mine?"

"You are my wife," he said. "What you do on my bed is my business."

"And what you do in the beds of others mine!"

"Oh come," he said. "Let us not diverge from the truth. I am away . . . in attendance on the Queen."

"Your good kind mistress . . ."

"The mistress of us all."

"But in one particular case . . . yours."

"You know there has never been that kind of intimacy between us."

"Arthur Dudley could tell another story."

"He could tell many lies," he retorted, "and when he says he is my son and Elizabeth's that is the greatest lie he ever told."

"It seems to be believed."

He threw me from him in his rage. "Do not evade the matter. You and Blount are lovers. Are you? Are you?"

"I am a neglected wife," I began.

"You have answered." His eyes narrowed. "Think not that I shall forget this. Think not that you can betray me with impunity. I shall make you answer for this insult . . . you and him."

"I have answered already for marrying you. The Queen has never once received me since."

"You call that payment! You will discover a great deal."

He stood before me—big and menacing, the most powerful man in the country. Words from *Leicester's Commonwealth* danced before my eyes. Murderer. Poisoner. Was this true? I thought of the people who had died at a time convenient to him. Was it merely a coincidence?

He had loved me. At one time I had meant a great deal to him. Perhaps I still did. He had come to me when he could; we had been well matched physically; but I had grown out of love with him.

Now he knew that I had a lover. Whether he wanted me still, I did not know. He was sick and feeling his age. I think at this time he only wanted to rest, but the hatred was there when he faced me. He would never forgive me for taking a lover.

I believed then that during those absences from home he had not been unfaithful. He had been in attendance on the Queen since his return from the Netherlands and I remembered that when he had been there he had wanted me beside him, decked out as his Queen.

Yes, I had had some power over him, for he had wanted me; he needed me; he would have been a uxorious husband if the Queen had allowed him to be.

And now I had betrayed him. I had taken a lover and one in what he would consider a menial post in his household. He would not allow any to insult him and escape. Of one thing I was certain. There would be revenge.

I wondered whether I should warn Christopher. No, he would show his fear. He must not know. I understood Leicester as Christopher never could. I would know how to act, I promised myself.

He said slowly: "I gave up everything for you."

"Douglass Sheffield, you mean?" I asked, determined to hide the fear I was beginning to feel by a show of flippancy.

"You know she meant little to me. I married you and braved the Queen's wrath."

"That was directed against me. It was not you who had to brave it."

"How could I be sure what would happen to me? Yet I married you."

"My father forced you to make it legal, remember?"

"I wanted to marry you. I loved no one as I loved you."

"And then you proceeded to desert me."

"Only for the Queen."

I laughed at that. "There were three of us, Robert—

two women and one man. It makes no difference that one was a queen."

"It makes all the difference. I was not her lover."

"She did not let you enter her bed. I know that. But you were her lover, nonetheless, and she your mistress. Therefore do not stand in judgment on others."

He took me by the shoulders; his eyes blazed and I thought he was going to kill me. There was violence in his eyes. I wished I could see what else. He was making plans, I knew.

He said suddenly: "We shall be leaving tomorrow."

"We . . . ?" I stammered.

"You and I and your paramour among others."

"Where shall we go?"

A wry smile touched his lips. "To Kenilworth," he said.

"I thought you were going to take the baths."

"Later," he said. "First to Kenilworth."

"Why do you not go straight to the baths? That was what your mistress ordered you to do. I can tell you, you look sick . . . sick unto death."

"I feel so," he answered. "But first I would go to Kenilworth with you."

Then he left me.

I was afraid. I had seen the look in his eyes when he had said Kenilworth. Why Kenilworth? The place where we had met and loved wildly, where we had had our secret meetings, where he had made up his mind that however he angered the Queen he must marry me.

"Kenilworth," he had said, with a cruel smile about his mouth; and I knew some dark plan was in his mind. What would he do to me at Kenilworth?

I went to bed and dreamed of Amy Robsart. I was lying in a bed and saw someone lurking in the shadows of the room . . . men who began to creep silently towards the bed. It was as though voices were whispering to me: "Cumnor Place . . . Kenilworth . . ."

I awoke, trembling with fear, and all my senses told me that Robert was planning some terrible revenge.

The next day we left for Kenilworth. I rode beside my husband and, glancing sideways at him, I noticed the deathly pallor of his skin beneath the network of red veins on his cheeks. His elegant ruff, his velvet doublet, his cap with the curling feather could not hide the change in him. There was no doubt that he was a very sick man. He was approaching sixty and he had lived dangerously; he had denied himself very little of what the world calls the good things of life. It was now apparent.

I said: "My lord, we should go to Buxton without delay, for it would seem you are in need of the beneficial baths."

He answered abruptly: "We are going to Kenilworth."

But we did not reach Kenilworth. The day was coming to a close and I saw that he could scarcely sit his horse. We stayed at Rycott, the home of the Norris family, and he retired to his bed and stayed there for several days. I attended him. He did not mention Christopher Blount. He wrote to the Queen, though, and I wondered what he said to her and whether he would tell her of my infidelity and what effect it would have on her if he did. I was sure that it would enrage her, for although she deplored my marriage, she would take it as an insult to herself that I preferred another man.

I was able to read that letter before it was dispatched. There was nothing in it but the protestations of his love and devotion to his goddess.

I remember it now, word for word.

I must humbly beseech your Majesty to pardon your poor old servant [he had drawn the two "o's" in the word "poor" as though they were eyes by putting dots in the middle of the circle to remind her of that affectionate nickname] to be thus bold in thus sending to know how my

*gracious lady doeth and what ease of her late pains she
finds, being the chiefest thing in the world I do pray for,
for her to have good health and long life. For my own
poor case, I continue still your medicine and find it amends
much better than with any other thing that hath been given
me. Thus hoping to find perfect cure at the bath, with the
continuance of my wonted prayer for your Majesty's most
happy preservation, I humbly kiss your foot, from your
old lodging at Rycott this Thursday morning ready to take
my journey. By your Majesty's most faithful and obedient
servant.*

R. LEICESTER

He had added a postscript thanking her for a gift she
had sent him and which had followed us to Rycott.

No, there was nothing there about my misdemeanor;
and of course he had written it from Rycott because it was
a place where, in the past, she and he had stayed often.
Here in the park they had ridden and hunted together;
here in the great hall they had feasted and drunk and
played at being lovers.

I told myself I was justified in taking a lover. Had not
my husband been the Queen's lover all these years!

I sent for Christopher and we met in a small chamber
apart from the rest of the household.

"He knows," I told him.

He had guessed it. He said he did not care, but that was
bravado. He was trembling in his boots.

"What do you think he will do?" he asked, trying to
appear nonchalant.

"I know not, but I am watchful. Take care how you go.
Do not be alone if you can help it. He has his murderers
everywhere."

"I shall be ready," said Christopher.

"I think he will revenge himself on me," I told him,

which threw Christopher in an agony of fear, and gratified me.

We left Rycott and traveled through Oxfordshire. We were not very far from Cumnor Place, I realized, and there seemed something significant in that.

"We should stay the night at our Cornbury house," I told Leicester. "You are unfit to go farther just yet."

He agreed.

It was a dark and rather gloomy place—a ranger's lodge really, in the middle of a wood. His servants helped him to the paneled room which had quickly been made ready and he sank onto the bed.

I said we must stay there until the Earl was well enough to continue his journey. He needed a rest, for even the journey from Rycott to Cornbury had exhausted him.

He agreed that he must rest and was soon deep in sleep.

I sat by his bed. I did not have to feign anxiety, for I was indeed anxious to know what was brewing in his mind. I knew by the manner in which he pretended to be unconcerned that he was planning something which affected me.

There was a hushed atmosphere in the house. I could not rest. I was afraid of the shadows which came with the darkness. The leaves were beginning to bronze, for September had come; the wind had brought many of them down and the forest was becoming littered with them. I gazed out of the windows at those trees and listened to the wind moaning through their branches; and I wondered whether Amy had felt a similar sense of brooding during her last days at Cumnor Place.

On the third of September the sun was shining brightly and he rallied a little. In the late afternoon he called me to him and told me that we would resume our journey the next day if the improvement persisted. He said we would sort out our differences and come to an understanding. We were too close, he said, to part while there was life in us.

Those words sounded ominous; indeed his eyes glowed with a feverish intensity.

He felt so much better that he needed food, and he believed that when he had eaten his strength would have revived sufficiently for him to continue.

"Should you not go with all speed to the baths?" I asked.

He looked at me intently and said: "We'll see."

He ate in his bedchamber, being too tired to come down to the dining hall. He said he had a good wine which he wanted me to try with him.

All my senses were alert. It was like a warning signal jangling through my mind. I must not drink this good wine. There was not a man in the whole of the country more skilled in poisoning than Dr. Julio, who worked assiduously for his master.

I *must* not drink that wine.

Of course he might have no intention of poisoning me. He might have thought of a revenge other than death. If he had kept me a prisoner at Kenilworth, perhaps giving out to the world that I had lost my reason, that would have hurt me more than sudden death. But I must be watchful. I went to his chamber. On a table was a jug of wine with three goblets—one had been filled with wine, the other two were empty. He lay back on his pillows; his face was very red and I think he had already drunk more than was wise.

"Is this the wine I am to try?" I asked.

He opened his eyes and nodded. I put it to my lips but I would not take any. That would be folly.

"It's good," I said.

"I knew you would think so." I fancied I heard triumph in his voice. I set the goblet on the table and went to his bed.

"Robert, you are very sick," I said. "You will have to give up some of your duties. You have done too much."

"The Queen will never allow it," he replied.

"She is concerned for your health."

He smiled and said: "Yes, she always was." His voice was tender, and I felt a sudden wave of anger to think of those two aging lovers who had never consummated their love and, now that they were old and wrinkled, still glorified it or pretended to.

What right had a husband blatantly to admire a woman other than his wife—even if she was the Queen?

My love affair with Christopher was justified.

He closed his eyes and I went to the table. With my back to him I poured the wine, which I had been afraid to drink, into another goblet. It was one which he used because it had been a gift from the Queen. I went back to the bed.

"I feel so ill," he said.

"You have eaten too much."

"*She* always said I did."

"And she is right. Rest now. Are you thirsty?" He nodded. "Would you like me to pour you some wine?" I went on.

"Yes, do. The jug is on the table with my goblet."

I went to the table. My fingers trembled as I lifted the jug and poured wine into that goblet which had previously contained that intended for me. What is the matter with you? I admonished myself. If he meant you no harm, then all is well, and he will come to none either. And if he did . . . am I to blame?

I carried his goblet to the bed, and as I handed it to him his page, Willie Haynes, came into the room.

I said: "My lord suffers from a great thirst. Bring some more wine. He may need it."

The page went out as Leicester finished the draught.

The next day stands out clearly in my mind, even after all these years. The fourth of September—the summer still

365

with us, the faint tang of autumn snuffed out by the sun at ten of the clock.

Leicester had said we should be leaving that day. While my women were dressing me in my riding clothes, Willie Haynes came to the door. He was pale and trembling. The Earl was lying very still, he said, and looked strange. He feared he was dead.

Willie Haynes' fears were proved correct. That morning, in the Cornbury Ranger's Lodge, the mighty Earl of Leicester had slipped away from this world.

So he was dead, my Robert, the Queen's Robert. I felt stunned. I could not get out of my mind the picture of myself carrying the goblet to the bed. He had drunk that which had been intended for me . . . and he was dead.

No, I did not believe that. I was distraught. It was as though part of me was dead. For so many years he had been the most important figure in my life . . . he and the Queen.

I murmured: "Now there are only two of us." And I felt desolate.

Of course there was the usual outcry of "Poison"; and suspicion was naturally directed against me. Willie Haynes had seen me give him the wine and mentioned this. That the man believed to be the arch-poisoner of his day should be caught with his own medicine seemed rough justice, if he had indeed been, and I knew that suspicion of having killed him would follow me to the grave. I was panic-stricken when I heard there was to be a postmortem. I did not know whether I had poisoned Leicester or not. It may well have been that the wine he had intended for me, and which I had given him, had been unadulterated. His health was such that he could have died at any time. I had not tampered with it. How could I be blamed?

It was a great relief when nothing indicating poison was found in him. But then Dr. Julio was renowned for his poisons which after a very short time left no trace in the body. So I can never be certain whether my husband intended to poison me and I turned the tables by poisoning him—or whether he died from natural causes.

His death is as mysterious as that of his wife, Amy.

Christopher was eager for us to marry, but I remembered the story of the Queen, Robert and Amy Robsart, and I had to restrain his youthful impulsiveness. Of course I was not the Queen, with the attention of the world on me; but I was now the widow of the most talked of man, not only in England but in the whole of Europe.

"I said I would marry you," I told him. "But later . . . not yet."

I wished that I had been at Court so that I could have seen how the Queen received the news. I heard later that she said nothing but stared blankly before her; then she went to her private chamber and locked the door. She would not eat, nor would she see anybody. She wished to be alone with her grief.

How great that grief was I could guess. It shamed me in a way. It made me realize the immense depth of her nature; of her capacity for love and vindictive hatred.

She would not emerge from her room of grief. At the end of two days, her ministers became alarmed, and Lord Burleigh, taking some others with him, had her door burst open.

I could imagine her feelings. She had known him so long—since they were children. I knew that it would seem to her as though a light had gone out of her life. I could imagine her facing her cold cruel mirror and seeing the old woman whom she had refused to look at before. She *was* old—no matter how the handsome young men danced round her; she knew they begged only for favors. Stripped of her crown, the light would be doused, and the dance of the moths would be over.

But there had been one, she would tell herself—her

Eyes, her Sweet Robin, the only one in the world whom she had really loved—and he was no more. And surely she would think of how different her life would have been if she had risked her crown and married him. What intimate joys they would have shared! Perhaps she would have had children to comfort her now. What pangs of jealousy she would have missed, and what joy it would have given her to know that I could never have shared his life!

She and I were as close as we had ever been. Her grief was mine. I was surprised how much I had cared for him, since in the last years I had turned from him. But I had done so because she had come between us. There was going to be a deep emptiness in my life now that he was gone . . . as there would be with hers.

But, as always in times of stress, she remembered at length that she was the Queen. Robert was dead but life went on. Her life was England, and England would never die and leave her alone.

I was in a state of anxiety because I feared that in view of Robert's discovery of my affair, he might have altered his will, and expressed his reason for doing so.

But no. There had been little time, and he had changed nothing.

I was the executrix, with his brother Warwick, Christopher Hatton and Lord Howard of Effingham to assist me. I had not realized how deeply in debt he was. He had always spent lavishly, and at the time of his death was having a gift made for the Queen which consisted of a rope of six hundred pearls on which hung a pendant. This pendant contained an enormous central diamond and three emeralds, encircled by a band of diamonds.

She was the first he mentioned in his will—as though she were his wife; he thanked her for her goodness to him.

Even in death she came first. I allowed myself to savor a certain jealous anger. It salved my conscience.

He had made his will while he was in the Netherlands and he had believed then that I was in love with him.

He had written:

Next to her Majesty, I will return to my dear wife and set down for her that which cannot be so well as I would wish it, but shall be as well as I am able to make it, having always found her a faithful and very loving and obedient, careful wife, and so I do trust this Will of mine shall find her no less mindful of my being gone, than I was always of her, being alive.

Ah, Robert, I thought a little sadly, how I should be mourning if it was as you believed then, and how different it might have been if you had not had a royal mistress. I loved you once and I loved you well, but she was always there between us.

I was dismayed to find his bastard, Robert Dudley, liberally treated in his will. He was now thirteen years old and on my death and that of Robert's brother, the Earl of Warwick, he was to inherit a great deal. He would also receive certain benefits when he was twenty-one, and he was to be well provided for until he reached that age.

Of course, Robert had never denied that this boy was his; but since he was also Lady Stafford's, I thought that she and her husband might have provided for him.

To me was left Wanstead and three small manor houses including Drayton Basset in Staffordshire, which I eventually made my home. Leicester House was mine including all plate and jewels therein, but to my sorrow and secret rage Kenilworth had been left to Warwick and on his death was to pass to the bastard Dudley.

Moreover, as I have said, Robert was more deeply in debt than I had realized. His debts to the crown were twenty-five thousand pounds. He had been very generous to the Queen, and his gifts to her had been responsible for a great part of his debts. I expected that since he had died in her service this would be remembered. It usually was in such instances.

Alas, she had no intention of relenting towards me one jot. She had her vengeance. She had come out of her solitude, determined that every pound of his debts should be paid. Her hatred towards me had not abated because of his death.

She declared that the contents of Leicester House and Kenilworth should provide the means to pay his debts, and lists of these should be made at once so that those selected for sale could be brought out.

She was merciless where I was concerned and I was enraged but could do nothing about it.

One by one the treasures had to be sold—all those things which had been precious to me and part of my life. I wept with rage over them and inwardly cursed her—but as always I must bow to her will.

Even so, those enforced sales were not enough to settle all the debts, but I felt it important to raise a memorial to him in Beauchamp Chapel. It was of massive marble and bore his motto *Droit et Loyal*. I had an effigy of him made in marble wearing the collar of St. Michael; and beside him was a space for me when my time came.

So passed the great Earl of Leicester. A year later I married Christopher Blount.

Essex

ESSEX,

Your sudden and undutiful departure from our presence and your place of attendance, you may easily conceive how offensive it is, and ought to be, unto us. Our great favours bestowed on you without deserts, hath drawn you thus to neglect and forget your duty; for other constructions we cannot make of those your strange actions. . . . We do therefore charge and command you forthwith upon receipt of these our letters, all excuses and delays set apart, to make your present and immediate repair unto us, to understand our further pleasure. Whereof see you fail not, as you will be loth to incur our indignation, and will answer for the contrary at your uttermost peril.

The QUEEN *to* ESSEX

For a time I reveled in my marriage and I was happy. I had a handsome, young, adoring husband who was not constantly in attendance on another woman. My son Robert, Earl of Essex, was fast becoming one of the Queen's first favorites, and it seemed likely that he would eventually take his stepfather's place.

"One of these days I will tell the Queen that she must receive you at Court," he told me.

He was very different from Leicester, who had always been so cautious and devious. Sometimes I trembled for him. He had so little tact and was not going to pretend to what he did not feel for the sake of expediency. This could be attractive in its initial stages, but could it last with a woman as vain as the Queen, and one so accustomed to adulation as she was? At the moment Essex was refreshingly youthful, an *enfant terrible*. He himself had always been inordinately vain, but was he overestimating his influence with the Queen?

I discussed this with Christopher, who was of the opinion that the Queen was so enamored of his youth and good looks that she would forgive him a good deal. Christopher's youth and good looks had done likewise for him, I reflected; but I should not be ready to endure insolence, however young and good-looking he might be; and I doubted Elizabeth would either.

I had thought it wise to wait a year before marriage in view of the rumors about Leicester's death and the fact that my new husband was some twenty years younger than I. The year that followed was a happy one.

We had always been a loyal family. One of Leicester's most endearing qualities had been devotion to his; and although my children had been on the best of terms with the first of their stepfathers, they were nonetheless ready to accept the second.

My favorite daughter was Penelope. She was something of an intrigante, as I myself was, and whatever her misfortunes, they never depressed her, and she was constantly looking around for exciting adventures. I knew, of course, that her life was not quite what it seemed. She lived quite decorously at Leighs in Essex and in Lord Rich's London home. In the country she appeared to be a model of virtue, devoting herself to her growing brood. She now had five children—three sons, Robert, Henry and Charles, and two girls, Lettice (named for me) and Penelope for herself. But when she came to Court she was full of plans.

She deplored the fact that the Queen would not receive me, and kept assuring me that Essex would lose no opportunity to get me reinstated.

"If Leicester could not do it, do you think Essex can?" I demanded.

"Ah," laughed Penelope, "do you think Leicester tried hard enough?"

I had to agree that he would have found it difficult to plead the cause of his wife, who was ostracized for the very reason that she *was* his wife.

They were often at Leicester House—my two daughters, my son Walter, and very often Essex. His friendship with Charles Blount, with whom he had fought a duel over the chess queen, had grown, and Charles, who was after all the elder brother of my husband, was very much one of the family. Frances Sidney was also a frequent visitor; and the talk round my table was full of vitality and sometimes wild. I did not care to restrain them, because I thought it would call attention to my age as they were all younger than I, although at times I wondered what the Queen would have thought could she have heard them.

The most reckless of them all was Essex, who was growing more and more sure of his domination over the Queen. Charles Blount warned him now and then he ought to have a care, but Essex just laughed at him.

I used to watch him with great pride, for I was sure it

373

was not just a mother's prejudice which made him supreme in my eyes. He was no more handsome than Leicester had been in his youth, and he possessed the same magnetism; but whereas Leicester had seemed to possess all the perfections nature could bestow on a man, Essex's very weaknesses were more endearing than Leicester's strength had been.

Leicester had always calculated the effect of what he did, weighing up the advantage to himself. Essex's very impulsiveness was appealing because it was dangerous. And honest—at least as *he* saw it. He could be very gay and then suddenly melancholy; he was vigorous and excelled at outdoors pastimes; then suddenly he would fall ill and have to take to his bed. He had a strange loping walk which made it possible to pick him out in a group from a long distance, and somehow it touched me deeply whenever I noticed it. Of course he was very handsome with that mass of auburn hair and those dark eyes—the coloring he had inherited from me—and of course he was very different from the other young men who circulated about the Queen. They were sycophants and he was never that. Moreover, he had a genuine passion for the Queen; he was in love with her in a way, but never did he subdue his own nature to suit hers. He would not pretend that she was all-knowing, if he disagreed with her.

I was very afraid as to where his impulsive steps would lead him and I was constantly begging him to take care.

When he sat with Penelope, Charles Blount, Christopher, Frances Sidney and myself, he would talk of what he hoped to do. He believed the Queen should be more bold with the Spaniards. They had suffered a bitter and humiliating defeat and it should be followed up. He was going to tell the Queen what course of action she should take. He had great plans. For one thing he wanted a standing army.

"Soldiers should be well trained," he cried, waving his

arms enthusiastically. "Each time we go to war we have to train men and boys anew. We want them ready. I am constantly telling her this. When I take my army to the war I want soldiers not plowmen."

"She will never agree to let *you* go out of the country," Penelope reminded him.

"Then I shall go without her consent," retorted my son loftily.

I wondered what Leicester would have said.

Sometimes, tentatively, I reminded him of how his step-father had behaved towards the Queen.

"Oh, he was like the rest," retorted Essex. "He dared not cross her. He pretended to agree with everything she said or did."

"Not always, and he crossed her more than once. He married me, remember."

"He never crossed her openly."

"He remained her favorite to the end of his life," I added.

"So shall I," boasted Essex, "but I shall do it my way."

I wondered, and continued to fear for him, for although Penelope was close to me, it was Essex who was my favorite. I thought how strange it was that the Queen and I should love the same men and that for so long the man who was of most importance to her should be to me also.

I knew that she still mourned Leicester. I heard that she kept a miniature of him which she looked at often; and that she had the last letter he had written her in a box which was labeled: *"His last letter."*

Yes, it was like a strange joke of fate that now my husband was dead the man she should most care about should be my son.

Essex was complaining that his debts were many and that, although the Queen showed her favor by keeping him at her side, she had bestowed nothing of value on him—

375

no titles, no lands, such as those she had given to his step-father; and he was too proud to ask her for them.

He was restive and longed for adventure of a kind that would bring him money. War was the answer, for, if it were victorious, spoils went with it. Moreover he was growing more insistent—and others agreed with him—that war with the Spaniards should be pursued.

The Queen agreed at length that an expedition might be sent out. Don Antonio, the ex-King of Portugal, had been deposed a year after he had come to the throne on the death of King Henry, and had been living in England ever since that time. Now King Philip of Spain had sent the Duke of Alva to claim Portugal for Spain. As the Portuguese were resentful of the Spanish usurpation, Portugal appeared to be a good battlefield. Sir Francis Drake was to take care of the fleet operations and Sir John Norris those of the land.

When Essex hinted that he should go, the Queen flew into a rage and he knew that it was useless to say more to her, but, being Essex, he was not deterred, and planned to go without telling her.

He came to say goodbye to me a few days before he left, and I was flattered to be taken into his confidence on this very secret matter, especially when the Queen was excluded.

I said: "She will be furious with you. It may be that she will not take you back."

He laughed at that. He was so confident of knowing how to deal with her.

I warned him, but not too seriously. To tell the truth, I was rather pleased at the thought of her anger and frustration at losing him.

How he loved intrigue! He and Penelope planned together.

The night he left he was going to invite Penelope's husband, Lord Rich, to his chamber to sup with him, and after his guest had left he would make his way to the park where his groom would be waiting for him with fleet horses.

"Drake will never allow you to board his ship," I told him. "He knows full well it would be against the Queen's wishes, and *he* is a man who would not risk offending her."

Essex laughed. "Drake will not see me. I have arranged with Roger Williams to have a ship waiting for me. We shall put to sea and conduct a campaign of our own if they won't let us join with them."

"You terrify me," I said; but I was proud of him, proud of that bold, reckless courage which I believed he had inherited from me, for it certainly had not come from his father.

He kissed me, all charm and concern. "Nay, dearest Mother, fear not. I promise you this: I shall come home so covered in glory and with so much Spanish gold that all men will marvel. I will give the Queen a part of it and make it clear to her that if she will keep me at her side she must accept my mother, too."

It all sounded very fine, and such was his enthusiasm that, temporarily at least, I could believe him.

He had written several letters to the Queen explaining what he was doing, and these he had locked in his desk.

He set out in the early morning for Plymouth and after riding ninety miles on his horse, he sent his groom back with the keys of his desk and instructions that these were to be given to Lord Rich, with the request that he should open the desk and take the letters to the Queen.

The fury of the Queen when she received those letters was so great that those at Court said it was the end of Essex. She swore about him, calling him all the unflattering names she could think of, and promising herself that she would show him what it meant to flout the Queen. I could not repress a certain gratification at her frustration and disappointment while at the same time I was apprehensive as to how deeply Essex had injured his chances.

She immediately wrote to him, commanding his return, but it was not until three months later that he came home and when he did he showed me the letters she had sent him. She must have been in a fine rage when she wrote them.

When the letters came into his hands after weeks of adventures—mostly disastrous—he did have enough wisdom to realize that immediate obedience was essential.

The expedition had been a failure, but Drake and Norris returned with cargoes of rich treasure stolen from the Spaniards, so it was not entirely a lost effort.

Essex presented himself to the Queen, who demanded an explanation of his actions, at which he fell onto his knees and told her how enchanted he was to see her. It was worth everything he had suffered to see her again. She might punish him for his folly. He did not care. He had come home and been allowed to kiss her hand.

He really meant that. He *was* delighted to be home; and she, in her glittering gown and her aura of regality, would have struck him afresh with her unique quality.

She made him sit beside her and tell her of his adventures, and she was clearly happy to have him with her, so that it was obvious that everything had been forgiven.

"It is as it was with Leicester," said everyone. "Essex can do no wrong."

It may be that Elizabeth, knowing that he had gone away to make his fortune, determined that he should learn to make it at home. She became generous to him and he began to grow rich. Most important of all she gave him the right to farm customs on the sweet wines which were imported into the country and thus presented him with an opportunity to reap a big income. This right had been one of her gifts to Leicester and I knew, through him, what an asset it had been.

My son was the Queen's first favorite and, oddly enough, he was in love with her in his own peculiar way. The question of marriage, which had occupied Leicester for so long, would never occur to him; but she fascinated him completely; he adored her. I saw some of the letters he wrote to her and they glowed with this extraordinary passion. This did not prevent his affairs with others and he was getting a reputation for philandering. He was, of course, irresistible—with his looks, his charming manners and court favor. I could see how he suited the Queen at this time of her life. She would never love him as deeply as she had loved Leicester, but this was different. This young man—who spoke his mind so freely, who detested subterfuge—had placed her on a pedestal to be adored and she was enchanted.

I watched his progress with delight, wonder and triumph because this was *my* son who, in spite of his maternal parent, had found his way into her heart. At the same time I was apprehensive. He was so rash. He did not seem to realize the danger all about him—or if he did, he did not care. His enemies were everywhere. I greatly feared Raleigh—clever, subtle, handsome Raleigh—beloved of the Queen, but never quite as she had loved my two—my husband and my son. Sometimes the irony of it all would present itself to me and I would be hysterical with laughter. It was like a quadrille. The four of us weaving our pattern to the tune which was not entirely of her making. One of the dancers had left the dance now, but the three of us remained.

Essex had no head for money. How different from Leicester! And Leicester had died deep in debt. I often wondered what would happen to my son. The richer he became—through the Queen's bounty—the more generous he was. All those who served him benefited. They declared they would follow him to the ends of the earth but sometimes I wondered if their loyalty would have been so firm if he ever lacked the means to pay for it.

My darling Essex! How I loved him! How proud I was of him! And how I feared for him!

It was Penelope who drew my attention to his increasing devotion to Frances Sidney. Frances was a very beautiful girl; her darkness inherited from her father, whom the Queen had called her Moor, was arresting; but because she was quiet she always seemed a little apart from the rest of the young who congregated around my table.

Penelope said that Frances appealed to Essex because she was so different from him.

"Do you think he intends to marry her?" I asked.

"It would not surprise me."

"She is older than he is—a widow with a daughter."

"He has always felt protective towards her since Philip died. She is calm and unobtrusive. She would not attempt to interfere with what he planned. I think he would like that."

"My dear Penelope, there is not a man in England who can have a brighter future than your brother. He could marry into one of the greatest and richest families in the land. He cannot choose Walsingham's daughter."

"My dear Mother," retorted Penelope, "it is not our choice but his."

She was right, but I could not believe it. Sir Francis Walsingham wielded a great deal of power in the country; he was one of the Queen's most able ministers, but she had never made him one of her real favorites; he was in the category which was acceptable for talent. The Queen would have been the first to admit that he had served her well. He had set up one of the finest spy systems in the world, and a great deal of this he had paid for out of his own resources. He it was who had been the prime mover in bringing the members of the Babington conspiracy to justice, which had resulted in the execution of Mary Queen of Scots. He was a man of great honesty and integrity, but he had certainly not amassed a fortune, nor had he gained great honors. But this Essex swept aside. He had decided to marry Frances Sidney.

Penelope and I with Christopher and Charles Blount talked to him, and Charles asked what he thought the Queen would say.

"I know not," cried Essex. "Neither would her disapproval deter me."

"It could result in your banishment from Court," Christopher reminded him.

"Good Christopher," boasted Essex, "do you think I do not know how to manage the Queen?"

"Pray do not even mention such a thing," begged Charles. "If such words were carried to the Queen . . ."

"We are all friends here," retorted Essex. "Leicester married, and she forgave him."

"But not his wife," I reminded him bitterly.

"Had I been Leicester I should have refused to go to Court without my wife."

"Had you been Leicester, my son, he would never have retained the Queen's favor throughout his life. I do beg of you, take care. Leicester was to her what no man ever was or will be, yet he knew he had to walk with care."

"I am to her what no man ever was or shall be. You will see."

Of course he was young and arrogant, and she had made much of him. I wondered whether he would ever begin to learn.

The young people admired him. They lacked my experience and approved of his boldness, and once again I did not wish to seem old and unadventurous, so I was silent.

Perhaps our opposition to the match made Essex all the more determined.

He came to see me on his return from Seething Lane, where Sir Francis was living, and told me that he had won his approval for the match.

"The old man is very ill," said Essex, "and I think he cannot last long. He told me that he has little to leave Frances for his debts are many. He said he doubted there would be enough money to bury him with dignity, so much had he spent in the service of the Queen."

I knew Walsingham was right and I thought him a fool for doing so. Leicester had served the Queen and made a very profitable affair of it—yet he also had died in debt, and at this very time I was bemoaning the loss of certain treasures which had had to be sold to pay them.

The outcome was that my son and Walsingham's daughter—who was Philip Sidney's widow—were married secretly.

I was shocked when I called on Sir Francis to see how ill he was. He was delighted, though, by his daughter's marriage. He told me that he had been anxious about her future. Philip Sidney had left little and he had little to leave either. "To live in the Queen's service is a costly matter," he said.

Indeed he was right. When I think of what Leicester had spent on New Year's gifts to the Queen—the diamonds, the emeralds, the necklaces of lovers' knots—I thought it was small wonder that my treasures had to go to pay for them.

Poor Sir Francis died soon after that and he was buried secretly at midnight because a proper funeral would have been too expensive.

The Queen was sorry and mourned for him. "I shall miss my Moor," she said. "Aye, miss him sadly. He was a good servant to me and I did not always treat him kindly, but he knew well that my respect for him went deep, and I was not the ungrateful mistress I might sometimes have appeared to be. I hear there is very little left for his poor widow and his girls."

After that she took a little interest in Frances and made her sit and talk to her. This had a rather unfortunate sequel because Frances quickly became pregnant.

The Queen was very observant of her women; she seemed to have an extra sense where their romantic attachments were concerned.

Frances herself told me what happened.

The Queen never minced her words and it often seemed that she tried to remind people of her father Henry VIII by a certain masculine coarseness.

She prodded Frances in the stomach and demanded to know whether she carried anything there which a virtuous widow should not. Frances was not the most subtle of women and she immediately flushed scarlet, so that the Queen knew her suspicions were correct.

That extraordinary interest in the sexual activities of those about her, which could flare into sudden anger, bewildered many. She behaved as though the act of love fascinated her while it disgusted her.

Frances said she received a sharp nip in the arm with a demand to explain by whom she was pregnant.

For all her quietness, Frances had dignity; she lifted her head and said: "My husband."

"Your husband!" cried the Queen. "I do not recall anyone's asking my permission to marry you."

"Madam, I did not think I was of sufficient importance to make that necessary."

"You are the daughter of the Moor and I always had a regard for him. Now he is dead your welfare is more than ever my concern. He married you in secret to Philip Sidney and excused himself with talk of no importance! I rated him sharply then, and you knew it. And have I not kept you here beside me since he died!"

"Yes, Madam, you have been most gracious to me."

"So . . . you thought fit to marry. Come. Tell me who he is."

Frances was terrified. She could only burst into tears at which the Queen's suspicions were aroused. Frances asked leave to retire that she might compose herself.

"You will remain," said the Queen. "Now tell me when you married, and I'll swear it was that the child you carry might be born in time. I tell you this: I will not have this lewd behavior in my Court. I do not treat this matter lightly." She then took Frances by the arm and shook her roughly, and when Frances fell to her knees she received a blow at the side of her face to remind her that she was withholding information which the Queen was demanding.

Frances was aware that sooner or later she would have to reveal her husband's name and that the Queen's fury would be great. She was old enough to remember what had happened when Leicester had married me.

Because of Frances's obvious fear, the Queen began to grow suspicious.

"Come, girl," she cried. "Who is your partner in this? Tell me, or I'll beat it out of you."

"Madam, we have long loved each other. Ever since my first husband was so cruelly wounded . . ."

"Yes, yes. Who? Tell me, girl. By God's blood, if you do not obey me, you will be sorry. I promise you that."

"It is my Lord Essex," said Frances.

She said that the Queen stared at her as though struck dumb, and forgetting she was in the presence of her sovereign, from which only permission should release her, so great was her terror that she rose to her knees and stumbled from the room, while the Queen just stood there staring at her.

As she ran away she heard the Queen's voice, raised and deadly.

"Send for Essex. Bring him here without delay."

Frances came straight to me at Leicester House in a state of collapse. I got her to bed while she told me what had happened.

Penelope, who was at Court, came shortly after her.

"All hell has broken loose," she said. "Essex is with the Queen and they are shouting at each other. God knows what will be the outcome. People are saying that before the day is out Essex will be in the Tower."

We waited for the storm to burst. I remembered so vividly the time when Simier had told the Queen that Leicester was married. She had wanted to send him to the Tower and had only been restrained from doing so by the Earl of Sussex. But she had relented. I did not know how deep her affection went for my son, but I did know that it was of a different nature from that which she had borne my husband. That had gone deep, entwined with the roots of her girlhood. I believed that which she bore my son was a more frail plant and I trembled for him. He would lack the tact of Leicester. He would show bravado where Leicester would have brought out his considerable diplomacy.

I waited at Leicester House with Penelope and Frances. In due course Essex came to us.

"Well," he said, "she is furious with me. She calls me ungrateful, reminding me that she brought me up and can as easily cast me down."

"A favorite theme," I commented. "Leicester heard it again and again throughout his life. She did not suggest sending you to the Tower?"

"I think she is on the point of doing so. I told her that much as I revered her, I was a man who would live his own life and marry where he chose. She said she hated deceit and when her subjects kept secrets from her it was because they knew they had something to hide, to which I replied that, knowing her uncertain temper, I had had no wish to arouse it."

"Robin!" I cried aghast. "You never did!"

"Something of the nature," he said carelessly. "And I demanded to know why she was so against my marriage, at which she replied that if I had come to her in a seemly manner and told her what I wished, she would have given the matter her consideration."

"And refused you permission!" I cried.

"And that would have meant that I should then have been obliged to disobey you instead of merely displeasing you."

"One day," I told him, "you will go too far."

I was to remember those words later, and even then they sounded like a tocsin ringing in advance to warn me of danger.

"Well," he went on, swaggering a little before us, "she told me that it was not only the secrecy which angered her but that I, for whom she had had grand plans, should have married beneath my station."

I turned to Frances, understanding her feelings. Had it not happened once to me? I wanted to comfort her and I said reassuringly: "She would have said that of anyone unless she were royal. I remember how she was ready—or said she was—to consider a princess for Leicester."

"It was an excuse to hide her fury," said Essex complacently. "She would have been mad with rage whomsoever I had married."

"The point is," said Penelope, "what happens now?"

"I'm in disgrace. Cast out of Court. 'You will want to dance attendance on your wife,' she said, 'so we shall not be seeing you at Court for some time.' I bowed and left her. She is in a vile mood. I do not envy those who serve her at close quarters."

I wondered how much he cared. He did not appear to

in the least at that moment, which was comforting for Frances.

"Think how much he loves you," I pointed out to her, "to incur the Queen's displeasure for your sake." Those words were like an echo coming down through the years —a repetition of the dance with Essex the Queen's partner now, instead of Leicester. There was the usual buzz of speculation at Court. Essex is out. What excitement for the others—men like Raleigh, who had always been at odds with him, and the old favorites. Hatton perked up considerably. Poor Hatton, he was showing his years, which was particularly noticeable in a man who had been so active and at one time the best dancer at Court. He still indulged and even took the floor with the Queen, as graceful as ever. Essex had outshone them all; and it was the younger ones like Raleigh and Charles Blount who stood to gain from his disgrace.

Poor Hatton did not benefit long from the decline of Essex. He became more and more weak during the days that followed and before long retired to his house in Ely Place, where he suffered acutely from an internal disease and died by the end of that year.

The Queen was melancholy. She hated death, and no one was allowed to mention it in her hearing. It must have been sad for her to see her old friends dropping from the tree of life like so many overripe plums, riddled by insects and disease.

It made her turn more and more to the young.

When Frances gave birth to a son we called him Robert after his father. The Queen relented. Essex might come back to Court, but she did not wish to see his wife.

So the Queen and my son were good friends again. She kept him by her side; she danced with him; they laughed together and he delighted her with his frank conversation. They played cards until early morning, and it was said that she was restless when he was not beside her.

Oh yes, it was like the old pattern with Leicester but, alas, where Leicester had learned his lessons, Essex never would.

I had at last accepted that fact that the Queen would never forgive me for having married Leicester and that I should always be an outside observer of the events which were shaping our country. That was hard for a woman of my nature to accept; but I was not one to sit down and mope. I suppose like my son and daughter I would fight to the end. I always felt, though, that if only I could have once met the Queen and talked to her, we could have repressed our resentment and I could have amused her in the way I had so long ago; then we could have come to some understanding. I was no longer Lettice Dudley but Lettice Blount. True I had a young husband who adored me, and that might displease her. She would think I ought to be punished for what I had done. I wondered if she had heard rumors about my having helped Leicester out of this world. Surely not. She would never have let that rest.

But I did not give up hope. Essex told me that on those occasions when he broached the matter of my reinstatement at Court her looks grew stormy, she became formidable and refused to discuss it with him, turning from him and not speaking to him for the rest of the evening. She had intimated that this was one subject which even he must not mention.

"I'll have to go warily with her," he said. "But I'll do it in time."

I guessed that she had been even fiercer than he implied, since she had made him realize that his insistence could bring about *his* banishment from Court. But I knew my Robert. He would not let the matter rest. It was, however, a question of her will against his.

So there I was—no longer young but still attractive. I had my home in which I took a pride. My table was one of the best in the country. I was determined to rival those of the royal palaces and I hoped the Queen would hear of it. I would myself supervise the making of salads from the products of my own gardens; my wines were muscatel and malmsey and those from Greece and Italy, which were often laced with my own special spices. The kissing comfits served at my table were the daintiest and sweetest to be found. I occupied myself with the making of lotions and creams specially suited to my needs. They enhanced my beauty so that there were times when it seemed it glowed more brightly as I grew older. My clothes were noted for their elegance and style; they were of silk, damask, brocade, sarcenet and the incomparable beauty of my favorite velvet. They came in the most delightful colors, for with every year the dyers grew more expert in their trade. Peacock blue and popinjay green; maidenhair brown and gentian blue; poppy red and marigold yellow. . . . I reveled in them all. My seamstresses worked constantly to beautify me and the result I must say—despising false modesty—was good.

I was a happy woman—apart from one great desire: to be received by the Queen. Being married to a husband much younger than myself helped to preserve my youth, and with a family who gave me so much affection—and among that family a son who was generally accepted to be the brightest star of the Court—I had good reason for contentment and must forget this need which overshadowed my life. I must forget the Queen, who was determined to punish me. I must take my life for what it was. I reminded myself that it was filled with excitement and my greatest delight was wrapped up in my son, who loved me devotedly and had made me the center of our family.

Why should I allow an aging and vindictive woman to come between me and my pleasure? I would forget her.

Leicester had gone. This was a new life for me. I must be thankful for it and enjoy it.

But I could not forget her.

Even so my family affairs provided perpetual interest. Penelope was growing more and more dissatisfied with her marriage, although she had borne two more children to Lord Rich. She was having a love affair with Charles Blount, and they met constantly at my house. I did not feel I could criticize them. How could I—understanding full well their feelings for each other? Moreover if I had, they would have taken no notice of me. Charles was a most attractive man and Penelope told me that he would very much like her to leave Rich altogether and set up house with him.

I wondered what the Queen's reaction to that situation would be. I knew that she would blame me. Every time Essex displeased her by a display of arrogance she would comment that he had inherited that trait from his mother, which showed that her animosity to me persisted.

Much that happened to my son is common knowledge. His was the sort of life which is an open book for all to read. So many of his emotions were displayed to the lookers-on; and when Essex rode through the streets people came out of their houses to stare at him.

He *was* arrogant, I knew; and very ambitious, but in my heart I also knew that he lacked the very quality to use his talents. Leicester had had that; Burleigh had it in excess; Hatton, Heneage, they all had stepped with the greatest care; but my son, Robin, liked to skate where the ice was thinnest. I sometimes think there was in him an inborn desire to destroy himself.

He told me that he despaired of ever realizing his ambition at home. Burleigh's one thought was to advance his own son, Robert Cecil, and Burleigh held great influence with the Queen.

I was amazed that my son should have dreamed of

taking over Burleigh's place in the State, which was of course the most important one of all. The Queen would never dismiss Burleigh. She might dote on her favorite of favorites, but she was always the Queen at heart and knew Burleigh's value. Often twinges of uneasiness would beset me when I was talking to my son, because he was fast believing that he was capable of leading the country. I, who loved him dearly, knew full well that even if his mental accomplishments had fitted him for that task, his temperament would have failed him.

During the few months he had lived in Burleigh's house, he had made the acquaintance of Burleigh's son, Robert like himself. But how different they were in appearance. Robert Cecil was very short; he had a slight curvature of the spine which the mode of dress at these times tended to exaggerate. He was very sensitive of his deformity. The Queen, who was fond of him and ready to advance Burleigh's son, was aware of his undoubted brilliance; however, she helped to call attention to his disability by giving him one of the nicknames she loved to bestow on her favorites. He was her Little Elf.

With Burleigh firmly in his post and unlikely ever to be removed from it except by death, Essex believed that his best way of advancing himself was through glory in battle.

The Queen was, at this time, much concerned with events in France, where, on the assassination of Henri III, Henri of Navarre had taken the throne and was having difficulty in holding it. As Henri was a Huguenot and Catholic Spain was still considered a threat in spite of the defeat of the Armada, it was decided to send help to Henri.

Essex wanted to go to France.

The Queen refused permission, for which I was glad; but I was worried, knowing what he had done previously and believing that he was quite capable of doing the same again. He was clearly becoming convinced that, whatever he did, the Queen would forgive him.

He sulked and begged and would talk of nothing but his desire to go, and at length she allowed him to do so. He took with him my son Walter and, alas, I never saw Walter again, for he was killed in the fighting before Rouen.

I have not written much of Walter. He was the young one, the quiet one. The rest of my children all asserted themselves, calling for attention in some way. Walter was different. I fancy the others resembled me, and Walter his father. But this gentle, affectionate boy was beloved by all of us, although we were inclined to ignore him when he was with us, but how we missed him when he was not! I knew that Essex would be heartbroken, and particularly so because he had persuaded him to go out and fight with him. It had been Essex who wanted to go to war and Walter had always wanted to follow his elder brother, but Essex would remember that, had he stayed at home as I —and the Queen—had wished him to, Walter would never have met his death. Knowing Essex well, I could imagine that his melancholy would match my own.

I heard news of him. He was brave in battle. Of course he would be, with his reckless, fearless nature; he cherished his soldiers and lavished honors on them when, Burleigh pointed out to the Queen, he had no right to. We were very anxious about him because men who returned home spoke of his absolute recklessness and oblivion to danger and how even when he wanted to hunt, he never hesitated about venturing into enemy country.

The loss of Walter and my fears for Essex made me very nervous and I even thought of begging the Queen to receive me that I might implore her to bring him home. Perhaps if I went on such a mission and somehow was able to have it conveyed to her why I came, she would see me.

I did not have to go as far as that, for she, sharing my anxieties concerning him, recalled him.

He made excuses about returning and I thought he was going to defy her, but finally he obeyed her. I saw little of him though, for the Queen would have him at her side through the day and far into the night. I was surprised when she allowed him to return to the field of action. I suppose she could not resist his pleading.

Frances visited me often, and we comforted each other. She was a gentle creature and she accepted Essex's wildness as she had Philip Sidney's passion for Penelope. There was a strength in her which contrasted oddly with her docility. She was a woman who had quickly learned to accept her fate with resignation, which was admirable, I supposed; and I thought of how I had raged against Leicester's absences and had revenged myself on him by taking a lover. Yet I could respect Frances's mildness and realized that it was a good crutch which carried her through the difficult periods of her life; but we are what we are, and I could never be like her.

Finally Essex came back unharmed. For four years he had stayed out of England.

The Road to the Scaffold

O God, give me true humility and patience to endure to the end, and I pray you all to pray with me and for me, that when you shall see me stretch out my arms and my neck on the block, and the stroke ready to be given, it would please the Everlasting God to send down His angels to carry my soul before His Mercy Seat.

ESSEX *at his execution*

To be a King, and wear a crown, is a thing more glorious to them that see it, than it is pleasant to them that bear it.

ELIZABETH

They were dangerous years. Although Essex rose high in the Queen's favor, I never knew a man so play with fire. He was *my* son after all. But I was continually reminding him of Leicester.

Once he said: "I wonder Christopher Blount does not object. You are always talking of Leicester as though he were a pattern of a man."

"For you, he could be," I said. "Remember that he kept the Queen's regard all his life."

Essex was impatient. He was not going to squirm and humble himself, he declared. The Queen, like everyone else, must take him as he was.

And it seemed she did. Oh, but he was surrounded by dangers. I knew Burleigh was against him now and determined to make the way clear for his son, but I was glad that Essex had struck up a friendship with the Bacon boys —Anthony and Francis. They were a clever pair and good for him, although they both suffered from resentment, fancying themselves both kept from high office by Burleigh.

Essex now had two more sons—Walter, after his sadly missed uncle, and Henry. He, alas, was a far from faithful husband. He was lusty and sensual and he could not live without women, and as he had never curbed his desires in any respect, it was natural that he should not in this. One woman was not enough for him, for his fancy strayed quickly, and being in the position he was, there was no dearth of young women ready to submit to him.

It was typical of him that, instead of choosing a mistress with care—someone whom he could visit secretly—he must become enamored of the Queen's maids of honor. There were at least four who were known to me. Elizabeth Southwell bore him a son who was known as Walter Devereux and that was a great scandal; then there was Lady Mary Howard and two girls named Russell and Brydges, all of whom were publicly humiliated by the Queen.

I was very apprehensive about his indiscreet behavior, because Elizabeth was particularly strict with her maids of honor, who were carefully taken from families selected by her—usually someone in the family had done her a service, and to take the girls was a reward. Mary Sidney was a good example of this, for she had been taken when her sister Ambrosia had died because the Queen was sorry for the family and Mary had, shortly afterwards and due to the Queen's efforts, made a brilliant marriage with the Earl of Pembroke. The parents of the girls were always delighted at the honor because they knew that the Queen would do her best to look after their daughters. If any of these girls married without her consent, she was furious; if she suspected any of what she called lewd behavior, she was even more incensed; and if their partner in disgrace should be any of her favorites, she would be wild with rage. Yet knowing this, Essex philandered, not only endangering his position at Court but causing great sorrow to his wife and mother.

I often wondered how long he would be able to steer himself safely through all the perils which he made no effort to avoid. Of course the Queen was old and clung more and more to the young; and when he was charming he was quite irresistible, as we all found.

Penelope had now left her husband and was living openly with her lover Charles Blount, who had become Lord Mountjoy on the death of his elder brother.

Penelope had never been a favorite with the Queen; she shared a lack of tact with her brother and of course the Queen would not accept from beautiful women what she did from handsome men. Moreover Penelope labored under the difficulty of being my daughter, and when the Queen heard that she had left her husband and was living with Mountjoy, while she was prepared to accept Mountjoy's departure from conventional behavior, for he was a good-looking young man, she did not apply the same leniency to Penelope, though not of her affection for Mountjoy, she did not forbid her to come to Court.

Penelope and Essex were fast friends, and she, being of a somewhat domineering nature, was constantly trying to advise him. She was very sure of herself. She was known as one of the most beautiful women at Court, as I had been; and Philip Sidney's poems which extolled her charms increased her good opinion of herself. Mountjoy adored her, and as Essex thought very highly of her also, she was a woman who could not but be pleased with her position, particularly as she had rid herself of a distasteful husband simply by leaving him.

It so happened that Penelope was staying with the Warwicks at North Hall when messengers came with the news that the Queen was not far off. Essex knew that Elizabeth would be displeased to find his sister there and might humiliate her by refusing to see her. He rode out to meet the Queen—a fact which delighted her, but she soon realized that his reason for coming was to warn her that his sister was at North Hall and to ask her to receive her kindly.

Elizabeth made little comment and Essex, as sure of himself as ever, thought she was naturally giving him what he asked. His dismay was great when orders were given that Penelope was to stay in her chamber while the Queen was at North Hall.

Impulsive Essex could never bear to be thwarted. He was devoted to his family and was constantly trying to persuade the Queen to receive me. That she should treat his sister in this way was insupportable to him.

After she had supped he asked her if she would receive Penelope. He had believed she had promised him that she would, he said, and he was hurt and bewildered that she should break her word. This was no way to tackle the Queen and she replied sharply that she had no intention of allowing people to say she had received his sister merely to please him.

"Nay," he cried hotly, "you will not receive her to please that knave Raleigh." Then he had gone on to say that she would do a good deal to please Raleigh. She would disgrace him and his sister for her love of that adventuring churl.

The Queen told him to be quiet but he would not be. He let out a tirade of scorn about Raleigh. She was in awe of the fellow, he said. He himself could find little pleasure in serving a mistress who was afraid of a low fellow like that.

This was all the more foolish, for Raleigh was of the party, and even if he did not overhear what was said, others soon would report it to him, so he was making of Raleigh an enemy for life—even if he had not already done so.

But the Queen tired of his tantrums. She shouted at him: "Do not presume to address me thus. How dare you criticize others. As for your sister, she is another such as your mother, and there is a woman I would not have at my Court. You have inherited her faults, and that is enough for me to send you away from here."

"Then do so," he cried. "Nor would I stay here to listen to my family's being slandered. I have no desire to serve such a mistress. I will remove my sister from this roof without delay, and since you are afraid to displease that knave Raleigh and he wants me gone, I will go too."

"I am weary of you, you foolish boy," said the Queen coldly, and turned away.

Essex bowed, retired and went straight to Penelope's room. "We are leaving here immediately," he told her. "Prepare yourself."

Penelope was bewildered, but it was necessary, he said, because he had had a disagreement with the Queen and they were in danger.

He sent her back to her home with an escort of servants

and declared he was going to Holland. He would be in time to join in the battle for Sluys and it might well be that he would fall. Never mind. Death was preferable to the service of such an unfair mistress, and he doubted not that she would consider herself well rid of him.

He then set out for Sandwich.

The next day, when the Queen asked for him, she heard that he was on his way to Holland. She sent a party after him to bring him back.

He was about to board a ship at Sandwich when they arrived, and at first he refused to return, but when he was told that if he did not they would take him back by force, he had to obey.

When he returned the Queen was delighted to see him. She scolded him and told him that he had been foolish and he was not going to leave Court without her permission.

Within a few days he was back in favor.

He had such good fortune, this wayward son of mine. If only he had taken advantage of it! Alas, it often seemed to me that he showed only contempt for the benefits showered on him. If ever a man tempted fate, that man was Essex.

One of his dearest wishes had been to get me reinstated at Court, for he knew how greatly I had desired this, and as Leicester had been unable to bring this about, I believe one of his reasons for wanting it was to achieve that which his stepfather had failed to.

It had always been a source of great distress to me that I could not be part of the Queen's circle. Leicester had been dead for ten years. Surely she could bear to see me now. I was a kinswoman; I was getting old; surely she could forget I had married her Sweet Robin.

I had given her her favorite man. Surely she must realize that but for me there could have been no Essex to disrupt and at the same time enchant her days. But she was a vindictive woman. My son was well aware of my feelings and had promised me that one day he would bring us together. He regarded it as a slight to himself that he could not persuade her to a reconciliation, and it was a challenge to his determination to enforce his will.

He was now acting as Secretary and she did not like him to be out of her sight. People realized that if they would please the Queen, they might be brought to her notice through this young man on whom she doted.

He came to Leicester House in a state of great excitement one day.

"Prepare yourself, my lady," he cried. "You are going to Court."

I could not believe it was possible. "Will she really see me?" I said.

"She has told me that she will be passing from her chamber to the Presence Room and, if you are in the Privy Gallery, she will see you as she passes through."

It would be a very formal meeting, but it would be a beginning and I was exultant. The long exile was over. Essex wanted the meeting and she could deny him nothing. She and I would be on civilized terms again. I remembered how in the old days I could often make her laugh, with some wry comment, some remark about people around us. We were old now; we could talk together, exchange reminiscences, let bygones be bygones.

I thought about her a good deal. I had seen her over the years, but never close. Riding on her palfry or in her carriage, she was remote, a great queen but still the woman who had defeated me. I wanted to be close to her, for only when I was near her could I feel alive again. I missed Leicester. Perhaps I had temporarily fallen out of love with him at the end but without him life had lost its savor. She could have put something back for me. We could have compensated each other for his loss. I had my young Christopher—a good, kind, devoted man who still marveled at his good fortune in marrying me; but I found myself constantly comparing him with Leicester—and what man could compare favorably with him! It was not Christopher's fault that I found him lacking. It was merely that I had been loved by the most dominating, exciting man of the age—and because she, the Queen, had loved him too, only now that I had lost him could I recapture that zest for life if she would take me into her circle once more— laugh with me, do battle with me—anything if she would but come back into my life.

I was overwhelmed with excitement at the prospect of going back to Court again. She meant so much in my life. She was part of me. I could never be unaware of her any more than she could of me. She was lost and lonely without Leicester as I was too. Even if I had deluded myself into believing that I had not loved him at the end, it made no difference now.

I wanted to talk to her—two women, too old for jealousy surely. I wanted to remember with her the early days when she loved and thought of marrying Robert. I wanted to hear from her lips how much she knew of the death of Robert's first wife. We should be so close. Our lives were entwined with that of Robert Dudley and it was to each other that we should tell our secrets.

I had not been so excited for a long time.

On the appointed day, I dressed with great care and restraint—not flamboyantly, but unassumingly, which was the manner I wished to convey. I must be humble, grateful, and show my deep pleasure in an unrestrained manner.

I went to the gallery and waited with a few others there. There were some who were surprised to see me and I noticed the discreet glances which were exchanged.

The minutes slipped by. She did not appear. There was a whisper in the gallery and more glances came my way. An hour had passed and still she had not come.

At length one of her pages came into the gallery. "Her Majesty will not be passing through the gallery today," he announced.

I felt sick with disappointment. I was sure that it was because she knew I was waiting there that she had not come.

Essex came to Leicester House later in the day.

He was distressed. "You did not see her, I know," he said. "I told her you had waited and had gone away disappointed, but she said she felt too unwell to leave her chamber, and she has promised that there shall be another time."

Well, it could be true.

A week later, Essex told me that he had so persisted that the Queen had said she would see me as she passed out of the palace to her coach. She was dining out, and it would be a beginning if I waited once more, and as she passed she would have a word with me. That was all I needed; then I could ask to come to Court, but until I had received that friendly word I was powerless.

Essex was suffering from one of his periodic bouts of fever and was in bed in his apartment at the palace, otherwise he would have accompanied the Queen and what would have made it easier for me.

However, I was no novice of Court ways, and once more dressed myself, as I thought, suitably, and taking a diamond worth about three hundred pounds from that store left to me after so much had been sold to pay Leicester's debts, I sat out for the palace.

Once more I waited in the anteroom where others, who sought a passing word with her, were assembled. After a while I began to suspect that it would be the same as before, and how right I was proved to be. After a while the coach was taken away and I heard that the Queen had decided not to dine out that night.

Fuming with rage, I returned to Leicester House. I

could see that she had no intention of receiving me. She was using the same treatment to me as she had given her suitors. One was supposed to go on hoping, go on trying and be prepared to meet with failure at every turn.

I heard from my son that when he had learned that she had decided not to dine out he had left his sickbed to go to her and implore her not to disappoint me again. She had, however, been adamant. She had made up her mind not to dine out and she would not do so. Essex sulked and returned to his bed with the remark that as no small request of his was worth consideration it would be better if he retired from Court.

He must have made some impression on her, for shortly afterwards he came with a message from the Queen. She would receive me privately.

This was triumph. How much better it would be for me to be able to talk to her, to speak of the past, to make a bid for her friendship, seated beside her perhaps. How different from a passing word!

I wore a gown of blue silk and an embroidered underskirt of a paler shade, a delicate lace ruff and a light gray velvet hat with a curling blue feather. I was becomingly dressed (for I could not give her the satisfaction of thinking I had lost my good looks) and at the same time discreetly so.

As I went into the palace I wondered whether she would find some excuse yet for turning me away. But no, this time I did come face to face with her.

It was a thrilling moment when I stood before her. I sank to my knees and remained there until I felt her hand on my shoulder and heard her bid me to rise.

I stood up and we took measure of each other. I knew she was aware of every detail of my looks and dress. I could not repress a satisfaction as I noticed how she had aged. Even the careful toilette, the subtle application of rouge, the red wig could not hide it completely. She was over sixty, but her slender figure and upright carriage did a great deal for her. Her neck showed the strains of age but her bosom was as white and firm as ever. She was in the white which she loved—a gown lined with scarlet and decorated with pearls. I wondered if she had given as much care to her appearance as I had. When she lifted her hand, the long hanging sleeve fell back disclosing the scarlet lining. She had always used her hands to effect. Beautifully white and still perfectly shaped, they showed little sign of age; they looked delicate, weighed down with the jewels which glittered on them.

She laid her hands on my shoulders and kissed me. I felt the blood rush to my cheeks, and I was glad, for she took it as emotion. But it was just plain triumph. I was back.

"It is a long time, Cousin," she said.

"Your Majesty, it has seemed an age."

"More than ten years since he left me." Her face puckered and I thought she was going to weep. "It is as though he is with me still. I still never grow accustomed to being without him."

She was, of course, talking about Leicester. I should have liked to tell her that I shared her feelings, but that would have seemed quite false since I had been married to Christopher for the last ten years.

"How did he die?" she asked. Obviously she wanted to hear again what she must know already.

"In his sleep. It was a peaceful ending."

"I am glad. I still read his letters. I can see him so well . . . when he was but a boy." She shook her head sadly. "There was never one like him. There were rumors at his death."

"There were always rumors about him."

"He was closer to me than any. My Eyes . . . indeed my eyes."

"I trust my son is a comfort to you, Madam."

"Ah, wild Robin." She laughed affectionately. "A charming boy. I love him well."

"Then I am happy to have borne him for your service."

She looked at me sharply. "It would seem that fate has played a trick on us, Lettice," she said. "Those two . . . Leicester and Essex . . . the two of them, close to us both. You find your Blount a good husband?"

"I thank God for him, Madam."

"You quickly married after Leicester's death."

"I was lonely."

She nodded. "That girl of yours should take a care or two."

"Your Majesty refers to Lady Rich?"

"Lady Rich . . . or Lady Mountjoy . . . I know not by which name we should call her.

"She is Lady Rich, Your Majesty."

"She is like her brother. They have too high an opinion of themselves."

"Life has given them a great deal."

"Yes, with Sidney moping over the girl and now Mountjoy stepping out of line for her."

"It tends to raise their opinion of themselves—as Your Majesty's kindness to Essex has shown."

She laughed. Then she talked about the old days, of dear Philip Sidney, who had been such a hero, and the tragedies of the last years. It seemed particularly cruel to her that after the defeat of the Armada when it was as though a great burden had been lifted from her shoulders —though another had been laid on them since by the same enemies—she should have lost the one with whom she could have shared her triumphs.

Then she talked of him, how they had been together in the Tower, how he had come to her when her sister had died. . . . "The first to rush to me, with the offer of his fortune. . . ."

And his hand, I thought. Sweet Robin, the Queen's

Eyes, how high his hopes had been in those days. She took me along with her, making me see again the handsome young man—incomparable, she called him. I think she had completely forgotten the gouty, bleary old man he had become.

And she seemed to forget me too, as she rambled on, living the past with Leicester.

Then suddenly she looked at me coldly. "Well, Lettice," she said, "we have met at last. Essex has won the day."

She gave me her hand to kiss, and I was dismissed.

I left the palace in a state of triumph.

A week passed. There was no summons from the Queen. I could not wait to see my son. I told him what had happened, that the Queen had talked with me and had been most friendly, even cousinly. Yet I had received no further invitation to go to Court.

Essex mentioned the matter to her, telling her how delighted I was to have been received in private. Now what I earnestly wished for was to be allowed to kiss her hand in public.

He looked at me sadly.

"She is a most perverse old woman," he cried; and I was terrified that the servants would hear. "She says that she promised me she would see you and this she has done. And that, she tells me, is an end of the matter."

"You can't mean that she won't receive me again!" I cried, aghast.

"She says it is the same as it ever was. She does not wish to receive you at Court. She has nothing to say to you. You have shown yourself to be no friend of hers and she has no wish to see you."

So there I was, back in the same position. That brief meeting had meant nothing. It might as well never have taken place. I pictured her laughing with her women, perhaps commenting on the meeting.

407

"The She-Wolf thought she was coming back, did she? Ha! She will have to change her views. . . ."

Then she would look in her mirror and see herself not as she was then, but as a young woman newly come to the throne, in all the splendor of her glorious youth and beside her her Sweet Robin, with whom none could compare.

Then to soothe her grief and add balm to her wounds which he had given her by preferring me, she would laugh afresh at my dismay at having had my hopes raised and dashed so that she could add to my humiliation.

I am now approaching in these memories of mine that time which is the most tragic in my life, for I believe, looking back, that that terrible scene between Essex and the Queen was the beginning of disaster for him. I am sure she never forgave him for it, any more than she ever forgave me for marrying Leicester. Faithful as she was to her friends, one could say she was equally faithful to her enemies, and while she remembered an act of friendship and rewarded it again and again, she could never forget an act of disloyalty.

I know that Essex gave great provocation. His close friend, the Earl of Southampton, was at this time in disgrace. Elizabeth Vernon, one of the maids of honor and a niece of my first husband, Walter Devereux, had become Southampton's mistress, and Essex had helped them to make a secret marriage. When the Queen heard of it, Essex boldly declared that he saw not why men should not marry as they wished and still serve the Queen. This displeased her.

Meanwhile Elizabeth was seeking to make a peace treaty with Spain. Her hatred of war was as strong as ever, and she often said it should be undertaken only in cases of dire emergency (as at the time when the Armada was threatening to attack) and at all other times every step should be taken to avoid it.

Essex took a different view and wanted to put a stop to negotiations for peace. He eventually won the day with the Council, to the chagrin of Lord Burleigh and Robert Cecil.

Essex started to work against his enemies with that furious energy which was typical of him. My brother William, who, now that my father was dead, had inherited the title, tried to dissuade him from his vehemence. Christopher worshiped Essex blindly and, although in the first place I had been glad of this accord between them, I now wished Christopher would show a little discrimination. Mountjoy warned him, so did Francis Bacon, who remembered what a good friend Essex had always been to him; but in his headstrong way Essex would listen to nobody.

The Queen disapproved strongly of what he was doing and showed this in her manner towards him. It was a hot July day when matters came to a climax, and I think that the first irrevocable step towards disaster was taken then, for Essex did that which the Queen would never tolerate and never lightly forgive: he assaulted her dignity and in fact came near to assaulting her person.

Ireland was a matter of great contention, as it always had been, and the Queen was considering sending a lord deputy there.

She said she trusted Sir William Knollys. He was a kinsman on whose loyalty she could rely. His father had served her well all his life and Sir William was the man she would propose for the task.

Essex cried out: "It will not do. The man for that task is George Carew." Carew had taken part in the expedition to Cádiz and to the Azores. He had been in Ireland and had knowledge of affairs there. Moreover he was a close friend of the Cecils and if he could be exiled from the Court, all the better from Essex's point of view.

"I say William Knollys," said the Queen.

"You are wrong, Madam," retorted Essex. "My uncle is quite unsuited. Carew is your man."

No one ever spoke to the Queen in that manner. No one told her she was wrong. If her ministers felt strongly about something, she was gently and subtly persuaded to change her view. Burleigh, Cecil and the rest were adept at this maneuver. But to say: "Madam, you are wrong" so defiantly was something which could not be tolerated—even from Essex.

When the Queen ignored him with a gesture which implied that the suggestion of this impertinent young man was of no importance, a sudden rage seized Essex. She had insulted him in public. She was telling him that what he said was insignificant. For a moment his temper got the better of his common sense. He turned his back on the Queen.

She had accepted his outburst—for which he would no doubt be reprimanded later and warned never to do such a thing again—but this was a deliberate insult.

She sprang at him and boxed him soundly on the ears, telling him to go and be hanged.

Essex, blinded by rage, put his hand to his sword hilt, and would have drawn it, if he had not been immediately seized. As he was hustled out of the chamber he shouted that he would not have taken such an insult from Henry VIII. No one before had ever witnessed such a scene between a monarch and a subject.

Penelope hurried to Leicester House to talk it over with Christopher and me, and my brother William joined us with Mountjoy.

William was of the opinion that it must be the end of Essex, but Penelope would not have it.

"She is too fond of him. She will forgive him. Where has he gone?"

"To the country," Christopher told her.

"He should stay there for a while until this blows over," said William. "That's if ever it does."

I was worried indeed, for I did not see how such an insult could be forgiven. To have turned his back on the Queen was bad enough but to have drawn his sword on her was outrageous and could be treason—and he had many enemies.

We were all plunged into gloom and I was not sure that Penelope really believed in the optimism she expressed.

Everyone was talking about the decline of Essex until a matter of great importance ousted my son from the public eye. Lord Burleigh, who was seventy-eight and had been ailing for some time, was dying. He had suffered terribly with his teeth (an affliction with which the Queen was in great sympathy since she suffered likewise) and of course he had been subject to strain throughout his life. With the meticulous care he had given to state affairs, he set his personal ones in order. I heard that he took to his bed, called his children to him, blessed them and the Queen, and gave his will to his steward; then quietly he slipped away.

When the news was taken to the Queen she was inconsolable. She went to her own chamber and wept; and for some time afterwards when his name was mentioned her eyes would fill with tears. Not since the death of Leicester had she shown such emotion.

He had died in his house in the Strand and his body was taken to Stamford Baron for burial, but his obsequies were performed in Westminster Abbey. Essex came up from the country, in black mourning, to attend these and it was noticed that none of the mourners looked as melancholy as he did.

Afterwards he was at Leicester House and my brother William Knollys was there with Christopher and Mountjoy. Although Essex had opposed William's appointment,

411

my brother realized that the family fortunes were tied up in my son. Moreover, Essex had a charm which very often overcame the resentment of those whom he had slighted or wronged in some way. Like my father, William was a far-sighted man and he was not one to let a momentary upset affect the future. So he was as eager as the rest of us to see Essex back in favor.

He said: "Now is the time for you to go to the Queen. She is broken down with grief. It is for you to go and comfort her."

"She is out of humor with me," grumbled Essex, "but no more so than I with her."

I retorted: "She has insulted me, but if she were to ask me to come to Court tomorrow, most willingly would I go. I beg of you, do not play the fool, my son. One does not consider personal affronts when dealing with monarchs."

William flashed a look of warning at me. My brother was like our father—a very cautious man.

"The more you stay away, the more she will harden towards you," Mountjoy warned Essex.

"She will have no thought for me now," retorted Essex. "We shall hear what a good man Burleigh was. How *he* never crossed her. Differences of opinion they had, but he never forgot he was her subject. Nay, I have no intention of going to Court to listen to a panegyric on the virtues of Burleigh."

In vain did we try to make him realize what would be good for him. His stubborn pride stood in his way. *She* must ask him to come, and then he might consider going.

He was unrealistic, this son of mine, and I trembled for him.

Mountjoy told me that the Queen had ceased to think of Essex, so deep in mourning was she for Burleigh. She would talk to those about her of that good man—her Spirit, she still called him. *"He* never failed me," she said.

She talked of how there had been a rivalry between those two dear men who had meant so much to her—Leicester and Burleigh. "I could not have done without either of them," she said, and wept again. Her Eyes, her Spirit, both lost to her. How different were the men of this age! Then she would talk about the goodness of Burleigh. He had been a good father to his children. Look how he had advanced Robert, her Little Elf. Of course, Robert was a clever man. Burleigh had known that. He had not tried to bring his eldest—now Lord Burleigh—to her notice because he had known he had not the wit to serve her. No, it was Robert the hunchback, the splayfooted Little Elf, who was the genius. And his good father had known it. Oh, how she missed her dear, dear Spirit.

And so it went on without a regret for the absence of Essex.

"I cannot compete with a dead man in the heart of a sentimental woman," he said.

His utterances were becoming more and more reckless We trembled for him—all of us. Even Penelope, who was constantly urging him to what I thought of sometimes as even greater recklessness.

However, we all agreed that he should try for a reconciliation with the Queen.

An opportunity came when the Council was meeting and he, as a member of it, was to appear. His haughty reply was that he would not do so until he had first been granted an interview with the Queen. The Queen ignored this, and he did not attend, but went down to Wanstead to sulk.

There was bad news from Ireland, where the Irish Earl of Tyrone was in rebellion and was threatening the English, not only in Ulster, but in other provinces of Ireland. The English commander, Sir Henry Bagnal, had been completely routed, and it seemed that if immediate action were not taken, Ireland would be lost.

Essex came up from Wanstead with all speed and attended the meeting of the Council. He had special knowledge of the Irish question, he declared, and because of the danger, he asked the Queen to see him. She refused and he fumed with fury.

His rage and frustration had their effect on him. Penelope came to tell me that she feared he was ill. One of those intermittent fevers had attacked him, and in his delirium, he raved against the Queen. Christopher and I, with Penelope, went down to Wanstead to nurse him and protect him from those who were eager to report those ravings to Elizabeth.

How I loved him! Perhaps more than ever at this time. He was so young, so vulnerable; and all my maternal feelings rose in anguish to see him so. I shall never forget the sight of him, his beautiful hair unkempt and the wild look in his eyes. I felt furious with the Queen, whose treatment of him had brought him to this state, while, at the same time, in my heart I knew he had brought it on himself.

Would he never learn? I wondered. How I wished that Leicester were alive so that he could have talked with him. But when had Essex ever listened to anyone? My brother William and Mountjoy—whose relationship with Penelope made him like a son to me—were constantly trying to warn him. As for Christopher he seemed to be possessed of such adulation for my son that anything he did was right.

The Queen, hearing that Essex was ill, changed her attitude towards him. Perhaps the death of Burleigh had made her feel lonely—who shall say? They were all dead now—Eyes, Spirit, Moor and Bellwether. There was still one left to love—the wayward, reckless but fascinating son of her old enemy.

She sent her physician to see him with orders that she was to hear immediately of his condition; and as soon as he was well enogh to travel—but not before—he was to come to her.

It was reconciliation, and he recovered quickly. Christopher was delighted. "None could resist him for long," he said. But my sober brother William was less euphoric.

Essex came to see me after he had been received by the Queen. She had been warm and expressed her pleasure to have him back at Court. He believed that everything was as it had been, and he was secretly elated that he could do that which no other would have dared and still regain her favor. At the Twelfth Night ball everyone noticed how he danced with the Queen and how delighted she seemed because he was with her.

Yet I was thoughtful, and I railed against her—in secret of course—for keeping me out.

Essex said he was going to Ireland. He was going to teach Tyrone a lesson. Nobody knew as much about the Irish question as he did, and he reckoned that his father had been ill served by his country. He had given all to the cause, and because he had died before he succeeded, he was considered a failure. He was going to avenge that. The Earl of Essex had died in Ireland and was said to have failed; now Essex's son was going to continue his father's good work; he was going to succeed and the name of Essex would be remembered ever after with reverence whenever Ireland was mentioned.

This was all very grand. The Queen, with one of her sly comments, reminded him that, since he was so concerned with his father's affairs, there were some debts of his which were still unsettled.

This reference to my first husband's debts sent a tremor of dismay through the family, and I was afraid that I might be called upon to meet them. Essex declared that if the Queen persisted in this rapacious manner—after all he had done for her—he would leave Court forever. This was

415

wild talk, for he knew as well as any that his only hope of future advancement was through the Court.

The Queen must have cared deeply for him because the matter was dropped and no more heard of it, and, after some reluctance, she gave Essex permission to go to Ireland and command the army there.

He was flushed with triumph. He came to Leicester House and told us of his plans. Christopher listened to him intently with that adoration in his eyes which he had once shown for me.

I said: "You want to go with him, do you not?"

"I will take you, Christopher," added Essex.

My poor young husband! He could not hide from me where his inclination lay, though he tried to. How different from Leicester! It would never have occurred to *him* to turn from what he might desire or what could be advantageous to him. Oddly enough I was inclined to despise Christopher for his weakness.

"You should go," I told him.

"But how could I leave you . . . ?"

"I am perfectly capable of looking after myself. Go with Rob. The experience will be good for you. Is that not so, Rob?"

Essex said it would be good for himself to have those about him whom he could trust.

"Then it is settled," I added.

Christopher was clearly relieved. Our marriage had been happy, but I had had enough of it. I was nearly sixty years old and at times he seemed too young to interest me.

In March of that year—the last of the century—my son, with my husband, marched out of London. The people came into the streets to see him pass, and I must say that he looked magnificent. He was going to subdue the Irish; he was going to bring peace and glory to England;

there was something godlike about him, and it was small wonder that the Queen loved him.

Unfortunately when the cavalcade reached Islington, a violent thunderstorm broke and the riders were drenched with the rain. The lightning frightened the householders into their homes where they crouched in terror, it was said, seeing in this sudden violent storm some evil omen.

I laughed at this superstition, but later even I began to wonder.

Everyone knows now of the disastrous results of that campaign. How much happier we should have all been if Essex had not undertaken it. Essex, himself, soon realized the magnitude of his task. The Irish nobility were against him, so were the priests, who held great sway over the people. He wrote to the Queen telling her that to subdue the Irish was going to be the most costly operation of her reign. There must be a strong English army, and as the Irish nobility were not averse to a little bribery, perhaps this would be the best way of bringing them to her cause.

There was an argument between the Queen and Essex about the Earl of Southampton, whom she had not forgiven for having made Elizabeth Vernon pregnant, even though he had made amends by marrying her. Essex and Southampton were close friends and Essex had made Southampton his Master of Horse in the campaign—an appointment of which the Queen did not approve. She ordered Southampton to be removed from the post and this Essex was bold enough to refuse to do.

I was growing more and more apprehensive as this news reached me, not only about the growing resentment of the Queen, but the danger in which both my husband and son had placed themselves.

Penelope was always the first to hear the news and she kept me informed of what was going on. I was comforted too to have the company of my daughter Dorothy and her children. Her first husband, Sir Thomas Perrot, whom she had married so romantically, was now dead and she was married to Henry Percy, the Earl of Northumberland. This marriage, however, was not turning out well, and she was glad to come to me; and we talked sometimes of the trials and pitfalls of married life.

It seemed to me that my family was not very successful in marriage. Frances, at any rate, loved Essex. It was strange that, no matter how badly he behaved, he seemed to bind people to him. His infidelities were common knowledge, and sometimes I think he indulged in them partly to spite the Queen. His feeling towards her was strange; he loved her in a certain way. Compared with all other women, she was supreme, and it was not only the fact that she was the sovereign. I myself felt that power in her; it was almost mystic. Was it not a fact that since she had made it clear that she had no intention of taking me back into her circle, life had lost its savor? Did she know this? Perhaps. I was a proud woman and yet I had made a great effort to please her. Was she laughing to herself, telling herself that her revenge was complete? She had won the last battle; she was revenged on me—the commoner who had dared become her rival and who had scored great victories over her.

Well, that was my family. Essex was philandering with several mistresses, and Penelope was living openly with Lord Mountjoy. She had even borne him a child who had been christened Mountjoy, and she was pregnant with another. Lord Rich made no attempt to divorce her as yet, and I supposed this was due to Essex's influence at Court. Had my youngest Walter lived he would have been the quiet one, the one who lived respectably with his family. But, alas, he was gone.

It was when Essex had a meeting with the rebel Tyrone and made terms with him that the storm broke. The Queen was furious that Essex had dared make terms with an enemy without first consulting her. He would do well to take care, she declared.

Essex then returned to England. How thoughtless he was! How reckless! When I look back I can see his walking carelessly step by step towards disaster. If only he would have listened to my warnings!

He reached Nonsuch Palace at ten in the morning, an hour when the Queen would be at her toilette. I think he must have been really afraid then. All his boasting about subduing Ireland was proving to be premature. He knew that his enemies at home surrounded the Queen and that they would be eager for his fall. He would let none deter him. He had to see the Queen immediately, before any could attempt to distort the facts and turn her against him. He was the great Essex, and if he wished to see the Queen at any hour he would do so.

How little he understood women!

In spite of my fears for him, I could not help laughing as I visualized that scene. A startled Elizabeth, recently risen from her bed, surrounded only by those women who were allowed to share the very intimate ceremony of her toilette.

A woman of sixty-seven does not want to be seen by a youthful admirer at such times. Essex told me afterwards that he scarcely recognized her. She was robbed of everything but her royalty. Her gray hair hung about her face, and no rouge gave the bloom to her cheeks and the sparkle to her eyes which courtiers were accustomed to see.

And there before her stood Essex—himself muddy from his journey, for he had not stopped to wash or change his clothes.

She was, of course, magnificent, as she would be in any circumstances. She gave no sign that she was not adorned, with painted face, wig, ruff and fine gown. She gave him her hand to kiss and said she would see him later.

He came to me in triumph. She was his to command,

he told me. He had burst into her chamber and seen her in a state of undress as, he had already heard it said, no man had seen her before. Yet she had smiled at him most graciously.

"By God, she is an old woman. I did not know how old until I saw her this day."

I shook my head. I knew what she would be thinking. He had seen her in that state. I could picture her demanding a mirror, and the misery in her heart when the reflection looked back at her. Perhaps for once she looked at herself as she really was and she could not in that moment, surely, pretend that she was as fresh as the young girl who had romped with Admiral Seymour and who had dallied with Robert Dudley in the Tower. They were gone, and she was left to cling desperately to that image of her youth which Essex had shattered that morning at Nonsuch. I did not believe she would easily forget that.

I begged him to go very carefully, but when she saw him again she was very gracious.

At dinner he was joined by his friends, among them both Mountjoy and Lord Rich, for neither of these two, in their friendship for Essex, bore any resentment towards each other—one being Essex's sister's lover, the other her husband. Raleigh, I heard, dined apart from them with his friends such as Lord Grey and the Earl of Shrewsbury— formidable enemies.

Later that day Essex was summoned to the Queen, who was no longer friendly. She was annoyed that he had left Ireland without her permission and she said his conduct there had been treasonable.

He was bewildered. She had seemed kind enough to him and had been gracious when he had burst into her bedchamber. Poor Essex, sometimes I think he was the most obtuse man I ever knew. Though it is true enough that many men can be said to be so concerning the working of the female mind.

I could picture that interview. She would be seeing not the glittering figure who at that time was reflected in the mirror of the Presence Chamber, but a haggard old woman, not long risen from her bed, stripped of her adornments, her gray hair hanging about her face. Essex had seen *that* and she could not forgive him for it.

He was told he must remain in his chamber. He was a prisoner.

Mountjoy came to me in great dismay to report that Essex had been judged guilty of disobeying the Queen. He had left Ireland against her wishes and had boldly forced his way into her bedchamber. The Queen could not tolerate such conduct. He was to be sent to York House and there he would remain until the Queen decided what should be done.

"The Court is going to Richmond," said Mountjoy. "I cannot understand it. She seems not to care for him any more. She has turned against him."

My heart sank with foreboding. My beloved son had gone too far at last. Yet I could understand her. She could no longer bear near her a man who had seen her as the old woman she was. I had always known that she was the vainest woman in her kingdom and that she lived in a dream where she was as beautiful as her sycophantic courtiers proclaimed her to be.

Essex *had* disobeyed her. He *had* made havoc of the Irish campaign. All that could have been forgiven. But having torn the mask of disbelief from her eyes, having looked on that which no man was intended to see, he had committed the unforgivable sin.

We were anxious about him. He was very sick. The dysentery which had attacked him in Ireland—and which those who did not believe Leicester had killed his father were sure had been the end of him—persisted. He could not eat; he could not sleep. We had this news from those who attended him, for we were not allowed to go to him.

Christopher returned in great haste to England. He came to me at once and I was glad to see him safe. But there could be no great joy in our reunion for both of us could feel very little but fear for Essex.

We were all terrified that he would be sent to the Tower.

Mountjoy was constantly at Leicester House. I knew that Essex had been, for some time, in correspondence with the King of Scotland, and Mountjoy and Penelope with him, to assure that monarch that they were in favor of his inheriting the throne on the death of the Queen. I had always felt this correspondence to be dangerous, for if the letters had fallen into the hands of the Queen she and others would have construed them as treason. Leicester would never have been so careless. I thought of those occasions when he had found himself in risky situations and how dexterously he had always made sure to cover his tracks. If only my son would listen to me; if only he would profit from what I had to tell him! But what was the use? It was not his nature to listen, nor would he have practiced caution if he had.

Now Mountjoy was making plans for Essex to escape from York House and go to France. Southampton, on whose account Essex had incurred the Queen's wrath, declared he would go with him.

Essex, however, scornfully—and wisely for once—refused to run away.

Poor Frances was in great distress. She wanted to be with him but he would not have her. In desperation she went to Court to sue for the Queen's clemency.

Essex's wife, who was disliked by the Queen, though not as fiercely as I was, of course, was the last person who should have attempted to plead with her, although certainly I, his mother, would have been even more unwelcome. But of course these young people didn't know

Elizabeth as I did. They would have laughed to scorn my certainty that Essex's present disgrace was in some measure due to the fact that he had burst into her bedchamber and seen her unadorned.

Frances was naturally sent away with orders not to come to Court again.

My son's case was tried at the Star Chamber. The accusation was that he had, at great cost, been given the forces he had demanded; he had disobeyed instructions and returned to England without permission; he had entered into conference with the traitor Tyrone and made terms which were not fit to be listened to.

This was the fall of Essex. A few days later his household was broken up and his servants told to look elsewhere for masters whom they could serve. He had become so ill that we despaired of his life.

I believed that the Queen's conscience would smite her. She had once loved him well and I knew how faithful she was in her affections.

"Is he really as ill as you tell me he is?" she asked Mountjoy, who assured her that he was.

She said: "I will send my doctors to him."

Mountjoy answered: "It is not doctors he needs, Madam. But kind words from Your Majesty."

At this she sent him some broth from her own kitchens with a message that she would consider visiting him.

During those early days of December we really thought he was dying. He was prayed for in the churches, a fact which irritated the Queen because permission had not been asked of her that this should be done.

She said that his wife might visit him and tend him; then she sent for Penelope and Dorothy and received them kindly.

"Your brother is a much misguided man," she said to them. "I understand well your grief and I share it."

I often think it might have been better if Essex had died

then, but when he saw Frances at his bedside, and understood that the Queen had given her permission to come to him and when he heard that Penelope and Dorothy had been received by the Queen, he began to be hopeful, and hope was the best medicine he could have had.

I was not allowed to see him, but Frances came to tell me that his health was improving and that he was planning to send the Queen a New Year's gift.

I thought of all the elaborate New Year's gifts Leicester had bestowed on her and how I had had to sell my treasures to pay for these. However, it was a good thing to send the gift, and I was eager to know how it was received.

It was neither accepted nor rejected.

It was pathetic to see the effect on him when he heard that his gift had not been rejected. He rose from his bed and in a few days was walking about. He looked better every day.

Frances, knowing how anxious I was, sent frequent messages. I would sit at my window waiting for them and thinking of the Queen, who would be anxious too, for she did love him. And I had seen with Leicester that she was capable of deep feelings. Yet she would not allow me, his mother, to go to him. She was almost as jealous of his love for me as she had been of Leicester's.

I heard, in due course, the alarming news that the Queen had sent his gift back to him. It was only when she feared his life was in danger that she relented.

Now that he was no longer sick, he must continue to feel the weight of her anger. So, though recovered from his illness, he was in equal danger from the Queen and her enemies.

Fate seemed determined to rain blow after blow on my poor boy. I wished that Leicester were living. He would have been able to advise and plead Essex's cause with the

Queen. It was heart-breaking to see this proud man dejected, almost—though not quite—accepting defeat. Christopher was of little use. Although we had been married so long, he seemed the boy he had been at that time when his youth had appealed to me. Now I longed for maturity. I thought constantly and longingly of Leicester. Essex was a hero to Christopher; he could see no wrong in him; he believed that everything that had brought him to this pass was due to ill fortune and his enemies. He could not see that Essex's greatest enemy was himself, and that fortune will not keep smiling on one who abuses her.

Events were moving to a swift and terrifying climax. There was a great deal of talk about a book which had been written by Sir John Hayward. When I read it, I could see how dangerous it was at such a time, for it dealt with the deposition of Richard II and the accession of Henry IV, the implication being that if a monarch were unworthy to rule, it was justifiable for the next in succession to take the throne. It was most unfortunate that Hayward had dedicated this book to the Earl of Essex.

I could see how Essex's enemies, such as Raleigh, would seize on this and use it against him. I could hear their telling the Queen that the book implied that she was unfit to rule. As it had been dedicated to Essex, had he had a hand in writing it? Did the Queen know that Essex, with his sister Lady Rich, had been in correspondence with the King of Scotland?

The book was withdrawn and Hayward imprisoned, and the Queen remarked that he might not be the author but was pretending to be in order to shield some mischievous person.

Penelope and I would sit together, talking of these matters until we slept for very exhaustion, but we arrived at no conclusion and could see no end to the problem.

Mountjoy was in Ireland, succeeding where Essex had failed, and Penelope reminded me that Essex had said

Mountjoy would be no good for the task, being too literary minded and caring more for books than battles. How wrong he had been! Indeed, had my poor Essex ever been right?

He was in debt, for the Queen had refused to renew the license on the farm of sweet wines which she had bestowed on him; and on this he was relying to pay his creditors. It seemed his fortunes could not be lower—but of course they could.

He had never been able to see himself clearly. In his opinion he was ten feet high and other men pygmies. I realized during those terrible days that I loved him as I loved no one else—since that time when I had been obsessed by Leicester. This was a different kind of love, though. When Leicester had coarsened and neglected me for Elizabeth, I had fallen out of love with him. I could never stop loving Essex.

He was in Essex House now and all sorts of people were congregating there. It was beginning to be known as the meeting place for malcontents. Southampton was constantly with him, and he was one of those who were out of favor with the Queen. All men and women who were disgruntled, who believed that they had not received their dues, gathered together and murmured against the Queen and her ministers.

Oh, my reckless, thoughtless son! In an access of rage against the Queen, in his anguish for lost favor, he shouted in the hearing of several that he could not trust her, that her conditions were as crooked as her carcass.

I wished that I could have reached him. I wanted to tell him that John Stubbs had lost his right hand, not because he had written against the Queen's marriage, but because he had said she was too old for childbearing. But it would have been useless. That remark could take him to the scaffold, I knew, if ever his steps should be turned that way; and of course he was rushing headlong towards it.

His great rival, Sir Walter Raleigh, seized on those words. I could imagine how they would be slipped into the Queen's ear. She would hate him the more because once she had loved him. She would still be haunted by the scene when he had slipped into her bedchamber and discovered a gray, old woman.

The rest of the story is well known, how the plot was made that he and others should seize Whitehall, insist on an interview with Elizabeth, force her to dismiss her present ministers and summon a new parliament.

It probably sounded simple when they planned it. How different it was to put it into action. Christopher was secretive, so I knew that something was afoot. I saw little of him during those days because he was constantly at Essex House. I learned afterwards that Essex was expecting envoys from the King of Scotland, in which case he promised himself he would have good reason for rising and hoping for help from the Scottish King.

It was natural that all these happenings at Essex House attracted attention. Essex's spies discovered that there was a plot afoot—with Raleigh at the head of it—to capture him, perhaps kill him, and in any case get him into the Tower. Whenever my son had ridden through the streets of London, people had come out to watch him and to cheer him. He had always been an object of interest and that charm of his had been a source of fascination. He believed now that the city would be for him, and if he rode out, calling the people to rally round him that he might right his wrongs and theirs, they would follow him.

On a Saturday night several of his followers went to the Globe Theatre and bribed the players there to perform Shakespeare's *Richard II,* so that people might see that it was possible to depose a monarch.

I was so alarmed that I asked my brother William to come to me without delay. He was as uneasy as I was.

427

"What is he trying to do?" he demanded. "Does he not know he is risking his head."

"William," I cried. "I beg of you, go to Essex House. See him. Try to make him listen to reason."

But of course Essex never had listened to reason. William went to Essex House. By that time some three hundred people were there—hotheads, fanatics, all of them.

William demanded an interview with his nephew, but Essex refused it, and because William would not go away he was hustled into the house and shut into the guards' room.

Then Essex did the foolhardy thing. He marched out into the streets with two hundred of his followers—my poor misguided Christopher among them.

Oh, the folly of it—the childish stupidity!

I feel sickened even now when I think of that brave, foolish boy, riding through the streets of London, with his inadequately armed men behind him, shouting to the citizens to join him. I could imagine their blank dismay as these worthy people hastily turned away and went into their houses. Why should they rebel against a Queen who had brought prosperity to them, who had triumphantly saved them from destruction by Spain—all because she had fallen out with one of her favorites?

The call of Rebellion went up, and in London and the neighborhood men were called on to defend the Queen and the country, and a force was quickly mustered against Essex. There was little fighting but enough for several to be killed. My Christopher was gored in the face by a halberd and fell from his horse so that he was left to be captured, while Essex retreated and managed to reach Essex House, where he quickly burned letters from the King of Scotland and any which he thought might implicate his friends.

It was night when they came to take him.

I was so angry. His friend Francis Bacon, whom he had helped so much, had spoken for the prosecution. When I thought of all Essex had done for Bacon I raved to Penelope and called him "False friend and traitor!"

Penelope shook her head. Bacon had been called upon to make a choice. He had to weigh up his obligations to the Queen and to Essex. Of course, said Penelope, he must choose the Queen.

"Essex would have chosen his friend," I pointed out.

"Yes, dear Mother," she replied, "but look to what his acts have brought him."

I knew my son was doomed.

Yet there was one bright hope to which I clung. The Queen had loved him, and I could remind myself how again and again she had forgiven Leicester. But Leicester had never raised an armed rebellion against her. What excuse could there be for Essex? I had to be reasonable and admit that there was none.

He was found guilty, as I had known he would be, and sentenced to death—and poor Christopher with him. I was bewildered and desolate, for I feared that I should shortly be deprived of a husband and a son.

It was a nightmare into which I had strayed. She could not do it. Surely she could not do it. But why not? Those about her would assure her that she must. Raleigh—always his enemy—Cecil, Lord Grey, all of them would explain to her that she had no alternative. Yet she was a woman of strong feelings. When she loved she loved deeply, and she had surely loved him. Next to Leicester he had been the most important man in her life.

What if Leicester had done what Essex had dared? But he never would have. Leicester was no fool. Poor Essex, his was a career littered with suicidal actions, and now there was nothing that could save him.

Or was there?

My husband and my son were condemned to death. I was her kinswoman. Would she have a little pity for me? If only she would see me.

I thought she might see Frances. She had always had an affection for her Moor, and this was his daughter. Moreover, Essex had been notoriously unfaithful to Frances, and the Queen would have pitied her for that, and that would surely have softened the hurt his marrying had inflicted.

Poor Frances, she was desolate. She had loved him dearly and had been with him near to the end of his freedom. I wondered whether he had been tender with her then. I hoped so.

"Frances," I advised her, "go to the Queen. Weep with her, and ask her if she will see me. Tell her I beg her to grant this favor to a woman who has been twice widowed and is likely to be so again. Beg her, in her mercy, to see me. Tell her I know that her great good heart is there beneath her stern royalty, and tell her that if she will see me now I will bless her throughout my life."

Frances was granted an audience during which the Queen had commiserated with her and told her it was a sad day for her when she had lost a great man in Sidney and married a traitor.

And, to my surprise, I too was granted an audience.

So, once again, I was in her presence. But this time on my knees to plead for my son's life. She was dressed in black—for Essex, I wondered—but her gown was covered in pearls; she held her head high above the ornate ruff and her face looked very pale against the too red curls of her wig.

She gave me her hand to kiss and then she said: "Lettice!" And we looked at each other. I tried to compose my features, but I could feel the tears coming into my eyes.

"God's breath!" she said. "What a fool your son is!"

I bowed my head.

"And he has brought himself to this," she went on. "I never wished it for him."

"Madam, he would never have harmed you."

"Doubtless he would have left that for his friends to do."

"Nay, nay, he loves you."

She shook her head, "He saw through me the way to advancement. Do not all of them?"

She signed for me to get off my knees and I rose saying: "You are a great Queen, Your Majesty, and all the world knows it."

She looked at me steadily and said grudgingly: "You still have some beauty left. You were very handsome when you were young."

"No one could compete with you."

Strangely enough I meant it. She had something more than beauty, and she still retained it, old as she was.

"A crown is becoming, Cousin."

"But it does not suit all who wear it. Madam, it becomes you well."

"You have come to ask me to spare them," she said. "I was of a mind not to see you. You and I have nothing to say to each other."

"I thought we might offer each other comfort."

She looked haughty, and I said boldly: "Madam, he is my son."

"And you love him dearly?"

I nodded.

"I did not think you were capable of loving anyone but yourself."

"Sometimes I have believed that to be so, but now I know it is untrue. I love my son."

"Then you must prepare yourself—as I must—to suffer his loss."

"Is there nothing that can save him?"

She shook her head.

"You plead for your son," she went on. "Not your husband."

"I plead for them both, Madam."

"You do not love this young man."

"We have lived pleasantly together."

"I heard that you preferred him to . . ."

"There are always evil rumors, Madam.

"I never believed you could prefer any other," she said slowly. "If he were here today . . ." She moved her head impatiently. "Life was never the same after he went . . ."

I thought of Leicester dead. I thought of my son who was condemned to die, and I forgot everything but the need to save him.

I threw myself to my knees again. I felt the tears running down my face, and there was nothing I could do to stop them.

"You cannot let him die," I cried. "You cannot."

She turned away from me. "It has gone too far," she murmured.

"*You* could save him. Oh, Madam, forget all the enmity between us. It is over and done with . . . and have either of us long to live?"

She flinched. As always she hated people to refer to her age. I should have known better. My grief had robbed me of my good sense.

"However much you hated me in the past," I went on, "I beg of you now to forget that. He is dead . . . our beloved Leicester . . . gone forever. Were he here with us today, he would be kneeling here with me."

"Be silent," she shouted. "How dare you come here . . . you She-Wolf! You ensnared him with your wanton ways. You took the finest man that ever lived. You lured him into deceit . . . and now this rebel son of yours deserves well the ax. And you . . . you of all women . . . dare come here and ask me to spare a traitor."

"If you let him die, you will never forget it," I said, all caution deserting me in this desperate need to save my son.

She was silent for a while, and I saw that the shrewd tawny eyes were glistening. She was moved. She loved him. Or once she had loved him.

I kissed her hand fervently but she withdrew it—not sharply, though, almost tenderly.

"You *will* save him," I pleaded.

But the Queen was replacing the emotional woman whom I had briefly glimpsed.

She said slowly: "I have seen you, Lettice, for Leicester's sake. He would have wished it. But even if *he* knelt before me now and asked this of me, I could not grant it. Nothing can save your son . . . nor your husband . . . now. They have gone too far. I could not, if I would, stay their execution now. There is a time when one must go forward. There is no looking back. Essex has walked into this with his eyes open and a determination to destroy himself. I must perforce sign his death warrant, and you and I must say goodbye forever to this foolish boy."

I shook my head. I think I was mad with grief. I knelt and kissed the hem of her robe. She stood looking down at me, and as I lifted my eyes to her face. I saw a certain compassion there. Then she said: "Rise. I am tired. Goodbye, Cousin. Methinks it is a strange matter this mad dance of our lives—mine, yours, and these two men we loved. Yes, we have loved two men, dearly. The one is lost to us; the other soon will be. There is no turning back. What is to be will be."

How old she looked with the marks of real grief on her face.

I was about to plead once more, but she shook her head and turned away.

I was dismissed. There was nothing to do but leave her and return in my barge to Leicester House.

I would not let myself believe that she would not relent. I told myself that when it came to signing his death warrant she would not be able to do it. I had seen it in her face that she loved him. Not as she had loved Leicester, of course, but still she loved him. My hopes were high.

But she signed the death warrant, and I was in despair. Then she recalled it. How happy I was—but, oh, how briefly so, for she changed her mind, urged no doubt by her ministers.

Once more she signed the warrant, and this time she did not withdraw.

On Wednesday, the twenty-fifth of February, my son, dressed in black, came out of his prison in the Tower and was taken to the high court above Caesar's Tower.

He was praying as he laid his head on the block.

There was mourning throughout London, and the executioner was seized by the mob and rescued just in time before they could kill him. Poor man, as though it were his fault!

The Queen shut herself away and mourned him, and in Leicester House I remained in my bedchamber and waited for news of my husband.

About a week after Essex's death, poor Christopher was tried and found guilty; and on the eighteenth of March he was taken out to Tower Hill, where he was beheaded.

The Old Lady at Drayton Basset

Blame but thyself that hast misdone,
And well deserved to have blame;
Change thou thy way, so evil begone,
And then my lute shall sound that same;
And if till then my fingers play,
By thy desert their wonted way,
        Blame not my lute.

SIR THOMAS WYATT
1503–1542

So I was once more a widow, and I had lost the son who, in spite of the follies I deplored, I had loved more than anyone. My young husband, who had been devoted to my comforts, was dead with him, and I must make a new life.

Everything was changing. The Queen no longer pretended to be young. I was sixty, so she must have been sixty-eight—two old women, who no longer cared very much about each other. It all seemed so long ago when Leicester and I made secret love and secret marriage and had feared her wrath.

I heard that she mourned for the men she had loved— chief of these being Leicester and Essex; but she still wept for Burleigh, Hatton, Heneage and the rest. There were none like them now, she was heard to say, forgetting that they had seemed like gods because she was then a goddess. Now she was merely an old woman.

Two years after the death of Essex, she died. She kept up her royal pride until the end, and although she had had several bouts of sickness, she would go on walking and riding as soon as she was up from her bed, so that people could see her. Finally she took cold, and decided to go to Richmond, which she considered the most sheltered of her palaces. Her cold grew worse, but she would not go to bed, and when Cecil begged her to and told her that to content the people she must do so, she replied with the familiar regal touch: "Little man, the word *must* is not used to sovereigns." And because she found she could not stand she had cushions brought and lay on the floor.

When we heard that she was dying a great silence fell on the land. It seemed an age ago when a redheaded young woman of twenty-five had gone to the Tower and declared her determination to work and live for her country. So had she done, never forgetful of her mission, even as she had vowed. It had come before everything, before love, before Leicester, before Essex.

When she was so weak that she could not resist she was carried to her bed.

It was the twenty-fourth of March in the year 1603 she died—on the eve of the Feast of the Annunciation of the Blessed Virgin, it was noted.

She had even chosen an appropriate time to die.

So they were gone—all those who had made life worth-while for me.

I was now the old woman—the grandmother, who must pass her time in retirement.

A new king had come to the throne—King James VI of Scotland had become James I of England—an untidy, not very prepossessing monarch. Gone was the brilliance of Elizabeth's Court, and I had no desire to be of the new one.

I went to my house at Drayton Basset and there I decided to live the life of a country lady. It was almost like being reborn. It was remembered of me that I had been the mother of Essex and the wife of Leicester, and soon I was holding court like a queen, which gave me pleasure.

My grandchildren visit me often. There are many of them and I take an interest in them and they like to hear stories of the past.

Only one event disturbed me during those years. That was when in the year of the Queen's death, Robert Dudley, the son of Leicester by Douglass Sheffield, tried to prove that there had been a legal marriage between his parents. Naturally I could not stand by and let him prove that, for had he done so, I should have been robbed of the major part of my inheritance.

It was an unpleasant case, as these cases always are, and there is always an element of fear in them that what is suggested may prove true.

This odious man insisted that his father and mother had

gone through a form of marriage and that he was indeed Leicester's legitimate son.

He had been with Essex at Cádiz, and it was when he returned, a widower, that the trouble began, for he married and his wife was the daughter of a very forceful gentleman, Sir Thomas Leigh of Stoneleigh. It was this man who urged him to take his case to court. This he did, and I am glad to say that it did not succeed, and so angry was he that he applied for permission to leave the country for three years.

This being granted, he left England, taking with him his beautiful cousin, who had to dress as a boy and pose as his page. He left his wife and children in England and never returned to them, so he was not a man to take his responsibilities seriously.

Penelope continued her colorful career. After the death of Essex, Lord Rich divorced her and she and Mountjoy married. There was a great controversy about this marriage, which was performed by Mountjoy's chaplain, Laud. Many said that Laud had no right to marry a woman who had been divorced. For years Laud bemoaned the fact that this had prevented his preferment, although he was to leap into prominence later.

Poor Mountjoy, though honors had been heaped on him and he became the Earl of Devonshire, he did not live long after his marriage. He died in 1606, three years after the Queen's death; and Penelope died one year after him. She left me several grandchildren, not only Lord Rich's but three by Mountjoy—Mountjoy, Elizabeth and St. John.

It seemed strange that I should live on and my vital daughter be dead. But that was my fate. Sometimes I used to think: I shall live forever.

My daughter Dorothy died in 1619, three years before her husband's release from the Tower, whither he had been sent at the time of the Gunpowder Plot, suspected of having a share in it. He had been deprived of all his possessions and was sentenced to stay there for the rest of his life; and it was sixteen years later that his release was brought about through his daughter's husband. It had been a most unhappy marriage and often Dorothy had come to me to escape from him. When she died I was approaching eighty, but *I* still lived on.

I have seen so much in my long life. I lived on after Sir Walter Raleigh had gone to the scaffold. He had been unable to charm James as he had Elizabeth. I heard he had said as he laid his head on the block: "What matters it how the head lies, so the heart be right." Wise brave words, I thought, from Essex's enemy.

I sat in my chamber at Drayton Basset, and thought of Raleigh as he had once been—handsome, arrogant and sure of himself. So are the mighty brought low.

And still I lived on.

The King died and his son came to the throne—dapper Charles, whom I saw once or twice—a man of great dignity. Life had changed. It could never be as it had been under great Elizabeth. There would never be another like her. How she would have been saddened to see her beloved England fall into the hands of these Stuarts. The Divine Right of Kings! How often did we hear that phrase! She had believed in it, of course, but she had known that the sovereign ruled by the will of the people, and never would she have displeased them if she could help it.

James . . . Charles . . . what did they know of the glorious days when the handsomest men of the Court had circled round the Queen—moths to the candle and the cleverest of them knowing how to avoid singeing their wings. Her lovers—all of them, for they had loved her and she had loved them. But they were her fantasies; her true love was England.

Her death had taken something vital from my life,

which was strange, for she had hated me and I could not say I ever loved her. But she was a part of my life, as Leicester was—and part of me died with them.

This sedate old lady in her manor house at Drayton Basset, caring for her tenants, playing lady bountiful, repenting her wild youth to make sure of a place in heaven, is this Lettice, Countess of Essex, Countess of Leicester, and wife of Christopher Blount? Poor Christopher! He did not really count. I had ceased to live dangerously and gloriously when Leicester died.

All this I lived through. These people flitted across the life of the times, played their parts and passed, while I lived on.

Now that I have written this story of the past I live it all again so vividly that it seems as though it happened only yesterday. When I close my eyes I sometimes feel that when I open them I shall see Leicester bending over me, raising me up to kiss him, to arouse in me that desire which we both found irresistible. I can fancy I am at the Queen's toilette, and that suddenly I receive a nip in the arm because I am dreaming and forgetting to bring her ruffs.

I see the three of us, side by side: Elizabeth and Leicester . . . myself in the background . . . important to them as they are to me. And then strangely enough Essex, the Queen, myself.

And they are gone and I live on.

I am over ninety. It is a very great age. I can be forgiven for fancying I am sometimes back in the past.

I like it best when my grandson, Essex, comes to see me. He is a man of great strength, punctilious in his zest for the right, a man who will do his duty, however unpleasant. He does not seek great honors. He is a great soldier—he could not be less like his father.

I hope my grandson will come to see me soon. Perhaps he will come for Christmas. I should like to see him then.

He talks to me a great deal about the King and the Parliament and the troubles with the Church. He thinks that one day there will be a disagreement between the King and the Parliament, and he will *not* be on the side of the King.

I tell him that he talks like his father, recklessly. But in truth he is far from reckless.

He sits there before me, his arms folded, looking into the future.

How I hope that he comes this Christmas!

EARLY ON CHRISTMAS MORNING IN THE YEAR 1634, WHEN HER MAIDS WENT TO HER BEDROOM IN DRAYTON BASSET THEY FOUND HER AS THOUGH SLEEPING PEACEFULLY.

SHE WAS DEAD.

LEICESTER HAD DIED FORTY-SIX YEARS BEFORE AND ELIZABETH THIRTY-ONE.

SHE WAS NINETY-FOUR YEARS OF AGE.

Bibliography

Aubrey, William Hickman Smith	*The National and Domestic History of England*
Beesly, E. S.	*Queen Elizabeth*
Black, J. B.	*The Reign of Elizabeth*
Camden, William	*Annals of Elizabeth*
Chamberlin, F. C.	*The Private Character of Queen Elizabeth*
Froude, J. A.	*History of England*
Gascoigne, George	*Princely Pleasures of Kenilworth*
Harrison, G. B.	*Life and Death of Robert Devereux, Earl of Essex*
Harrison, G. B.	*An Elizabethan Journal 1591–1594*
Harrison, G. B.	*A Second Elizabethan Journal 1595–1598*
Harrison, G. B.	*A Last Elizabethan Journal 1599–1603*
Hedley, Olwen	*Royal Palaces*
Hume, David	*The History of England*
Hume, Martin	*Courtships of Queen Elizabeth*
Hume, Martin	*Two English Queens and Philip*
Jenkins, Elizabeth	*Elizabeth the Great*
Jenkins, Elizabeth	*Elizabeth and Leicester*
Neale, J. E.	*Queen Elizabeth*
Rawson, Maud Stepney	*Penelope Rich and Her Circle*
Rouse, A. L.	*The England of Elizabeth*
Rouse, A. L.	*Elizabeth and Her Subjects*
Rouse, A. L.	*The Expansion of Elizabeth and England*
Salzman, L. F.	*England in Tudor Times*
Stephen, Sir Leslie, and Sir Sidney Lee, edited by John	*The Dictionary of National Biography*
Stow, from the text of 1603 with introduction and notes by Charles Lethbridge Kingsford	*Survey of London*
Strachey, Lytton	*Elizabeth and Essex*
Strickland, Agnes	*Lives of the Queens of England*

Timbs, John, and Alexander Gunn — *Abbeys, Castles and Ancient Halls of England and Wales*

Wade, John — *British History*

Waldman, Milton — *Elizabeth and Her Times*

Waldman, Milton — *King, Queen, Jack*

Williams, Neville — *Royal Homes*

Wright, Thomas — *Elizabeth and Leicester*

Isaac Bashevis Singer

Winner of the 1978 Nobel Prize for Literature

SHOSHA	23997-7	$2.50
SHORT FRIDAY	24068-1	$2.50
PASSIONS	24067-3	$2.50
A CROWN OF FEATHERS	23465-7	$2.50
ENEMIES: A LOVE STORY	24065-7	$2.50
THE FAMILY MOSKAT	24066-5	$2.95

Buy them at your local bookstores or use this handy coupon for ordering:

FAWCETT BOOKS GROUP
P.O. Box C730, 524 Myrtle Ave., Pratt Station, Brooklyn, N.Y. 11205

Please send me the books I have checked above. Orders for less than 5 books must include 75¢ for the first book and 25¢ for each additional book to cover mailing and handling. I enclose $_____ in check or money order.

Name_____
Address_____
City_____State/Zip_____

Please allow 4 to 5 weeks for delivery.

James A. Michener

Winner of the Pulitzer Prize in Fiction

The Bridge at Andau	23863-6	$1.95
The Bridges at Toko-Ri	23856-3	$1.95
Caravans	23832-6	$2.25
Centennial	23494-0	$2.95
The Drifters	23862-8	$2.75
The Fires of Spring	23860-1	$2.25
Hawaii	23761-3	$2.95
Iberia	23804-0	$2.95
Kent State: What Happened and Why	23869-5	$2.50
A Michener Miscellany	C2526	$1.95
Rascals in Paradise	24022-3	$2.50
Return to Paradise	23831-8	$2.25
Sayonara	23857-1	$1.95
The Source	23859-8	$2.95
Sports in America	23204-2	$2.50
Tales of the South Pacific	23852-0	$2.25

Buy them at your local bookstores or use this handy coupon for ordering:

Victoria Holt

Here are the stories you love best. Tales about love, intrigue, wealth, power and of course romance. Books that will keep you turning the pages deep into the night.